WHAT READERS ARE SAYING ABOUT
THE ONE THAT GOT AWAY

★★★★★
'Clear your schedule. Once you start reading,
you won't be able to stop'

★★★★★
'All the twists and turns kept me guessing
until the very last page'

★★★★★
'The ending is incredibly hard to predict'

★★★★★
'Wow, is all I can say for this book'

★★★★★
'An incredible novel that drew me in and didn't let me go'

★★★★★
'What a thrilling read'

★★★★★
'Dark, twisted and utterly unpredictable. A must-read!'

Egan Hughes was born in North Devon and grew up in Hampshire. She is now based on the South Coast of England and works in marketing as a freelance copywriter. An early version of *The One That Got Away* was shortlisted for the First Novel Prize, and the 2017 Richard and Judy Search for a Bestseller Competition.

THE ONE THAT GOT AWAY

EGAN HUGHES

sphere

SPHERE

First published in Great Britain in 2020 by Sphere as a paperback original

1 3 5 7 9 10 8 6 4 2

Grateful acknowledgement is made to Cath Deeson of Cath
Deeson Linocuts for permission to print lines on p135.

A CIP catalogue record for this book is
available from the British Library.

ISBN 978-0-7515-7678-8

Typeset in Caslon by M Rules
Printed and bound in Great Britain by Clays Ltd, Elcograf S.p.A.

Papers used by Sphere are from well-managed forests
and other responsible sources.

MIX
Paper from
responsible sources
FSC® C104740

Sphere
An imprint of
Little, Brown Book Group
Carmelite House
50 Victoria Embankment
London EC4Y 0DZ

An Hachette UK Company
www.hachette.co.uk

www.littlebrown.co.uk

To David and Lucy

For never, ever looking bored when I talk about writing.

There are three truths: my truth, your truth and the truth.

Chinese proverb

My truth is a deep, dark truth with no escape. It's a corrosive secret I can't tell anyone. Your truth is something else entirely. You know too much and it adds up to trouble. What happened that night could ruin my life, and keeping it secret will ruin yours.

He said no one would love me the way he loved me. He had me believe I deserved a better life, but he bent reality to suit his purpose. His warped reality became my warped reality. That's the thing with gaslighting, not that I'd heard of it back then. This person you love becomes your world and what should be right goes wrong. It creeps up by stealth until you're so far gone you've lost your way. It's called coercive control, now there's a law against it.

He said I was unhinged, but he made me that way. It's no wonder something terrible happened. Fear prickles on my skin. I breathe it in and out. We're two of a kind, you and I, brought down by him. Everything rides on whose version of the truth they believe.

PART ONE

MIA

Panic gripped me when they said he'd died. The floor listed at a woozy angle.

'Someone shot him on his boat,' the man said.

I shut my eyes and pictured the gun. His gun. I gasped for breath, as if the air had been sucked from the room.

'You okay, Mia?'

I opened my eyes and tried to calm myself. I wanted the shaking to ease off, along with the blotches in my vision.

'Take your time. I know it's a shock.'

The two officers in navy suits filled my sofa with their combined bulk and cigarette smell. I burned from their scrutiny. Before all this happened I never said my ex's name, because I wanted to forget him and forget what happened. Then the police turned up and he was everywhere.

'We need to ask you some questions as part of the murder investigation.' The female officer sat with her notebook poised. 'When did you last see him?'

It was all I could do to keep breathing. My throat tightened and thoughts of him crowded in. 'About two years ago.'

'You took out an injunction, is that right?'

At least my vision was coming back to normal. The panic attack began to ease. I managed them better now, so I didn't look like someone falling apart. The trick was to slow your breathing and focus on something solid. I studied a cobweb on the fireplace, willing the police to leave. I didn't want them looking at me and seeing the damage.

'Mia? Did you take out an injunction against him?'

'I just ... as a precaution. I didn't ...' My voice was jagged, I tripped over the words. I never could hide my feelings.

'Drink your tea.'

I took a gulp and set it back down. Despite my shaking hands, I managed not to spill any.

'He threatened to kill you. Is that right?'

'I don't think he meant it.'

She gave me a wearisome look.

'It got bad before we split up. We weren't right for each other.' I had this urge to explain, so they'd see I wasn't the sort of person to get death threats. I wanted them to know how he came along and made me happy. It was like a gift. But it wasn't mine to keep because it wasn't real. Not that they cared.

Darcy lay sphinx-like at my feet, one Alsatian ear pricked and the other flopping down. Mr Darcy, my guard dog; both of us wary of people we didn't know.

'You did the right thing to take out an injunction. It can be dangerous when you leave a man like him. He'd have wanted to keep you under his control.'

'What happened is ... it's awful, but I don't know him any more. I didn't know he'd remarried.'

To be fair, I never knew him. He mostly pretended to be someone else, someone better. There was more to him beyond the surface, none of it good. My teeth worried at a fingernail, and the officers watched me in silence.

My panic subsided a few more degrees. The woman drummed a biro on her restless leg, her hair scraped into a thin ponytail. Her rugged colleague who'd made the tea might have been my type, once upon a time. The younger me would have looked into his eyes and imagined hidden depths, because that's how I was back then.

'So you last saw Rob Creavy two years ago. Yes?' he asked.

'Yes.'

We held each other's stare. I blinked first and steeled myself for more questions. They exchanged a glance, and the woman snapped her notebook shut.

'That's everything,' the male officer said. 'You've answered our questions ... for now.' He lingered over the last two words, and my heart dipped at the thought of them coming back.

He gave me a business card with his number, in case I thought of anything relevant. I nodded and studied it, even though I wouldn't be calling him. They walked into the evening gloom. I shut the door and leaned against it for a long time. Then I sat on the stairs and gave in to the shaking.

Time passed while I stared at a patch of black mould on the

wall. My thoughts swirled; clammy hands wedged themselves between my knees. I'd escaped from Rob when everything turned bad, but now I'd been plunged back in.

Mr Darcy nudged my elbow until I wrapped my arms around him. He nuzzled against the side of my face, a furry blanket of reassurance. I'd hold on to what was good and find a way through. He flopped down beside me, watching with concerned brown eyes.

'It's okay, Darce.' I stroked the fur between his ears. He closed his eyes and murmured under his breath. When I got him as a puppy, both ears flopped down. One learned to stand up, but the other never managed to join it. 'We'll be okay.'

A glass of wine would help my dry throat and numb the anxiety. I could finish that open bottle in the fridge, not to get off my head, just to escape it for a while. But even that wasn't enough to move me from the hall where I stayed hunched, as if shackled.

I used to think the past would settle behind me, but it crept up and pulled me back where I didn't want to go. I went over what I'd tried to forget, what my memory kept alive, because even in death he had this hold on me. He gained the upper hand by manipulating me. I didn't notice at first, and then I was in too deep to walk away.

My mobile rang. Ben's voice jolted me back to reality, asking about my day. I stood in the shadowy hallway and told him about the police visit, not wanting to talk about it, but he was my boyfriend, after all.

I'd been single for a while after leaving my ex. A wariness

hung around, although my resolve weakened when I saw happy couples. I'd look away, wanting it for myself but not wanting it. Then Ben came along and took me away from the highs and lows. He made things right just by being him and wanting to be with me. I didn't need big gestures and wild promises. I just needed him.

'I'm coming over,' he said, voice filled with concern.

He arrived soon after, with Stan lumbering in after him. Ben hugged me tight and I buried my face in his moss-green fleece. Stan and Darcy circled round us in their own doggy greeting.

'Do you want to talk about it?'

I rubbed my eyes and shook my head. My mouth stayed dry, my throat choked up. He knew about the disaster of my marriage, even though I'd spared him the details.

'You've got an early start tomorrow. Let's go to bed.'

When we turned off the light, Ben held me in a sleepy embrace. He smelled fresh from the shower, but still with an earthy trace of soil from his gardening work. We spent three or four nights a week together, at my place or his, two miles away. We'd talked about living together, but hadn't made the move.

Ben murmured to me until his words trailed off into sleep. I stared into the darkness. My thoughts took on an intensity I couldn't tone down. I heard Rob's voice in my head, and saw his vivid blue eyes when I closed mine. Wine would have taken the edge off, making it blur so I could fade into sleep, but then I'd have woken in the early hours, and those were the worst.

Ben slept soundly, same as always. But it wasn't the same because everything had changed. He'd no idea, lying there so peacefully. A snag of pain took hold. *Don't leave me.* I couldn't bear it. I went breathless. It felt as real and sudden as if he *had* left. I'd made such a mess of things. A part of me thought he would understand, but I had too much at stake to tell him. Tears stung the back of my eyes.

I replayed my lies to the police. Of course I knew about Rob's new wife, the woman younger than me who he loved more. I'd said I hadn't seen him for two years, which was also a lie. Part of me had wanted to come clean, but I didn't trust them to see it the way I did.

Had the officers read the fear in my eyes, telling a story all of its own? They didn't ask for my alibi, didn't ask where I was when he died. What if they came back and asked those questions? I'd nearly passed out when the police turned up. Could I lie again?

JESS

December 2014

His brilliant blue eyes. That's what I notice most, glinting with interest as I walk towards him in the marina bar. I take in his lightly tanned face and glance away. I can't help smiling when he keeps watching. That kind of scene plays out in bars everywhere, but it feels significant. Perhaps I'm giving it more meaning than it deserves. It's two nights before New Year's Eve and the promise of new beginnings.

Minutes earlier, conversations played around me and I'd checked the time. My friends weren't boring, just samey in the post-Christmas slump. I'd tried to back out, but Becca wouldn't let me. She said I'd enjoy it, in the soulless bar not properly on the waterfront, with not even a moonlit sea view to shake me from my disengaged state. At that time of night, there was only the occasional ferry churning through the dark to Portsmouth. Jonathan sat at our table of five and talked about his New Year's resolution to increase his pension contributions. He was part

11

of our group who met up now and then, and one reason for my reluctance to turn out on a cold night.

'Thank God for alcohol, eh?' Becca took a fortifying swig of her drink and ruffled her red head of curls. 'I resolve to have more fun.'

My gaze drifted round the bar. A couple walked past in their own world, holding hands and laughing. Why didn't I have that? I had friends, a home and a career, but I wanted more. I'd wanted more since Sachi from work got married last summer. I shared her infectious joy until the reading of 'Today I Married My Best Friend' and I choked up a little. Why does that kind of togetherness elude me?

Becca said I didn't try hard enough, but I wore myself out trying. I gave up after dating Rick for three months. We'd booked a trip to Barcelona and I couldn't wait, thinking it marked the start of something more serious. Then a friend told me he'd checked out her online dating profile and 'liked' it.

'Show me,' I said.

She called up his profile. *I'm single and honest* it said, and his status was *online now*. My heart sank. When I'd asked him, he said, 'Why would I limit myself?' I cancelled the holiday, crushed that he thought so little of me.

Becca met her husband at uni, in simpler dating times. She says I should get on and find someone. But I don't want someone, I want 'Today I Married My Best Friend'. Is it wrong to hold out for a warm, funny, sexy man who feels the same about me?

Then I see him, the blue-eyed man. He's looking right at me, taking me in. His smile speaks to my restlessness. He doesn't look away, and I don't mind because I like his interest, and his tousled hair, and those gorgeous eyes drawing me in.

There are enough of my friends not to miss me, and I need a break from Jonathan, who's offering to cook me an omelette sometime. 'I'm a very good cook', he says. He'd probably claim to be a good lover too. I break away. Becca makes a thing of me abandoning them for some bloke, but I can't even chat properly to her, not with Jonathan eager for a way into our conversation. I'll make it up to her. The man goes to the bar, and so do I, as if I've been waiting for him all along. He smiles as I approach him, and something inside me comes alive.

'Need a refill?'

'Thank you.'

'Your friends might seem more interesting after a couple more drinks.'

'They'll have a better time without me.'

'I doubt that. Your admirer isn't very happy.'

I glance over at Jonathan, who nurses a possessive look. 'He's just a friend.'

'He likes you. I can see why he doesn't want to lose you over here.'

He smiles an easy smile, and the barman pours our drinks. Up close, I admire the contours of his toned chest and strong arms, visible through his shirt. We make our introductions, clink glasses and then sit in a quiet corner and talk. I warm to his attentive chat and thoughtful little pauses, and the way he tilts his head when I speak.

'I used to keep my boat in the marina here,' he says.

'Ah, so you sail.' It suits his weathered good looks, the muscular arms from winching in sails. He looks at ease with taking on the elements. I picture him sailing into the wind on a sunny day.

'Do you ever sail?' he asks.

'I've never tried. I like being near the sea, though.'

'Would you like a go? You can come out on my boat when it warms up.'

'Sounds good,' I say, my voice all smudgy with alcohol.

He rests his elbows on the table and gazes intently at me. 'What do you like to do?'

'I like going to new places, weekends away. There are so many places I'd love to see. Where do you sail?'

'The Greek islands are my favourite.' His face lights up, eyes faraway. 'The beaches are wonderful. You can sail to a little bay, have a sandy beach to yourself and swim in crystal clear water.'

'Sounds amazing.'

He leans closer. I lean in too and catch a subtle drift of aftershave.

'So, if your admirer's just a friend,' he says, 'are you seeing anyone else?'

'Not right now. Work keeps me busy. I haven't put myself out there for a while.'

'Well, if you fancy putting yourself out there' – he looks down at his hands, less sure of himself – 'I'd love to go out with you sometime.'

I have a sudden urge to touch him, this complete stranger who I pretend not to find intoxicating. His deep voice draws

14

me in. He talks, and I look at his lips, thinking he'll be a good kisser.

Back home that night, I lie awake with a big grin on my face, though it strikes me I might not hear from him again. But he calls the next afternoon, and I like him even more for calling, not texting. It's real. Not like dating apps.

'Hello, is that Jess?'

'Yeah ... yes, it is. Hi.' I attempt to sound cool, not letting on that my heart's going a mile a minute.

'It's Rob. I really liked getting to know you last night.'

I grin down the phone.

'I'd love to see you again,' he says. 'You'll probably have plans on New Year's Eve, but if not, I know a beautiful spot on the waterfront ...'

I should say I have plans, try not to seem keen, but I *am* keen. So I say yes.

Even that early on, my future feels wrapped up with his. As midnight chimes in the New Year, it feels like a fresh start. I resolve to say yes to some new experiences. He leans in and tucks my hair behind one ear, his fingers trace my jawline, his gaze on me. My sapphire blue dress is silky against my skin, his hand warm on the small of my back.

I lean in to kiss him, struck by a thrill of anticipation. I was right: he is a good kisser. He puts his arms round me and rests his forehead on my forehead, which seems sweet and intimate. Later he'll just smile and I'll smile too, neither of us needing to say anything. Mine is the smile of someone who can't believe her luck.

He says I'm special. A while back, I'd have pulled away from

15

a man talking like that, but not now. You have to hear him say those things to know the resonance, or maybe you just have to be me. I'm physically attracted to him, but there's more to it – a hidden depth drawing me in, a quiet intelligence that speaks to me, and a sense of fun to carry me along. His relaxed confidence says everything's going to be fine. Your heart knows the real thing. It just knows.

'I bet he's good in bed,' Becca says, two weeks after New Year, when we meet up at her place.

'I expect so.'

'Hasn't he made a move?'

'We're getting to know each other. He's old-fashioned like that.'

'*Old-fashioned?*' Becca says, incredulous. 'You sure he's not a player?'

Normally the one to resist advances for a few dates at least, he caught me off-guard when I first stayed over. He was six years older than me, assured and experienced. *You can see he's lived*, Becca had said. We lounged on his sofa and drank sauvignon blanc, him casual and sexy in dark jeans and a shirt that I wanted to unbutton. Wine had never tasted so good, the mood seductive even before he lit candles in the bedroom.

He gave me one of his soft cotton shirts that nearly reached my knees. He went to clean his teeth and I slipped the shirt on. When he came back, he rolled up my sleeves that had frayed round the cuffs.

'It's lovely and soft,' I said.

'You look better in it than I do. Let's go to bed, I just want to hold you.'

It sounded like a line, but he did hold me, arms curved round me, face nuzzling my hair. It can be strange, sleeping with someone the first time, awkward and polite. With him, it felt natural. He said he couldn't get enough of me, but we had plenty of time.

The attraction burns strong and a slightly longer wait gives me even sweeter thoughts of him. I like his old-fashioned approach to romance: the way he phones instead of texting, and how he takes things slowly in the bedroom. He's genuine, and it's not what I'm used to, which makes him all the more intoxicating.

MIA

I woke up, my mouth all furred. The window rattled in the wind. When your bedroom has a sloping ceiling and a badly fitting window, you notice what the weather does. Too jaded for a shower, I pulled on yesterday's clothes. At least I didn't need to be anywhere. Ben had already walked the dogs and taken Stan to work with him. Darcy sprawled on his dog bed.

I worked at my desk, planning a local awareness campaign for my newest and now biggest client. They'd bought new sports equipment for the local school and pitched in at beach clear-ups, but hardly anyone knew their long list of good work. Locals blamed them for the rise in traffic that came instead from a neighbouring business. We had to change that now they needed planning permission for a factory expansion.

People advised me not to become a freelance PR consultant. They thought I didn't need the stress after everything else. They didn't know how much I wanted it to work, because I'd already screwed up enough. I pushed forward to distance myself from the past. I no longer trusted anyone with my livelihood, even though Ben bore no resemblance to my ex. His landscaping business kept him grounded, and he wasn't one for taking off and cutting ties.

After three hours of solid work, I stretched and looked out at the rain-lashed day. My little garden was bathed in grey January light, the dormant shrubs battered by winter weather. A sharp knock on the front door startled me. Had the detectives come back? I thought that was the worst that could happen, until I answered the door.

'Mia?'

'Yes?'

'My name's Rachel. My husband . . .' Her voice tailed off.

Teardrops of rain scattered her face and her honey-blonde hair. She didn't care about the rain or didn't notice. I hid my panic and asked her in. The house was a mess and so was I, with ratty hair and crumpled clothes. I still hadn't made it into the shower. Not how I'd choose to meet my ex's new wife, but there were bigger things to worry about.

She brought in the damp from outside. I offered her tea or coffee, which she didn't accept or decline as she followed me through to the kitchen. I put the kettle on, needing something to occupy my unsteady hands. We could have done with something stronger. Barely noon, and I already craved a real drink.

'Would you like a towel to dry off?'

She brushed the offer away with a small shake of her head, and leaned into the doorway, arms clutched round herself. Why was she here? I didn't have to let her in, but I wanted to find out what she knew about the murder, since the police hadn't given much away.

'How did you find me?' I asked.

'Rob had your details written down.'

I hadn't given him my address. He'd kept track of me, even after I'd taken out the injunction.

We sat on the sofa, where the detectives had questioned me yesterday. I settled my surprise, forcing it into the pit of my stomach. She angled politely towards me, her face unnaturally pale and her eyes glassy from too much crying or too little sleep.

It bothered me that he'd had enough charm left to snare her. The charm he could tap into at will or turn off when it suited him. How dare he? How dare he drive our marriage off a cliff and leave me smouldering in the wreckage while he found someone even younger to prey on? Not that it should matter, but it bloody well did.

'Have the police spoken to you?' Her voice was so soft, I strained to hear. She gripped her mug and stared into it as if the answer would come from there.

'Yes, routine I think.'

'They said there were similarities with our relationships.' A hopeless melancholy hung behind her words.

'I didn't have it as bad, and I left before anything was repossessed.'

I'd said too much, but only what the police had told me, probing for a raw nerve to get me talking, not that it worked. She closed her eyes and in the stillness, I heard her breathing. She looked as if she could hardly bear the pain.

'I'm sorry. It must be terrible.'

'I need to ask you something.' She glanced at me, purple smudges of sleeplessness under her eyes.

I froze. She'd seen me with him before he died. That's why she was here. She'd come for a better look before telling the police. *Stop panicking. Deny it. Keep it simple and don't say much. That's what you're supposed to do, isn't it, when you lie?* I was a terrible liar.

She only saw me from behind at a distance as dusk fell. It could have been anyone. He'd seen her there. He'd looked past me, further along the shore and told me it was her. I'd turned. A woman with her back to us had clipped purposefully up the concrete steps built into the sea wall, her body rigid, as if she'd seen us and marched off. She disappeared behind a scrubby patch of brambles and I lost sight of her. Now he was dead and she was sitting beside me.

'The police are looking for evidence to charge me,' Rachel said. 'If they do, will you be a defence witness?'

'Me?' The question floored me. 'What good will I do? We don't know each other.'

She gazed back into her tea, swaying a little, steadying herself. I saw a trace of myself in her. I pushed away memories of leaving him. How many women had he done this to?

'I thought you might say you loved him. And that you'd never have killed him.'

'How would that help your defence?'

'You said your marriage had similarities to mine. Rob could be difficult, but I didn't kill him, same as you didn't when you

21

were married to him.' She looked through the window at the rain-darkened day, her eyes wide as if willing herself not to cry. 'They think I did it because of how he was, but I loved him. He wasn't well towards the end. I just wanted him to get better.'

'But why would the police charge you?'

'I found his body. I touched him. His blood was all over me.'

Jesus. She looked ready to crumple. Pity seeped through me. I'd escaped from him, so he ruined her life instead. And just like me at first, she couldn't see it. My throat tightened and when I spoke, the words came out all choked.

'It won't do any good, me giving evidence. I didn't stay because I loved him. He controlled me. He made it hard to leave.'

I fought the urge to confide anything else. I shouldn't be talking to his widow like this. Even if she didn't see me that day, I was already in too deep. 'It won't help, me giving evidence. I'll make it worse.'

She looked at me, hollow-eyed.

'I'm sorry for everything you're going through.' I stood up to break the tension, wanting her to leave. 'Will you make it home okay?'

She stood up too, looking relieved to be going. Thank God she didn't ask anything else, since I couldn't take much more.

'Wait,' I said as she turned to leave. 'Give me your number.'

She looked grateful and reeled it off for me to tap into my phone. When she left, I poured a glass of wine and drank it quickly, one hand flat on the kitchen worktop to steady myself.

I used to lie awake trying to dream up the perfect murder.

Never mind that blood made me queasy and I'd rather guide a fly outside than kill it. But he killed something in me, and it turned out I wasn't such a softie after all. Some things you can't forgive. Thoughts like that can consume you and turn you into the sort of person you never expected to be. I could hardly swear in court that I didn't want to kill him. Given the evidence, no jury would believe me.

JESS

February 2015

Last night, Rob asked me to marry him. I smile sleepily, not quite awake but holding the thought close. So perfect I might have dreamt it.

'Happy birthday,' he murmurs, easing his warm body against mine. He'd said it earlier, at five-past midnight at the rooftop bar in Rome. We'd been drinking champagne, looking out at silhouettes of old buildings. He took my hands in his.

'Marry me?'

I caught my breath.

'We're good together,' he said. 'Will you marry me?'

I said yes, and he kissed me. He held my hand and slid a ring on my finger.

'I had it made specially for you.'

'Oh wow,' I said, looking at the diamond ring. It was dainty and charming, not what I'd have chosen, but he'd had it made for me, which meant more than buying one in a shop.

After a late night, now we lie wrapped up with each other, slipping in and out of sleep. When daylight shines through the curtains, I blink in the morning light, happier than I ever thought possible. Room service arrives, and we feed each other croissants, roll around on crumpled sheets, and then have a shower together in the vast marble bathroom. He gets dressed, and I stand at the window with a view across Rome. The ring feels foreign on my finger and I hold it to the light. I take a photo of it against the backdrop. Perhaps I'll post something on Facebook or Instagram. I don't share my whole life online and never had much reason to show off, but I like having something good to shout about for a change. He comes up behind me.

'What are you doing?'

I lean back against him and show him my Facebook page. 'Shall we let people know?'

'I didn't think you were that sort of person.' He kisses my neck, and the kisses carry on down to my shoulder. 'People pretending how perfect their lives are, trying to outdo each other. All the pressure to look good.'

He's right. I know he's not into social media. I close my phone and turn in his arms.

'There's nothing fake about us,' he says between kisses.

We take to the streets of Rome. My first time in Italy. We saunter through crumbling alleys into little Renaissance piazzas, some with a fountain in the middle or a statue of lovers. Stalls dotted around sell kitsch Madonna and child figurines, adding to the charm, in my rose-tinted view. A couple pose in front of the Trevi Fountain with a selfie stick.

25

'It's a shame when people experience everything through a screen,' he says softly, so only I can hear.

'Especially somewhere beautiful like this,' I say.

He only uses his mobile for texts and calls. I like the way he finds me more engaging than his devices. I tuck my phone away and focus on us, determined to break the habit of checking it during every lull.

The sunshine fades as we head for the Vatican, leaving a chill in the air. Gathering clouds turn the skies dark, and rain splatters the pavement. We shelter in a doorway but the rain keeps on, heavy and persistent, leaving the streets awash. But even rain has a touch of noir romance in this slightly unreal film version of my life. Rome can do no wrong, even when it pours down.

Rob hails a boy in a hooded mac with an armful of umbrellas. 'How much? Um, *quanto costa*?'

We buy an overpriced umbrella and run, splashing round puddles to find the Vatican entrance. Closed. Something to do with official business. We squint through pelting rain at a time-table beside the locked doors.

'Bugger.' He clutches me round the middle. 'Shut till Monday. I wanted to show you the Sistine Chapel.'

'Next time. Let's have a coffee.'

We dash to the nearest café. I breathe in wafts of aromatic coffee as we cram in at a small table alongside an Italian couple with a sweet baby. We coo at the *bambino*, who smiles gummily at us.

'Do you want children?' he says with a look of encouragement. 'Guess we should've talked about this before I proposed.'

'Yes. I would like children.'

'Good. Me too.' He kisses me, which I take as some kind of agreement, and then he goes to lean on the counter. I tuck my damp hair behind my ears and watch him turn his charm on the waitress. He looks back at me and she reluctantly follows his gaze.

He says *grazie* and bounds back. I go to ask what he'd said, when she weaves through the tables towards us, her shining dark hair swinging from side to side. She holds a slab of cake with a candle burning in the top, singing a theatrical *'Appy Birthday*. People near us clap and smile.

He smiles back and says in faltering Italian, *'Le chiedo di sposarmi ... e lei risponde di si.'* He turns to me and says, 'I asked her to marry me, and she said yes!'

More clapping and approving murmurs. I kick his leg.

'Bella signora, much beautiful!' He throws his arms wide and leans over for a theatrical kiss.

'Stop it.' But I can't help smiling.

We return home to reality, and the next day, I only just make it to work on time. Work has slipped from my focus, pushed aside for him.

'How was Rome?' Sachi asks.

Helen looks over from her desk, but I blank her. Her competitiveness and tendency to steal ideas don't go down well with me. I pull off my gloves and show Sachi the ring.

'You're engaged!' she squeals. 'Let me see.'

She examines the ring, her brown eyes wider than ever. Just

as well our boss isn't in, who expects us to pretend we don't have personal lives. I've always done the job at full tilt, loving the buzz of meetings on the fly, the frenzy of emails and a flow of marketing materials to produce.

'It feels weird. Like it's not really happening.'

'That's because you've been single for a while. Enjoy the excitement while it lasts.'

It was Sachi who'd married her best friend last summer. She offers to bring her stack of wedding magazines in. I prefer her response to Becca's, who I've avoided since his proposal. She'll only put an edge on it. I'd sent her a text from Rome and she'd fired back an incredulous, *WTF?! Phone me as soon as you're home.*

I haven't phoned, so she calls me at work.

'Hello, stranger.' She draws the vowels out to make a point.

'Hi, Bec.' I grimace.

'I've been phoning you. Thanks for your text. Were you drunk?'

'Why?'

'"In Rome, in love, engaged."' She reads my text, deadpan.

'Rob took me to Rome and proposed.' I splay my fingers and look at the ring that I want to show and hide from her in equal measure.

'Are you getting married?'

'At some point, yeah.' I balance the phone between my shoulder and ear, ready to zone her out with quiet typing.

'Remember to mention it to me afterwards.'

'I didn't expect him to propose. It happened so quickly—'

'Well yeah, since you hardly know him.'

28

'*Mum?* Is that you?'

'What?'

'Nothing, sorry. Forget it.'

She tuts.

'You know, it's usual to offer congratulations when your best friend gets engaged.'

Out of everyone I knew, Becca understood that I didn't want to stay single and stuck in a cycle of crappy dates that go nowhere. On Christmas Eve, just days before first meeting him, Becca and I had a late night present-wrapping session for her children. Fuelled by rioja, she took on a badgering tone.

'You deserve someone nice,' she slurred, her lips stained with wine.

'As if it's that easy.'

'Leave it too long and the good men will have been taken.'

'You'll be saying I'll lose all my teeth next.'

'And your marbles. I've been saving baby things for you.'

'Really? Give them to charity.'

'But you want kids. You're good with Jake and Ellie. When you meet the right person, it'll be at least two years before you're settled and both ready.'

'I'm not that desperate I'll settle for anyone.'

'If you don't mind me saying, sometimes you don't give it a good enough chance.'

I went to defend myself, but she kept on.

'No one's perfect. God knows, Adrian isn't. All I'm saying is don't hold out for some notion of a perfect soulmate. Find a decent man who wants to commit.'

Becca's drunken heckling had echoed what I quietly believed. I did sometimes end relationships at the first sign of trouble, but now I was making a go of it with someone who wanted commitment. I'd found my perfect man, so why couldn't she be happy for me?

MIA

I fumbled with the door key and rushed to pick up the ringing landline. Mr Darcy barked to welcome me home. I rattled in, dropping keys and bags to lunge for the phone, shushing the dog.

'Hello?'

'Darling, it's Mum.' She sounded breathless, still struggling after having a stroke. She'd been rushed to hospital just two days before the murder. 'Have you seen the papers?'

The knot inside me tightened.

'That poor girl. You still there?'

'What's happened?'

'Rachel, her name is.' She paused for breath after every few words, her speech slow and laboured. 'I keep thinking it could've been you.'

'What?' I hunched over the phone, my body tensing.

'She's been arrested on suspicion of murder. Well, it says a woman of thirty-two has been arrested, so it must be her.'

'Must it?' I tried to sound calm.

'I saw her photo in the paper when they covered the murder last week.' Mum paused to take a few breaths. 'It said then his wife was thirty-two. They didn't have enough evidence to charge her before now.'

Two weeks since the murder. They must be under pressure to make arrests.

'It says police divers retrieved a gun near the boat on their second attempt to find the murder weapon.'

I sank to the floor and sat on my heels, gripping the phone.

'Are you there?'

'The gun was in the water?' I screwed up my face, confused.

'Well, yes, if divers retrieved it.'

My heart pounded in my throat.

'Where did she get a gun?' Mum asked, her voice cracked and vulnerable.

I knew exactly where she'd got the gun. 'Do they seriously think she did it?'

'All it says is something about . . . hang on.' The newspaper rustled. 'Forensic evidence. She's a slight little thing. Doesn't look capable.'

She didn't look capable, but he might have driven her to it. The police must think Rachel did it, giving me a twist of guilty relief. Had she simply incriminated herself? I pictured her pale face and self-contained vulnerability when she'd visited.

'You should tell the police what he was really like,' Mum said.

'They already know. Don't talk to anyone. Please. We'd better keep quiet.'

Not so long ago she'd have speculated about it to friends, brimming with indignation. I didn't expect her to say the wrong thing now, not with the fight gone out of her. My mum, previously a woman of barbed comments and forthright views, had become a reduced person because of me.

I told her the police had it covered so she needn't worry. She responded with a defeated sigh, probably worn out by it all. I put the phone down and pressed my palms to my face. In the dark, I saw his dead body splayed in a louche pose. I jolted in shock, as if I stood right there, him dead before me and all that blood. My mind played tricks like that, taking me where I didn't want to go.

Darcy whined for attention. I ruffled the fur around his ears. When my head stopped swimming, I took him for a walk and made a plan. First, I'd have to go online and trawl the news to pre-empt Mum, who must have been scouring the papers. Then I'd get a handle on why the police had arrested Rachel. Not yet though. The less I knew the better with Ben due over. He phoned my mobile just as I came home from the dog walk.

'Hey you,' he said.

'Hi, are you still coming round?'

'Yeah, I just wanted to check you're okay. I saw online that the wife's been arrested.'

'I know. It's awful.'

'And you said she looked so fragile.'

I'd told Ben about Rachel's visit, but hadn't gone into detail.

'There's nothing you can do, okay?' he said. 'I'm coming over. I'll get a takeaway.'

Ben arrived a bit later. Stan padded in alongside him, both with matching sandy hair and loyal brown eyes.

'How are you doing?' he said.

'I'll be all right.'

'Course you will. Let's relax. You choose a film and I'll do the food.'

Ben watched the film, and I quietly despaired. Why did they arrest Rachel, and what if she pointed the finger at me? She might have seen me on the beach and come here to check it was me. She didn't confront me, but if she told the police, they would know I'd lied. But I'd be in deeper trouble if I told them the truth.

Ben and I held hands. The credits rolled and he flicked over to one of those 'setting-up-home-in-the-sun' programmes. I sipped wine, trying not to glug it down. I sensed his eyes lighting up at the coastal shots.

'Fancy a holiday? Be good to get away.'

'Um ...'

'Somewhere hot. So you can relax.'

'Yeah. No ... Sorry, I can't. Not now.'

'Maybe in the summer, then. We'll find somewhere good to explore, get cheap flights.'

'Hmm.' I needed a break, but couldn't manage a week or two of uninterrupted Ben and trying not to fall apart over the murder investigation. Too much free time and I might confess all to him in the boozy warmth of a beachside bar. He held off asking questions, but it wouldn't last. I could almost hear his mind whirring.

'Mexico was good, wasn't it?' Ben said.

That was last year, when I still expected his personality to change and the mind games to start. I remembered the warm night when a band played at the beachside hotel. We danced barefoot on the moonlit beach to the strains of music and the shush of seawater lapping the beach. I used to search for his hidden agenda, until I accepted he didn't have one and started to relax.

'It was lovely. We'll have a holiday . . . later.'

When the programme finished, we went to bed and he held me close. It reminded me of when I first got Darcy. He would snore beside me in a contented heap, and I wouldn't want to cry so much. After a while, I started sleeping instead of thinking up elaborate revenge fantasies, but lately I'd gone back to having no control over the darkness inside my head. I'd been the one storing up stone-cold revenge, yet the police had gone after Rachel. No one had asked for my alibi yet, and I was all too aware I didn't have one.

When I did slip off into sleep, the dreams pressed heavily. My ex came for me and instead of running, I drifted with no ground beneath me. I woke with a start, panicked arms flailing, trying to turn on the bedside lamp.

Ben's arms found me in the dark. 'Hey, shush, I've got you.'

His whispered breath on the side of my face reminded me that it was him and it was okay. 'You're safe now. He's gone. You can put the past behind you.'

Sometime later, I woke up standing next to the window, whispering to myself. I must have opened the blind in my sleep, as if trying to shed light on something. Ben pulled me back to bed. He slept and I drifted in and out, the nightmares ready to take over.

In the morning, we had breakfast, and Ben talked about South East Asia for our next trip.

'When your mum's better,' he said. 'I know you won't want to venture too far until she's recovered. It's been a tough month for you, what with the murder and your mum's stroke. How's she doing?'

'She's tired and her speech is still slow. I'll make her some soup later and drop it in.'

After we'd cleared away the bowls and mugs, I switched on the computer at my desk in the corner. In the two weeks since the police visit, I'd forced myself to stay in control and keep working. Darcy and Stan slumped at my feet, their presence settling me.

Ben made another cup of tea, and I rubbed my eyes as the emails loaded.

'Any excitement in the world of PR?' Ben asked.

'Plenty. If councillors touring a factory counts as excitement. I've advised the client to stop viewing the council as the enemy and start talking to them instead.'

I scanned down the replies to the factory invitation, until the subject line of an email made me pulse with fear.

I know your secret.

My heart hammered in my chest. I clicked on the message. It opened to a blank email. Nothing except that subject line. Who'd sent it? The email address meant nothing, just spammy-looking letters and numbers from a Gmail account. It might have been random, I told myself. I deleted it before Ben looked over my shoulder.

JESS

February 2015

We walk along the blustery shore to see his boat. Wispy clouds breeze through the sky and sunlight reflects off the green sea.

'I like the sea when it's wild and windswept. Maybe it's the drama,' I say.

'You'll like sailing then.' Rob's face is animated and he's keen to show me the boat.

'But I only want to look out at it when it's stormy. And I don't like deep water.'

'Can you swim?'

'Not that well. My dad taught me. He wasn't very patient.'

'You don't have to be a good swimmer. I'll keep you safe.' The salty wind gives his hair a tousled look. 'How old were you when your dad left?'

'Twelve. He left on Christmas Eve, which was just like him.' I'd told him a little about my parents' marriage. 'Causing maximum disruption.'

'Must've been tough on you. We both had difficult child-hoods. That's why we understand each other.' He hugs me into his big sailing jacket. He'd told me about his mum dying of cancer when he was a teenager. His dad had remarried soon after.

We reach the boatyard. He takes my hand and helps me aboard. 'I can't wait for you to see inside.'

He leads me down the little staircase. The sleek interior surprises me, all contoured wood and cream furnished interior.

'This is the galley,' he says, full of enthusiasm.

'The kitchen?'

'We call it the galley on board.'

'Right.' I open the door alongside me. 'Oh, a little shower room!'

'It's called the head.'

I snort. 'Why?'

'I don't know.' He doesn't react to my amusement.

'Call it the shower room, then.'

'It's the head.' His eyes shine when he talks about sailing. I can see his passion runs deep and I stop my teasing.

'It's beautiful, but I don't think I'll ever be into boats the way you are.'

'Just wait till we're sailing, then you'll get it. You can't beat the feeling of racing through the waves on a hot summer's day.'

He leads me down a narrow hallway and opens another door.

'Through here's the aft cabin.'

'The bedroom?'

'It's our cabin.' He raises a suggestive eyebrow, and pulls a duvet from a divan drawer. We undress messily. He covers me in the duvet and holds my shivery body against his warm skin.

'How are you so warm?' I say. 'It's freezing in here.'

We kiss. Despite the cold, damp cabin, I warm into his touch, the sweet intensity and feeling so close to him. My first time on a yacht. I imagine us on a balmy day, the boat's gentle sway in tune with us. He likens sleeping on a boat to being cradled in the womb. Proving the point, he drifts into a nap. I lie awake, looking at my engagement ring, becoming used to it. I rest my head in the crook of his arm, breathing his musky warm smell and the faint sea-spray scent of his aftershave. When he wakes, we light candles in the afternoon gloom and he uncorks a bottle of champagne to celebrate Valentine's Day.

'It's not my thing, Valentine's Day,' I say. 'It's cheesy when you're a couple, and you feel a failure when you're single.'

'You're no failure. I'm lucky to have you.'

Propped up in bed, we gaze at candlelit shadows flickering on the cabin walls. He gives me a present wrapped in tissue paper and a bow. 'I know you like books.'

I unwrap a book on sailing. Not my usual reading material, but I like that he wants to bring me into his world. A bright photo on the cover shows an athletic couple on a boat racing through the waves. Rob plays with a strand of my hair and talks about the time he dived into the sea, unaware of rocks under the water.

'It nearly paralysed me. They warned me before the surgery that I might not walk again. All that time flat on my back in hospital, I put my life right, in my head at least. I promised myself I'd get better and make the most of every minute.'

He'd told me about it before, how he'd recovered from the injury, and it gave an added dimension to his ambitions.

'Sailing brought me back. Made me realise how good it was to be alive.'

I solemnly clink his champagne flute.

'What about you?' he asks. 'What do you want from life?'

'For us to always be like this.'

'What else?' He draws me closer.

'To enjoy life . . . To have a decent place to live.'

'We will. Why don't we go house-hunting? Buy some-where bigger.'

'Sell both our houses?' I ask.

'And find your dream home.'

He lives in a Modernist deckhouse on the coast, raised on stilts to make the most of sea views. A cluster of them stand at the quiet end of a windswept harbour. He likes the unconventional style, along with the view. Londoners mostly own the others as weekend crash pads by the sea. It's more like a bolthole than a home, and my tiny terraced house is too far from the sea, his work and the boat, so neither would work for us to move into together.

Rob arranges for us to view a cottage in the Sussex countryside that Saturday.

I gasp when we pull up in front of it. Drifts of narcissi surround the flint cottage, and smoke puffs from the chimney. 'Can we afford it?'

'Don't worry about that.'

So I don't. A grinning estate agent opens the door and welcomes us into the homely sitting room. Logs burn in an open fire. I long to kick off my shoes and settle on the sofa in front of it. The agent shepherds us through to the kitchen, with views of the garden, a low flint wall at the end and fields beyond.

'It's a proper farmhouse kitchen, with an Aga,' he says, stepping back for us to see.

An Aga won't suit my life of rushing in and out, microwave pinging, running late. But I'd get the hang of it. The agent directs us up the creaky staircase.

'There are three good-sized bedrooms. Do you have children?'

'Not yet.' Rob winks at me.

'But don't you want a sea view?' I ask, my voice low.

'The best sea view is from a boat. We're not far from the water. So long as we've got room to breathe, I can live in the countryside.'

He hates being hemmed in, and a family home by the sea round here costs a fortune. If he gives up his sea view for me, I'll sell my place to live here. Stepping out of the back door, the sound of a child playing in a nearby garden carries to us. I can't help imagining our own children playing here.

Out of earshot of the estate agent, he pulls me close. 'I love it. What do you think?'

'It's perfect.'

'So are you.' He hugs me into his chest. 'Would you like to live here?'

Of course I would, with him, the man I've been holding out for. Happiness wells up. I marvel at finding my way to him, both of us unattached at the right time.

MIA

Mia Fallon is a cold-blooded killer.

I stared at the email in horror. The same address as the strange email from a few days back. I steeled myself and clicked on it, expecting another blank message, but it got worse: She fucks with people's heads. She led him on and shot him. If the police don't come for you, it will be an absolute travesty of justice.

Who is this? I fired back.

Someone who knows what you're capable of.

Fuck. Fuck. Fuck. I shut down my emails and pushed away from the desk. Darcy followed me to the hall, where I pulled on my winter jacket and clicked the lead on to his collar. I slammed outside and marched away from the house, the computer and the poisonous words still there.

We took our usual route to open fields and Darcy ran free. I slowed and the drizzle cooled my mind. Two messages in a week. I had no idea where they came from, and that made it worse. Who suspected me, and what did they want?

We circled the field and then headed towards home, where I sat on the stairs in my boots and jacket and scoured the internet on my phone for any new details of the murder investigation. The news trail had gone quiet, but I picked up a small mention that stated Rachel had been released under investigation. I felt light-headed, so put my phone down and stayed on the stairs until Ben dropped in soon after, Stan at his heels. He hugged an armful of travel brochures to his chest.

'You just got home?' He looked at me still in my outdoor gear.

'I was checking for news.' I picked up my phone to show him the headline about Rachel being released.

'Oh yeah, I saw.'

He must be keeping tabs on the news too. I kicked off my boots and followed him through to the kitchen.

'Do they still think she did it?' Ben asked.

'God knows. They haven't charged her. Maybe they need more evidence.'

'Or maybe they're looking at other suspects.'

I stiffened. Did the police have me on their radar? The doorbell rang and I jumped, looking in fear towards the door. Ben gave me a strange look and went to answer it. Just someone collecting for charity. I placed a hand over my beating heart and told myself to get a grip.

'He sounded like trouble, your ex,' Ben said as he came back into the kitchen.

'The police said he was going to prison.' Or had they? The memory of their visit blurred. I'd known of his looming prison sentence but who'd said what and when had become muddled in my head. I'm pretty sure he'd told me on the day he died. But the police might have said it too.

'Prison?' Ben looked shocked. 'What for?'

'A scam. Conning someone.'

'Was Rachel involved? Is that why she shot him? Maybe she was tangled in his scams and it got out of hand.'

'We don't know if she shot him. She's been released. More likely he misled her too.'

It gnawed at me, Rachel being released under investigation. I couldn't help thinking she had a hidden motive for coming here the other day, as well as asking for my help should she be charged. The news report said she'd been released two days ago, so the emails could be from her. But what could she gain from tormenting me, rather than telling the police? It didn't make sense, unless the emails came from someone else.

'The police haven't been back, have they?' Ben asked.

'No. But they might now Rachel's been released.'

'Did they ask where you were when it happened?'

'I'm sorry – what?' I tidied the kitchen to detract from my edginess, shunting his hopeful sunny brochures to the edge of the counter. Easier to look up holidays online, but brochures were harder to ignore than a website. 'Are you saying I need an alibi?'

He turned to face the window overlooking my wintery garden. 'Shame we didn't have plans that night, then you'd be covered.'

Ben's rational mind had a knack of finding its way to the truth. I picked up a sharp knife and gripped it.

'Not that you need one, obviously,' he added.

Clutching the knife, I opened the plastic around one of his brochures and blindly flicked through.

'Are you annoyed with me?' He eased the knife from my grip.

'No, but talking about it makes me twitchy.'

'Sorry, I'm being insensitive. It's all those crime podcasts I listen to. Course you don't need an alibi.'

Don't I?

I flipped the brochure shut, and then opened it again, trying to mask my unease.

He wrapped his arms around me. 'Are you okay? You look tired.'

'Mmm. Are you staying tonight?' My words were muffled against the padding of his jacket. He stroked my hair.

'No. Early start tomorrow. I'm behind on everything. My schedule's gone to pot from all the rain. Will you be all right? I'll stay if you want.'

'I'll be fine.' I patted Stan goodbye, wanting to make up for my mood.

He called for Stan to follow, and they retraced their steps through the narrow hall. Darcy and I stood at the front door as Ben unlocked his bike from the drainpipe. He left to cycle home in the cold evening, Stan trotting alongside.

Darcy watched me double lock the front door and try

the handle to check it was secure. I muted my mobile and had a bath.

Lying in bed later, my mind fell back to the time Rob and I went to a busy pub beside the River Hamble. A woman with sun-kissed hair and a glowing outdoorsy face had walked in, her face untroubled until she glanced our way. He tensed, she took a protective step back, and then disappeared.

I looked at him. 'Something you said?'

'I used to know her.' He pursed his lips and busied himself with the bar menu.

I'd marked her down as a spurned lover. But now I realised it was because he had form. She'd reacted just as I would have if I'd bumped into him after I left. Was she reading about Rachel's arrest too, wondering if that could have been her?

After leaving Rob, I avoided everywhere we'd gone, and everywhere he might go, not just to steer clear of him but to escape the memories that hurt so much. I wanted to remove all trace of him. Then all that changed. When I found out he'd done, two days before the murder, the past came crashing back. It went beyond the other ways he'd tried to ruin my life. I had swung to the other extreme, furiously seeking him out. Sometimes even good people are pushed too far. I used to consider myself a decent person. Now, I'm less sure.

The night carried on, silent around me. I curled up and intrusive thoughts dominated my mind. Thoughts of the murder, the gun, the blood. If only I'd stayed away from him the night he died.

JESS

March 2015

'One more day, and then we'll be in the Med,' he says before leaving for work.

I pull out my summer clothes for our trip to the Canary Islands. It puts me behind, and then rush hour roadworks hold me up. I arrive twenty minutes late and catch sight of my boss unexpectedly in the office. *Bugger.* I stride in to a flurry of good mornings.

Everyone lays on a busy performance for Liz. She sits bolt upright at her computer, carefully positioned so she can see us all. The blood-red lipstick on her pursed lips stands out against her pale face. She glares at the clock and picks up a folder from her desk.

'Jess? A word please.' She fixes her gaze on me. 'Now you're here.'

I groan inwardly. She click-clacks from the open plan area to the meeting room. Helen looks smug at her desk. Teacher's pet. We sit down and Liz opens the folder.

'I'll get straight to the point.'

Brochures slide from the folder onto the table, the same one in several foreign language versions. File copies of the latest brochure I worked on. We have digital versions and use hard copies too.

'Notice anything?'

I pick one up to examine, with a sinking feeling.

'Oh God, the logo.' They've used the wrong bloody logo. It's the old one, from before our corporate rebrand.

'Yes, the logo.'

'I don't know how that happened.'

'You signed it off.'

'I missed it. I'm sorry. The printer must have used old artwork.'

'It's a huge print job. Thousands of copies.'

I want to bury my head in my hands. Thousands of copies already shipped around the world. How did that happen? I take pride in attention to detail and making everything run smoothly, or at least I used to.

'We have limited resources, *as you know*, so it can't be rectified.' She shuffles the brochures back into the folder, her mouth a disapproving line. 'How did we come to be in this situation?'

'I've been busy. I'm back on top of everything now. It won't happen again.'

'We're here to do a job. I do my job and I expect you to do yours. Understand?'

'Understood.'

'We should also look at your timekeeping.'

Should I tell her I was too busy having sex? I almost laugh. Last night flashes into my mind, when I'd rushed home from work and Rob arrived back not long after.

'What a day,' he'd said. 'I couldn't wait to get back to you.'

He loosened his tie and undid the buttons of my shirt.

'I need a shower,' he said, 'with you.'

We undressed each other on the way. I'd never been into shower sex, but everything felt good with him.

I zone back in to Liz and her sanctimonious tones, pursing my lips like hers. She only joined the company last October. She must have preferred me before I met Rob in December, back when work came first.

'We'll review your performance in a month. I'll sign off all your print jobs from now.'

Back at my desk, I despatch several emails in brisk succession. The first one goes to my print rep, asking why an obsolete logo found its way onto a massive print job. Their mistake, but I hadn't spotted it.

'Helen?' Liz calls over to my colleague. 'Can you take over the New York trade fair?'

That's my trip. My first business trip somewhere exciting. I let out a tortured breath. Six months of building relationships in the US, all the legwork and planning, and now Liz snatches it away. Helen bounces in her chair, trying not to do a victory lap round the office. Liz asks Sachi to rebook the flights in Helen's name. She checks they're business class. I hide my dismay, but my mood sinks.

Liz makes a long phone call, and Sachi brings me a mug of coffee.

'You okay?'

My vision clouds and I take a jagged breath. 'Not really.'

'Why'd she give New York to Helen?'

'I screwed up. She's being spiteful.'

'She should watch that. Someone might spit in her coffee.' Sachi turns on her heel and returns to her desk.

I pass my files over to Helen, avoiding eye contact. I try to engross myself in an advertising budget spreadsheet. The columns and figures swim, despite my efforts to keep it together. All I want is to be with Rob. I fight the urge to walk out and never come back.

On our last full day in the Canaries, I watch his broad, muscular shoulders as he winches in the sails. The Canary Islands are even better than Rome. Each day the sea breeze takes us to a new beach or harbour, under a never-ending sky of forget-me-not blue. He shows me how to take the helm and steer towards our destination, and I love going barefoot on the sun-drenched boat.

'You're a natural,' he says.

A boat carrying a family passes us, and the children wave from the deck. We wave back.

'Kids love sailing,' he says.

'Did you sail as a child?' I remember he'd said about learning in his twenties.

'No, my dad never took us to the beach or on holiday. I never set foot on a boat as a kid.'

He didn't talk much about his dad. I guess his life took a difficult turn when his mum died and his dad remarried.

'Do you ever speak to your dad?'

'He's dead.'

'Oh ... I'm sorry. I didn't realise.' I knew they'd fallen out over his stepmum, but he didn't mention that he'd died.

'It's fine. We weren't close.'

We drop anchor in a new bay and I swim in the shallow turquoise water over milky-white sand. He jumps in with his snorkel gear and bobs up, sleek as a seal. He snorkels after little fish, and the sea splishes lazily against the boat. I float on my back, making silvery ripples with my fingers. He surfaces now and then to offer up the mask or tread water and chat alongside me.

'Isn't it perfect?' he says.

'Picture perfect.'

I climb out and dry off by lying on the deck. He follows and lies beside me.

'This is how it's meant to be,' he says with a look of pure contentment.

'Shame it's only for a few days.'

'We can come back for longer. Take off for our honeymoon and explore the islands. Let's go to the Greek islands. I'd love to take you sailing round there.'

'That'd be amazing.' The wooden deck beneath me feels so warm it could lull me to sleep.

That evening, we watch the sunset with a beer.

'So what's your verdict on sailing?' he asks.

'I like it. And we didn't drown.'

'I knew you'd take to it.'

'Shame we have to fly home tomorrow.' I gaze at a beach resort in the distance, prettily lit up.

He drapes his arm around my shoulder. 'It is.'

'We should live like this forever.'

'Let's teleport our lives over here,' he says. 'Then we won't have to go back.'

'Cool. Can we do that?'

'Not in the real world. But we could live here,' he says. 'Though I suppose you'd miss your life back home. Your job.'

'Mmm.' I don't want to think about my run-in with Liz. I've hardly checked my phone since we came away. Work keeps me connected to the online world, but his views on messaging and social media have rubbed off. This digital detox has a lot going for it. It's freeing to engage with the world rather than stare at a screen. I can be someone different out here. Start afresh.

'You're right though,' he says. 'If we lived like this, I'd be so happy. Let's go to the Greek islands for our honeymoon. Sail our boat over. Ours is better than this crummy charter boat.'

'I can only take two weeks off at a time.'

'I was thinking three or four months.'

'Ha! You haven't met my boss. She'd never let me go for that long. Nice thought, though. If only we could take off for months on end.'

'Your boss needs to relax. If she had what we had, she wouldn't care about a stupid logo. Have you thought about working for yourself? Then you won't be tied down.'

'I'd love to if it meant coming places like this.'

He pulls me into a hug. 'We could run a business together. Wouldn't that be great?'

It would be great. He makes everything sound achievable. The sun dips below the horizon and I allow myself to imagine us together in the future, settled and running a successful business together, with a family, in a beautiful location like this.

MIA

Darcy chased after a ball in the park and I ploughed through my options. Instinct told me to lie low, but I longed for some insight into the police investigation. They hadn't rearrested Rachel. Did that mean they were pursuing other lines of enquiry? I couldn't ask the police, but what about asking Rachel? Media coverage of the murder went cold after the report of her release from custody. She was the only person I knew with a connection to the murder, and I needed to uncover if she was sending the emails. Should I call her? She'd been the one to approach me and had looked relieved when I'd asked for her number. I could leave a message and let her call me back if she wanted.

Darcy trotted back, ball in mouth and tongue lolling out to signal he'd run around enough. He flopped at my feet, and I scrolled through my phone to Rachel's number. So much I wanted to ask, but I stayed torn. My rational mind told me to steer clear of anyone involved with the murder, so I checked emails instead. Another anonymous message pinged through. I read it with a fist pressed to my mouth.

You're a dark horse. Wasn't there a brunette with him the day he died? Soon everyone will know the truth.

My blood ran cold. I put a hand to my dark hair. Who was sending these? I scanned around the park as if someone was watching me. I couldn't report the emails to the police, not when they would expose my lies. Everything would unravel. I walked home, deep in unsettled thoughts.

When Rachel had come to see me, I'd recognised myself in her. We had a strange affinity. I could still see her pale face and dark eyes, robbed of her future by him. If she went to prison, it gave her no chance of moving on. At least I'd pushed myself forward after leaving him, although not far enough. I walked indoors to the landline ringing.

'Hello?' I answered the phone.

'Did he have a gun when you knew him?' Mum went straight in for the kill. Her struggle to get the words out didn't stop her. 'It's just I've read about the murder weapon in the paper.'

Mum had the local paper delivered and accepted it as gospel.

'Don't worry about it,' I said. 'You're better off staying out of it.'

'I keep thinking of that poor girl. *Rachel.* It could've been you.'

Yes, it could.

'Let's not think that, and don't talk to anyone else about this. *Please.* I don't want the police coming back. And you need to rest.'

'But you should tell the pol—'

'You don't need to worry about the gun. About any of this.'

I didn't want her stressed out, not after her stroke. Not after everything else. Stroke or not, I couldn't have her confiding in anyone about the marine gun. It was hardly coffee morning chat. I'd have to trust her to keep quiet, from shame more than anything. Who wanted a daughter mixed up in murder?

Fuck lying low. With Mum fretting about the gun and someone sending me threatening emails, I couldn't avoid being a part of it. I had to take control so I phoned Rachel. It rang several times.

'Hello?'

'Rachel? It's Mia.'

'Oh ... Mia.' I heard the drifty hesitation in her voice.

'Sorry, did I wake you?' I checked the time. It was past 11 a.m.

'No ... it's just ... I don't know whether I'm coming or going.'

'No wonder. Are you okay?'

'The police arrested me. They kept me in a cell. I didn't think they'd let me come home.'

'That must have been terrible. But they've let you go. Does that mean they've ruled you out?'

'They still think I did it, but I didn't even know he had a gun.' Her voice sounded thick and woolly. 'My solicitor says there's evidence he was being blackmailed.'

'Blackmail?' My mind raced. I heard a male voice talking to Rachel in the background. 'Who was blackmailing him?'

'I can't talk now.' Her voice sounded distant, as if it might fade away. 'I'll phone back tomorrow.'

She ended the call. She must be exhausted. It took me back to the wreck I'd been when I left him. Now the devastation surged through Rachel's life. How many women had fallen for his lies? And which of them had been brave enough for retribution?

JESS

March 2015

On my first day back from the Canaries, I'm stuck in rain-lashed traffic on the M27. I zone out the local radio bulletins of overturned lorries and major road works, and picture us sailing away from everything.

At least Liz isn't at work when I arrive. The New York trip still hurts. What if she takes away my next prized project? I push through the bad days, same as everyone, but now I question whether work makes me happy. I spend the day catching up, and keep imagining us getting away from everything and running a business together.

Back at his place that evening, I climb the wooden steps and let myself in. There's something refreshing about the minimalist style of the deckhouse. The only ornaments are a model sailing boat on the windowsill and chunky candles in tasteful shades of white. My own furnishing style is more homely, but his pared-back approach helps clear my mind. I crave comfort food and put a shepherd's pie in the oven. He walks in an hour after me, looking worn out.

'Bad day?' I ask.

'Yeah. Technical problems with the client. They've insisted on a system so overloaded with features that efficiency's compromised. Now it's my fault. I told them this would happen, and I'm the one lumbered with sorting it out.'

'Can you look for another contract?' He'd told me he can take on new work when it suits him.

'This one will finish soon, but I wish we were still on holiday.' His dissatisfaction ripples towards me.

He stands behind me and kneads my achey shoulders. I groan a little from him releasing the tension. I've never felt so connected to anyone else. He finishes on my shoulders and goes to stare through the patio doors onto the balcony and the inky sea beyond. He loves being near the sea. On stormy days, you hear it indoors and taste its salty tang outside.

'I've been thinking about what you said in the Canaries, about us staying out there,' he says.

'Staying out there?'

'We could go away again. Find a sunny place to live.'

'That would be amazing.' I mean it in the same way as winning the lottery would be amazing. I carry the steaming hot shepherd's pie from the oven to the table.

'Just think: dips in warm water, sunset views, romantic suppers on a bobbing boat. When you're in a lazy mood, you can stretch out on deck and read novels. All those books you don't have time to read. I'd take you to my favourite islands in

Greece. Just you, me and the occasional dolphin. Our haven from the rest of the world. No evil boss, no stress.'

'No money,' I say, dishing out big spoonfuls onto our plates.

'I've got money. We'll have enough for the trip. We can sell up and build our dream home. It's cheap to buy land. We can choose a plot with a sea view. You said your boss is a pain in the arse.'

'I don't need to emigrate to avoid her.' My head swims. Island hopping really would be incredible, but I don't want to live on a boat for months. And the idea of not having much money bothers me after working so hard to make it onto the property ladder. Rob had put an offer in on the country cottage, but he came in much lower than the asking price. He said it was a game, buying property. The glint in his eye said he loved doing a deal, but then someone else snapped it up. I tried to keep a lid on my disappointment.

'This looks lovely.' He sits opposite me at the table. 'Wouldn't it be great if we could be our own bosses?'

'We can't just take off.'

'No, you're right. We need a plan. We could do something that combines our skills.'

'Could we?'

'Course we can. What sort of business would we have?' He looks at me with shining eyes.

'Um . . . we could set up a yacht charter company?' I hesitate, not really believing we could.

'That's a brilliant idea.'

'We could use your boat to start with. Keep the overheads low.'

'You can market it and sort out the bookings. I'll run the

nautical side of things. You can do what you want with the logo. Balls it up to your heart's content.'

'Thanks.' I ignore the dig, since I like the thought of not answering to my boss any more.

'Wouldn't it be brilliant though?' he keeps on between forkfuls. 'In charge of our destiny. We'd have more time together.'

'Yes, but . . .' I feel the urge to slow things down. This is only wishful thinking, not a realistic option, surely? 'What about house hunting round here? I thought we'd look at other cottages, and we need to fix a budget for the wedding.'

'Sure, but Greece is only three hours on a plane. We can build a big house, and everyone can come and stay. If the business does well, we'll keep a place over here and fly back off-season. Then we'll call England *and* Greece home.'

'Doesn't Greece have a financial crisis?'

'It's under control. They've had bailouts. We'll keep our savings in the UK if you're worried. Loads of tourists go to the Greek islands. It'll always be popular. We can aim the business at people like us going on holiday.'

'Are you sure there's enough business out there?'

'God, yeah. It's rammed in the summer.'

I can't help warming to the idea of us going away. Rome was fantastic, just the two of us wandering round, and the Canaries showed me the freedom of living on a boat. The thought of us setting up in business buzzes round my head. I want us to create something – a shared life, a family, a business – and it'll be even better out there. We can sail round the islands and find a home. My mind jumps ahead to us settled in the future.

'It's meant to be,' he says. 'You've sold the house, neither of us are happy at work. It just feels right.'

You hear stories of people unable to sell their homes, but I had been offered the full price just days after mine went on the market. It would take another couple of months for the buyers to complete.

'Don't you think the universe is sending us signs?' he asks. 'It's as if the obstacles are moving out of our way.'

'So fate's giving us a helping hand?'

'We both need to relax more. I've been swallowed up by work and forgotten what life's about. I like the idea of us going away. We can make our own future. And if you don't love it, we'll come back. Start a business here instead.'

He reaches over to hold my hand. 'When you've had a brush with death and you're told you might not walk again, it changes you. You go for it, because you have a second chance. I'm lucky to have you. We're on the same wavelength.'

A framed watercolour of a sailing boat hangs on the wall, with a quote about daring to dream and sailing away from the safe harbour to explore. I'm tempted by the pull of a long barefoot summer, warm sea breezes, sand under our toes, like those childhood summers that went on and on. I don't want to end up like Liz in twenty years, all steely-eyed disapproval, cut off from the people around her. It's a big step, though.

'We're lucky to even consider it.' He clears the dishes away. 'I want to be with you no matter what, but sometimes a leap of faith brings the best rewards, and I'll look after us.'

I didn't intend to go off on a boat with a man I've only known a few months. It wasn't my plan. But looking back to the time before we met, when I very much had a plan, life was flat and monochrome. I had my home, my job, my life, but now we have something better. We have each other, and our life is flowing in a new direction.

I can't sleep that night. I keep picturing us going away, having all that freedom. I sit up in bed and hug my knees. He reaches out to stroke my back in the semi-darkness. In the warm buzz of our engagement, I know it'll be okay because he makes everything okay.

'Let's do it,' I say, turning towards him. 'Let's go away and be happy.'

He switches on the light and we blink at each other.

'It's meant to be.' He pulls me back to him. 'That first time I kissed you on New Year's Eve, I thought . . .'

'Mmm?' I lean closer.

'I thought if we got together, I'd want us to have everything. And I'd never give you up.'

MIA

After the strange, muted phone conversation with Rachel, I went over to Ben's. We sat in his garden on the weathered wooden bench, both of us bundled against the crisp day, although the sun warmed us.

'Have you heard any more about the police investigation?' Ben asked.

We'd only just sat down. I didn't blame him for wanting to know, but talking about the murder made me tense.

'They've found his marine gun,' I said. I'd told Ben what I knew about the gun after the police visited me.

'It was a banned gun,' Ben said. 'I googled it.'

I glanced at him, startled. It seemed my mum wasn't the only one reading up on the murder coverage.

'Apparently it can be converted or modified if you know the right person,' he said.

'He told me it was a marine gun. He kept it on his boat.'

'He told you a lot of things. A marine gun sounds legit, like something Jacques Cousteau would clip on his diver's belt. He's described as a "cynical swindler". They don't know the half of it.'

I could manage my mum's reaction to the press coverage by saying we shouldn't stress her out. Ben wouldn't be fobbed off so easily. He might be laidback, but he could be like a dog with a bone when something caught his interest. I'd worked out that it wasn't a marine gun ages ago, even if I'd chosen to believe that when Rob first showed it to me. I hated admitting that I'd been involved with someone who kept an illegal gun.

'You okay?' he asked.

'I've been getting panic attacks from reading about it.'

'What? Why didn't you tell me?' Ben looked at me as if he'd caught me covering up again. My anxiety increased.

'It's just when I get stressed. When I read about the murder I feel a rush of panic, so I stop and do breathing exercises.' You're supposed to slow your breathing when you have a panic attack. Easier said than done when it feels like I'm about to faint or throw up or have a heart attack. Anyway, a paranoid part of me didn't want to search too much online and leave an incriminating trail. The police did that, didn't they? They checked searches and used them against you.

'What about the nightmares? You still have the ones where you're drowning?'

I couldn't deny it when they woke him up. My jaw tightened, making it hard to speak.

'I don't want to talk about it. I'd rather forget him. Forget it happened.' I bit the side of my lip. I never saw the point of talking when I'd rather have killed him with my bare hands.

'A lot of people would be angry after what he did.'

'I was angry.' I didn't tell him that I'd lie awake thinking of ways to kill Rob. He'd isolated me in our time together and it kept on after his death. I buckled from the weight of not telling anyone what happened the night he died. What I knew circled in my head and what I didn't know chased close behind. Not talking about it constricted my lungs and came out in my nightmares.

'He's dead now. You can move on.'

Dead or not, I hated Rob still having a hold on my emotions. My hands wouldn't stay still in my lap.

'I want you to be okay.' He put an arm around me, and we stared out at the garden. Ben's phone buzzed with a text. We both smiled at his iPhone wallpaper of us posing with the dogs, Darcy and Stan wearing felt Christmas antlers. We looked happy, just weeks before the murder and my life caving in all over again.

I leaned into him. 'Let's do something good at the weekend.' Something to distract me from the police investigation, the weight of wondering if they'd return to question me.

'Why don't we drive to the New Forest with the dogs? Have a pub lunch.' Ben agreed enthuastically. 'And look, don't read about the murder if it gives you panic attacks. I'll check it out and let you know the important stuff.' He glanced at his phone and then hesitated, as if working out how to phrase his next words. 'The police are asking for anyone with information to come forward. They say he was seen with a woman on the beach the day he died. A woman with dark hair.'

My hand covered my shocked mouth. The police were looking for a dark-haired woman. For me? Had the person behind the emails tipped them off? It suddenly felt overwhelming.

'You okay?'

I nodded and let my hand drop to my lap, not wanting him to suspect me.

'I reckon the murderer is someone shady who made it look like a deranged lover,' he said. 'There must've been people wanting him dead, people who know how to cover their tracks. Thank God no one tried it when you were with him. The police might have pinned it on you.'

Did Ben think I was the woman on the beach? He'd always been trusting, but what if he suspected me? He would think I couldn't leave it alone, and he'd be right.

Rachel had sounded so otherworldly on the phone that I didn't expect her to call back. But she texted and asked to come round for a chat. It was risky, but I couldn't turn down the chance to find out more. I said yes and she turned up an hour later. At least it was a weekday morning, so Ben wouldn't walk in on us.

'Are you taking time off work?' I asked as the kettle boiled.

'I've been on leave since Rob passed away.'

'How are you managing?'

'Holding it together, thank you.' She sounded more in tune with reality now, even if she still carried her air of fragility. 'I was out of it when you phoned. I hadn't slept all the time in custody. Then the exhaustion hit me when I came out, and the grief of it all. I still can't believe he's gone.'

'You sound better.' I wanted to find out so much, but every question seemed like an intrusion. We sat at the little kitchen table.

'I saw him with a woman on the beach.' She looked properly at me for the first time. 'Just before he died.'

I gasped. *She saw me. Oh fuck. That's why she's here, and she'll tell the police.*

'I think it was Sky,' she said.

'*Sky?*' Surprise overwhelmed my panic. 'Why was Sky there?'

'After him for money, as usual.'

My mind spun from the news that all three of us had been circling round in the hours before Rob was killed. It made a twisted kind of sense. Drama followed him around in the form of Sky. It sounded like she had kept on stirring up trouble, and that Rachel shared my dim view of her.

'Are you sure?' I hadn't seen Sky since splitting up with him, and it shocked me to think she'd been there too.

She let out a tortured breath. 'Pretty sure. I didn't speak to her. She hates me.'

'What about him ... did you ask him what she wanted?'

'I already knew. She used to turn up and do her sweet little sister act, wanting him to feel sorry for her and give her money. Money we didn't have. Did she do that when you were with him?'

I nodded and looked at the dripping tap.

'The first time I met her, she turned up unannounced at his boat. She had her boyfriend in tow. I was at home and Rob brought them in. He said, "Meet my half-sister." It was the first

I'd heard of her.' She gave a weary sigh and a small shake of her head. I returned her look to say I knew the whole screwed-up scenario. He'd sprung her on me in a similar way.

'What happened?'

'She seemed quite sweet at first. They came in for a drink and she smiled and hugged me. It was a hot weekend, so we sat on the balcony and had a beer. Rob and I were married by then, but he acted as if it were perfectly normal to introduce her to me completely out of the blue.'

I bet he did. Him and his parallel universe. He'd acted as if his behaviour was normal and the rest of us were out of step. Rachel had clearly received the same treatment.

'She called him "big bruv" and hugged him in a possessive way, like she was staking a claim on him. He indulged her. I remember he pointed out the view to her boyfriend and then when their backs were turned, she looked me up and down as if to say, "You're not so special."'

I found myself nodding at her description of the Sky I remembered. Rachel spoke in her quiet voice in a way that implied hurt rather than anger. She had bigger things to be angry about, or perhaps she didn't have the energy. Her fingers toyed with a loose thread on the cuff of her jumper.

'I didn't bother with her after that. And the boyfriend didn't seem to like Rob, which made it all a bit frosty. Did you meet him?'

'No. I heard mention of a boyfriend, but they weren't getting on back then.'

'After they left that first time, Rob called him a dick. He

said so long as Sky's happy, he didn't care. She didn't look happy, though. I think she'd come to check me out and found me lacking.'

'You and me both.'

'And it was all downhill from there,' she said.

'The day he died ... did you speak to him after you'd seen him with Sky?'

'I didn't get a chance. I went looking for him and ... that's when I found him.' Her voice shook. Her hands stayed anchored to her mug.

'What do the police say about Sky?'

'They're looking into it. I just hope they find some evidence.'

'If she's guilty, they'll find evidence, or she'll trip herself up. She was a motormouth when I knew her, so she might incriminate herself.'

'When did you last see her?'

'A week or so before I left him. She brought it all to a head. Gave me some home truths. She was quite spiteful. What's she like now?'

'Vindictive enough to kill him and blame me.'

We sat in silence for a few moments. My phone buzzed.

'I'd better go,' Rachel said, getting up. 'Thanks for the coffee. I'm sorry for bothering you. It's just ... we have this shared history. You knew him as well as I did, and you've met Sky.'

She walked towards the door. 'It helps to talk to someone who knows what she's like. And well ... I'm scared I'll be charged.'

'It's a lot to deal with.'

After Rachel left, I tried working it out. Her visit had raised more questions than it answered. Rachel must be thinking ahead to a possible trial, and maybe she still wanted me to be a witness. Whatever her motives, talking about Sky brought out my buried hostilities. I didn't know Rachel well enough to trust her. Even so, it sounded like her experience of Sky mirrored my own.

Rachel may not have seen me on the beach, but what if Sky had? It made sense for the emails to be from someone who knew me. And no one else I knew had any reason to send me malicious emails. It was a bit of a leap to suspect someone I hadn't seen for years, especially with no evidence. The kinder version of me would write it off. Sky once referred to me as 'small fry' and she might well have forgotten all about me.

But ... but if Rachel was right about Sky being there, she could be the one tormenting me. It would be just like her. She'd been spiteful towards me in the past. What if the murder prompted her to pick up where she'd left off? I pictured her typing it in a fury from a secret email account. All that anger directed at me.

I reached for my phone to google her, and nothing came up, so I went and dug around in the cluttered spare room wardrobe to find my stash of old photos. Rachel didn't tell me anything concrete. Despite her vested interest in blaming Sky, I knew enough to take the same view. Was she trying to ensnare one of us?

At the back of the wardrobe, I pulled out the pack of photos. It seemed old-fashioned to have hard copies of photos, but my ex harboured a distrust of the online world. No smartphone photos for him. He only used a 'real' camera with real film. Now I understood that he didn't want identifiable photos posted online.

I sifted through the pictures, and paused over the only one I'd taken of Sky and him. It was impossible to think of what went wrong without thinking of Sky. In the photo, they're flushed with heat on the boat, Sky laughing helplessly and collapsing into his arms. Their secret was so obvious now.

JESS

March 2015

He has it all mapped out. We'll sell our homes and cars, use some of the money to fund the trip and the rest for setting up in Greece. He talks about it as we lie in his bed that Saturday morning.

'I can see us in a white stone house on a hillside,' he says. 'We won't be indoors much. We'll eat outside at a wooden table. Slow meals in dappled sunshine.'

'Is it by the sea, this romanticised home of ours?'

'Romanticised? I'm deadly serious.' He drapes an arm around me. 'Is everything okay with your house sale?'

'The legal stuff's underway.' I look around at the pale, exposed wood and large window framing the coastal view. 'What about selling this place?'

'Haven't we agreed that? We decided to keep it as our crash pad for trips home.'

'Did we?'

'We talked about it.'

'I don't remember.' But we've had a lot going on. 'Why don't we keep mine?'

'You've got a buyer. And your place is older, so more can go wrong. You said the boiler's dodgy and roof tiles are falling off. This is low maintenance and we can rent it out when we're not here.'

'Oh ... okay.' But is it? Should I really sell my home for an imaginary one in a country I've never visited? 'I need to go home and catch up on things.'

'You're not coming on the boat?' He leans over and kisses my shoulder, slowly working his way down with tender kisses. He pulls back the covers, stroking and nuzzling as I lazily trace my fingers over his muscular arms and chest. He still gives me butterflies.

'Did I tell you I love you?' he says.

'Not for ages. Days, actually.'

'I love you, and I've been thinking about our new life together.' He leans on his elbow and looks intently at me.

'Mmm.'

'I want to go away with you as my wife.'

It throws me, and I stare wide-eyed at the ceiling. A shotgun wedding isn't what I envisage. 'Let's take a drive out to the church where I was christened. I'd like us to get married there.' I imagine the people close to us filling the space, light filtering through stained glass windows as I swish down the aisle to him.

'I don't want us to have a church wedding. It's too formal.

You're stressed about the house sale, but I don't want to lose sight of us. I just want you to be happy.'

I go to answer but he cuts in. 'Let's get married so we know we've got each other and you're looked after. Let's do it right.'

'We leave in two months. There's not enough time.'

'There is. We'll do it just before we leave.'

'Why don't we scope out a venue before we go away? Book it for next year.' It's a fair compromise.

'Next year?' He looks crestfallen. 'Let's do it before going away.'

'But everything needs organising—'

'We'll keep it intimate and simple.'

'Intimate and simple still needs to be organised.'

He pulls back and looks at me with serious eyes. 'Promise you won't freak out.'

'Why?'

'I phoned the River Hotel. You love it there. They do civil ceremonies, and they can do the Friday before we go away. I've spoken to a photographer. She'll do us tasteful black and white wedding photos, like we talked about. The hotel put me on to their florist. They hire out white rose bushes in pots. They can do us table decorations, all in white. I'll sort the invitations and help you with everything. We can do it together, it'll be fun.'

His eyes shine in the way they do when he imagines something good. I can't see the point of rushing, but it means so much to him that I agree to go in and have a look.

'You're amazing. I love you and I want to marry you.' He

looks like so much hinges on it. 'Think of the honeymoon we'll have, sailing to lovely sandy beaches. It'll be perfect if you come away as my wife.'

'Hmm.'

'I can see you on our wedding day in a fitted cream silk dress, with your hair down, how I like it.' He traces a finger over my cheekbone. 'Because life's too short to wait till next year.'

He goes to check on the boat, and I phone Becca.

'What's new with you lovers?' she asks in a droll voice.

'We've been talking about the wedding. We haven't decided.'

'Will Ellie get to be bridesmaid?'

'Does that mean you're coming round to it?'

'She is your god-daughter.'

'I don't think we're having a church wedding. It'll be low key.'

'Have a country house wedding. He can afford it. He must earn good money, what with his yacht and sea-view pad. What is he again, some kind of high-flying consultant?'

She talks above a little whiny voice in the background. I lift the blinds with one finger and peer through, in case he forgets something and comes home. 'I'm not bothered about his money.'

'Ha! Wait till you have kids who are always hungry and always growing.' She breaks off to hiss, *'I'm on the phone,'* then returns to me. 'Money matters. *Go and ask daddy.*'

'I'm not sure which part of that was for me.'

'Sorry. Money matters when you have kids.'

'We're not having kids yet.'

'No, because you've only known him five minutes.'

I sense the roll of her eyes, and cut the call short. She might go on about money and practicalities, but I have something money can't buy and it feels good.

MIA

Three weeks since the murder and I was worn out from too much worry and not enough sleep. I organised my notes for a client meeting. It should be straightforward, but my mind kept straying into darker territory. I typed a quick agenda to keep my focus on the meeting. The doorbell rang. I ignored it and kept typing, but it rang again. Thinking it might be a delivery, I went to the door.

Rachel stood on the doorstep, looking drawn.

'Oh, hi Rachel.'

'Can I talk to you? It can't wait.'

She seemed more together now, as if she'd called upon some inner resolve. I checked my watch. 'I'm leaving soon for a meeting.'

'I'll only be five minutes.'

I let her in. I could spare five minutes if she told me something to my advantage. She followed me through to the kitchen.

'What's it about?'

'Sky.'

'Any news?' We both sat at the table.

'That's the thing. I can't find anything out. I thought she might talk to you, since she won't talk to me.'

I drew back. 'What makes you think she'll talk to me?'

'She sees me as competition. I doubt that's changed.' Her quiet air of fragility still hung around, but she wasn't taking the murder accusation lying down.

'What am I supposed to ask her?'

'Ask what happened that day on the beach. Why she was there. What the two of them had going on.'

'She won't tell me.'

'She might if you say you don't like me either. The two of you united against me.'

I shook my head and exhaled at the enormity of it. 'It's not that I don't want to help ...'

Rachel looked bereft.

'But she'll have it in for me too.' And Sky might not even be involved, I thought to myself. Rachel said she'd turned up before the murder, but the police hadn't arrested her. The Sky I'd known was capable of sending malicious emails, but I had no evidence they came from her. She might have mellowed since then.

Rachel stared out at the garden. 'I didn't tell you before, in case it freaked you out.' She turned back to face me. 'You're on the police's radar.'

'How do you know?' I clasped my shaking hands under the table.

'Because they asked questions about you.'

'What questions?'

'Whether I'd met you. Whether you still had contact with Rob.'

'Isn't that routine? They asked me the same questions.'

'They took an interest in you. My solicitor says you're a person of interest in the investigation.'

'Even more reason for me to stay out of it.' I didn't like the way this was going. I wanted to know if the police suspected Sky, not me.

'If Sky can't pin it on me, and she finds out you're in the frame, she'll go for you instead.'

Rachel seemed more likely to do that, since she was the prime suspect. Her vendetta against Sky made me uneasy. Was Rachel trying to push the blame onto her?

'I haven't seen her for years,' I said. 'Anything she says about me is hearsay.'

'You could ask the police about her if they interview you again.'

I turned clammy at the thought of them coming back. 'If she did it, what's her motive?'

'Someone like Sky doesn't need a motive. She's unhinged. She killed him,' Rachel said in a quiet, urgent voice, palms pressed on the table. 'There's no other explanation. But if the police ask her about you, she'll have you in her sights. You know how determined she is. If they drop the charge against me, she'll try to pin it on you.'

Now it was my turn to stare out of the window. Her words echoed what I already feared.

'And they're looking for the brunette woman on the beach,' she kept on. 'I *know* it was her. But what if she says it was you?'

I looked at Rachel, eyes narrowed. What did she know?

'Why would she do that?'

'She was jealous of you,' Rachel said. 'She talked about you once, in a gloaty way to me, as if she resented you for being with Rob. Coming after you would be revenge if she can't stitch me up.'

Would it? It sounded tenuous, to say the least, but something about Rachel's words rang true.

'What do you have in mind?'

'Go and see her. Find out more.'

It was one thing to find out about Sky, but something else entirely to go and see her. 'I can't just turn up on her doorstep. She'll slam the door in my face.'

'I don't go looking for trouble. But my husband's been killed, and I think Sky did it. If I'm found guilty, she gets away with it and I go to prison.'

'What does your solicitor say?'

'He gives me reassurances, but he's not the one being accused.'

'The police told me Rob was abusive towards other women he was in relationships with.' The detectives had said it when they came round. Then they watched for my reaction. I'd been too panicked to take it in at the time, but fragments of the conversation came back to me. If they'd said it to get me talking, it hadn't worked. I took it as a bad sign, the police testing me out, although everything was a bad sign. I never used to be this paranoid.

'Our marriage wasn't great.' She looked down at the table, shrinking into herself. 'I guess your time with him wasn't always a walk in the park, but did you leave at the first sign of trouble?'

'I wish I had.'

'We had our problems, but I loved him. It's the most awful thing, the police coming to arrest you.' She looked lost, her face haunted. 'They can come any time ... in the middle of the night. They have all the power. We have none.'

She shook her head at the futility of it. *They could come for me too.* It hung unspoken between us. Maybe they'd come today. It wouldn't surprise me.

'I didn't kill him,' Rachel said.

I nodded and went to the desk to shove my papers, phone and laptop in my bag. 'I'll be late.'

She stood up. 'We're both at risk. If we take the same approach, we can fend her off.'

I hated not having any control over what might happen. I knew I shouldn't get involved, but I needed to find out more. Besides, with Rachel focused on Sky, it meant she was less likely to suspect me.

We walked to the door and down the path together. 'I can't find anything about her online,' I said. 'Was Sky even her real name?'

'I've only ever known her as that,' Rachel said. 'But I wouldn't put it past her to lie.'

'Sorry, I have to go.'

I left Rachel, my mind whirring. *Sky.* It had been so long

since I'd thought about her. She'd been a nasty piece of work, but she was nothing compared to the monster my ex became. But what had Sky become in the years since we'd seen each other? Was she capable of murder?

JESS

March 2015

I arrive home to the SOLD board looming outside my house. I sit in the car, nagged by a creeping sense of displacement. It says 'subject to contract' in tiny print, but it no longer feels like home. *And that's okay*, I tell myself, because of our new life together.

When I walk through the front door, the red answerphone light flashes with accusation. Messages play and I sift through a pile of post. The dry cleaner reminds me about suits to collect from last year. My shoulders sag from polite recriminations, and then Mum's voice fills the narrow hall.

'Jess? It's only me. You didn't come back about hats. Shall I buy one for the wedding? Now it's the start of the season and John Lewis has more to choose? And did I tell you about Madonna?' She pauses after each question, as if waiting for the answer. 'We have to do something about her weight. She came in the lounge with the cat flap stuck round her middle. Shall I ask the vet?'

I can hear my stepdad whistling to music in the background

86

of the phone message. 'Doug needs to lay off the biscuits,' she says in a louder voice, presumably so he can hear, 'otherwise he won't fit into his wedding suit.'

She rattles on, and I wince at a letter threatening a summons for an unpaid water bill I've forgotten. Fighting a losing battle with the clock, frustration frays at my edges. I don't have time for my old life any more, and look forward to leaving the hassle behind.

At least I make it to Becca's for a coffee. 'We might have the wedding at the River Hotel,' I say.

'There's no rush though,' Becca answers, with a slight frown.

I don't tell her our plan to marry in six weeks, because she'll only give me a hard time. I know my life will never be the same, but I like the idea of him taking me somewhere different. Why can't I throw caution to the wind this once?

'Will you cope with living on a boat?'

'We won't always be on a boat.' I blink and smile, glancing at my engagement ring.

'Do you get seasick?'

'Sailing in the Canaries was okay.'

'You only went for a few days. Have you handed in your notice?'

'Tomorrow.'

She gives me a strained expression and blows on her coffee.

'It's not going well with my new boss,' I say. 'I need a change. If it doesn't pan out, I'll find another job.'

'You know I care about you,' Becca says. 'I don't see why you have to change your whole life to be with him.'

How has it got so serious? Her attitude starts to grate. If the tables were turned, I'd accept her choices. I look away. 'Don't.'

'What?'

'Act like it's a mistake.'

'Okay.' Becca bites into her cream cake and motions towards mine untouched on the plate. 'Not hungry?'

'I'm putting on weight.'

She looks at me with concern, but I've let my workouts slip. Lack of exercise and all our boozy romantic meals mean my clothes feels tighter. He'd patted my stomach the other day and pulled a face.

'Do you think I'm fat?' I'd challenged.

'There's just a little more of you to grab hold of.'

'No wonder when I don't have time for the gym.' I pulled away. 'And you're always plying me with booze.'

'Hey.' He drew me back to nuzzle the side of my face. I breathed in his familiar musky smell, wanting to be annoyed but liking his body pressed against mine. 'I think you're sexy. I love your curves, but I can see you don't like putting on weight.'

Insecurities bubbled to the surface and I resolved to lose the extra few pounds. As for Becca, she doesn't see his wayward charm. To me, he's assured and confident, which I admire.

That afternoon, back with Rob at his, I mention seeing Becca and he rolls his eyes.

'Don't be like that,' I say.

'She's jealous.'

'She's not.'

'Life just happens to her and Steady Eddie. They don't go anywhere exciting.'

'They've two children. They can't just take off.'

'You've got me now. You don't need unsupportive friends.'

I turn silent on the subject, with him, at least.

When Becca calls the next day, I can't hide my feelings. At least Rob isn't around to hear me talk about him.

'If I didn't agree with your relationship choices,' I say, 'I'd still try to be supportive.'

'I'm only saying don't rush in.'

'Because you don't like him.'

She tuts.

'Maybe you're jealous.'

'Did *he* say that?'

'I'm sorry but it's up to me who I choose to be with.'

She sighs as if drawing on reserves of patience. 'Okay. Good luck, then.'

Nobody's universally liked, but most people like him. He doesn't have friends as such because he travels a lot, but he's friendly with men from the boatyard. And I notice the way women respond to him. Not that he flirts. He's attentive and interested, so you feel good about yourself. Becca's attitude makes me want to defend him. He's right, I realise. I don't need unsupportive friends.

MIA

I parked near my client's office and stepped out of the car. Rachel's visit had rattled me, but I turned my attention to the meeting. Ten minutes until it started, so I had time to dodge the rain showers and run to the cashpoint.

'Mia?' A man in a suit came striding towards me. I froze, car keys mid-air.

'Can I have a chat, please?'

Detective Sergeant Thornley. I only knew his name and rank because of the business card he'd given me when he turned up with his colleague about the murder. Rachel's words from earlier came back to me. *You're on the police's radar.* Had he come to arrest me?

'Shall we?' He motioned to my front passenger door. Before I could respond, he'd tucked his large frame into my Golf.

I got back in. Had someone told him they'd seen me on the beach? My hands twisted and fidgeted in my lap until I checked myself and stopped. It felt awkward this close to him. People passed by in the busy street, their noise muted behind the rain-speckled windscreen.

'You followed me?' I tried to gain some ground on his intrusion.

'Not at such. I pulled into your road just as you drove off. The station's near here. We went the same way.'

Did we now. Give him an inch and he'd be all understanding, and then watch me swallowed up by the law. I forced my hands to rest on the steering wheel. All other effort went on calming my thudding heart and strangled breathing.

'It's about Rob Creavy's murder.'

A panic attack welled up. I wanted to open the door and gulp down cold air. Throw up in the gutter.

'What do you know about the gun he kept on the boat?'

My mouth dried out and I struggled to swallow. Dark vultures circled inside my head. I had to hold the panic at bay. I could beat it by breathing deep and staying in the present so my mind didn't go haywire.

'He had it back then, I presume?'

My heart raced, not helped by his burning gaze. Sweat and unease prickled on my spine. 'Sorry ...' *Breathe.* I wanted to take off my jacket, but I stayed still and held the steering wheel to stop my hands from shaking. 'I've had panic attacks ever since I was with him. Talking about him brings them on.'

'Take your time.'

The worst of the panic eased off. Okay, the gun. I could handle it, so long as he only wanted to know about that.

'He never used it, as far as I know. He said it was a marine gun. He kept it out of the way.'

The detective looked satisfied at getting something out of me. It was a bad move to talk about the gun, but I couldn't deny it all. Knowing about the gun wasn't the same as shooting him with it.

DS Thornley looked kindly at me. 'Why didn't you tell us?'

'I didn't think ... It was a shock, when you said he'd been murdered.'

'You could've phoned us when it stopped being a shock.'

'There wasn't anything to tell you. He never used the gun. He said boats that go abroad have marine guns.'

'Shall we start from the beginning?' He cocked his head, patient and encouraging, not that he fooled me. He looked less tired this time, his brown eyes flecked with hazel and framed by long lashes. No cigarette smell, it must have been the other one.

He pulled out his notebook, more relaxed without his side-kick, or using a different tactic. I tested out the fear of telling him what I knew. *Say it. Just say it. Stand on the cliff edge and hurl yourself off.* For a terrible moment, I thought I'd actually told him. I breathed in and pulled back from the brink. He looked suspiciously at me. My head swam. I cleared my throat.

'He kept the gun hidden on the boat,' I said. 'He showed it to me once.'

It had been the first time we'd sailed on his boat, just out in the Solent. He'd showed me all the nooks with concealed storage. Perfect, as it turned out for someone like him. He'd opened a cupboard door and lifted a floorboard to reveal the smallest of spaces. We'd crouched down and the tang of freshly carved wood scented the air. I'd opened my mouth to speak, and then saw inside the compartment and the words died on my lips.

'What is it? An air gun?' Not that I'd ever seen one, but the other option had been so far from my life, I couldn't comprehend it.

'It's a marine gun.' He lifted it out and opened it with a practised air, the bullets sliding into his palm.

The words sounded safe. A marine gun. Not a real gun.

'Could you kill someone with it?'

'Yes, God forbid.'

'But it can't be legal. Why have you got it?'

'Boats that go abroad sometimes have them, to fend off pirates. The police turn a blind eye if you sail abroad.'

I looked at him, none the wiser, despite his efforts to normalise it. 'There aren't pirates where we're sailing.'

'No, don't worry. I just wanted to show you where it is. No secrets, right?'

We stood up and he tried to hand it to me, but I stepped back. 'Where did you get it?'

'It came with the boat.' He laid it back in its hiding place.

'*It came with the boat?* That's ridiculous.'

'The previous owner kitted it out for the Indian Ocean. You're on your own out there, so it's useful for protection. Then he had health problems and sold the boat.'

'You could've said you didn't want the gun.'

'If you'd been with me we'd have said that, because you think ahead. Whereas I'm a boy at heart. I see a gun and I'm a seven-year-old playing cops and robbers.'

'But . . .'

'Don't worry. It's back-up we'll never need, like having life jackets on board. And we might make it to the Indian Ocean one day. Their best weather is our wintertime, so we could take off over there.'

I'd prickled with unease. A gun on board represented an element of danger I didn't want to acknowledge. He realised and distracted me in other ways, flooding my brain with feel-good chemicals to pull me back to him.

He'd tested me with the gun. I saw that now. My reaction told him to play it down and keep it hidden. I should have known that a man who kept an illegal gun might not be the person to trust with my life. I'm not sure when I abandoned rational thought. It blew away in the rush of being with him. I'd been wrong to trust him, but not alone. He'd seduced other women, taking them sailing. He'd probably shown the others the gun as some kind of power trip.

'It freaked me out, to be honest,' I said to DS Thornley. 'He made it seem okay for people who sail abroad to have a gun for protection. I never expected him to use it. He said we'd put it away and forget about it.'

Thornley made notes in between nodding. When I paused, he gave me a kind smile that transformed his face. The face I'd thought spoiled by cynicism. His face said *trust me*. No chance of that.

'My meeting's about to start.'

'Okay. Phone me if you think of anything else.'

We opened the car doors in unison. He gave me his kind

smile again, and walked to a dark blue Audi. I hadn't noticed him following me. *Keep on your toes*, I told myself. At least he'd arrived on my street after Rachel left. Seeing us together might have prompted more awkward questions.

I walked into the meeting and a sudden memory hit me. The time we went sailing with Sky came back to me. The two of them argued. In a fury, she tore below deck and searched for the gun. She threatened to shoot him.

JESS

April 2015

A cold wind sweeps through the car park at work. The sound of Rob's voice and the taste of his lips linger in my senses from his kiss goodbye an hour ago. Work is the only time we spend apart. I tuck my free hand in my coat pocket, pleased I won't need a wool coat in Greece. My fingers brush against a little papery package. I pull out a yellow post-it note folded round a chocolate turtle. I pop the turtle in my mouth and read the note. *Have a great day. Love you x.*

My smile lasts until the meeting I've scheduled with Liz. I've avoided her since our run-in over the wrong logo.

'I'll get straight to the point.' I sit down and borrow her clipped tones. 'I'm handing in my notice.'

'You're leaving?' She leans back in her chair to better assess me, and purses her dry red lips. She wears a sharp black suit that fits her neat frame. I'll be free to live in casual summer clothes soon.

'I'm going away.'

'Have you been offered another job?'

'No, I'm going sailing with my fiancé.'

'*Sailing?* I didn't see that coming.'

'We leave in May. I'll work a month's notice. It's been a tough decision—'

'Right then. We'll have to manage without you.' She stands up, and I do too, taking covert pleasure in admitting to more enjoyable priorities.

'I didn't know you sailed.'

'I don't. Rob has a boat.'

'It's quite macho, sailing. Guys who sail can be gung-ho. Make sure you're safe, life jackets and all that.'

I don't like her lumping him in with 'guys who sail'. She presumes to know his type, just as Becca thinks she has him sussed. Liz strides off in the other direction, and I tell Sachi on the way back to my desk.

'Lucky you! You've found an escape route.'

I'm following a dream that so many others harbour, of giving work the slip. Marcus in product marketing asks questions about the boat, most of which I can't answer. Sachi and the others fixate on how I'll be basking in sunshine, puttering round markets and enjoying cheap wine.

'It's a big step,' I say to Sachi. 'Uprooting to another country.'

'I moved down here from Derby to marry Liam. It's not another country, but I left my job and everyone behind. With him in the Navy, I didn't have much choice. My parents moved here from Sri Lanka. They took a leap of faith. You make it work if you want to be together.'

I nod in agreement.

'If you love someone it's not such a compromise.'

People uproot themselves all the time to be together. I push aside Becca's concerns and bask in Sachi's approval instead.

'You should start an Instagram account for your travels,' Sachi says. 'Make us all jealous.'

'We'd rather go off-grid.'

I don't mention his aversion to social media. 'If we're going to do it,' he'd said when we made plans, 'let's make it just us and the great big world. There won't be wifi everywhere. Think you can handle being offline?'

We agreed to live simply and travel on a shoestring.

'And I hate all the Big Brother implications of being tracked online wherever we go,' he'd said.

'I doubt anyone wants to track us,' I'd teased.

'But life's better when it's just us. Let's not have a travel blog or anything braggy. No one wants reminders we're having a great time when they're stuck in the same rut.'

My grasp on work loosens. My colleagues stop asking me to meetings and copying me in on emails. I'm lost without the cut and thrust of work, so I look busy scribbling to-do lists and reading up on sailing theory. My old life slips away and I prepare for Rob's carefree world, where the sun always shines and the sea invites us in.

MIA

Darcy welcomed me in as I returned from the client meeting. At least I was home, where I could disappear inside and escape people's interest in the murder by screening calls and ignoring the doorbell. Darcy went to snuffle in the garden while I checked emails. I homed in on one and my insides twisted. The same Gmail address as before.

I know what you did on the day of the murder. Hell hath no fury. Bitch.

I reeled back from the screen. Someone knew I'd been there, angry with him. I forced myself to look closely at the message, but it held no clues to the sender. What did they want? Would it escalate beyond the emails or was it a prelude to reporting me to the police? I gritted my teeth and clicked and dragged each accusing message from my inbox to a separate folder. Should I tell DS Thornley, or would it expose me? Better to stay away from him.

My mind cast back to Sky on the boat, that time I thought the two of them would come to blows. She knew about the gun, threatened to shoot him with it. I thought it was just histrionics at the time, but all the same. And that night I overheard her referring to me as a bitch. *That bitch is small fry.* No one has ever called me a bitch apart from Sky. *Hell hath no fury. Bitch.*

A text pinged through from Rachel, asking to come over. I should have said no, but DS Thornley's questions combined with the latest email had put me on edge.

Rachel arrived half an hour later. We sat at the kitchen table, drinking tea in silence.

'Have the police been back since they let you go?' I asked, since she wasn't forthcoming.

'No, but they can pull me in any time. It's the not knowing that gets to me.'

The not knowing got to me as well.

'They're building a case against me. My solicitor says they go for the most likely scenario based on what evidence supports it. When they've enough evidence, they can charge the person.'

Despite my recent suspicions, I still thought Rachel was clutching at straws by blaming Sky. 'Do they know if Sky was there?'

'There must be evidence, like CCTV of her driving in the area, but she's acting the innocent victim.'

'If she pulled the trigger, isn't there forensic evidence?'

'The police have made up their minds that I did it. The way it's going I'll have to wait a whole year before it comes to trial.

My solicitor says I'm likely to get off, but I don't want to go through it all.'

'How will you get off?'

'They only have one piece of evidence that isn't circumstantial. My jacket had blood spatters on it. The police say it's from firing the shot that killed him. But I wasn't there. My defence team can prove the blood didn't come from firing the shot.'

'Where did it come from?'

'I found his body. I crouched over him to check if he was breathing and a kind of ... *mist* of blood came out of his mouth.'

I leaned back in my chair, queasy. I tried not to think of his dead body, splayed out from the gunshot. All that blood.

'That happens sometimes, apparently. The final breath is still in their throat. If you disturb the body, it can come out. It was air mixed with blood that bubbled up and came out on me.'

My hands gripped my thighs to steady myself. 'Can it be proved?'

'We've an expert witness to dispute their forensics. It's been used as a defence before. If that's all they've got on me, it's not enough.'

'What's the circumstantial evidence?'

'Three days before he died, the police barged in with a search warrant. They told me the worst of what he'd been up to. They can build a case around me looking like the wronged woman. But I was still in shock from the police turning up. I wasn't ready to admit the marriage was over.'

101

Rachel had the trial sewn up when she hadn't even been charged with murder. I could imagine a jury taking her side. She had an innocence to her, so calm and softly spoken. She didn't try to win me over. She said everything as a simple matter of fact that made me believe her.

'It won't go to trial if they think you'll get off.'

'They're under pressure to secure a conviction, so they'll build a compelling case. I can't take another year of this.'

Nor could I. I hated it hanging over me and I hadn't even been through Rachel's ordeal with the police.

'I've got Sky's address,' she said. 'We could go there together, and you could talk to her.'

'I can't face seeing her.'

'Nor can I, not really, but I have to do something. I don't want to deal with a trial. You seem like a resilient person.' She looked at me, worry etched on her face. 'If I can handle seeing her, we both can. Tell her you want to know what happened, for closure or whatever.'

Was it better to join forces with Rachel than be alone and accused farther down the line if the case against her was dropped? Right now, she had a vested interest in finding out whether Sky did it. I hadn't seen Sky for five years, and couldn't rely on Rachel's opinion. It was futile to try and make Sky confess, but I didn't want Rachel focusing on me.

Her phone pinged with a text. She pulled it from her pocket and I caught the screen shot of her pressed close to Rob on what looked like their wedding day. She wore a simple silk dress, her honey hair tumbling down in a Californian beach wave. He smiled at the camera. Her smile was hazier, her head resting on his shoulder.

She checked the message and lay the phone down.

'Is that from your wedding?' I nodded towards the phone screen.

She smiled and touched his face with her index finger. 'We were so happy. I couldn't get enough of him. He was everything I wanted.' She looked sideways at me. 'I'm sorry. I know it didn't work out for you. Sometimes even when you love someone and want it to work, that's not enough.'

Her eyes clouded over. I didn't know if that comment was about her or me. She'd hinted that their marriage had suffered by the time of his murder. DS Thornley had hinted at it too, in his earlier attempt to get me to talk.

She kept staring at her phone. 'I've been getting strange emails. Anonymous ones, saying I'm the killer.'

God, so it wasn't just me being targeted. Rachel was getting them too, confirming my hunch that she hadn't sent them. I suddenly didn't feel so threatened and isolated. 'Me too.'

She stared at me. 'Really?'

I nodded.

'They're from Sky,' she said.

'How do you know?'

'One of them said something about me that only she knew. That's why I want to see her. She's trying to scare me. I shouldn't let her upset me, but she might stop if she knows I'm on to her.'

She swiped and tapped at her phone and held it shakily towards me. I leaned in to read the email she'd called up.

He didn't watch his back. Now it's time you watched yours.
The police are closing in.

'It's like the ones I've had. Same email address.' I pictured Sky in a rage, pulling the cabin apart in search of the gun. I didn't tell Rachel, it would only fuel her determination. 'They brought out the worst in each other, him and Sky.'

'You'd think she might be different now he's gone, but not if these emails are anything to go by.' She sank back in her chair. 'It's strange. His things are all around the house. His clothes still smell of him, but he's not there. I can't get used to him never coming back. I still make us two coffees in the morning, and end up tipping his down the sink. Isn't that stupid?'

I thought of the softness in Rachel's voice the first time we met, when I refused to help her. The polite exterior and helpless face that nearly undid me. It matched her sad acceptance of everything. Was that why she stayed with him until the bitter end? I'd tried to recalibrate Rachel from a different perspective, removed from the quiet, fragile person I'd met. She intrigued me. The image of her as a killer didn't work.

'What about sailing?' I asked. 'Are you into boats?'

She shook her head. 'I went along with it at first. He said I'd be a natural, but I didn't like it. We had a honeymoon trip around the Med. Then we came home and I haven't been on the water since.'

'Me neither, not since leaving him.'

'There was this one time we got caught out in a storm,' she said. 'We lost radio contact and I thought the boat would

104

capsize. We were out in it all night. The waves were huge.' Her wide eyes relived the fear. 'I thought I could at least trust him on the boat. He was such a keen sailor, but he took risks. We could've died that night.'

Her words transported me back to the stormy times. She looked so hopeful in that wedding image on her phone, in her cream silk dress beside her adoring new husband, before it all turned bad for her.

JESS

April 2015

We get married in the hotel's Georgian drawing room. Patio doors face onto a bluebell meadow with a stream meandering by. Rob kisses me and everyone claps.

'Hello wife,' he says, softly.

Is this actually my wedding day? I stand beside my husband and wait for reality to kick in. To the casual observer I might look serene. Sachi says I'm ethereal. If Becca had come, she'd have said I was away with the fairies. She couldn't arrange time off work, with it being a Friday and at such short notice. I'm torn between disappointment that she didn't try harder, and relief that she's not here creating an atmosphere. He looks adoringly at me and I can see my family beaming at him out of the corner of my eye.

'Smile!' Sachi says, her phone poised to take a photo. I lean my head against Rob's shoulder and we smile.

As a small child, I dreamed of my wedding. I would draw

elaborate pictures of my Cinderella ballgown, with a tight bodice and dramatic long skirt. My actual wedding dress is cream silk, chosen by him. It skims my curves and sweeps to the floor. I wear pearl earrings, though my superstitious mum advised against it. She says pearls stand for tears. The dress doesn't resemble the one I'd dreamt of as a child, just as the wedding isn't what I'd imagined. No wonder, when I barely had anything to do with it. If I'd disagreed on the finer points, then I expect we would have compromised, but he swept me along. He said that getting married was the main thing, not a showy ceremony.

It's too chilly to pose outside for photos in the late April gloom when I don't have a coat, just an elegant covering of silk. We stand indoors by the French windows in the beautiful oak panelled room. People congratulate us, and we all sip champagne and eat tiny little versions of sausage and mash canapés.

'I'm so lucky to have Jess as my wife. I can't believe she chose me,' he says in his speech, looking at me. 'I love you so much.'

Everyone says *ahhh*.

Sachi looks gorgeous in a peacock blue silk dress. It makes her Sri Lankan features even more stunning. I don't know when I'll see her again. Leaving work last week didn't seem any more real than getting married, as if I'd been clearing my desk ready for a holiday and would be back with a suntan in two weeks.

'He's devoted to you,' Sachi says. 'Wherever you are, he watches you.'

I turn and see him across the room. He winks and raises his glass in a salute. Is this how a bride should feel? While I've known other brides to nearly lose their minds over the details, the most I did single-handedly was book a hair appointment and manicure, and then do my own make-up.

I waft through the day on a heady scent of lily of the valley from my bouquet, putting my glazed state down to the champagne. I feel strangely disconnected, as if I've dressed as a bride to play a role. It's not wrong, just not what I'd envisaged. Perhaps it hasn't sunk in yet, and I can hardly complain when I agreed to it all.

We don't have an evening reception. Everyone leaves by late afternoon, all smiles, glowing from champagne and lunch. I'd suggested to Rob that we spend our wedding night at the hotel.

'No need for that,' he said. 'You'll always be my bride. We've got our whole lives together.'

Back home, he gives me a bright red sailing jacket as a wedding present. We change into jeans and drink more champagne. Lounging in jeans on our wedding day makes it seem even more unreal. I touch the platinum wedding band on my finger to reassure myself this is really happening. He won't wear a ring, even though I'd said it was important to me. He said rings got in the way of sailing.

MIA

My conversation with DS Thornley had unsettled me. He'd basically accused me of withholding information. I'd better show willing and tell him about Sky and the gun. If it made her a suspect, well, I couldn't help that. I opened the wardrobe, put on a pair of smart trousers and a shirt, and grabbed the pack of old photos. I placed the one of Sky on top of the pile, drove to the station and asked for Thornley.

I expected the woman on the reception desk to say I couldn't see him without an appointment, but she made a call. Then she nodded at the plastic chairs screwed to the floor and told me to wait there. Thornley might tell me whether they saw Sky as a suspect. After only a minute, he arrived in the waiting area and held the door open.

'Come on through,' he said.

I followed him down a corridor. He led me into a room with comfy chairs and a coffee table. Not what I'd expected at a police station. We sat opposite each other and I reached into my bag for the photos.

'After we spoke, I remembered something about the gun. It's about Sky.'

'Sky,' he said with a grimace.

'We were on the boat, just before I split up with him. They had an argument on deck. It got so bad, I thought he might chuck her overboard. She stormed down to the cabin, saying she'd shoot him with the gun.'

'Then what?'

'He went after her and calmed her down.'

'What was the row about?'

'Money probably, but he was tight-lipped. I was scared she'd shoot him, both of us even. He told me she didn't know where he'd hidden the gun. I said to chuck it in the sea, but he wouldn't.'

Thornley motioned to the pack of photos. 'What's that?'

I took out the photo of the two of them, of Sky laughing with Rob. 'It doesn't prove anything. It was taken a day or two before that. They were very up and down. Friendly one day and she was at his throat the next.'

'Can I see the rest?'

I handed him the photos and he shuffled them onto the coffee table.

'Tell me where they were taken,' he said. 'Take me through them.'

I leaned forward and did my best to recount the times and places to him.

'Can I borrow them?' he asked.

'Sure. Why do you want them?'

'We're building a clearer picture of what went on, hence our need to talk to people like you. He was camera shy. We don't have many photos of him that aren't police mugshots.'

'How's the investigation going?' I kept leaning forward, my business suit making me strident. Thornley might take me more seriously if I came across as professional.

'We're making progress.'

'Is Sky a suspect?'

'I can't discuss details of the investigation with you.'

But was Sky there? He wouldn't tell me that either, and I couldn't ask without admitting I'd talked to Rachel, which wasn't a wise move. Nor could I ask about the dark-haired woman in case he thought it was me.

'Why do you suspect Rachel?' I said.

'I can't discuss it at this stage.'

'I can't imagine her doing it.'

'I thought you didn't know her.' He frowned at me, the cynical look creeping back. 'You said you didn't know he'd remarried.'

I was losing him. *Pull it back.*

'I've found out about her since. When you came to see me, you said her situation was similar to mine. I assumed they had money problems. It made me wonder if she was involved in his scams.'

He looked hacked off. I'd gone too far, so I gave a little smile and played with the sleeve of my jacket.

'Leave that side of things to us,' he said.

I met his eye and nodded.

'What do you know about his scams?' he asked.

'Nothing. When I questioned anything, he'd explain it away. I never added it up.'

Thornley watched me, his dubious mouth downturned. 'Is there anything else you haven't told me?'

'No. I forgot about the gun.'

He arched an eyebrow. 'Is there any other suspicious activity you can think of?'

I shook my head, perhaps too quickly. What if I admitted my own suspicious activity? Just said the words. The unsayable words.

'Are you okay?' he said.

I blinked several times and dug my fingernails into my palms, dragging my mind back.

'Do you like sailing?' He rifled back through the photos to one of me gripping the helm, deep in concentration as the boat tacked at an angle. I hated everything that photo brought back.

'I prefer dry land,' I said, in an attempt to sound lighthearted. 'Were there other women?'

He paused, as if unsure of how to answer.

'I mean, other women he manipulated ... ones he might have taken away on the boat?'

'Yes.' He shuffled the photos back into the pack. 'I can't tell you any more than that.'

His answer didn't surprise me, but it tore at me all the same that he'd used the same seduction techniques on me as any number of women. I stood up to leave.

'Thank you for your help,' he said.

I smiled and he escorted me out. Back in my car, I covered my eyes, no clearer about the investigation. Were they going for the easy target with Rachel? She might have the biggest motive, but that didn't make her guilty. At least Thornley didn't know what happened. Not yet anyway. I'd been driven to the edge that day on the beach. It terrified me to think how close I'd come to being discovered.

JESS

April 2015

I pull the front door of the deckhouse shut, preparing to walk to the marina. Rob's sold his car and he drove off in mine earlier, to show it to a potential buyer. Neglected planters dotted around give the outdoor space a forlorn and barren air. Becca pulls up on the grass verge and steps out of her car. I come down the steps from the house, surprised to see her.

'Hello, stranger,' she says.

The top of Ellie's head is just visible in her car seat. She must be asleep or she'd be running towards me by now.

'Hi. I'm just leaving. Mum and Doug are coming to see the boat.'

'I'll only be a minute.' Becca crunches up the gravel path. 'I couldn't have you disappear without saying goodbye.' She fishes in her bulging handbag and pulls out a card and a small box. 'And I wanted to give you this.'

We sit on the wooden steps, the place deserted apart from

us. It's probably less desolate in the summer. I read the card, tactfully written to us both. A winsome tugboat on the front battles on a dark wavy sea. The poetic caption underneath is about staying safe from waves and thunderstorms. A silver heart pendant nestles in the box.

'It's a talisman for your travels. Look what's on the back.'

I turn it over. The engraving says *Never Give Up*.

'It's gorgeous. Thank you. Do it up for me.' I pull my hair into a high ponytail for her to fasten the clasp.

'How's it going with you two?'

'Okay.'

'You're done.' She pats my back. 'Only okay?'

I look down at the meaningful inscription on the pendant. 'No, it's fine. We're fine.'

Her silence says *good luck with that*.

'I know you don't like him, but we're married now.' I've had enough of justifying it, but I stay reasonable.

'You say I don't like him, but it's more about his problem with me.'

I turn to face her.

'I couldn't work him out when I met him at your place. He was okay till you went to the loo. Then I made some innocent remark about how he'd swept you off your feet and he said, "Are you jealous?" He gave me this warning look, but I'd just been making small talk.'

It had seemed strained that time she'd dropped in soon after I'd met him, but I wrote it off as a personality clash. 'He must've taken it the wrong way.'

'Why would I be jealous? It threw me. Then you came back and he was nice again, so I let it go.'

'But you haven't let it go.' I can see her point, but her entrenched view puts me on the defensive. There's a wedge between us, and Becca knows it too. Our lives are heading in different directions.

'Are you annoyed with me?' she asks.

'No.' I give a rueful smile. 'Thank you for the card and the present. They're lovely. Is that Ellie waking up?'

Ellie writhes in her car seat and flings her arms above her head. Becca goes to her.

'Phone me. Any time,' she calls through the open car window, grimacing as she manoeuvres out of the narrow road. Ellie kicks restlessly in the back. I can see her strawberry blonde mop of curls as she arches in the car seat. I wave them off with a pang of loss.

I walk to the marina in thin sunshine, keeping the necklace to myself under my jumper. A car pulls up – it's Mum and Doug. Doug lowers the window and Mum cranes over, both of them in nautical sweaters with navy and white stripes.

'You're going the wrong way,' I say.

'We've already been.' Mum leans against Doug to see me. 'The boat's lovely!'

The two of them look animated, with the youthful glow they had in the early days of them becoming a couple.

I frown. 'You're early. We said four o'clock.'

'We arranged it for three o'clock. We thought you'd had a better offer,' she says.

'Becca came round, but I wasn't going to be late. Weren't you coming at four?'

'No, definitely three. But don't worry, I know you're busy,' Mum says.

'Not too busy to see you. Come back now and have a cuppa.'

'Sorry love, we can't. We're eating early. I've got WI.'

Doug nods and studies the empty road in front of them. 'Don't want to get caught in traffic. It's a smart boat. We like it.'

'It's given Doug ideas. He'll be buying us a yacht next!'

They hoot with laughter.

'Come to us next time, both of you.' Mum settles back into her own seat. 'If you can fit us in!'

I wave them off. She's certainly come round to the sailing trip. When I first broke the news, her pinched face said that people like us didn't leave our jobs to go sailing.

At the marina, I pull myself aboard. 'Ahoy!'

'Ahoy yourself.'

I stand on tiptoes and hold on to him for balance as we kiss.

'They've been and gone,' he says.

'I saw them down the road. Did you get the time wrong?'

'It was three o'clock.'

'You told me four,' I said. He'd arranged it when he helped Doug with his laptop.

'You must've got the wrong time.'

'I don't get times wrong.' He'd said four o'clock, I'm sure of it. Had I misheard?

'Don't worry, I handled it,' Rob said. 'I put your mum's mind at rest. She was surprised by the boat, especially the beds.'

'Did she think we'd sleep in hammocks?'

'Probably. They went away happy. I thought you'd forgotten.' He kisses me again.

'Becca dropped round as I was leaving.' I want to change the subject, but mentioning Becca is also contentious.

'Becca? Good. Did you patch things up?'

'I think so. I feel bad about it.' We stay in our clinch, looking like the newlyweds we are. I feel the pendant under my jumper and for some reason want to keep it to myself.

'Why do you feel bad?'

'Because I've sidelined everyone for you – for us,' I correct myself, not wanting to upset his good mood.

He surprises me by being pleased I've made peace with Becca. I bury my face in his chunky sweater, liking our togetherness. He goes back to repairing something and I set about cleaning the cabin. I've just started when all at once he's there behind me, slipping his arms around me.

'You're sexy in those rubber gloves.'

'I'll wear them more often.'

We help each other undress and then spill onto the bed. The boat sways as we forget the time, along with everything still to be done.

Afterwards, he wraps both arms around me. 'My mate's buying your car. You dig out the documents. Leave the rest to me.'

I like him sorting it out. It's one less thing to worry about. He's agreed a decent price, which seems too good to be true.

'How's he going to pay me?' I roll onto my side to face him

in the dim cabin light. The overhead hatch and portholes round the side of the cabin cast him in shadow as the light outside heads towards dusk.

'He'll pay it straight into my account.'

'Not mine?'

'I didn't know your account number.'

'You could've asked me.'

He takes a deep breath. 'I've got a few bills to sort before my final invoices get paid. Can I use the car money for now and wherever we end up, I'll buy you a better car.'

It comes out as a statement rather than a question. I nod in vague agreement. It makes sense to merge our finances now we're married, especially as we'll be travelling and running a business together. Our lives aren't separate now.

'Let's go home and I'll cook,' he says. This pleases me, since he rarely takes a turn in the kitchen. He's preoccupied with boat maintenance and goes off for hours to source boat parts or obscure books on navigating the French canals. Instead of finding parts on eBay, he has to seek them out and look them over the old-fashioned way. He spends entire days in London, finishing off his IT contract and 'finalising things'.

Back home, he chops vegetables. I like it best when we cook together. He'll insist he knows some great recipe then we'll make a mess of it and laugh a lot.

'Are you okay?' he says. 'You seem a bit quiet.'

'Is the money situation all right? I know you're laid-back about money, but now we're not earning any ...'

'It's an expensive time. I've bought some major stuff for the boat. It's left me short, but we'll have my final contract payment soon. It's just a hitch till then.' He pours oil into a pan.

Money is the only thing we don't entirely agree on. We'd agreed to put equal amounts in a joint account to last the summer. I'd made a show of transferring a lump sum from my house sale to encourage his share to materialise, but he hasn't matched it. He reminded me of the assets in his house and the yacht, so he's hardly penniless. He's had spare cash until now, and he's always been generous.

'I'll pay the expenses to start with. When your money comes through, you take a turn.' I find myself saying it because it doesn't matter in the scheme of things. It's not an issue when you trust someone.

MIA

DS Thornley came back a few days after I saw him at the police station. Did he never make appointments? Perhaps he turned up unannounced in an attempt to catch me out. I'd better not meet Rachel here again, just in case. Nervous anticipation rippled through me. I made two mugs of tea and we sat on the sofa. He held my photos in his hands. Darcy lay at my feet, forever watchful.

'Here's your photos back. Thanks for bringing them in.' He laid the pack on the coffee table.

'Were they any use?'

He shrugged as if to say maybe, maybe not. 'Rob Creavy wasn't on social media, so it's useful to see photos that build a picture of the life he led.'

'Why? Is that the key to how he died?'

'Most murder victims are killed by someone who knew them.'

I saw this as my opening to ask about Sky and Rachel, but he looked pointedly at me.

'How did you first meet him?'

'In a bar at Clear View marina.'

He nodded slowly. I tried to forget the early days, especially that first night when our paths could so easily not have crossed.

'Why do you ask?'

'He also met Rachel Harman at the marina. He had a pattern of behaviour for meeting women there. He scoped out targets near marinas, hoping their proximity to yachts made them amenable to sailing.'

Targets. I burned with shame, hating how he'd lured me in. Another woman to fulfil his requirements.

'Will you make any more arrests?'

He cocked his head. 'Why do you ask?'

'You say murder victims are often killed by someone who knows them. I keep thinking about Sky and the gun. Maybe she's involved.'

His face was inscrutable. 'How well do you know her?'

I aimed for the right level of nonchalant interest. 'Hardly at all. I couldn't work her out.'

He nodded and returned my deadpan look. He sat back and drank his tea, not asking anything more about her. I couldn't help myself though. 'So is she involved?'

'We're piecing it together. How everyone fits.'

'But she's not a suspect?'

'Rachel Harman is the only person who's been arrested, but we're following up leads.' He said this in a careful way and I went hot.

'What sort of leads?'

'Your ex conned people out of money. Some of it happened when he was with you. What do you know about that?'

'Nothing. I'm sorry.' I felt the implied criticism. His sins mine by association. 'He kept a lot secret from me. Who did he con?'

'People who can't afford to lose the money.'

His answer made my stomach churn. I was about to say that none of us could afford to lose money, when a key turned in the lock. I stiffened. Ben let himself in. Stan plodded in too and Darcy stood up, wagging his tail. I went to the hallway, faster than necessary.

'Hi.' Ben looked in on Thornley.

They acknowledged each other before I pulled the door shut, leaving Thornley in the room. I clutched the handle as if hiding a secret lover. I'd expected Ben to drop in, so brought the police into the little sitting room for a degree of privacy. It was harder to avoid him if we sat at the kitchen table.

'The police are checking some facts. Can you give us a few minutes?'

'Okay. Shall I make a brew or something?'

'You go ahead. We've got one. Won't be long.' I pasted on a smile, my entire body rigid. I didn't want him asking DS Thornley awkward questions. Ben looked sideways at me. I returned to the detective and closed the door behind me.

'My boyfriend.'

Thornley sat back and drank his tea, in silence

I took a sip of mine to keep up the charade of looking normal. 'Yes, so,' I said.

'It must have been hard when you left him.'

'I wasn't in a good state back then.'

'Because of the abuse?'

'Yes, but I moved on and took back the control. He had no say any more.'

'Did it help to change your name?'

With a thud to my stomach, I thought of Jess.

Did it help to change my name?

Yes, because Jess was an idiot. Her heart ruled her head since your head didn't get a look-in when you were crazy in love. I knew because I *was* Jess. At least, I used to be.

PART TWO

AFTER

I was christened Jessica Maria Handley. My dad chose Jessica. Maria was my grandmother on my mum's side. I shortened Maria to Mia and that's what I became. MIA, missing in action. He tracked me down regardless. He wanted to make the point that he'd found out my new name. I ignored his power games. I'd done it for me, as part of moving on.

To see me now, you wouldn't place me in the mould of hopeless romantic, but Rachel hadn't been the only besotted one. I pictured my sun-burnished husband on the swaying boat in an expanse of perfect blue and wondered how closely Rachel's experience mirrored mine: the engagement in Rome, the impromptu wedding. What I'd considered special moments were ticks on his checklist. Rachel barely mentioned the darker elements of her marriage. Was she still in denial, as I'd been?

Mia Fallon. Fallon for falling, failing, fallible, I don't know. A reminder not to screw up again. Ben knew, as did Becca and my mum and Doug, of course. DS Thornley's words came back to me from that first time he visited me about the murder.

Mia, you married Rob Creavy under the name Jessica Handley, is that correct?

I hadn't been able to speak. That's when the panic attack had crept up. I thought they'd come to arrest me.

'You're the Jessica who married him in April 2015, aren't you?' Thornley had asked again.

I'd nodded in confirmation and Thornley had left it at that. Until he came back with the photos. I thought Thornley was on my side after I'd shown him the photos. I dropped my guard a bit, but then he paused and gave me a measured stare.

'What's your shoe size?' he asked.

I seized up. Footprints. Mud. Drizzle. Boat by the towpath. I'd kicked off my shoes before climbing aboard. *Christ. Look normal. Breathe. Stay calm.*

'Five.'

'Do you know why I asked?'

I shook my head and kept my mouth shut. All I'd left at the boat that night were squelchy footprints. I'd hoped rain would wash away the evidence.

'We believe this crime was committed by a woman who knew him. Hardly surprising is it, Mia? When he treated you all so badly.'

I was still reeling, almost giddy from his words. He suspected me, I was sure of that now. It'd been a mistake to ask questions, to draw attention to myself. Rachel had it wrong. They were looking for another suspect. The footprints clearly weren't hers, but they might be mine.

'Is that everything?' I asked.

His eyes hadn't left mine, even as he stood to leave. He must think he knew it all, he'd seen it all, and he had me sussed. He was probably right. My footprints at the murder scene didn't mean I'd killed Rob, but I knew how it looked. After all, wasn't that what I'd set out to do – commit the perfect murder? So perfect that Rachel had been stitched up.

When Thornley left, I leaned my forehead and one hand on the door, taking a moment to steady myself for Ben. His footsteps came through from the kitchen. I sat back down and cradled my head in my hands. I'd come up for air soon. Just not right now.

'Was that a detective on the murder case?'

I nodded into my hands.

'What did he want?' Ben sat beside me and placed a steadying hand on my back.

'Just checking some facts.' I lifted my head and took a slow breath.

'You look strung out.'

'No, I'm fine, it's just, you know.' I waved my hand in the direction of where DS Thornley had sat.

'It's serious, isn't it? The police coming here.' He looked at me with grave eyes, and shook his head as if he didn't understand.

I took hold of his hand, our fingers interweaving. Mine looked small and pale in his gardener's hand, his skin rough and scratched. His fawn-coloured jumper had snags where branches and rough edges had caught it.

'What are the photos of?' He saw the pack Thornley had left on the table.

'They're old ones. He wanted to see photos of the boat.'

'Do you think you're a "person of interest"?'

'How do you work that one out?'

'Well, they've been back to see you. Rachel is the main suspect but they can still be interested in other people.'

His words echoed my own fears. 'When did you become the expert?'

'Sorry, sorry.' He held his hands up. 'Too many true crime podcasts. Police documentaries. It's interesting though ... the reasons why people commit murder. Will you need to be a prosecution witness?'

I sighed. Clearly he wanted to talk about it, and I didn't want to keep biting his head off.

'There isn't a trial date yet. They haven't charged anyone. I just want it to be over.'

'I need you to tell me what's going on. The less you say, the more I worry.' He tried to catch my eye, and I kept looking at our entwined fingers.

'You don't have to worry. That whole time was a mistake. I'm better off focusing on the present.'

'You're not, though. You jump out of your skin when the doorbell goes. You have night terrors. You're scared of what you might read about the murder.'

He saw through my attempts to hide it, but how could I tell him I'd been caught up in something bad, something dangerous? I couldn't.

'I'm getting through it the best I can.'

'If someone shot my ex-wife dead, I'd be talking to you. I'd be leaning on you, trying to make sense of it, but you won't tell me anything about him.'

I let go of his hand and rubbed my forehead.

'I'm on your side, or I would be if you didn't push me away. You can tell me.'

I can't though.

His hand went back to holding mine. I lifted it to my lips and kissed it. He leaned against me.

'I don't want to poison us with it. I'd rather forget him.'

'You can't forget him. You woke up the other night saying his name. The name you hate hearing and avoid saying when you're awake.'

What else did I make known in my sleep? All those dark secrets preying on my mind. When Ben brought up my night terrors, I'd pretend not to remember, brushing away his concern.

'I'm too complicated.'

'You're not complicated. Your past is, and we can't have a conversation without you getting jumpy.'

'Let's give it time to settle. Are you hungry?' I went through to the kitchen and took an onion out to chop, needing to ease my nervous tension. 'Shall we go away at the weekend? You choose.'

I tried to sound normal, but my mind spooled ahead, taunting me with what-ifs. What if they arrested me? What if I was put on trial? Could I defend myself if the evidence stacked up? Would I go to *prison*? I couldn't shake off thoughts like that.

Ben took the frying pan out and leaned sideways on the worktop so he could see my face. 'Why are you wincing?'

'What?'

'The look on your face. What are you thinking?'

I nearly blamed it on the onions making my eyes sting, but he deserved more than my usual brush-offs. 'I should've made Rob dispose of the gun.'

He didn't give me a hard time, but I knew he would mull it over, ask more questions. I couldn't tell him what happened. How the past came crashing down on the day of the murder and I'd acted in a way that no rational person should have. If he knew, he might want me to do the right thing and tell the police. I didn't mention that Thornley had asked my shoe size.

I changed my name to escape my past, but Rob had pulled me back to him and the boat. It made sense for him to die on the boat, the place where he said he belonged. People in my world didn't get killed, but his murder wasn't surprising. It was a terrible thing to say about the man I'd married, but it had to happen. And if the police knew the whole story, I would be more than a 'person of interest'. I'd be a suspect.

BEFORE

April 2015

He insists we sleep on the boat the night before leaving the country. It's like arriving at the airport the night before an early flight when you live ten minutes away. We settle in to our new cramped quarters and go to bed.

'The sheets are damp,' I say. 'I only put them on today.'

'It's the sea air.'

The cabin sways. He sleeps, and I listen drowsily to the slap of water on the side of the boat. Until now it's been a novelty, but the rocking motion will become my new way of life. The boat creaks and the air's full of eerie *ting-ting*ing of metal halyards clanking on masts. I fall asleep in the early hours, and we get up not long after.

The engine shudders into life, disturbing the quiet marina. Droplets of dew rain down on us from the sails. The pre-dawn air is colder than it should be for late April. We slide away from the pontoon.

I wear my new red sailing jacket with a big yellow oilskin jacket over the top and awful matching dungarees tucked into wellies. With my hood up, I have to swivel ninety degrees to look sideways. I'm not much practical use, but at least I can't drown, since I'm wearing a harness with a built-in life jacket.

'I've never been so weighed down by clothes.'

'You'll need the wet weather gear and thermals. And take a couple of these.' He fishes a pack of seasickness tablets from his jacket pocket. 'It's rough out there.'

The wind pits the waves. Within minutes, the biting cold turns my fingers blue and I can't coil ropes, tie knots or do anything else I've learnt.

'It won't usually be like this,' he says. 'We'll be in the Greek islands soon.'

I can just about helm without falling over. Despite the sea not playing along, he has me believe the rest will be plain sailing. As we head into the Solent, the darkness lifts into a dull gloom. The day is a monotony of grey layers, one of those days that never gets properly light. We sail under bleak skies on a sea whipped up by a fierce wind. It takes my breath away.

The boat tips around, making me clumsy and lacking in balance. For great swathes of time, I gamely hang on, eyes watering from the bitter wind. Pummelled by the weather, we squint through sea spray. The waves splash wildly at us, and my feet stay numbingly cold despite the ridiculous layers of clothes. I stand frozen to the helm in dripping oilskins. The seasickness tablets aren't working. I didn't need them in the Canaries, but the Channel is so much rougher.

'It won't always be this bad,' Rob shouts through the wind.

I keep telling myself the same thing, like some crappy mantra. He's everywhere at once, a frenetic mass of energy tearing round the deck to untangle the rigging or get a better view from the bow. What would happen if he fell overboard?

The wind gathers strength, howling round the mast, battering the boat and us. A swift gust catches the sails and the boat flies across the waves, my stomach lurching with it. God knows how I'll ever enjoy it. I keep reminding myself that the Canaries wasn't this bad. Seven relentless hours later, nausea and sea spray have worn me down. He makes steaming mugs of tea and I take a hot gulp.

'Tastes of saltwater.' Everything does.

Seasickness creeps up. My stomach lurches in time with the boat bumping through the waves. It intensifies over the hours, spreading to my throat. Rob produces a bucket and I throw up. Then I slump onto the cold fibreglass seating.

'It won't always be this bad,' he says. 'Have I already said that?'

I don't care if he's said it before. I catch it in the wind and hold on to it. I want to be anywhere but on this bloody boat with its endless swaying. The words on Becca's card echo round my head: *Little boat on the sea, keep the waves away from me, keep me safe, keep me warm, keep me dry from thunderstorm.* Trust her to know better than me.

We zig-zag through the water, which he says is called 'tacking' to keep the wind in the sails and us tearing through the sea. When the boat tips to one side, the metal boom swings over, ready to knock out anyone in its way.

'What's it for?'

He says something about it changing the angle of the sail.

'That's insane! What if it knocks you overboard?' But there isn't much sanity in sailing.

A violent gust rips through the worn old mainsail, tearing it into uselessness. We'd stowed away a savagely expensive new set, which I'd paid for. I could hardly believe I'd shelled out so much for it. Marcus at work had likened yachting to standing in a cold shower tearing up fifty pound notes. People laughed at the time.

'It's too rough to fit new sails. We'll have to motor instead.' Rob's disappointment is at odds with my relief. The motor keeps us on an even keel, not tipping over at crazy angles.

The ripped sail flaps melodramatically until he winches it in. The afternoon passes in a blur of nausea, then fading daylight adds to the chill factor and still it drags on. As we heave into darkness, we pick out an uneven row of lights in the distance: at last, France.

'When will we get there?'

'Half an hour or so. Then we'll grab a shower at the marina and find a restaurant. There, see?' He hugs me with one arm, his other hand on the helm. 'We've nearly made it.'

The engine noise becomes loud and erratic. It judders, splutters and dies. He leaps to the ignition, swearing and trying to restart it. I feel his ferocity, and daren't speak. He storms down to the engine with a torch, but can't get it working. The boat drifts and his fury builds. He snarls under his breath. I've never seen him like this before. It makes me wary. He gets on the radio to ask the French coastguard for help.

'They're coming to give us a tow.' He clutches the top of his head.

'But that's good, isn't it?'

'What good is a broken engine?' He glares at me. Dark tension pulsates from him.

Lingering nausea leaves me drained and with no inclination for his bad mood. The coastguard boat cuts through the waves. The men on board tow us to the harbour. Safely moored, he goes to check the engine, and I peel off wet layers. At least a shower will warm me back to life.

'I'll go and find the showers,' I say, but Rob ignores me. I lurch off the boat like a queasy drunk and find my way to the shower block. The swaying sensation stays with me. The showers are locked and in darkness. When I sway back, the coastguard says in broken English that all the restaurants have shut for the night. Today feels like a bad omen. Have I made a huge mistake or will it get better?

Can I tell you a story? It's about an older man. Let's call him Rob, because that's the name he goes by, except when he's scamming someone out of their life savings. He made a play for a girl of nineteen. She'd been to a girls' boarding school and spent the holidays holed up in the countryside. You wouldn't call her streetwise. She trusted the wrong man and trusting him came at a high price.

That girl was me, even though older men aren't my thing. I wish someone had told me what he was really like. But I found out the hard way, the lonely way, and it ruined my life. He ruined my life.

Mummy met Rob at Cowdray when they both watched the polo. She introduced him to me as her friend, but they were more than that. He was younger than her, but still old. She knows lots of people in the polo set.

When I left school, I became the stable girl at home and looked after our horses. I didn't do well with academic stuff because of my dyslexia, but I loved the horses and lived in the little barn conversion beside the stables. Rob took an interest in the horses and we hit it off. He even helped with mucking out. We had a laugh and I liked him more and more. He made me feel special.

'You're not like other girls,' he said. I was the one he chose when he could have nearly anyone. Rob asked if wanted to spend my whole life cleaning up after horses. He said there were loads of things I

could do, but I hadn't found my niche. He encouraged me to get out in the world and spread my wings. He had this way of making you think anything was possible.

He said he would take me sailing round the Greek islands, just the two of us. I imagined the gorgeous beaches, a lovely big boat, lots of sunshine. I fell for him and the life he said we could have.

I thought we could love each other and it would be okay because I'd seen all those romcoms where the sweet, awkward girl ends up with the guy who's right for her. What we had was more than a fling. It was the real deal and everyone would come round eventually. That's what he said.

AFTER

Another email came through, and I flinched at the words.

You were with him on the beach. I know you shot him.
Do you remember that other trip to the beach, when you
found out his secrets? You were just as angry back then. I
bet the police will be interested to hear about it.

Sky? Did Sky write that? The last time I saw her flooded
back. I pictured her in Corfu that searing hot day as she
revealed his secret life, the venom in her brutal home truths.
She'd pushed me to breaking point and left me devastated.
That's what I thought at the time. Looking back, I could see
now that it was him. But she'd colluded, hadn't she? She'd been
brazen, cruel. Perhaps she still was. The Sky I knew was more
than capable of sending the emails. And she was the only other
person with me on that beach in Greece, the only person who
knew, unless she'd told someone else.

I had to do something while I still had the chance. DS Thornley had scared me, asking about my shoe size and staring me down. I half expected him to come back and arrest me. Rachel texted to ask again if I'd go with her to see Sky. I said yes, ignoring my resolve to distance myself from Rachel. I wanted to see how much of a threat Sky posed. The old her would have sent the emails, and the old me might have ignored them. I had to get the measure of her and find out what the fuck she was playing at. Then I'd warn her off, in case she thought me a pushover.

Rachel and I met at the station and boarded the train to London.

'How did you find Sky's address?' I asked as we sped through the countryside.

'Same place I found yours. His little black book. It had "Jess" crossed out and "Mia" written over the top.'

'Does that bother you? The way he kept track of his exes like that?'

Rachel shrugged and looked out of the window. Surely she wasn't still in thrall to him? Was she in denial? She wanted answers, but she didn't seem to feel the rage that I did. She was no pushover though. The police must have told her to stay away from potential witnesses since she was the chief suspect, so she had steely nerves to risk seeing Sky and to contact me.

Rachel took out her phone and scrolled through photos. 'I like looking back on the better times.' She leaned in and showed me a wedding photo of them posing outside a stately home. At least they didn't marry at the River Hotel.

'It's Goodwood House.'

'Lovely.' I scrolled through the photos with my index finger. Not the simple and intimate wedding that he'd sold to me. I was fascinated and repelled all at once, but mostly I wanted to take the phone and smash it.

'Did he mind you having photos on your phone?'

'He hated it.' Her smile turned indulgent at this personality quirk. 'Such a perfect day. My parents wanted to do it in style. My dad's traditional like that.'

The train hurtled through Surrey, and her gaze misted off to a field in the distance.

'You didn't take his name when you married him?'

She squirmed in her seat. 'He wouldn't wear a wedding ring. Silly really, but I didn't take his name because of that. It was my own little protest.'

'Fair enough.'

So she wasn't entirely compliant. I didn't change my name either. In the whirlwind of him racing me up the aisle, I didn't have time to change my passport before we went away.

'When did it start going wrong?' Curiosity needled at me.

Her face clouded and she slid the phone into her pocket. 'On the boat.'

'Same for me.' Though to be honest, things were never right in the first place.

'He had a temper. He said it was stress. He was quite controlling.' Her voice faded out. 'And a bit aggressive.'

'Do you think you're playing down how bad it was?'

She twisted her wedding ring back and forth.

'I'm only asking because I did the same.'

'He made it seem like my fault for expecting too much. He said I was too emotional.' Her voice thickened. 'So I'd take my mind off somewhere else. Pretend it wasn't happening. I guess it wasn't such a good thing.' She brushed a tear away.

'I'm sorry.'

'No, it's fine. Every now and then it hits me that he's never coming back. The wedding photos remind me of when we were happy. I wish I hadn't found his body. It's awful. I keep picturing it.'

Me too.

She suppressed a sob and delved into her coat pocket for a tissue. 'I like photos of him when he was happy and healthy.'

We sat in silence for a while. The green landscape gave way to commuter belt towns. How awful for Rachel if she really was innocent, forced to seek out the murderer because the police didn't believe her.

'What do you want to know from Sky?' I asked.

'Why she was on the beach. What she wanted from him.'

My heart sped up at the thought of confronting Sky. My instincts told me I was straying too deep, which is why I hadn't mentioned it to Ben. I'd told him I had a client meeting, so he'd taken Darcy to work for the day. Guilt stabbed at me. If Ben knew we were going to see Sky, he'd be shocked. Rachel's visits to see me were one thing, but confronting Sky went way beyond that.

'She'll think we're ganging up. She won't admit anything.'

'This is Sky we're talking about,' Rachel said. 'She can't keep her mouth shut where he's concerned. She'll be guarded with the police. But she acts superior to us, which means she might say too much and put her foot in it.'

Be strong, I told myself. Keep breathing so you don't have a panic attack. I'd been optimistic to think I could face seeing Sky of all people. At the very least, I thought I could suss out Rachel's and Sky's shoe size. And if we got Sky talking, she might say something to my advantage.

Rachel's feet were small in brown Chelsea boots. 'What shoe size are you?' I asked. 'Your feet look tiny.'

'Size three. I can wear children's shoes.'

She wiggled her feet and we smiled at each other.

'I'm glad you're here,' she said. 'It's daunting doing this on my own. She'll be easier to handle with two of us.'

'Is there any evidence of Sky killing him?'

'Not at this stage. They haven't arrested her yet, and we won't see what evidence there is against her unless it comes to trial.'

The train pulled in at Victoria and we walked to Sky's flat. Rachel navigated her way there and we arrived at the housing block shrouded in gloom. It was so close to the train line into Victoria, we could hear the trains rattling through, but I felt no sympathy for Sky. I'd last seen her at the lowest point in my life. My ex-husband had caused the worst of it, but Sky proved herself a willing accomplice. I hadn't come to make amends.

'What's your plan?' I asked Rachel as we reached the entrance of the tower block. A delivery man came out and held the door open. Rachel checked a piece of paper that had the address on and directed us up the stairs.

'Knock on the door and ask if you can come in for a chat. I'll wait round the corner.'

'What?' I stopped in the stairwell and looked at her. 'You're not going to speak to her? She won't tell me anything.'

'I – I can't. Not now we're here. She's more likely to talk to you. She hates me. Tell her she was seen on the beach and watch for her reaction. She might kick off and say something stupid.'

'I don't want her to kick off.'

'You can handle her. Say you're upset about the murder and you want closure. Then record her on your phone.'

I stared dumbly at her.

'Here, let me do it.' She took my phone and set it up to record. 'Just get her talking and see what she comes up with.'

I regretted coming, but I took a breath and walked down the corridor to her flat. Rachel tucked herself into a recess where Sky wouldn't see her. I knocked on the door and moments later, Sky flung the door open. She stood in front of me, looking more polished than before, her hair cropped into a severe, copper-coloured bob.

'Hello, Sky.'

She stared blankly at me. 'It's me, Mia ... I mean, Jess. I changed my name, but I was Jess back then.'

She tilted her head in silent recognition.

'Can I talk to you?'

She kept staring, her blue eyes splintered with ice, her face hostile. She reminded me of him. That icy stare.

'Why?' Her mouth twisted in a sneer.

I felt my face flush. I'd better not trip over my words and go to pieces in front of her. I glanced at my feet and remembered to look at hers. Barefoot, electric blue toenails. About the same size as mine.

'I ... I just want to know what happened. He hurt me so much, back then. I wanted nothing to do with him.' My voice cracked and I sounded vulnerable. 'But now he's dead and I need to know why. Please. You knew him better than I did.'

She slouched a little, assessing me through jaded eyes.

'Rachel shot him. He should never have got involved with her.'

'Why did she shoot him?'

'Ask her.' She went to shut the door.

'Wait!' I put my hand out before she slammed the door. 'Someone's been sending me anonymous emails. Threatening ones. I'm going to show them to the police.' I stared hard at her.

She shrugged as if it was of no consequence. '*Mia,*' she sneered again, looking me up and down. 'Trying to reinvent yourself, are you? You're not so special. You never were.'

She slammed the door shut.

'Fuck you!' I shouted through the door and stood back, shaking all over.

If Sky had sent the emails, she would know I suspected her. She'd given nothing away, but I still felt good about challenging her. I wanted her to know that she couldn't walk all over me again.

I went back to Rachel, pissed off that I hadn't responded with something better than 'fuck you'. Rachel took the phone from me and turned off the recording.

'Who does she think she is?' I said, still fuming.

'Rise above it. She thinks she's better than us, but you had the last word.'

We walked back to the station. Rachel linked arms and leaned against me as if we were firm friends.

Pre-rush hour and the train should have been quiet, but Victoria was crammed with commuters staring at the information screens. An announcement said a signalling problem had been resolved. We boarded our train a minute before it pulled away, and stood in a crush of people. I was still shaken from seeing Sky and I held tight to the handrail. So long as I didn't have a panic attack, I'd be okay. Rachel placed a hand on my arm.

'Let's talk when we get back.'

When we arrived back at the station, Rachel offered to drop me home. We walked to her car, and I called a client who'd been trying to get me all day. The phone conversation lasted until we pulled up at my house, and I promised to email him in the morning.

'I don't know about you, but I need a drink,' Rachel said. 'There's a bottle of wine in the back. I thought we'd need it after seeing Sky.'

She looked wrung out, and I felt the same way. She followed me in with a bottle of red wine from her car. I opened the wine and we sat at the table with the bottle between us.

'You did really well to talk to her.' She took a sip from her glass.

'Not that she said anything worthwhile.' I drank the wine to ease my tension. I'd laid off the booze lately. The wine tasted velvety smooth and slid down easily.

'What colour is her hair now?'

'It's copper.' I hadn't wanted to tell her, in case she suspected me of being the woman on the beach instead of Sky, but Rachel could have sneaked a look at her when she opened the door.

'It was an ordinary shade of brown when I saw her on the beach. She changes it a lot. It was the same shade as Rob's when I first met her. She must have changed it after the reports of the other woman.' She topped up my wine. I'd nearly finished the glass.

'I wonder what Rob would make of all this?' she said.

He'd revel in it. His final selfish act made sure he left drama in his wake, leaving us to pick up the pieces after his wrong-doings caught up with him. But who had pulled the trigger? Rachel had looked angry when I saw her stomping away. Sky supposedly went there demanding money, if she was there at all. And I'd gone there wanting payback. All three of us had a motive.

'Did he ever mention me?' I asked.

'He said you were unhinged.'

I took another glug of wine.

'Join the club.' She topped up our glasses. 'He called me unhinged when we argued.'

We fell into silence until Rachel changed the subject.

'Well done for mentioning the emails. She might lay off them now. The police weren't interested when I told them. She sends them from a Gmail account. You can't track them down.' She rested her elbows on the table and traced her forefingers over her eyebrows as if trying to smooth away her tiredness.

'Perhaps we're fixating on Sky because we don't like her,' I said. 'She might have nothing to do with it.'

'If she didn't do it, who did?' She looked at me, eyes red from a heavy day. 'Because I didn't shoot him.'

'What happened, after you saw him and Sky on the beach?'

'I didn't want Sky making a scene, so I came home and waited for him. I thought he'd get rid of her, but he never came home.'

'And?'

'I went looking for him. He wasn't on the beach, so I went to the boat.' She pressed her hands to her mouth so her words came out muffled. 'He was dead.'

'Was the gun there?'

'No. The police found it in the water. They think I shot him because of how he treated me. But I didn't do it.'

'Did you ever feel like killing him?' My words slipped out, oiled by the wine.

'He was awful at times. I tried to make it work. People say marriage is hard, and it takes compromise and sacrifices. That's why it's called the labour of love.' Her eyes filled with tears and she gave a sad smile. 'The things we put up with. It's no wonder people commit crimes of passion.'

I ran one finger up and down the stem of the wine glass. We weren't that different, Rachel and I. Neither of us knew what we'd let ourselves in for.

'What about you?' She delved in her bag for a tissue, and then gave me a look of solidarity. 'Did you ever want to shoot him?'

149

'I had dark times. One time I could've killed him in the heat of the moment.' I immediately wished I could snatch the words back. I'd let my guard down, relaxed from the wine.

'And then someone did kill him,' she said in a low voice.

'I still can't believe it.'

'What happened when you wanted to kill him?'

'Let's not go there.' I felt queasy and pushed my glass away. I'd drunk too much and said too much.

Rachel took her phone out. 'I'd better go. I'll get an Uber and leave my car parked up the road.' She tapped at the screen. 'Will you be okay?'

'My boyfriend's coming over. He's had my dog today.'

When the cab arrived, she hugged me at the door just as Ben came down the path with Darcy. I introduced them.

Ben shook her hand. 'I'm sorry for your loss.' He said it awkwardly, unsure if it was a loss.

'Thank you.' She gave him a grateful smile and walked to the cab.

Ben came in and shut the door. 'What was she doing here?'

'Updating me on the investigation.'

He looked at me as if I'd gone mad. 'Is that wise?'

'I'd rather hear from her than read it online or wait for the trial.'

'She's been accused of murder. You might get dragged in.'

'They haven't charged her. And what if she's been wrongly accused?'

'All the more reason to leave it to the police. Since when have you been friends?'

'We're not friends.'

'Good. Keep it that way.'

I folded my arms, annoyed by his tone. '*Rob* tried to come between me and my friends. I don't put up with that shit any more.'

'Mia—'

'I'm not friends with her, but it's my choice, not yours.'

'Fine.' We stood awkwardly in the hallway.

'Are you coming in?'

'No, I'll head home, early start tomorrow.'

He kissed me on the cheek and turned to go without making eye contact.

'Thank you for having Darcy.'

'He's no trouble. Did your meeting go well?'

'Yes thanks,' I lied, not wanting to mention Sky.

When Ben left, I realised how reckless I'd been, telling Rachel I'd wanted to kill my ex. He was still her husband, after all. But I'd only said I *felt* like killing him, not that I'd set out to kill him. And she hadn't seen me go to the boat that evening, or fleeing soon after. If she realised it was me on the beach, it would incriminate me.

BEFORE

April 2015

What's that? The rocking and floating sensation feels like a dream. The boat dips from side to side and I wake up a little more. Lifting up on my elbows, I crane towards the perspex hatch and see him leap off. The boat settles back to a drunken sway. Early still. I shrink back under the duvet for warmth.

Sleep eludes me, so I pull on clothes from a jumble in the corner. My head throbs. I emerge from the cabin wanting coffee, but with no idea how to work the gas cooker. I straighten up the mess from yesterday's English Channel crossing until he clambers noisily back. No need for a doorbell when the boat announces every coming and going.

'Shall I make coffee?' I ask.

He shows me how to work the strange little cooker so we can boil water. Still wobbly from the rough crossing, I go to the shower block and grimace at my pasty face in the mirror. A hot shower revives me. When I come back, he's lying beside the engine, doing a messy oil change.

'Need any help?' I say to his back.

'There isn't room for two of us.'

I put the kettle on the hob. He grunts when I leave him a second mug of coffee.

'You're welcome.'

I only speak to his back for the rest of the day and he hardly says a word. I stare through drizzle at the concrete marina, trying not to crowd him, this mechanic I don't know. *Bonjour* boredom. I call Mum from my mobile.

'Jess! You've made it. We keep wondering how you're getting on.'

At least I can have a conversation with her, even if all we do is establish everyone's well, and then compare their rain with ours.

Sachi and a few friends have texted *Bon Voyage* messages. I'd primed everyone that we wouldn't be posting updates or sending flurries of messages, so I send quick replies to say I miss them, adding things like, *The weather's awful, but it'll heat up soon.* Why did I only talk about the weather to people back home?

Stay warm! xxx Sachi replies. *Still better than being at work!*

Not really! I want to say. I already miss the warm office and Sachi.

'It's all right for some.' Rob appears from the engine, splattered in oil.

'What am I supposed to do?' I look up from the phone. 'I've cleaned, I've lugged food back. You're busy. I'm in the way if I come near you.'

'It was a joke.' He looks at me as if to say *don't start* and goes back to the engine.

It rains disappointment and takes three days of repairs for the boat to cough back to life. He stops tinkering on the third night and slumps down with a beer. We hardly speak. So this is married life. I don't expect passion forever, but our shared wavelength seems a distant memory.

'What's going on with us?' I rub his shoulder, wanting to bring back the closeness. 'It's like you've switched off from me.'

'I've been up to my elbows in engine oil.'

'You're shutting me out.' I don't want to go to bed on an argument. 'Let's start as we mean to go on. We can deal with it together.'

'We'll be fine when we're in the swing of things.' He rakes his hands through his hair, distractedly mussing it up. 'It's just the engine breaking down. And you're adjusting to big changes. Relationships ebb and flow.'

The next morning, we motor into brisk, salty air and along the coast to the waterways. The French canals will take us to the South of France and the Mediterranean. Drizzle comes horizontally at us, the sky drained of colour. We battle against the wind.

'It's nearly as rough as the Channel crossing,' I say.

'Take your seasickness pills.' He stares straight ahead.

What's happened to the caring man I fell for? *Early days. Give it time to improve.* Little mantras help me to hold on. I feel queasy most of the day from the throb of the engine and smell of boat diesel. We chug through steel-grey water until darkness falls and we reach a grim industrial area. Clouds of black smoke billow from old factory chimneys.

'Smells of burning rubber,' I say, and I cobble a meal together from what we have in the cupboards. The oily taste of diesel coats my mouth, even after we've eaten. I go to bed and huddle in the frigid cabin.

A while later he clambers in, smelling of whisky.

'God, you're freezing,' he mutters.

'I've been freezing since we left.'

'It'll warm up soon, then you'll say it's too hot. C'mon, snuggle up.' He shifts over and I hold him close. My inner voice says to stick with it, since it can't get much worse. Warmed by his body heat, I fall asleep.

Next morning, I wake up to him moving in the bed, and for a moment I think we're back home. Then the boat rocks and I remember with a sinking feeling. I go to budge up closer, but seconds later, he's up, dressed and on deck without a word. He does that every day. I lie on my back puffing out white plumes of cold breath. A salty dampness permeates the boat. The warmth goes from the bed so I dress quickly.

We set off and chug along, but the engine strains to get going. It judders and cuts out in a replay of the Channel crossing. He tries the ignition. It won't start. The current pulls us towards the concrete canal wall.

'Fucking hell!' He turns the ignition on and off.

He panics about the boat being wrecked, and hurls out the anchor to stop us hitting the wall. The chain jangles after the anchor, and still our collision course keeps on. A crushed boat means we can come home. *Wreck the boat. Wreck the boat.* The chant fills my head. We can haul ourselves onto the canal bank and watch it sink.

'It's not taking.' He clutches the top of his head and stares after the submerged anchor, his body rigid.

Wreck the boat. We slide towards the wall.

'I don't fucking believe this,' he says.

I hold my breath and will disaster to strike. My expectations have sunk so low we might as well write off the boat and the whole trip.

The anchor gets traction just in time. I breath out my disappointment. Short of firing bullets through the hull, we're stuck on the boat. His emergency repairs nurse the engine back to life, and angry frustration leaches out of him. By twilight, my head's pounding again and we limp back to where we'd started this morning. The boat commandeers his time like a sick child, and I brave the galley for an attempt at Thai curry to cheer us up.

We eat huge platefuls with red wine and I do my best to be positive.

'At least the weather will improve the further south we go,' I say.

He eats in silence.

'You tan easily. I bet you'll be really brown by the time we reach the Med.'

More silence, as if he's indifferent to anything other than boat repairs. *Come back to me*, I want to say. I only drink enough for a mellowing effect on my head. He finishes the two bottles we have left and doesn't come to bed until after I've fallen asleep.

AFTER

Ben and I walked the dogs along the beach in bright sunshine. Darcy and Stan chased each other in and out of the shallow water, shaking themselves off on the shingle and racing round. We liked it here on Sunday mornings. The shush of the waves soothed my mind, endlessly churning over the murder. The not knowing scratched away at me. I hadn't answered the door since Rachel came over last week.

A family walked towards us in the distance. The dad carried a little girl on his shoulders, who bounced with his strides. She laughed in that infectious way of small children. The sound carried to us on the sea breeze. A woman walked with them and smiled as the dad ran headlong towards the water. The girl squealed and he pitched forward at the water's edge, pretending to tip her into the sea.

Ben threw a stick for Darcy, the dog's fur wet from the sea. The family came closer, and the man looked familiar. DS Thornley. It felt exposing, seeing him close to the spot where

I last saw my ex. Thank God I hadn't taken Darcy with me on the day of the murder. The report of another woman was bad enough, but one with an Alsatian would have pointed the finger straight at me.

I'd veered between keeping a low profile and wanting Thornley to contact me again so I could find out more. Not that he'd tell me anything. I hadn't forgotten his pointed question about my shoe size. I stared for too long, intrigued by this different side to him, a family man. He seemed oblivious, no doubt wanting to keep work from tainting his personal life.

When we walked round the shore and headed back to the car, they were sitting in bright sunshine on the sea wall beside a café. The child licked an ice cream cone, despite it being February. He wiped a melting dribble of pink ice cream from her hand and grinned at her. Then he took a big lick of her ice cream to stop it dripping more.

'Is that the detective who came round the other week?' Ben said.

People milled around by the café and Thornley ignored us.

'Yes. He looks happier out of his work suit.'

'Looks a nice guy,' Ben said. 'Aren't murder detectives supposed to be divorced heavy drinkers with shambolic personal lives?'

I smiled and threaded my arm through his. The path to the car park led us further round the shore. 'They are on the cop shows you watch.'

'Any update since then?'

'No.'

'Would you tell me if there was?'

I stared out to sea, the lapping water a reminder of the past. The Isle of Wight stood in the distance, its blurred outline marking where my ex and I once sailed.

'You seem better informed than I am.'

'Only because you don't tell me anything. Your ex-husband was murdered. It's a big deal.'

'Can we stop going on about it?' It came out all hard and defensive. I took a breath and tried to tone it down. 'It's lovely here. Let's just relax and enjoy it.'

When we got home, Ben put on the news and thumbed through his travel brochures. He wore his specs low on his nose, making him look endearing – reassuringly Ben, the kindest man I knew.

'Look, please let's go away. Take your mind off what's going on here,' Ben said.

'I can't just yet. Work's busy.' I wanted to make things better between us, but I couldn't face a holiday with the investigation unresolved.

'Would you be so driven if you weren't your own boss?'

'It's not just that. I don't want to go away until Mum's better. But yeah, I've always worked hard.' I scrolled through a client's press coverage online. I couldn't concentrate on TV, but work kept me going. Clients trusted me. I'd proven myself a safe pair of hands and should apply them to my own crisis.

'I can't imagine you sailing.' Ben watched the local news, fascinated by a clip of a round the world yachtswoman from Lymington.

My heart constricted at the sight of her on a boat. 'I was never in her league.'

The woman shouted above the whistling wind. It pounded her sideways, her reddened face just visible inside a storm-proof jacket. I tasted saltwater in the back of my mouth, remembering times when waves battered the boat, the decks flooding while I clung on. Sailing into a storm was exhilarating, that's what my ex would say. He saw danger as part of the attraction.

'Were you ever out in seas like that?' Ben asked.

'I've been in apocalyptic weather. They say worse things happen at sea. It's true.'

'What's the worst you've been in?'

'We spent a day and a night battling a storm in Italy. All I could do was hope we'd get through. And hang on.'

Seeing the woman on TV dredged up bad memories. Rob had promised it would be plain sailing, but I became used to the changing quality of the ocean. We set off one morning on a feisty Italian sea, and a storm spent the day creeping up until it had us surrounded.

We battled through churning water and arching waves until we stared into a furious night-time storm that raged out of control. By midnight, I called on some higher power for help. It wasn't the coastguard, since we'd lost radio contact.

'The boat might roll, so go with it,' Rob had shouted above the howling wind.

'Roll?'

'Turn 360 degrees. It's okay, we'll come back up.'

'Won't we be dragged under?'

'We'll come back up.' He scanned for tankers that we wouldn't see until too late. We hung on and as the sun rose, the sea began to relax. My muscles stopped tensing after hours of being hyper-alert, and we limped to the nearest harbour.

Within days, he talked up our drama on the high seas. He liked to be seen as an adventurer. It turned out we'd sailed through a notorious stretch of water that seasoned sailors knew to avoid. While he boasted about the night we nearly died, I resented him for risking our lives.

'You're overreacting,' he'd said. 'Why are you so negative? Is it because I love sailing, and you're trying to spoil it for me?'

'We could've died out there.'

'Do you seriously think I'd endanger our lives? I know you're scared of the water, but can't you see I'm keeping us safe? You don't give me any credit. We got through that, didn't we? We can weather anything.'

But weathering the storm of our marriage was harder. I tried avoiding a row, and made more of an effort, as if that would make it better. As if I could make it right by being me.

'You were away for a long time,' Ben said.

'It never felt like a holiday.'

'Can I see the photos? The ones you showed that detective?'

'I should throw them out.' I'd meant to, but they turned up in a packing box when I moved here, and I'd shoved them in the back of the cupboard, perhaps as a cautionary reminder.

This time I would throw them out. I went upstairs and pulled out the photos from the so-called holiday. We'd only taken a reel of thirty-six for all our time together. So little to represent

161

so much. I shuffled through them as if looking at someone else's life. In one, I wore a red swimsuit and held the large metal wheel of the helm. Taken on a dazzling day at a drunken angle, the wind swirled my hair around and my eyes scanned the horizon.

'Look at you,' Ben said from behind me. He drew close. 'You're like the woman on TV.'

'Hardly. I'd never have sailed solo.'

'Look at your face. You're so young.'

'It's only five years ago.'

'You look different.'

He had no idea how much I'd changed.

Sky had taken one of the photos when she'd come for a holiday on the boat. We were sitting on deck wearing sunglasses in bright sunshine, his arm slung round me, looking like we smiled out from one of Ben's travel brochures. *Look at the happy couple holidaying on a yacht. You too can have a fabulous time like them.*

Before Instagram filters and Photoshop, they said the camera never lied. But it's possible to lie to the camera. Nowadays you could cut and paste my smile, but I'd been brought up to smile in photos. The smile didn't always reach my eyes, though. No one saw the darkness, but look closely and it was there in my eyes.

At Rob's request, his divorce solicitor had asked for a copy of the photos. I said I'd destroyed them. Like he nearly destroyed me. It hurt to see the person I'd been that summer, when my world fell apart on that little boat. The storms weren't even the worst of it. It flooded back to me – the way he isolated me, his mind games that kept me controlled.

Despite initially shunning news stories about my ex, I returned to my daily habit of scrolling through my BBC News app to stay informed of current affairs for work. Now and then, I came across a random article about a charismatic con artist who mesmerised a woman, and then took her money and a whole lot more. He might claim to be a millionaire or in the SAS, and the hapless victim might tough it out for years. Other times, it was just long enough for her to sign over her life savings. I'd told Thornley I didn't know about my ex's scams, but I knew enough to hate how the women in those stories became the losers and victims. Before the murder, I always wanted to hear of an avenging angel getting her own back.

BEFORE

April 2015

I wake before Rob in the morning, a headache still nagging at my temples. He stirs and I snuggle in to keep him from jumping out of bed. He's been lost under all that engine oil, and I want him back. He winds an arm round me. I wish he'd kiss me on my nose or my lips or anywhere really, the way he used to.

'I've got a splitting headache,' he groans, killing my romantic mood before it can spread.

'That's the wine. I've had one for days.'

'Can you get me some painkillers?'

I've lost the ability to get through to him. I never had to try before, when we radiated the heat of passion back home. I pull on my jeans, leaving on the crumpled sweatshirt and socks I've slept in. The smell of engine oil hangs around, and industrial noise comes from a shipyard in the distance.

I expected the first flush to meld into an everyday together-ness. I expected we would lean on each other through the tricky times. This is our testing ground. A few weeks ago, I'd have said it would bring us together. I pad through to the galley for paracetamol and room temperature juice, since the fridge only works when the engine runs. We sit in bed and share the juice, gulping down a couple of pills each. He pulls on his jumper, ready to go off again.

'I'd like us to talk . . .' I pull my knees close to my body.

'Not now. I've too much on my mind.'

'So what's on my mind doesn't matter?'

'That's not what I said.'

'I'm struggling with this—'

'I'm struggling too,' he says.

'Okay, we're both struggling and it doesn't feel like we're in it together.'

'We *are* together. You're too sensitive. Give it a chance. The Canary Islands were good, weren't they?'

I look at him in silence.

'We'll have that again,' he says. 'In Greece.'

He stretches and groans as if his back aches, and then goes to do something dull. I dig around in the recesses for the leather-bound journal my colleagues gave me as a leaving present. Sachi had written *Jess's Ship's Log* inside it. I sit with it open and blank on my lap, missing her. Free of work commitments, my escapist fantasy now takes me back to the office.

I can't commit what I really think to paper in case he reads it. And writing about the trip will give an outlet to the troubled voice inside me. I silence the voice and go in search of groceries. When he'd talked about the French canals, I'd pictured us exploring quaint little towns together and picking up freshly baked bread from a *boulangerie*. No bakeries round here, but I find a supermarket and stagger back with enough food to last a few more days.

We have the mast lowered by a towering crane so we can pass under the bridges spanning the canals. He's worried it'll wreck the boat, and his uptight mood transfers to me. The crane drips globs of dense black oil over the deck, and the mast overhangs both ends of the boat, lashed down until we reach the South of France. I help my dismayed husband clean the deck. I don't like him calling me oversensitive, so I'll prove myself reasonable.

Perhaps I do expect too much. Even the most together couples would get on each other's nerves in this small space. With a love like ours, we'll get through this rough patch. Other couples settle into married life, which isn't an immediate option for us. You can't settle when you're on the move. And when his money comes through, we'll celebrate with a weekend honeymoon in a Paris hotel.

Life isn't clear-cut and love isn't black and white. Things don't always work out how you want, but you keep going. That's what I tell myself. I stifle my inner voice until it's barely a murmur. My stubborn heart refuses to give up.

I organise things below deck, and look for Rob's passport so I can put mine with his. It's nowhere obvious. He's gone to find a boat part, so I rummage round to see where he keeps everything. It takes ages to find his passport in a storage space below a seat cushion.

I open it and my gaze falls on the written details. My

stomach twists. I hold the passport in both hands and chew on my lip. It brings into focus something that niggled from our wedding. I'd glimpsed it from his birth certificate, but it hadn't quite registered in the rush of the day, and then I'd forgotten. But it's there in black and white. The boat rocks from his return and I face him with the evidence.

'What've you got there?'

'Your passport.'

'Oh yeah?' Feigning lack of interest, he unpacks lager bottles from a plastic bag.

'Yeah. They got your age wrong.'

He clicks the lids off two bottles. 'No, they didn't. I'm forty-seven.'

'You told me you'd just turned forty.'

'Yeah, well.'

It's even worse to hear it confirmed in his indifferent tone. As if it doesn't matter that he lied.

'When you said how old you were, I thought I'd better make out I was younger. And that guy was flirting with you.'

'What guy?'

'When we first met. The one trying to pull you. He kept giving me evil looks. I couldn't let him have you.'

Jonathan.

'You lied,' I say.

'A white lie.'

'You let me think you were forty. We talked about what you did for your fortieth as if it had just happened.' The boat closes in. I need air.

'I wanted to tell you, but I didn't have the heart when you started going on about my fortieth.' He seems sorrier now, and shakes his head as if owning up to his mistake. He rubs his hands over his stubble, deep in contemplation. 'Then I meant to say something before the wedding, obviously, but I forgot in the rush.'

'You were never going to tell me. Didn't you think I'd find out?'

'I don't want you snooping through my stuff.'

'It's not snooping.' I keep my voice steady. 'Even though you hid it from me, along with your real age.'

'Calm down.' He grips the galley worktop with one hand and takes a nonchalant swig of beer.

'You lied to me.'

'Come on, Jess, I'm not an axe-murderer. I told a white lie to keep you interested and it worked.'

I walk up on deck and perch on the edge of the cold fibre-glass seating, holding on to steady myself. I don't want to speak to him or be near him. I let the shock dissipate. He isn't six years older than me. He's thirteen years older. He appears from below deck. The grey sky has darkened into dusk.

'Your beer's here, shall I bring it up?'

I ignore him and go to the bow of the boat to stare out at the darkening horizon. When it turns cold, I come below deck.

'Okay, pussycat?'

I return his smile with a blank look.

'Hungry?' He's laid the table and lit a candle. He guides me to a seat and pours a beer. We eat in silence.

'It was stupid of me,' he eventually concedes.

In the flickering light, he looks every one of his thirteen years older than me. *You only have to look at him to see he's lived*, Becca had said. The crinkles round his eyes used to say he laughed a lot and loved sailing on a bright, windswept day. Now they say *older man*. I'd found his weathered face attractive. Now I don't know what to think. He tries to take my hand. I pull it away.

'I wanted to be with you and I couldn't have you think me too old. Then it was never the right time and I thought you'd be angry.'

'Which I am.'

'I didn't mean to hurt you.'

Not quite an apology, but he doesn't say sorry because he's never wrong. He fusses over me for the rest of the night in an attempt to be the man I fell in love with. I barely speak and go to bed before him, pretending to be asleep when I'm too hurt for sleep. So much for not going to bed on an argument.

AFTER

After a late night of scrolling through the internet, I woke with tired eyes and a fuzzy head. I'd only just sat at my desk when Detective Sergeant Thornley phoned.

'Can you come back to the station and help us with a line of enquiry?'

'What line of enquiry?' My mind jumped straight to the footprints.

'We can talk when you get here. Eleven a.m. okay?'

'Um ... yes.'

He thanked me and rang off. Did he want my help again, or was there evidence against me? I did an online search of Thornley. A web page from last year showed a photo of him accepting an award. DETECTIVE HONOURED FOR TACKLING DOMESTIC ABUSE. I scrolled down and read a quote from him talking about a new offence of controlling behaviour in relationships.

One in four women experiences domestic abuse. It's often hidden, but it's likely we all know someone who's been affected. It's

170

important to recognise the signs of control, such as isolation, blaming the victim and distorting their perception of events. It's coercive control, also known as gaslighting.

He seemed to understand why the victim didn't always leave, and why they concealed how bad the situation had become. I liked him for that, and kept reading.

The new law will help victims who are coerced and manipulated psychologically, and whose finances are controlled. I've seen how deeply it's instilled in these women, because it usually is women who fall victim.

Something of a dark horse, DS Thornley, not that his domestic abuse credentials helped Rachel. Seeing him on the beach yesterday softened his hard edges. A month after the murder and I only had scattered pieces of the puzzle. I could tell him how my ex had controlled me, taken my money for a business that didn't materialise, and worse. Then Thornley might tell me more. I weighed up my need to know with the fear of him seeing me as a suspect. Having answers would ease the gathering darkness inside me, so long as it didn't implicate me. But everything I knew implicated me.

Too amped up for work, I went for a coffee on the way to see Thornley, and then at the station, I waited. I could ask about his domestic violence award, but then he would know I'd checked up on him. He took longer to appear this time. With nothing to do, my mind roamed back to just before the sailing trip, when I'd tripped over a cable at the boatyard.

I didn't remember hitting the ground. The world came back into focus with my husband kneeling over me, supporting my wobbly head with his hand. He'd stroked my hair away from my forehead.

'I'm fine,' I murmured. 'Just need a lie down.'

'You've cracked your head open. I'll grab a towel to stem the blood. We'll take you to A&E.'

Inside the treatment cubicle, I slumped woozily on the bed. Blood seeped from my head wound.

'She fell over,' he said. 'Tripped up and knocked herself out.'

One of the nurses gave the other a knowing look and ushered him back to the waiting room.

'Did someone do this to you?' the nurse asked as she cleaned the wound.

'No, I caught my foot on a cable and fell over.'

'Is he your partner? The man who brought you in?'

'He's my husband. We've just got married.' I touched my wedding ring. 'I didn't want to come, but he thought I might be concussed. He said we should get it checked out.'

'Okay. This might sting a bit.'

I winced from a liquid she dabbed on the wound. At the same moment, it hit me that she thought him an abusive partner. I'd found it unthinkable. A part of me still found it unthinkable.

Rachel must surely be in denial to have stayed in the marriage, the same as I'd been. Ben read up on domestic abuse and said victims went through a stage of denial. He'd said it when I told him a little about my ex. I'd said Rob didn't physically hurt me, not really. But according to Thornley, emotional abuse was a form of control that built up over time. Victims felt as if they trod on eggshells and had to keep the peace.

After waiting so long at the police station, my nerves crept up. Why was he keeping me here so long? More minutes passed before Thornley came out and wordlessly held the door open for me. I followed him to a stale little interview room in which everything was chipped. What happened to the room with the comfy chairs?

The woman with the tight ponytail walked in; the detective constable who'd turned up with Thornley the first time. I'd been introduced to her that time and had instantly forgotten her name. She placed a notepad and phone on the table, and didn't say a word. Sitting opposite them in a police interview room felt formal and ominous.

'Thanks for coming in,' Thornley said. 'DC Roper is going to play you a recording.'

The DC picked up her phone, tapped, swiped and tilted it for us to listen.

A woman's voice played out, 'Did you ever want to shoot him?' The muffled recording sounded like Rachel talking in hushed tones.

'I had dark times,' another woman said.

That's my voice. It hit me with an electric shock. *It's me.*

'One time I could've killed him in the heat of the moment.'

'And then someone did kill him,' Rachel said in a low voice.

The officer tapped the screen to end the playback. I stared dumbly at the phone.

'Was that your voice?' Thornley asked.

I looked at him, open mouthed.

'Was that you talking to Rachel Harman?' he said.

'Yes, but . . .' I tried to take it in. 'That's not the whole conversation.' My mind scrabbled back to that evening with the bottle of wine, after I'd seen Sky. 'Can you play the bit before that?'

'That's all there is.' The DC folded her arms and stared at me.

'But wait . . . hang on . . .' I pressed my fingers to my temples, trying to remember. 'Rachel was the one who said she'd wanted to kill him. I felt sorry for her. She brought a bottle of wine and plied me with it. Where's the rest of the recording?'

'I said that's it.'

Fuck. Had Rachel killed him after all and set me up? I should never have let her in. They couldn't use a covert recording as evidence, especially not one edited by the accused, but it aroused enough suspicion for them to dig for a motive.

'Tell me about all the contact you've had with Rachel Harman,' Thornley said. The woman sat poised to take notes.

I told him about Rachel's first visit, when she asked me to give evidence if she went on trial. And that I'd refused. Then how she'd wanted us to visit Sky, which I didn't want to do, but I'd been getting anonymous emails that Rachel said came from Sky.

'You went with Rachel to see Sky?'

'Yes,' I admitted, since it wasn't a crime. 'Rachel didn't go near her. I only wanted to tell Sky that if the emails were from her, she had to knock them off.'

The woman wrote something down. 'Do you think the emails are from Sky?'

'Probably. One of them said something only she knew.'

Thornley looked at me, stony-faced. 'Can we see them?'

I took my laptop from my bag and pulled up the emails in their own toxic folder. 'It's not true. None of it's true.'

Mia Fallon is a cold-blooded killer.
She fucks with people's heads.
She led him on and shot him.
Soon everyone will know the truth.

They peered at the messages and then forwarded them to the detective constable's email. I resisted the urge to tell them again that it wasn't true.

'Will you be able to trace them?' I asked.

'They're from a Gmail account. They're not easily traceable,' she said.

'But surely you can do something. What about the IP address?'

'That's the thing with Gmail. It's encrypted so users can hide their IP address.' She sounded matter of fact, as if they could do nothing to trace them.

'Have you only had these? Any letters or phone calls?' Thornley asked.

'Just those.'

'Why didn't you tell us?' DC Roper raised her eyebrows as if it proved something.

'I thought you had enough to deal with. I wanted to warn Sky off and see if they stopped. Which they have now. When Rachel and I came back, she wanted some wine. That's when she recorded our conversation. I spoke to my boyfriend afterwards and we agreed that I wouldn't talk to her again.'

'You need to stay away from her,' DC Roper said. 'Don't have any contact with her.'

Thornley leaned forward, his elbows on the table. 'Regardless of what Rachel might have said, why did *you* say you could've killed him?'

'I – I don't know.' My mind froze and my face burned. I saw the distrust in their faces. 'It was a figure of speech.'

'Sounded like a confessional.'

The airless room closed in. I wanted to leave, but they didn't look finished with me.

'Am I under arrest?'

'You're helping with our enquiries.'

'How can you use that against me? She was the one talking about his murder, how he'd treated her so badly that she considered killing him.'

'She said you'd been the one to talk about killing him, but by the time she started recording you'd nearly finished saying it.'

'She's lying.'

'A lot of people lie in a murder investigation, Mia. It's up to us to find out the truth.'

But the truth was a slippery thing. The police only needed something provable. If they proved I'd been there with a motive, I could look as guilty as Rachel. I couldn't believe she'd set me up.

'Why are you in touch with Rachel? You hadn't met before, had you?'

'No, I just … I felt sorry for her. We both went through the same thing. He gaslighted me, kept me under his control.

Rachel acts as if she's still brainwashed by him. He probably fed her the same lies he did to me, how he wanted a family, a happy home. He did that to me, and then took my money to fund his sailing trip round the Med.'

'Didn't you go too? You showed me the photos.'

I flinched. He knew about the injunction, so I assumed it didn't need spelling out that my marriage had been bad. 'Yes, but we went to find a base for setting up a yacht charter business. That's how he convinced me to sell my house and car. But he just wanted to leave the country. And Sky was in on it. Then when I tried to leave him, it got bad. He said all my money was gone. He kept my passport and bank card.'

'Why didn't you tell me this before?'

'I don't want to be seen as one of his victims.'

'No?'

'I made a mistake and I've moved on.'

'So why tell his widow you felt like killing him?'

'It didn't mean anything. I shouldn't have got involved with her. I only let her in the first time because I was curious and she knew what was happening with the case. She thinks Sky was up to no good.'

'Rachel is the only one who's been arrested in connection with the murder.'

'But Sky argued with him before he was killed, according to Rachel.'

They exchanged a dark look.

'Is there anything else you want to tell me, Mia?' Thornley said.

'No. Can I go now?' I stood up to leave, my legs nearly buck-ling beneath me. *Please don't arrest me. Please let me go.*

The DC showed me out. I glanced over my shoulder at Thornley who stood back and assessed me with his hands in his pockets. I couldn't believe Rachel had come into my home, acting the victim while she secretly recorded me. I walked out of the police station grateful for my freedom but shaken to the core.

BEFORE

May 2015

Our days start early in the French pre-dawn. The engine's judder and vibration drowns out the chill rustle of wind through the trees. With the mast taken down, we won't sail again until reaching the Mediterranean. The waterways have hundreds of locks, tiering their scenic way up and down the countryside. As we come close to the latest one, I waver with a rope in my hand, ready to jump off and tie us up before the boat scrapes against the canal wall.

'Jump,' Rob shouts. *'Jump!'*

'It's too far.' Anxiety swells round me at the risk of falling in the oily canal water.

'Jump or we'll hit the wall.'

In dread of falling in, I brace myself to leap off and tie us up. How has he turned so mean? He only cares about the boat. Our frayed tempers rub together like sandpaper. My head and heart pound from the grief of it all.

'This is the worst trip of my life,' I say, my clothes damp and smeared with oily lock mud. We wait for the lock water to drain away and match the lower level on the other side.

'It's the working part of the trip. It'll be different in the Med. You're always having a go at me.'

'I'm not having a go. I'm saying let's relax now.' The stress of work is replaced with the stress of getting the boat through France. I could live with his tortured, brooding ways if we laughed every now and then. His determination excludes me, as if the trip isn't about us at all. Any doubts I voice are passed off as my inability to enjoy any of this.

'If you trusted me instead of complaining, you'd be okay and I could relax. You've just got to adapt to life on a boat.' He goes to steer us out of the lock.

A hired canal boat careens towards us and knocks against our boat. The tourists on board laugh at their ineptitude in steering it.

'Sorry!' One of them waves cheerily.

'You fucking wankers!' Rob shouts at them. 'You think it's funny? Getting pissed and wrecking my boat?'

An appalled silence descends. I bite my tongue and stare at the canal wall, mortified. He speeds us out of the lock too fast, leaving the other boats caught in a wash of water.

'That was your fault,' he rages. 'You keep having a go at me and complaining. I can only take so much.'

'I didn't have a go at you.'

'It's already pressured, going in the locks and trying to control the boat with all those idiots around. Think before you stress me out.'

I hate arguing, so I go down to the cabin. I'd rather walk away to avoid it getting out of hand. He usually insists we're both on deck all the time the boat's moving, him at the helm and me navigating our way though, in more ways than one. As far as our relationship goes, there's no navigational aid. Is it really my fault? He says I'm having a go at him, but I don't mean to. All I know is that I can't bear him making another scene like that. I'll have to try harder to keep the peace.

On our way to Rouen the next day, I still haven't recovered from his outburst. He pulls me towards him, one hand still on the helm, his free arm clutching my waist. We watch the river ahead. At least we're making progress, under a dishwater-grey sky. His urgency pushes us forward. Instead of slowing into French rural life, he fights against the *escargot's* pace. He only wants to get to Greece, while I want a way back to us.

'"William the Conqueror and Joan of Arc died in Rouen",' I read from the guidebook. The sights stay out of reach with his insistence on motoring ahead. Since Rob calls it the working part of the trip, I treat it as a job, albeit a shitty unpaid one that I didn't apply for. Plans for the business keep me going. I question him on our strategy. He's sketchy on figures, but I use the journal from Sachi to scribble down notes. When we set it up, he can obsess about the boat and I'll mix with other people on dry land to keep my sanity.

We arrive at the pontoon in Rouen and I go to the shower block. When I come back, I look for my phone to charge, since we have an electric point for the night. It's not in the drawer where I'd left it. He must have put it away somewhere, so I look in the cubbyhole where we hide the cash.

He comes down the steps to the cabin, towelling his hair dry from the shower. 'What are you doing?'

'Looking for my phone.'

'Ask me before you go snooping around.'

'It's not snooping. My phone's been moved. Have you seen it?'

'Why do you want it?'

'To charge it, since we're hooked to the electrics.' I stand with my hands on my hips. 'Have you seen it?'

He towels his hair more vigorously. 'I had an accident with it.'

'An accident?'

'I dropped it overboard.'

'How come?' I stare at him, incredulous.

'Mine wasn't working. I wanted to check on that payment. They said they'd email when it was in my bank account. I brought yours up on deck and it had a signal, so I opened the back to swap the SIM. It burst open and I dropped it in the river.'

'When?'

'Yesterday. You weren't around or I'd have asked. It was getting dark so I held it towards the light and then dropped it.'

'You're saying we don't have a functioning phone between us?'

'You and your phone. You're like an addict. We'll get one in Paris. I hate phones anyway.'

'All my contacts are gone.'

'You can track people down. You know your mum's landline. Forget about it. Let's go for a night out. We deserve it.'

'Why didn't you tell me?'

'Because I knew you'd react badly. It was an accident. We'll get you another one. Come on, let's go out.'

I stand rigid, and he hugs me.

'Let's go.' He takes my hand for our walk into the city.

There must be more to it, but I need relief from the pressure cooker environment of the boat. Going out for the evening is a welcome change, as he usually just uses the time to tinker obsessively. At nightfall, we usually tie up somewhere remote and he starts on the maintenance. I've become good at cooking on the wobbly little stove in the dingy galley. It puts me in control of a small part of my life, breathing in simmering aromas, comforted by stirring the pan. But tonight we can forget about the boat.

We take in the city and he chats the way he used to, as if to compensate for screwing up. On our second round of drinks in a swish bar, he eyes a platter of *fruits de la mer* at the next table. 'Let's eat here.'

'It's pricey. I think we passed some cheaper places.' I motion back the way we came.

'No, let's treat ourselves.'

So we stay until late, talk like a normal couple and drink too much. The bill is steep, but we hold hands on the way back, as we did in happier times. I tell myself the stress has got to him, and it'll improve. That's easier than contemplating the alternative. I know marriage comes with flaws. It's just that your husband's flaws are more endearing when you love him. But the man I married has become a stranger and I don't know how far I have to go to get the love back.

AFTER

After my sobering visit to the police station on Monday, I stopped opening the door to unexpected callers. I wanted to shut out the drama and make things right again with Ben. I came back from a walk with Darcy and saw Rachel getting out of her car. Christ, she had a nerve.

'Hi, Mia.' She came and crouched down to pet Darcy. She looked thinner and even more fragile than before.

'Are you here to record me again?'

'What?' She looked up at me, her face confused.

'The police called me in and played it.'

'Played what?'

'Our conversation after we'd seen Sky. When you plied me with wine and asked if I'd ever wanted to kill him.'

Her hand covered her mouth. 'They didn't! Oh my God, I'm sorry.' She got up from Darcy.

'Don't pretend. You set me up. First Sky, and now me. I'm not playing your fucked-up games.'

'No, no, no.' She shook her head and huddled her arms around

185

herself. 'I came to tell you I went back to see Sky. I was going to phone you but the police came back and took all my devices. They've still got them. They said it'll take six weeks to go through the records as they've got a backlog. They must have found the recording on my phone.'

'But you recorded me!'

'I do it to keep track of things when I'm tired. I haven't been sleeping and I was worn out from the stress of us going to see Sky, and we drank all that wine.'

'You edited out your own admission.'

'No ... but did the police?' She cocked her head, perfectly reasonable. 'That sounds like a police tactic to focus on the person they're interviewing. They just played you that snippet.'

'I gave you the benefit of the doubt because I felt sorry for you, but not any more.' I went to walk past her with Darcy.

'I'm sorry. I'm trying to get through this, but it's hard ... Rob's murder, the accusations. Listen—' She came after me. 'I won't bother you again. I just wanted to tell you about Sky.'

'What about Sky?' We came to a halt at my front gate.

'I told her I saw her on the beach before he died.'

A chill went through me, thinking of Sky on the beach and Rachel watching from the shadows.

'I caught her unguarded. Her face dropped. You should've seen it, the fear in her eyes. She knew I'd caught her out.' She spoke in hushed tones, as if scared of Sky. 'She looked shocked that I knew, so I don't think the police have challenged her. She's getting away with it. Makes you wonder how they go after one person and ignore the rest.'

'Did you mention the emails?'

'Through the door when she slammed it in my face. She didn't reply.'

'What about the gun?'

'She'd deny knowing about the gun, but even I knew about the gun.'

'Did you?' I looked sharply at her. 'You told me you didn't know about it.'

She faltered and half raised her hands in an awkward apology. 'I'm sorry. My mind was a mess when I said that. I didn't know whether to trust you. But now I know you, we're like kindred spirits.'

'Bullshit. Ben was right. I should never have got involved with you.'

I went inside and slammed the door. That's what came of giving people the benefit of the doubt. Thank God I didn't contact her after the police warned me not to. They would have known and I'd have incriminated myself even more. The emails might not be from Rachel if the police had her phone and laptop, since she could hardly risk sending them under that kind of scrutiny, even with a new phone.

She'd lied about the gun. It made me furious that she might have recorded everything I'd said and the police now had it all. What a shitstorm, and my fault for buying into her 'Poor Rachel' act.

I had a missed call from Becca, and I played back the voicemail. 'Hi, I've sent you a link. You need to brace yourself and read it. Call me back.'

I steeled myself and typed in the web address. My wifi turned sluggish and indifferent to the urgency. The page loaded in increments. I cursed at the wait.

MURDERED LOVE-CHEAT CONNED WIDOW.

I saw the headline and my vision speckled. The rest of the page opened sporadically. A photo came up of a woman with a wretched stare. She posed in a neat little living room. A committed Christian of fifty-eight, Margaret had met my ex-husband at a hospice open day. She'd signed up for a sponsored skydive in memory of her husband, who'd died of lung cancer. My ex had sponsored her with a big-hearted hundred pounds.

I thought it was incredibly generous when he'd only just met me. He left a lovely message on the Just Giving page that my son set up for me. I emailed back to thank him, and it went from there.

He lured her in with romantic lunches and walks along the beach. She considered him a kindred spirit when he talked of his own grief since his wife died. That part turned me cold. He introduced her to his sister, who expressed her happiness that he'd found someone special. *Sky*. The article didn't name her, but it had to be Sky.

His sister told Margaret how close he was to her young daughter. His niece had *been a bit poorly*, so he bought them a car to make the hospital appointments easier. Her condition improved, and Margaret lit candles for the girl that she'd seen a photo of – *A sweet little thing who looked like them both*.

'Fucking con artists,' I muttered, scrolling down. Sky had always been there, stirring things in the background.

His generosity towards his niece touched her, especially

when he'd said, *If you can't spend your money on your nearest and dearest, then what's the point?* He quoted from the Bible: keep your life free from love of money, and be content with what you have.

She believed he was selling his IT business for £2.5 million. As the sale neared completion, he wanted Margaret to share in his success. He said they should go on a cruise, since she was nervous of small boats. I read with distaste, his motives transparent, yet the man I once considered true to himself had taken us all in.

He'd put on more of an act with Margaret, since he usually only went for younger women. Shame that few of us younger women had enough cash to prop him up for long, hence his need to change tack when things became desperate. Is that what he did – fleecing older women and running off? Then he played a slower game with the rest of us. We were easily controlled and without much tying us to home. He could isolate us on the boat where he called the shots and played mind games.

He'd used a false name, and showed Margaret the website of his IT company, which turned out to be owned by someone else. Arranging the company sale took so much of his time that she hardly saw him, but he promised her a long holiday to deepen their relationship. Déjà vu caught in my throat, along with irritation at the tone of the reporting. The reporter seemed to think no man could catch her out. She referred to it as 'romance fraud', where men like him targeted naïve women.

The company sale went smoothly until he needed a sudden £82,000 for professional fees. He'd thought the fees weren't due until the sale completion. The financial aspect became complicated because the buyer was from the Far East. He sat with Margaret and made frantic phone calls to his bank and business contacts, but he couldn't raise the funds before the sale went through. He asked her what he should do, and she liked that he confided in her.

She saw his anguish and offered her savings, squirreled away for her retirement. It made her uneasy but it would only be for a few days, two weeks at the most. He promised to share the profits, starting with their cruise of a lifetime. He transferred her savings overseas and disappeared.

A distraught Margaret contacted the police, who failed to trace him. She never saw him or the money again. He'd conned her a year before meeting me. After five years of internet searches on 'conman' and similar, she read about the murder and recognised his photo.

The double page spread included a craggy-faced police mugshot of him, and one of his wedding to Rachel, in her cream silk dress with her hair down, how he liked it. I stared at the pictures, trying and failing to equate him with the man I fell for.

The article talked of Rachel's turbulent relationship with her husband. It mentioned other cons during their short marriage, suggesting he'd needed the money to maintain their lifestyle. When she discovered the betrayal, it probably devastated her in the same way he devastated me.

BEFORE

May 2015

The grey skies melt to reveal a warm sun in Normandy. We've stopped in Giverny, since I've pushed to stay for a day or two where Monet painted his water garden. We only take time off to 'rest the boat', usually in a built-up area close to a *supermarché* and places to find mechanical bits. Then we motor past vineyards and medieval towns. But I stand my ground and he relents, for a day.

We've moored on a river with a millpond quality. The purity of light gives the scenery an unreal sheen and the sun low in the sky casts everything in a golden light. The unspoilt setting makes me want to speak in hushed tones. In the stillness, I watch the glass-like reflections of the riverbank until he ruins the peace by running the engine.

'Coming to Monet's garden?' I ask.

'No fear. It'll be swamped with naff coach trippers.'

He gives the same response to any sightseeing that involves

stepping off the boat. I shrug off his indifference and leave him to it.

'See you later then.'

I set off through the sleepy town, off-kilter as I rarely go anywhere without him, having morphed from a capable person into his shadow. He's right about the coaches. The entrance swarms with tourists. It's odd to be surrounded by people after watching life go past at a distance from the boat. I turn back and circle round the little church and graveyard, and spend the unused entrance money in a *boulangerie* and grocery store. Then I return to the boat in case he's finished tinkering and wants to move us on.

'You know I'm trying to make up time,' he snarls when I climb aboard, 'and you go wandering off like that.'

'But I asked if you wanted to come.'

'Some of us have to work on the boat so it doesn't break down again. I didn't know how long you'd be.'

'If we had mobiles—'

'We don't need two mobiles. I'm working hard so we'll have the life we want, and you're slowing us down. We need to get to Greece and make a go of it. The longer we take, the more it costs. You go on about money, but you want a holiday in France. You can't have it both ways.'

I stow the groceries away to prove that I pull my weight. His undercurrent leaves its trace even when I go off without him. I think of my mum, who had been the same, nerves frayed. We always had to be back before my dad, ready to put dinner on the table. I didn't question it as a child and I certainly never challenged him. His volatile moods scared me and I would retreat inside myself. Then he walked out on us, blaming Mum and me for being impossible to live with. My upbringing is my undoing, with my damaged template for marriage. I'm good at keeping the fragile peace.

We plough on. That balmy Sunday evening, we tie up at a pontoon. Our boat nudges the one in front, flying a Red Ensign to show it's British. The couple on board drink wine on their deck, a folded newspaper and bottle of rosé between them. The man strikes up a conversation with Rob, and they compare their boats.

The woman introduces herself as Marilyn and invites me aboard. She says they live near Weymouth. 'Come and have the tour.'

I follow her below deck. 'It's more homely than ours. Oh, you've got cushions!'

'Yes darling, see—' She peels a cushion away from the banquette seating. 'Velcro backing to keep them in place in rough weather.'

It fascinates me to see how another couple manage their lives on board. 'Do you like living on a boat?'

'It's a good way to see new places.' She pours me a glass of rosé.

'That sounds like a tactful *no*.'

'When we first got together, I loathed sailing. We'd be in the middle of the Solent, and Roger would get stroppy with me for doing something wrong and I'd want to get off. I'd stand there and shout at him, "I've had enough. I want to get off *now*." We'd be an hour from land. So we'd carry on and make it up, then go out again the next weekend.'

'Why would you carry on?'

'Darling, I adored him. And he adored sailing so it was either that or not see him all summer. I read sailing books. I went on a course with a load of youngsters, and made an idiot of myself learning how to navigate and what to do with the sails. I kept going on the boat and it got better. You get out what you put in.'

When I fell in love, I liked the way he didn't care about football or rugby and didn't spend hours roaring at his team on the TV. Sailing was refined by comparison. I agree about making the best of it, but no previous boyfriend expected me to give up my life for football.

Marilyn's friendliness feels good after a month of his patchy company. I'm sorry to say goodbye to her that night. No one else keeps pace with us, so we won't see them again, not when we're leaving at daybreak. I miss having friends. I don't know what made me think I can live without them. When I spritz my favourite perfume, it wraps me in warm memories of nights out with Becca. Since leaving home, I've no choice but to zero in on him.

'I like Marilyn,' I say as we get ready for bed. I've thrown myself into boat life, but it doesn't make either of us happy. At least Marilyn does it on her terms. Chatting to her lifted me up and I've a sudden urge to get in touch with friends back home.

'Did you see what they've done below deck?' He curls his lip. 'It's homely. She's put her stamp on it.'

'It's a pot-pourri floating caravan. That's not your style.'

194

'They're happier than us.'

'You always do that, measure yourself against other people. It's a sign of insecurity.'

'I'm not insecure.'

He comes up close to me in the cabin and strokes my hair from my face. His hand lingers at the back of my neck. 'You have a problem with attention and validation. Your dad walking out affected your self-esteem. It's not your fault. You were only young, but we've got each other now.'

'I'm buying a new phone in Paris.'

'We don't have money to waste on texting and phoning.'

'Are we short of cash?'

'You know I'm working on getting the money we're owed.' His jaw tightens because I'm not following the script, accepting what he says. His fingers knead into my neck.

I pull away. 'The money I've put in will cover a phone plan.'

'There's that phone obsession again. Did you forget what we agreed about not being attached to phones? I thought that's what you wanted. This is our time to switch off and make a go of it.'

'We did agree but—'

'You were single a long time before we got together. You relied more on your friends. That was understandable, but we're married now.'

'We can be married and have friends.'

'When we're in Greece, we'll know lots of people and you'll have friends. Greek people are friendly. Your friends from home can come and stay. But me and you are a solid unit. I'll always look out for you. I love you more than anyone will ever love you.'

195

His words don't bring me comfort. Perhaps I am too reliant on other people and just need more time to get used to married life.

We arrive in Paris the next day, and stop at a marina close to the Bastille. The warmth intensifies into an oppressive heatwave. Becca's heart-shaped pendant burns against my skin under my sleeveless top. I hold my hand over the reminder of her.

We tie up and he goes to find a payphone to chase up his contract payment. Too grubby to explore Paris, I do the drossy jobs before going out to buy the phone. I take a huge pile of laundry to the marina washing machines. When I look out of the laundry room window, Marilyn and Roger glide past on their boat. I come out and help them get tied up, only a few berths away from ours.

'I didn't expect you to catch us up.'

'You inspired us to get a move on. Isn't Paris fabulous? We're going to visit the Louvre and have some café life,' Marilyn says.

'Sounds wonderful.' I coil a rope on their deck.

They co-exist better than us in their own small space. She calls Roger '*mon petit chou*' and he chuckles in reply. My own '*little cabbage*' returns as I trade paperbacks with Marilyn. I clutch the Patricia Highsmith novel she gives me.

'*The Talented Mr Ripley* will get you in the mood for Italy,' she says.

The boat's less claustrophobic when I escape into novels. I only read after finishing all the work, since he dislikes my attention being elsewhere.

'I can see why you fell for such a handsome smoothie-chops.'
Marilyn motions to Rob, who is rigging up the smart blue
canopy on the boat for some shade.

I smile.

'Here, let me read your stars. What sign are you?' She reaches
for the paper I'd seen the day before, peering through her glasses.

'Aquarius.'

'"The May lunar energies are full of love and romance."' She
cackles merrily. I smile along, and think of being like her in
thirty years, resigned to the sailing life, struggling to remember what I used to enjoy back home. I've put my needs on the
back burner, going along with Rob about the 'working part of
the trip', but I climb back aboard our boat with an urge to right
the wrongs.

'I see the old folk chased after us,' he says.

'They got a move on so they could explore Paris. I bet they
have a better time than us.'

He refuses to meet my gaze, and organises things around me.
'They're retired. They can zimmer along like geriatrics. And
they're going to Spain. It's closer. When we reach Greece, we'll
do all the holidaying we want. I've got a call to make.'

'Again?'

He jumps off the boat and strides away. The shops will close
soon, so I'll sort out the phone tomorrow. In the heavy heat, I
lug more washing to the laundry room. Waiting for the cycle to
finish, I flick through a discarded English language magazine
and read a feature on 'Ways to rekindle your romance'. It rec-
ommends saying at least five positive things to every negative.

Seeing as he dismisses nearly everything I say, I move to the next tip about drawing out each other's hopes and dreams, as he'd done with the country cottage we'd viewed when he might as well have offered me the moon.

I toss the magazine aside and haul the laundry back on board, my body slick from heat. The cabin will be suffocating tonight. He arrives back as I lower myself and the washing down the tight wooden stairs.

'Where've you been?'

'I can't get the money sorted,' he says. 'I walked round for a while.'

I catch a hint of booze from his breath.

'What's happening about the money?'

'They're dragging their heels. I can't chase them properly when we're out here. This heat's killing me. I'm going for a shower.'

No good will come of challenging him, not when he's been drinking. He might sneer at Marilyn and Roger's boat, but I like its atmosphere, untainted by his oppressive ways. I've been reduced to living on the edge of his life, accompanied by the background hum of tension. His presence crowds out the confined space. The boat closes in on me.

AFTER

Becca invited me over after I'd read up on Margaret.

'Can you believe the lowlife scum?' She opened the door and kissed me on the cheek. 'And quoting from the Bible. Nice touch, Billy Graham.'

I had to smile, despite it all. At least Becca and I stayed close, despite my ex coming between us. I struggled to pick up with other people I used to know. Apart from Becca, old friends left me feeling like the ghost of my past, tapping on the window of my old life.

Darcy and I followed her through to the messy kitchen-dining room. He found a plastic ball and sprawled with it held between his teeth. We could dissect the details, since Ellie and Jake were asleep in bed, and Adrian was on a business trip.

'And what about the poorly niece? Made me sick reading that bit.'

'That's the most fucked up part,' I said. 'Him and Sky.'

'It's a shame nobody thought to kill Sky.'

Good old Becca.

'I can't believe you didn't shoot her when you had the chance.'

'It took a lot of restraint.'

'She's slippery,' Becca said. 'The one that got away.'

'With what? Murder?'

'She sounds more capable than Rachel. Maybe she murdered him and framed Rachel.'

In other circumstances I might stick up for Sky, because why blame her when he was the real villain? His actions were far worse, but I caught on to Sky's underhand ways on the boat. Her sly looks and furtive plotting were designed to undermine me so she came out on top.

'There's more to Rachel than meets the eye,' I said.

'What if Sky was under his spell too? What if she had an attack of conscience and made amends with Margaret? Then they became allies and cooked up a plan to kill him.'

'Interesting theory. Perhaps Rachel joined forces with them. I feel left out.'

'It's like that Agatha Christie whodunit. The murdered man was such a git that they all did it.'

'What if Mr Darcy did it to avenge my honour? My doggy assassin.'

'Oh God, Darcy,' Becca said to him. 'Did you leave paw prints at the scene?'

Darcy sat bolt upright and cocked his head.

We cleared a space at the computer for an online search of Sky. I'd already followed the links and search phrases that Becca tried. It was worth the duplication if she found out anything new.

'You'd think she lived on a mountaintop,' she said when the searches drew a blank. 'And as for *the bastard*, did he even work in IT?'

'More or less. It wasn't as lucrative as he made out.'

'He might've known it would all catch up.'

'And he couldn't handle it when it did.'

'The web piece said he was going to prison for fraud.'

'Hmm.'

'Did you know?'

I hesitated a little too long. 'The police told me.'

I must stop saying that. I don't think they did tell me. My ex told me before he died.

'How does it feel to know he had other marks?' Becca said.

'Marks?'

'It's how conmen describe their victims.'

'That's not how I want to be seen. I feel sorry for Margaret. Ensnared by him.'

'And you weren't?'

Reading about Margaret took me back to when I first met him, those early days, the rooftop engagement in Rome. I'd never say it aloud, but what we had was a living, breathing thing. He'd wanted it to work, but it only worked when I went along with his fantasy. He hated me seeing his true colours.

'He didn't use me like he used her.'

'Okaaay.'

'He didn't target me for money. He talked me into leaving my job. We had no income. He liked me for who I was.'

'Mia, he stitched you up and kept you controlled.'

'Yeah, but I didn't have enough money to be one of his "marks".'

'Enough to take him island hopping in the Med. Typical of his short-term approach. An extended holiday for him, subsidised by you, never mind the consequences.'

'He wouldn't have married me if he didn't love me.'

'It was another ploy. Without the marriage, you'd have left him sooner.'

For better or worse, I'd taken my wedding vows seriously, even if he hadn't. 'I didn't have a widow's inheritance.'

'Okay, so let's say this is his MO—'

'MO?'

'Modus operandi. His method.'

'I know what it means, but you sound like a criminal profiler.'

'Let's say he's a sociopath and chancer: charming on the surface, but underneath he's out for what he can get. He marries you, then Rachel, because both of you boost his ego. He runs out of cash to maintain the lies, so he targets older women to prolong the fantasy. Anyone hurt is collateral damage. He didn't see marriage like the rest of us. It was a tool to get what he wanted.'

Her theory stabbed at my heart. It hurt more than it should, that he never loved me, as if it mattered now. He'd made me murderous, but until I found out about the other women he'd treated badly, I had believed he'd wanted us to have a future. His manipulation went so deep that I couldn't shake off my conflicted feelings, even after everything he'd done.

'I'm having a go at him, not you. You need to be prepared. That coverage is tame. After the trial it'll be open season.'

I sighed. 'I'll deal with it when it happens.'

'If it makes you feel better, then believe he loved you, but don't tell anyone or you'll look as much of a victim as Margaret.'

She had a point. I saw how the two detectives looked at me when I'd said I didn't think he'd meant the death threats. Perhaps my mind was still warped by him. Had he wanted to be with me, or was it the thrill of the chase? He couldn't manage an honest relationship when he built his life on lies. And he loved himself more than he loved me. It only went well in the early days because I reflected his self-love back at him.

'He was a sociopath,' she kept on. 'He wasn't capable of real love.'

We'd been over that ages ago. Something wasn't right with him, as if a part of his brain was missing, the empathy part that made you human. Becca helped put a name to it. When I looked up a list of sociopathic personality traits, it read like a character assassination of my husband, the smooth manipulator with a parasitic lifestyle, who lied and lacked remorse so long as he achieved what he wanted.

We settled on the sofa. Becca drank more wine and I sat with my knees tucked in, feet touching hers.

'When did you first put it together about his lies?'

'After we went sailing. Even then, I didn't see the full picture. He always had a plausible answer.'

'Just think,' Becca said. 'If the police had tracked him down after he screwed Margaret over, you might never have met him. He'd have been festering in prison.'

And my life would have taken a different turn. I left for

203

home, okay to drive as I'd only had one glass of wine. My eyes flicked to the rear-view mirror and my mind churned. Nothing felt right.

Back home, I double-locked the front door and left Darcy to sleep. Always on edge, a proper deep sleep eluded me, and tonight would be no different. Becca's theories circled my head in a creepy merry-go-round, driving me to distraction.

I used to read stories like Margaret's and wonder what those women were thinking. After joining their ranks, my judgements eased. If they were anything like me, they held on to the better times as a reason to persevere, not that it did any good. I'd had my own store of happy times to call on that helped excuse the bad.

I'd no idea if Sky killed my ex, or even if she was there the day it happened. I just knew the way she'd entangled herself in his con tricks. I'd seen Sky's bad intentions and volatile state before I knew much about her. She was tied up in everything bad about him. And why had Rachel recorded our conversation? Did she think I would confess and get her off the hook?

BEFORE

May 2015

Roger welcomes us aboard that evening in the sultry heat of Paris. He clutches a jug of Pimm's, his open-necked shirt exposing a sunburnt chest.

'Jess, you look in need of a drink.'

'I've been melting all day.' I accept a Pimm's and clink his glass. 'Lovely that you caught us up. We were saying how you two go sightseeing while we plough ahead.'

'Well, you're young and energetic.'

'We're out to enjoy what France has to offer,' Marilyn says. 'That's part of the adventure.'

I'd been holding out for us to enjoy Paris as newlyweds, which seems unrealistic now. Even drinking in company makes Rob tense. He gulps his drink stonily.

'Isn't it pretty?' Marilyn motions to our twilight view of the Seine, illuminated by ornate street lamps.

'Here's to *Paris*,' Roger pronounces it the French way.

I feel my husband's judgemental cringe.

'We're lucky to be here, especially those of us who are kept men.' Roger winks at me and I stiffen, my emotions pulled taut. So much for wanting them to lighten the mood.

'Wonder how long this heatwave'll keep up?' Marilyn jumps in.

I take a fortifying gulp of Pimm's, then rub Rob's knee to say, *Relax, it's no big deal.* He pushes my hand away. We leave soon after and return to our boat.

'What the fuck did you tell Roger the Cabin Boy?' His face contorts with rage.

'Nothing.'

We speak through gritted teeth in the cabin so our argument doesn't travel in the voyeur's paradise. Boats touch either side of ours and twenty more bob about within earshot of a shouting match. The private dramas of other couples fascinate me, but ours is strictly off-limits.

'You said something to make them think you've bank-rolled me.'

'It was harmless chat. Marilyn asked how we could go away for so long. She asked what we did for jobs. I must've said about selling my house.'

'You'd no right to tell her,' he hisses. 'It's none of her business.'

'If I'm offered company, I'll take it, since you're not interested in me.'

He clenches his fists. The light accentuates an angry pulsing vein in his neck. He comes close, eyes blazing. In a blinding moment, it's as if he'll lash out. I shrink away and he grabs the back of my neck, his face inches from mine.

'Keep your mouth shut in future,' he snarls, eyes burning.

I wrench away. Rob swipes my sunglasses from the table and hurls them down the galley. He stomps up on deck and the boat rocks and jolts from him jumping off. He disappears into the night.

I knock back a large glass of wine, shocked by his outburst. I knew there was something a bit wild about him, a bit raw. Maybe that was part of the attraction, so it became part of the deal. But this is something else. We skirt round him feeling demeaned by spending my money, although not enough for him to remedy it. So what if I told Marilyn that we funded the trip by selling my house? Why should I collude in his illusion of an alpha male providing for his younger wife?

I face the prospect of going home without him. Can I give up so soon, with nothing to return to? On top of the Pimm's and in the heavy night-time heat, tiredness overwhelms me. I curl up in bed, unsteady from the argument and the booze. I'll work it out tomorrow. I'll ask Marilyn if she fancies a walk and coffee at a street café.

Early next morning, I wake to the engine shuddering into life. The boat slides from the pontoon before I make it on deck. He's moved us on, putting distance between Marilyn and me. I know this time I'll never see her again.

We push on like fugitives from the law, motoring along the Seine to leave Paris behind. He fetches drinks and makes small talk in an attempt to compensate for last night. I sit listless from the pressing heat, a dull hangover pulsing behind my eyes.

'We'll get used to the heat,' he says as the sun beats down.

He carries on as if nothing has happened, but he's rattled. The crags of his face look deeper, his mouth downturned. I know to keep a close eye on him.

I view my desolate emotional landscape from behind scratched sunglasses. I should have replaced my phone in Paris, where the shop staff are more likely to speak English. I thought we'd have another day before moving on.

'It'll be like this in Greece, but with more of a sea breeze.'

He stands at the helm and we chug down the Seine. The scorching heat begins to ease, along with my hangover. In our role reversal, his hand lingers on the small of my back and he listens attentively when I answer him in monosyllables.

'You overreacted about me talking to Marilyn,' I eventually say.

'Loyalty's important to me.'

'Loyalty?'

He stares ahead. 'My mum left me. My stepmum threw me out. We need to be loyal to each other.'

'I am loyal to you.' I say it carefully, despite losing patience. 'Because of my so-called loyalty, I'm out here with no friends.'

'You know I said you can be insecure? The way you look to other people for opinions. You don't need to do that.' He keeps his gaze on the waterway ahead.

'I can't carry on like this.' I think of Marilyn, breezing round Paris. It brings me round to missing Becca with such an intensity it becomes a physical ache. He's put an ocean between me and everyone I care about.

'Don't leave me, Jess.' It's a plea, but it could be a warning.

We motor on in oppressive silence. I toy with my pendant and consider leaving him. Not that I can take flight here, in the middle of nowhere. My emotions are too scattered to decide what to do for the best.

We arrive at a mooring that evening. I don't know where it is and don't care, since we'll only stay until daybreak. I walk to the town square to call Mum from a payphone.

'We were wondering when you'd phone.' Her voice sounds tight. 'Whereabouts are you?'

'We left Paris this morning.'

'*Paris?* We thought you'd have made it through France by now.'

'It's taking longer than we thought. What's wrong?'

She pauses and I think I've lost the connection. Then she takes a laboured breath. 'Doug needs help with his laptop.'

I almost laugh. 'Can't you take it to PC World?'

'The men need to talk to each other, since they chose it together. Can you put Rob on?'

'He's not here. He's on the boat and I'm at a payphone.'

'Can you get him?'

'Not right now.'

'Tell him to call us. It's important.'

I sigh. 'What's actually wrong with it?'

'If he phones, I'll put Doug on.'

I finish the call and go back to tell him what she said, knowing it'll add to his bad mood.

'Tell him to take it to a repair shop,' he says.

'I did. Why's she so stressed?'

'She's going batty. I don't mind helping Doug when I'm in

the country, but we can't give him computer lessons out here. He needs someone back home to sort it.' He climbs off the boat. 'I'll see if I can get some sense out of the people who owe me money. I was getting somewhere yesterday.'

'Can you phone my mum as well?'

'Let's not.' He starts walking away. 'It'll just irritate us both. They'll sort it out.'

'But—'

'If we leave it, they'll fix it and realise they can manage without us.'

A while later, he walks back along the riverbank, raking his fingers through his hair, deep in thought and muttering under his breath.

'Did you sort out the money?' I ask.

'What?' He glances at me, distracted. 'I'm working on it.'

He has the slippery look I've seen before, the one where he gets tetchy over money. It reminds me of his attitude to bills back home. Before going away, when anything official came in the post, he would frown and study the envelope. Then he'd grimace and rip it open, or more likely, shove it in a carrier bag he kept in the hall cupboard.

One Saturday morning, when he couldn't stuff any more unopened brown envelopes in the bag, he disappeared into his garage with it. I followed him to the doorway. He tipped the contents into a bin bag next to a tired old filing cabinet. He saw me watching and made light of it, saying his accountant sorted it out. He had me believe it was a harmless quirk. It didn't matter because he made good money, or so I thought, and his accountant dealt with what he clearly loathed. Sometimes assumptions come back to haunt you.

'I'm not sure what to make of the money situation.' I choose my words carefully to avoid lighting his short fuse. 'And I don't think either of us is enjoying this.'

'It'll get better. I promise.' He sits beside me.

'How?'

'When the money comes through we can relax. And you'll love Greece. It'll be like the Canaries again.'

'We're a long way from Greece.'

He takes my hand. 'Once we're in the Med it'll be better. We're over the worst now.'

'I don't like what happened in Paris.'

'That was a turning point. The heat, the money ... it got to me. When people let me down I take it badly. Look, why don't I cook tonight and you take it easy? Read a book or something.'

He goes to the galley and starts clanking pans.

When people let me down I take it badly. Is that aimed at me or the people who owe him money?

'You took it out on me.'

'Roger pissed me off, not you.' He fills a pan with water. 'It'll get better. Trust me. We'll put France behind us. Read your book and I'll do us some pasta.'

Roger's comment *was* badly timed, what with the payment not coming through. At least Rob's being honest with me. At least we're talking about it. I tell myself it'll get better. It has to get better.

211

That night, I wake to the faint trilling of his mobile. I sit up in bed and look towards the saloon.

'What's wrong?' he says, his voice heavy with sleep.

'The phone. It's ringing.'

'It's not. You dreamt it.'

I can't hear it now. 'It's stopped.'

'It wasn't ringing.'

Perhaps I had dreamt it. *Oh, I don't know.* Hot and drowsy from sleep, I lie back, disorientated and not trusting what I heard.

'You're imagining things. You just need to relax.'

My dreams turn feverish, of faraway ringing phones and sinking underwater. I can't see through the murky depths, wanting to cry for help but no sound comes from my mouth. So weak. My limbs too heavy, I can't fight it. *Stop imagining things.*

Rob and I spent more and more time together, mostly at the stables, or sneaking off to other places. He made it fun and I guess we both got off on the excitement of keeping it secret. He knew Mummy and I weren't especially close. We didn't share secrets and I never went to her with boy troubles as she'd only say, 'You're wasting your time, darling, just leave him.'

When she caught on to us, she got arsey. Rob said to rise above it and not tell her anything because she was jealous. I didn't think she was jealous of me, but I pretended nothing was going on. He said I was young and gorgeous, which was worth more than all her money. She cut him out of her life and told him not to come near us. Then she banned me from seeing him, as if I was like, fifteen or something.

'Sod that,' he said to me. 'You're nineteen and old enough to make your own decisions.'

We loved each other and I wanted it out in the open. Going to Greece meant we could be together without her giving us grief.

'It'll be liberating,' he said. I trusted him completely and felt like a rebel for taking off with him.

We flew to Corfu and he bought a grotty little boat. It was nothing like the spacious, luxurious boat he'd described. He said a small one would be easier for me to learn to sail. And we had to start with an old one so it didn't matter if we bashed it about. He said he had his eye on a better boat for when I was proficient.

'I need to call Mummy,' I said, 'to check the horses are being looked after.'

'"I need to call Mummy",' he mimicked in a horrid high-pitched voice.

I cringed. Did I really sound like that?

'Isn't it time you stopped calling her "Mummy"? You sound childish. Adults don't talk like that in the real world.'

I made a point of calling her 'Mum' after that. I missed her and I didn't mean to fall out with her. I missed Chester, my pony, too but it was only for the summer until things settled down. Love's hard when you have to make tough choices.

Rob said to throw my phone away so Mum couldn't contact us. He might be tech-free but the rest of us aren't. I don't go anywhere without my phone. I always thought that was strange, the way he hated mobiles and the internet. It made him seem even older. I said we could block her number, but it wasn't enough for him, so we got a new SIM and changed my number. He hated me texting anyone. I'd sneak below deck and text my friends when he was busy with the bloody boring boat. I wanted to hang out in the resorts and drink at the beach bars, but he didn't like other people. He wanted it to be just us.

And then I found out the real reason he wanted to be with me. Someone back home had said I had a trust fund that I could cash in at twenty-one. It hit me hard. He only wanted my money, but I didn't have any. There was no trust fund. He found out and that's when the trouble started. It turned bad. I never told anyone how bad.

AFTER

I hadn't wanted another man in my life after the divorce. Darcy and I did our own thing. We'd been rambling along a South Downs walk one bright Saturday. Darcy's ears pricked up at something behind us and he darted off to investigate. I spun round. Him again.

'Hello.'

'Hi.' I pushed my hair away from my face.

He breathed fast, as if he'd run to catch up. He wore a rugby shirt that suited his athletic build. We'd met a few weeks earlier, when his Labrador bounded over and tried to hump Darcy.

'He doesn't take after me,' he'd said, that first time.

He had kind eyes and a sweet, lopsided smile. I grinned back, despite promising myself not to trust another man so easily.

'They haven't even been introduced.'

'Neither have we. I'm Ben.'

We walked in separate directions and I thought nothing of it. Then he caught up with us again. This time, we carried on along the same path, awkward at first. The dogs romped about. He had a bounding enthusiasm, similar to his Labrador.

'Does Darcy just belong to you?' he asked.

'Yes, he's mine. Or I'm his.'

'This is my favourite walk. I come up with friends sometimes.'

I negotiated a fallen tree trunk. He went to offer me a hand, but I'd already clambered over.

'Does your other half ever come with you?' he said, keeping it casual.

'No. It's mostly just Darcy and me.'

He ran out of polite ways to dig, so I helped him out. 'I'm single.'

'Really? Why isn't someone like you in a relationship?'

'I like it on my own, but thanks for the compliment.'

'Fancy meeting for coffee sometime?'

I stared into the distance.

'Just friends,' he added.

'I can't be with anyone right now.'

'That's fine. How about we both walk this way next week?'

We had another walk, and another, talking for hours. And he was just so kind. He admitted doing that walk several times in the hope of seeing me again. After a while, I relaxed enough for an easy familiarity to grow between us.

I set small boundaries, only seeing him at the weekends, and then with a weekday evening in between. He knew a little about my disastrous marriage but I didn't dwell on it, and he didn't seem to mind me hauling emotional baggage. I liked Ben's openness and honesty, which had come to mean a lot.

Travel-wise, he aspired to nothing more than a few weeks in the sun every year. He'd tried sailing at school and 'didn't get it'. It used to take a frisson of excitement to capture my interest, but not now I had him. He disarmed me with likeability.

Ben drove us to a village near Petersfield to work on his latest landscaping project. The rain had put him behind on hard landscaping, so I offered to help him catch up now the weather had improved. The sun dazzled through the windscreen on the crisp March day. We passed the turning to Kingley Vale and my heart lifted as it always did. It was still our favourite walk; the one where we first met. I thought I'd come a long way since then, although not far enough.

'It's a sensory garden, did I tell you?' Ben said, changing gears. 'It's for a retired couple. The man's virtually blind, so it's designed to evoke the other senses. I'll make a ridge around the path to help guide his way with his stick. He likes to brush against the plants.' Knowing Ben, he would pick plants with fragrance and texture, and ones that rustled in the breeze.

We arrived outside an Edwardian rectory. Ben's supplier had dropped off a bulk delivery of brick paving and compost on the drive. We unloaded the van, piling garden tools into his heavy-duty wheelbarrow. I filled the smaller barrow with compost from the bulk bag and followed Ben round the back of the house. I welcomed the distraction. Six weeks since the murder and the anxiety sometimes threatened to engulf me.

When Ben and I first dated, he'd asked about my garden, which I'd planted from scratch. It helped me create new roots.

The lilac, jasmine, and honeysuckle restored hope to the waste-land of my life. It surprised me how much pleasure I found in wet soil squished between my fingers and new life bursting forth. That first summer, I would sit in the garden with a pot of coffee, alone but not lonely, remembering how to be myself. I didn't tell him any of that. I just said I loved the mix of colour and fragrance.

Ben had plotted out the sensory garden and dug a strip of bare earth winding from the patio to the summerhouse. It would become a brick path.

'Can you fork compost into the borders?' he asked. 'There's a cold snap coming, so the frost will break it down. Then I'll plant lavender and the other scented plants in the spring.'

The owners didn't mind Stan and Darcy coming along. The dogs stretched out in bright sunlight on the lawn, noses twitch-ing in the fresh air. Ben started on the paving, and called over to check I was okay. The sun brightened his sandy hair as it fell in his face. I smiled back. Maybe one day we'd potter round our own shared garden.

The couple came to the back door. The woman held her hus-band's arm, talking to him. He spoke and she threw her head back and laughed. I felt a surge of what they felt, picturing Ben and me in the future, laughing together and settled in a home we'd made our own. I glanced at Ben, and then kept working the soil, my eyes blurred with tears.

'I like us working together,' he said when we stopped for coffee. 'If you ever fancy a career change.'

'Thanks, but I'm a fairweather gardener.'

When I finished preparing the borders, my phone trilled from deep within my jacket's internal pocket. By the time I'd rubbed soil from my fingers, it had stopped ringing, so I sat on the cool ground and freed the phone from my pocket. One missed call and a voicemail that I played back.

'Sweetheart? It's Mum.' She sounded flustered. 'Have you seen? In the paper? His poor wife's been carted off by the police. They've charged her with murder.'

I gasped.

'And they're keeping her on remand until the trial.' Her voice trembled. 'Isn't it awful? I'll call you back.'

I deleted the message and stayed with the phone in my hand. I took slow breaths until my heart calmed. The shock of it stayed with me. *They've charged her with murder.* It took the heat off me that someone, anyone, had been charged.

The sense of peace in the open air with Ben had been shattered. We climbed into his van not long after and drove in silence back to my house. I didn't mention Rachel, needing to process it first. We pulled up on the street outside.

'Thank you for saving me,' he said, which made me want to cry all over again.

'I enjoyed it.' I looked at the dirt on my fingernails. *You're the one saving me.*

He touched my arm. 'You okay?'

I nodded and leaned in to kiss him goodbye.

'You want some company tonight?'

'No, I'll have a soak in the bath. Love you.' Darcy and I clambered out of the van and I waved Ben off.

Inside the house, I sat on the bottom stair, wanting to know more about Rachel's arrest. Perhaps she'd been locked up for contacting Sky and covert recording of potential witnesses. Darcy came and nudged me. I crouched down to ruffle his coat and rest my head against his. My gorgeous boy.

The kitchen tap dripped. I rubbed my sore eyes and a watchful Darcy groaned. I stroked his soft fur. The trust in his eyes snagged at my heart. Darcy and I had a bond, that's what Ben said. No one knew Darcy's routine like I did. No one could read his looks and interpret his ways. I couldn't be separated from him. I couldn't go to prison. He'd think I'd abandoned him, and my heart would split in two, not to mention the impact on Ben and my mum. I must stop thinking like that. Rachel was the one they'd locked up, not me.

'It's okay, Darce. I won't leave you.' Although could I promise that? Staying here was the only outcome I could handle, but I had to stop hiding from it all.

When life with my ex turned bad, I blocked out what I couldn't face. After the murder, it became a kind of superstition: if I didn't mention his name and tried not to think of him, then I wasn't part of it. It hadn't worked and I couldn't avoid being part of it.

A professional viewpoint might help me see more clearly. I called Adam, a solicitor I knew. We'd met at some awful networking evening, and it turned out we had a client in common. I'd given him pointers for improving his website, and now I swallowed my awkwardness in the hope of him returning the favour without asking too many questions.

'Do you know the case about the man who was shot dead on his boat?' I asked. 'The one where his wife's been arrested?'

'Ah, yes. Awful business. He sounded like a nasty piece of work.'

'I know her through a friend. It's been preying on my mind. I wondered if you knew what her options are.'

'It's not my field,' he said. 'But the courts are becoming better at going easy on women who kill abusive partners, particularly if they're provoked by fear.'

'Even if it's premeditated?'

'Possibly. Battered woman syndrome has been used as a defence in murder cases, where a cumulative effect of abuse can be shown. It depends on the case against her.'

'It's not actually called battered woman syndrome?'

'I believe it is, yes.'

'Wow. Okay.'

'And there are new laws about coercive control in relationships, where a pattern of controlling behaviour is a criminal offence. How do you know her?'

'Friend of a friend. Why would they keep her on remand?'

'Ah, well, there must be more to it,' he said, as if anticipating a scandal. 'If you don't have inside information, it'll come to light during the trial. You're unlikely to find out anything official before then. Once a case is under consideration by the court it can't be discussed publicly. You won't be reading anything salacious in the *Daily Mail* until the jury's verdict is announced.'

Salacious? I couldn't imagine anything salacious about

Rachel. 'What if she denies killing him and says she loved him, even though the police have evidence against her?'

'She might get a lesser sentence if it's shown she was under diminished responsibility, but she has to demonstrate it, not plead innocence.'

'What about intent to kill?' I tried to use the right words. 'Say, if she went to kill him, but someone else got there first?' My voice veered out of control. I clung to the phone. 'Could she be held responsible?'

He stifled a laugh. 'Unusual hypothesis. I'm not sure I follow.'

'What if he attracted enemies? She might've had reason to kill him, but someone else did it and covered their tracks. Then she turned up and found him dead.'

'Depends on the weight of evidence. Juries have convicted people of murder on seemingly flimsy evidence. If your friend had a motive to kill this person, and there's evidence she was at the murder scene, then I would advise her to seek very good legal representation.'

We ended the call, Adam's words ringing in my ears. Because, of course, I hadn't asked for Rachel. I'd asked for myself.

BEFORE

June 2015

After leaving Marilyn in Paris, I don't get close to anyone, least of all my husband. I don't want him offending anyone else I might like. In my adult life, I've never spent so much time with one person and I've never been so alone.

I go off without him to a phone shop in a rural town. He says we can use the boat radio for emergencies, but I want my own mobile. My French doesn't stretch to asking about the finer points of an international SIM card, but I come away with a functioning phone. I leave a message on Mum's answerphone with the new number, relieved to avoid a strained conversation with her.

As the confined space of the boat closes in, I look to nature. Last night, the sky turned vibrant pink and orange, darkening to a starry midnight blue against the silhouettes of trees lining the waterway. The moon lit up the silky dark water. Small pleasures along the French waterways keep me going, like early morning birdsong today in the misty air, and the rustle of wind in the trees before the engine drowned it out. Part of me isn't on the boat any more. I lose myself in clouds and ignore the harsh reality.

We doggedly chug along the waterway under a canopy of trees and dappled June sunshine. He takes the helm while I make tea and carry the mugs up on deck.

'What's that?' I tilt my head, tuning in to the faint trilling of a phone. I turn back to locate the sound. It's not my new phone, which is turned off and tucked away in the cabin with my debit card.

'What?' he says.

'Sounds like a mobile.'

'The phone's not working.'

'Listen.' I look at him, puzzled.

Nature surrounds us and there's no one on the riverbank. It can only come from the boat. He makes a face and shrugs. The trilling stops.

'You're hearing things. Ringing in your ears.'

Am I hearing things? I can't say now the ringing's stopped, similar to the night after leaving Paris when the phone rang in my sleep. We moor a couple of hours later, and he talks to a man on the boat closest to us.

Rainclouds threaten and the sky darkens. I go below deck and hear their voices through the open hatch. He talks and I check the cubbyhole hiding places under the floorboards and behind the seating. One of the little cupboards is awkward to reach, so I contort and angle my arm inside. Feeling around, my hand closes onto a cold hard shape. I pause, checking for voices and then snatch out his old-fashioned mobile.

In the murky cabin light, the screen shows a signal, a missed call, and a voicemail. The missed call has a UK dialling code. I go to access the message and then stop myself, not wanting him to know I've found it. But who's called him and why keep the phone secret?

It pains me to put it back, but better to wait and see what he's up to. He'll turn the phone off when I'm not looking. I jolt at footsteps on the deck and shove the phone back in a frenzied rush. He comes down the steps. Swearing under my breath, I fit the little wooden door back on the cubbyhole and swing round to face him.

'What you up to?'

'Dusting.' I flap the duster and cough. Rather than wave the evidence in his face, I give him a chance to come clean.

Rain patters on the deck. He clicks the hatches shut.

'Is the phone working now?' I dust around the shelf of paperbacks.

'No.' He looks suspiciously at me.

'Do you want to check in case it's picked up a connection? Because I heard a phone ringing earlier.'

'It wasn't a phone.'

Oh, but it was. The way he's acting doesn't feel right, but nothing feels right and my judgement clouds. Everything's foreign to me, including him.

'Where is the mobile anyway?'

'It's not working,' he says.

'I'll take it to a phone shop. See what they say.'

'It's no use.' He shakes his head at me not understanding this simple fact. 'I already checked in a phone shop. Why do you doubt me on everything?'

'Because you're a liar.' I sit down, clutching the duster to my thudding heart, feeling bold and scared all at once. 'I found the phone. I did hear it ringing.'

'You could ask me before snooping around. It's like you're trying to catch me out.'

'Why would I catch you out?'

'See? You don't trust me. Seriously, Jess, you're a nightmare when you're like this. Get a grip.'

It's pouring with rain. I go to the aft cabin for a breather from him, and sit on the edge of the bed. Large parts of my childhood were spent hiding out in my bedroom, retreating from my dad's anger at life, my mum, and me.

A minute later, he strides in and looms over me, 'What are you doing, sulking in here like this?'

'What? You upset me.'

'You've upset yourself. This is no way to deal with things, running off in here.'

'I don't want to argue.'

'That's rich when you started it.'

Did I start it? I feel small with him bearing down. He looks ready for a fight. Tears sting the back of my eyes and I push past him. He follows me back out and I stand with my hands covering my face.

'This can't go on. I've had enough.' I wipe my eyes and look at him.

He purses his lips and then his face relaxes into caring husband mode. 'It's been getting to me too.' He guides me onto the banquette seating and sits beside me. 'But we're nearly through it. We're nearly at the Med and then we'll be okay.'

'This isn't right. None of it.'

He takes my hands and nudges up close. 'I've been trying to sort out the money. I didn't want to worry you. That's who's calling, and I need to fix it for us.' He talks as if it's hard to admit. 'Living on the boat's getting to you, I can tell. You've changed, but you're not used to it, that's all. We'll take it easy soon, like we did in the Canaries.'

He looks so sincere, as if everything depends on him making it right. My mind processes it, but it's all so strange. He's so strange.

'Come on, Jess. We can't give up. What would your mum say about us coming back so soon after leaving our jobs? Do you really want to crawl back to your boss, tail between your legs? What would Becca and the others think? We can make a go of it. We owe it to ourselves after coming this far. We're nearly at the Med, then we can set sail and it'll be better.'

'Will it, though?'

'It's because we're confined to the canals. I hate that we're not sailing properly. They say living on a boat is a pressure cooker environment. I'm used to it, but you're not, so I need to take that into account. Everything's intensified. It feels like the end of the world, when it's not. It's really not.'

I don't like the dull ache spreading through me. Here I am, miles from home, technically homeless, certainly jobless, too proud to admit I've screwed up. It could have been different. I tried to begin with. I learned about the boat, how to tie sailor knots and cook on the wobbly stove. I used the stupid, wanky names for everything, and raised my game so I'd know enough for our yacht charter business. I came away on the promise of us starting a new venture, but his secrecy makes me wary. He thinks we can turn it around and somehow wipe out the knowledge that he makes a habit of lying to me. I've a different vision of how it'll turn out, with me not trusting him.

He returns to his obsessive tinkering. I'm stuck out here with a man I don't know. From the moment we set sail, the fire went out of our marriage. The fight seeps away from me. I just need things to be okay. We've nearly reached the South of France, where we'll sail in open seas beside Cannes, St Tropez and Nice. I cling to that, as if a change of scenery will fix us. We need to be around other people on dry land, so I can feel normal again and make my own decisions. Better to keep going for now. That's easier than contemplating the alternative, because I'm scared of how he'll react if I leave.

He ploughs on, putting the fights behind us. Days later, the boat chugs away from the final lock, and the waterway opens out and gushes towards the free-flowing Mediterranean. We leave behind the soupy canal water for an irresistible pull towards the sea.

'Look how fast we're going!' he shouts from the bow, arms wide. He's so animated that it reminds me of the old him and brings a chink of hope that we might just move on from the bad times. 'We'll see the Med any minute!' He beams at me.

And there it is, spread out under the South of France sun. He can't wait to raise the mast, and my heart lifts at the sight of glittering ultramarine. The tang of sea spray hits us, and I dare to believe everything will improve.

AFTER

The doorbell rang. I ignored it and kept working, but someone kept a determined finger pressed on the bell. Darcy's thunderous bark drowned it out. I checked out of the window. The man on the doorstep looked like a police detective, with a receding hairline, grey at the temples, wearing a dark raincoat.

Darcy lurched at the door, all paws and claws trying to get through. I pulled him through to the kitchen and he quietened down. The letterbox rattled and I watched in horror as the man's fingers pushed through and held the metal flap open.

'Mia! We need to talk.'

Jesus Christ. I recoiled. 'Who are you?'

'Rachel's father. Alan Harman. Please, Mia.'

I put the security chain on and opened the door the few inches it would allow. There wasn't much of Rachel in his face, except a refined quality. He had sharp eyes, where hers were distant. He looked the sort to take a quiet pride in his family, until this happened. He hadn't been in the wedding photos that Rachel showed me, since they were only of the happy couple.

'Can I come in?'

'I let your daughter in and she recorded me. The police played it to me. She tried to set me up.'

'Did she?' He looked pained. 'She didn't mean for that to happen. She's been utterly bereft. Doesn't know whether she's coming or going. You were helping her. She saw you as someone on her side.'

I kept hold of the door handle, immune to the Harman family's bullshit.

'When was this?' he asked.

'Last week. After we'd been to see Sky.' I'd no interest in his opinion on the covert recording, but I let him keep talking in case he said something to my advantage.

'I'm in close contact with her defence team and I can assure you that Sky is the main person of interest. I wanted to thank you for helping Rachel. It's been a difficult time for us all, including you. Can I come in?'

'Say what you have to say here.' He must have come here because of the murder charge, so I couldn't take any risks.

He leaned closer and lowered his voice. 'Rachel's been charged with murder. She needs the best fighting chance. That, that, *monster* is dead and it won't serve any purpose to lock up an innocent girl. Whoever killed him did the world a favour, but it wasn't my daughter.'

I studied him. Did Rachel know he was here? She might have sent him in her place after being locked up.

'I knew he was bad news the day Rachel brought him home. Diane was taken in by the charm offensive, but I could see the sort of person we were dealing with. I told Rachel she'd regret it. She said it was meant to be, which sounds like some rubbish he'd fed her.'

I winced for Rachel, and for myself.

'She said I didn't see the real him. She looks for the good in people, even now. But we can't change the past.' He shook his head, nostrils flaring, mouth downturned. 'I just knew he wasn't right. They think she's lying because he was such a brute. But that's the thing with abusers. He'd conditioned her to go along with him. He took advantage of her kind nature.'

'Why do the police think she did it?'

'A dog walker heard screams and found her in a heap on the towpath, covered in blood. She'd been cradling his dead body on the boat. She went looking for him when he didn't come home. She found his body and the shock of it took over.'

His words brought it back: the body, the blood, the shock. If I closed my eyes, I'd see it, so I pushed past the sickly fear and kept my gaze steady on Rachel's dad.

'The boat was about to be repossessed. He hid it out of the way so the bailiffs wouldn't find it. If he'd kept it in a marina, someone would have heard the gunshot, and there would've been CCTV.'

I'd no idea if my movements were caught on camera. Even more to fear.

'My wife thinks Rachel saw something and blanked it out from shock or terror. I disagree. The murderer knew what they were doing and would've killed any witnesses. Thank God

Rachel wasn't there the same time as Sky, or she might have shot Rachel too.'

'What are you doing about Sky?' He could give her a hard time instead.

'I know what I'd like to do.' Anger built in his voice. 'How dare they not press charges against her?'

'What evidence do the police have against Rachel?'

'Circumstantial. It's a complete fit-up, when you consider that he owned the gun illegally. You know about his past, I presume?'

'Yes, well, he kept a lot hidden. As I'm sure he did from Rachel.' I braced myself for more anger.

'Which brings me to why I'm here.'

He gave me a piercing look. My mouth went dry in anticipation of him coming to the point.

'I'm looking for a motive. The police don't care about the truth. They want an easy conviction. It's not enough that we've disproved their forensic evidence, so it's up to me to find the real culprit.'

I swallowed, needing a drink of water.

'We've used a private investigator to do some digging, but he hasn't turned anything up yet.'

'I can't help you with this—'

'You can help us. You can definitely help us. Rachel wasn't the only one he abused. The police say he had a pattern of going after attractive younger women, ones with careers and a few assets. He'd pretend to be a high earner and suck them in on the promise of starting a new life together. Then he'd control them through fear, get them to take out loans. When he'd bled them dry, it would all fall apart.'

I looked at my shoes. Did Rachel have assets for him to liquidate? She was younger than me, but her family might have helped buy her first home. Another reason to anger her dad.

'And there were older women he conned, purely for money. You knew him before we did. Leaving Sky aside, who can you think of from his past who wanted him dead?'

I wanted him dead. I very much wanted him dead.

'I can't help you.'

I shut the door and went to the window. He walked to a black estate car and drove off. I couldn't stay under the radar, not with his urgency to find the killer. He would do anything to pin it on someone else, making them the guilty one, not Rachel. I hadn't even considered her family, but of course she had parents desperate to help her. When Alan Harman said his wife was taken in by the charm offensive, it reminded me of the first time my new fiancé met Mum and Doug. I'd told Mum about our engagement after we'd returned from Rome.

'You're not pregnant, are you?' she'd said.

I'd expected her to dislike Rob on sight. In my teenage years, there was often a boy on the phone and me rushing to answer before she got there. She'd pass waspish judgements, calling them scruffy, or saying she didn't like the cocky ones. She could be difficult like that. My dad probably caused it, not that I excused her.

'Relax,' he'd said when I mentioned that she wanted to meet him. 'I'm good with mums.'

'She can be quite annoying.'

'I'm marrying you, not her. It doesn't matter what other people think.'

We visited her and Doug. They took to Rob with ease, while I watched in suspicion. My mum poured him tea.

'Thank you, Rose. You make tea just how I like it,' he said.

He munched on homemade cake and chatted to Doug about the England cricket team, when I never knew he followed cricket. Mum told him how she'd visited the shops near where he lived.

'A man was playing a harp outside M&S,' she said. 'Even the beggars are posh.'

'You means buskers,' I said.

'How did you two meet?' he asked them.

'In the Post Office,' Doug beamed.

'Outside the Post Office,' Mum said.

'You left your stamps at the counter.'

'I went to buy stamps, and left them there.'

'She always leaves things behind.'

'I'm worried about losing my purse, so I make a point of putting it away—'

'Then she leaves something else behind,' Doug said. 'I was next in the queue. It gave me a reason to talk to her, even though I lost my place. I caught up with her outside a café. She was pleased to have her stamps back, so I said, "I'm just going in for a cuppa, would you like one?"'

'And I said yes.' More smiles. 'Doug wants one of those lapdog computers. He's after some advice, since you work with computers.'

'I'll help you choose a lap*top*,' he said. They talked about Rob's work in IT, and then he grinned at me.

'I'm so lucky to be marrying Jess,' he said. 'Isn't she lovely?'

They murmured in approval.

My mum phoned the next day and compared him to Warren Beatty, 'because you can tell he's a man who loves women'. It pleased me that they didn't take against him. Would things have been different if they had? They didn't have the foresight of Rachel's dad, not that it did Rachel any good. Even so, I wished they'd doubted him, for their sakes.

After Alan Harman's visit, I had a soak in the bath to ease my tension. Feeling less fraught, I lay on the bed in my bathrobe and checked my inbox.

You're the one that got away. His wife wasn't so lucky.

My whole body tensed. It struck me that the email might be from Rachel's dad. But surely he wouldn't send it so blatantly after coming here? He'd hired a private detective, so he might know more about me than he let on.

I got up and opened the curtain a crack. Whoever sent the emails could be out there. The back of my neck tingled at the thought of someone watching from the shadows. My skin crawled at the thought of Alan Harman staking me out and sending them.

Bitch. Killer. I know what you did. Soon everyone will know the truth.

BEFORE

July 2015

We round the French coast under a perfect sky. The boat scuds across white-capped water and the sun reflects off the waves of the Côte d'Azur. And it is azure. His eyes match the blue of the Med.

'This is as good as it gets,' Rob calls from the bow.

After weeks of sluggish motoring, we've raised the mast. He revels in unfurling the sails, cutting the engine and letting the wind take us. I cast off my grubby layers and go barefoot on the boat.

'You look amazing.' He gets his camera and takes my photo, the first of the trip, a proper holiday snap of me at the helm in my red swimsuit.

The smell of sun cream mingles with sea salt. I emerged from my wet weather gear newly svelte from our frugal lifestyle. My pasty skin has turned dark gold. The sun tinges our hair shades lighter and I've acquired blonde streaks. My hair's longer, and without a hairdryer, the natural movement comes out. I may look carefree, but I don't feel it. I stay guarded from his lies and moods.

He comes up behind me and wraps his arms round my waist, resting his chin on my shoulder. My hands stay on the helm, steering a steady course.

'How long shall we stay?'

'Just a night or two,' he says. 'Seeing as we've lost so much time.'

He wants us to forge ahead to Greece, but I need a few days on solid ground to see who we are off the boat. Can we repair our marriage? A plane descends towards Nice airport, reminding me of a business trip I'd taken to France. I'd forsaken that life on the promise of something different. Regret nagged at me.

We cruise into the harbour and I take in the A-list villas sprawled on the hillsides. We pass swanky boats, nudging our much less expensive one into the marina of shiny yachts and powerboats, all gleaming white and reflecting off the water. I change into shorts and a top for exploring the town and water-front. It feels good to be somewhere vibrant. His face falls when I come back on deck.

'What?'

'Aren't they a bit loud?' He eyes my bright red top and orange shorts.

'I'm in the mood for colour. Shall we go?'

'The boat needs to be sorted.'

'Can't we do it later?' Stupid question really, when the boat comes first.

'These lines are a mess and I need to check the engine.'

I open my mouth to retort, but something in his expression stops me. His tightly wound tension is a storm cloud brewing. I coil ropes and clean up, retreating behind my protective veneer of indifference. The boat gleams from daily scrubbing, and my brightness fades away. I'd put up with rigorous cleaning on the grimy journey through the canals, but now we're in this hedonistic other world, I want to stroll around the beachfront and restore some balance.

I tidy things away, just like I did growing up with my dad. Days out would end abruptly with him a mass of seething resentment because we didn't meet his expectations. Everything revolved around him, with my mum intent on keeping the peace. The quieter I was, the better. I didn't expect to end up with someone like him, but I start making the connection.

'I'm going for a walk.' I'm ready to see things, to paddle in the sea and escape the confined space.

'We'll go together.' He smartens up and comes with me. We walk round the old town and along a little side street, shaded from the last rays of early evening sunshine. In awkward silence, we dip in and out of tiny galleries and craft shops.

'This is good, just wandering round.' I touch a row of coloured glass pendants dangling down outside a boutique.

'It's fake.'

'I like the buzziness.' And I like having things to look at other than sea.

He takes my hand. Part of me wants to snatch it away, but the two of us sauntering round reminds me of our trip to Rome. How has so much changed in just five months? We circle round to the beach, still teeming with people late in the day. 'I'd like a swim before we go tomorrow.'

'All these people.' He screws up his face as if I have low standards to like it here. 'Just wait till we're in Greece. We'll have an entire sandy bay to ourselves. You'll never set foot on a crowded beach again.'

As the sun sets, we sit outside at a restaurant on the bustling waterfront and order the *plat du jour*. The stars come out and his mood begins to lift. The waiter brings us plates of grilled fish and tops up my wine.

'*Merci beaucoup*.' I like the opportunity to practise my French, even if I don't always get it right.

'That waiter's hacking me off,' Rob says. 'He's looking down his nose at me.'

I sip my wine and gaze out at the waterfront. 'He seems fine to me.'

The sky darkens and we eat in silence. When we finish the wine, I pay the bill.

'*Garçon*, here's a tip.' Rob stands up. 'Show some respect.'

I look at him in dismay and walk off.

Rob catches up. 'He asked for it.'

I stare ahead and stride back to the boat, leaving unsaid everything that'll make it worse. *He didn't ask for it. You were rude. Why spoil a lovely evening?*

He grabs my hand and walks in time with me. When we reach the pontoon, an Italian man who's crewing on the motor-boat next to ours says, 'Hello'.

'Hi, how are you?' I say, desperate for some cheerful company.

My husband winds a possessive arm around me.

'I like your boat,' the man says. 'I sailed one like this from France to the UK.'

'It's a good boat. It suits us.' Rob deems him worth talking to since he's taking an interest in our boat.

'I'm Rafael. Do you like to come aboard? The boat owner is out for dinner.'

We make our introductions, kick off our shoes and walk up the gangplank. Rafael shows us the living area below deck. I admire the lovely curved seating area of soft leather and the huge windows. He asks questions about our boat, so Rob invites him back for a beer. We climb on board our more modest boat and Rafael tells us how he's crewed racing yachts. His amiable company lifts the mood. Over drinks, he tells us about a yacht he'd sailed with a crew that included a married couple. 'We all know the wife had an affair with the skipper. Then her husband find out,' he says in his lilting accent.

My husband shakes his head, his accusing eyes on me. 'I hope you're listening to this.'

My face betrays the hurt. 'But darling, I'm already sleeping with the skipper,' I say, my jaw as tight as his.

Rafael snickers into his beer, unaware of the simmering tension. After he leaves, I open another bottle of beer and go through to the cabin, pulling off my top. Rob follows me in.

'I'm taking off this slutty outfit you like so much.'

He grabs my arm, whisky on his breath. 'Don't wear it again.'

The boat tilts a little and he lets go with a push. Unsteady from booze and the rocking boat, I land back heavily on the

241

bed. He didn't shove me as such, but I heard his warning tone and saw the same look in his eyes after his outburst in Paris. He walks out. The door swings shut behind him, leaving me with a sobering sense of unease.

I could have packed a bag and headed for the airport. The exits weren't barred. I could have left but I couldn't. Back home, I had been decisive, independent, but that seemed a long time ago. I'd replaced the phone he'd ditched, but I couldn't bring myself to call anyone.

I'd accepted long ago that part of married life was the tension behind closed doors. As a child, I would lie in bed hearing raised voices, my dad taunting my mum, who sometimes responded with a rare outpouring of emotion. I thought they argued because he didn't like me. But he didn't like anything. I'd stay as still as possible, gnawing a thumbnail in the dark, the sudden silences worse than the shouting. Back then, I didn't have a choice of who I lived with, and now it seems I'm in the same position. Trapped.

'Let's stop at Monaco,' he says the next morning.

He plays the part of doting husband while I absent myself, mentally at least. It's a deluded existence all round. I don't face up to our sham of a marriage, having invested everything in it. I parcel up the hurt and shut myself down. A dense mist of denial settles around me, throwing a blanket over the despair. Perhaps I think it will muffle me from the worst, but mostly I don't think anything. I stare glassy-eyed into the middle distance while sweeping views of the South of France pass us by.

Rob said he had some cashflow issues, so why didn't I get a credit card and we could treat ourselves? He promised to make it up to me. I went along with it and signed the credit card application form. They gave me a £1,500 limit. We burned through it in a month before it was refused and we couldn't pay it off. We'd only used it for essentials, like food and boat fuel, and phone credit to keep me sane.

I ran out of phone credit and my friends stopped texting because I couldn't text them back. Rob became my whole world, so I relied on him more. He said I was clingy, and it made him push me away. It was better back home. He treated me better and I had my own life. He went from making me feel good about myself to making me feel awful. I missed Chester like mad, and I wished myself back home looking after the horses. At least they weren't moody like him.

Rob was part of the polo set, so I thought he was sorted money-wise. That's how he had all that free time to bugger around at polo matches and come away with me. He covered it up at first. He said he wanted to be with me, when really, he wanted my family's money. He'd planned to rack up debts in my name for the mythical trust fund to pay off, until he found out I didn't have one.

After saying I couldn't call home, he made me call home and ask for money. My mum wasn't having any of it. He said she'd soften up, but she cut me off. She taught me a lesson and it hit hard. I wished I *did have a trust fund, so we needn't worry about money and could go back to being happy. He acted as if I'd been the one to mislead him. I cried nearly every day.*

AFTER

Cooking smells wafted over from the kitchen, where Adrian and Ben were at work. I laid the table, pleased to spend an evening with Becca and Adrian at their place.

'Heard any more about Rachel?' Becca came in after settling Ellie in bed. We sat on the battered sofa at the end of the kitchen-dining room.

'She's still locked up.'

'I'd love to find out what really went on. Aren't you dying to know?'

'Hmm.'

'In the absence of real information, I've constructed my own theory.'

I tutted under my breath, wanting facts rather than speculation.

'Oh shush. Do you want to know or not?'

'Go on then.' Once she'd had a drink, there was no stopping her.

'It's weird, the police having her on remand. When they arrested her, I thought they were going for the easy target. They can't find the real killer, so they go on fishing expeditions with you and Rachel. Now I reckon the police have something on her. Even if she's guilty, that's not enough to lock her up ahead of the trial. She's done something.'

'Like what?'

'Let's assume she tracked you down through an internet search.'

'It's not a crime to knock on someone's door.'

'But what else has she been looking up online? You hear about it in murder trials. Some people don't realise they leave a trail. They think it's impermanent, like flicking through TV channels. I had to show Adrian how to clear the history so the kids don't find the stuff we look at.'

'What stuff?'

'Just stuff,' she said, with a minxy grin.

'What are you talking about?' Adrian called over from the hob, where he poured stock into a sizzling pan of risotto.

'Nothing,' she sing-songed before lowering her voice. 'Some people are clueless. When I showed my mother-in-law how to find recipes online, she thought a real person looked them up for us. She wanted me to type "thank you" when the internet person came up with the recipes.'

'And you've passed those genes on to your children.'

'I know,' Becca said. 'Scary.'

'What if the police haven't investigated properly?' They didn't ask for my alibi, I nearly said. 'It might be Sky.'

'Sky killed him?' Becca said.

'She might've done it and set Rachel up as the killer. We know she's good at making stuff up.' But she might not have even been there. I should stop fixating on her, but I knew how she used to stir things up.

'Interesting,' Bec said. 'So why have the police got Rachel on remand?'

I opened my mouth to answer, but Becca cut in to answer her own question.

'She's either got previous convictions, which I can't find mention of, or the police think she's a danger to the public.'

'Or the police have it wrong.'

'Or she really did kill him.'

'How do you work that out?' I asked.

'Well.' She leaned forward, brightening. 'Maybe he drove her to it. Coercive control is a powerful thing, especially from a manipulator like him.'

She was probably right about Rachel's internet use, since the police confiscated her devices before locking her up.

'Need a top up?' Ben came over. 'What are you two plotting? It all seems very cloak and dagger over here.'

'You know us,' Becca said, holding out her glass for more gin and tonic, before Ben went back to helping Adrian.

'What if Rachel's dad did it?' Becca said.

'He wouldn't see her locked up on his account.'

'She's only on remand. There might not be enough evidence to convict her.'

I wrinkled my nose, unconvinced. Alan Harman was trouble,

but my own stepdad had a bigger motive. I held my ex responsible for Mum's stroke. The damage he'd done to them both, not that I let on.

'Rachel wants babies and a happy home.' Becca knocked back her gin. 'She finds out his debts won't fund her life plan, so she cuts her losses and kills him for the insurance money.'

'The insurance policy?' I studied her. 'Was it in the papers?'

'No, just being an armchair detective. Is there an insurance policy?'

Me and my big mouth. 'No. I don't know, I didn't, I just thought you'd read about it.'

She looked strangely at me. 'Was there an insurance policy when you were with him?'

'God, no.'

Adrian sliced garlic bread, hot and pungent from the oven. Becca and I looked over at the two of them in the kitchen. Ben grinned at us. My heart tugged.

'You'd never have given Ben a second glance five years ago,' said Becca in a low voice.

'Huh?'

'He adores you.'

I hoped so. I couldn't bear him feeling betrayed by me.

She sipped her drink. 'Are you and Ben okay? You seem agitated.'

'Is it any wonder? With the past stirred up?' Perhaps she would take the hint.

'Don't let it get you down, you've got Ben, and you're normal again.'

'Normal?'

'Not like before, with *him*.' Her voice sped up, laced with alcohol. 'I was shocked how quickly you gave yourself over to him. We were worried about you throwing your life away.'

'Do I want to hear this?' I looked at a partly demolished Lego house in the corner.

'No, but I want to say it.' She slurred a little, and the alcohol made her bolshie. 'His murder dredged up memories for me too. I was there for you when he screwed you over, even though you sidelined me for him. You sidelined everyone for him. You couldn't see the control he had over you.'

She'd never let me off the hook for choosing him over her.

'I'd nothing against you falling in love, but you turned your back on everything else. If I said a word against him, you twisted it round to be jealousy. You acted like years of friendship didn't mean shit.' She sat back and her chest heaved in and out with an overdue breath.

Where had that come from? But she had a point. Back when my heart glowed like a pink neon sign, I abandoned everything, including Becca. I didn't notice the danger signs. Beware handsome, charming men. His enthusiasm carried me away, along with the promises he never kept. It threw my judgement into question that I went along with him. What was I thinking? Maybe I wasn't. But I didn't need that intensity any more, the manipulation dressed as love. I just needed Ben. We were good together. Real.

'Grub's up.' Adrian carried the pan of seafood risotto to the table.

'Are you all right?' she said. 'I don't mean to bring it up. It's just that his murder's brought a lot back.'

I nodded. 'You know I'll always be grateful for what you did ... afterwards?'

'What's done is done.' She stood up and waved her hand as if it didn't matter after all. 'You know my biggest regret? Not shooting him myself.'

'You sure it wasn't you?'

'Guilty.' She held up her hands and stumbled over a Lego brick. I steadied her.

'Sorry. I'm a moany old cow for mentioning it,' she said.

'Not moany. Just drunk.'

'I won't blether on. You know what it's like when you start dwelling on the past.'

I knew.

Later, Ben and I walked back to spend the night at his house.

'You and Becca were having a good chat,' he said.

'Yeah. She'd had a lot to drink.'

'Adrian was talking about your ex,' he said.

'Really? Becca was giving me a hard time about him too. What is it with those two?'

'I asked him.'

'Why?'

'You're so secretive. Feels like you're covering up, or holding back from me. So don't blame me for talking to Adrian. Your ex was killed with a gun he had when you were married. Why wouldn't I want to know?'

I didn't answer, not wanting to turn it into an argument.

'Any more news on the investigation?'

'No.' I didn't mention my visit to the police station, the emails or Rachel recording me. I hated lying to Ben, not that it was lying. Just omission of detail, which proved his point.

'Will the police keep you updated?'

'Doubt it. They haven't told me anything.'

'You can always talk to me.'

'I know.'

'Everyone has a past, but I get a glimpse of yours and you slam the door in my face.'

'Not everyone has the police coming over to ask about their past.'

'Exactly! So what aren't you telling me?'

I walked right into that one. *Stay calm. Don't get stressed.*

'Like what?'

'What was he doing with the gun? Did he shoot anyone?'

'God, no! He never used it, as far as I know.'

'At least Rachel's been locked up, so she can't bother you.'

'Her dad is instead.'

'What? Her dad's hassling you?'

I shrugged. 'He's been round, sounding off about the police fitting Rachel up.'

'What did you do?'

'Nothing.'

'It's a murder investigation,' he said. 'Are you mad?'

I recoiled away from him in the silent street, empty at that time of night. It was what Rob used to say to undermine me.

251

'You can't go talking to her dad now she's locked up. Stay away from them.'

Something sparked up in me. A flare of anger. 'Fuck's sake, Ben! Do you think I need this right now?'

He looked at me in shock. He reached over and held me by the waist so I couldn't avoid him. 'It's getting too much, isn't it? When you're having a bad night, you wake up in terror, as if you're in danger. You do it over and over. I want to help. You just need to let me in.'

But I can't. 'This is how I am right now.' I chewed on a fingernail and turned my head away. It didn't help either of us, him wanting to know too much, and me avoiding his attempts to find out.

He kept hold of me, his voice steady and reasonable. 'If you just relaxed a bit—'

'A holiday won't help. I can't expect you to handle all of this.'

He looked at me, his mouth downturned. 'If I had a court case hanging over me, would you want to help me?'

'Yes.'

'Then stop being so stupid.' He wrapped his arms around me and dipped his head to nuzzle my hair. Rob isolated me on the boat, putting distance between me and other people. Even in death, he kept me at a distance from Ben and everyone else.

Alan Harman's visit had left me unsettled. I felt his urgency in wanting to blame someone else. The not knowing drove me to distraction. Ben held my hand and we walked to his house in silence.

BEFORE

July 2015

He noses the boat into the neat, square marina lined with mega-yachts. The guidebook says Monaco has the highest density of millionaires in Europe. It's described as a sunny place for shady people, which might explain why my husband wants to stay there.

A speedboat races towards us, driven fast by a slick man in a dark uniform and shades. You know at a glance not to argue with him, even before he starts shooing us away with sweeping arm movements.

'Let's go,' I say.

But Rob can't resist a red rag. In the glaring midday heat, he engages in a pointless standoff. We clearly aren't getting in alongside the pimped-out motorboats. He eventually turns around and motors on, hurling abuse over his shoulder. His bad temper simmers away and comes out in angry bursts. I rub a livid bruise on my arm. I keep slipping and tripping over things, clumsy these days, so he says. Or was it from him grabbing me last night to make a point, his fingers digging in? It's better to keep the peace so I don't provoke him.

France merges into Italy and we sail resolutely past Rome. It would have been sad going back there. We sail towards the Amalfi coast, passing vine-covered cliff tops. Sun-baked houses and cypress trees cling to the edges. We rarely see people or have any hint of other lives unfolding, although we sometimes cross paths with gnarled men in painted fishing boats. If we weren't in such a rush we could have explored Tuscan hills and villages, but I don't suggest it.

'We left home three months ago,' I say as we sail along a never-ending stretch of craggy coastline, too far from land to see anything interesting. 'And we haven't even swum yet.'

Rob wears swimming shorts most days when the sun shines, and I'm in a swimsuit. He takes the sails in and ties a long rope to the stern. 'There you go – swim.'

'I mean swim from a beach, not miles from land.'

I've been reading *The Talented Mr Ripley*, which Marilyn gave me in Paris. Last night I reached the scene where they go out in a boat, with San Remo a blur in the distance. Ripley's tension is palpable. When they stop for a swim, I turned the pages, heart in mouth, expecting something bad to happen.

Rob dives in and bobs straight up. 'Come on, you wanted a swim.'

I peer through the murky depths and shake my head, no.

'Why do you do that?' He grabs the metal rung of the ladder and shakes water from his face. 'You complain, so I try to make it right, and then you don't want to know. You just sulk, go all passive aggressive.'

Passive aggressive? I see it as avoiding arguments. Is that how I come across?

'I don't sulk.'

'Of course you don't. Why trust anything I say? Come and swim.'

I clench my teeth and lower myself from the ladder into the deep, dark water. Waves slap the boat with menace. It's more turbulent than it seems from standing on deck. I swim away from the waves colliding with the boat. He launches into a fierce front crawl. I squint against the dazzle of sun and the saltwater stinging my eyes. If the sea weren't cold, I'd be sweating.

I have the wild idea that Marilyn gave me the book as a warning, but I shake it from my head. That's ridiculous. Ahead, Rob stops at the ladder and climbs aboard. He shakes off the seawater and starts the engine.

What the fuck? The propellers grind into action.

In a bracing cold moment, I envisage him leaving me at sea. I'm not a strong swimmer, but I push myself back with all my might, fuelled by a desperate urge to get on the boat. I grab the ladder, panting. The water churns from the propeller and my heart pumps like crazy.

He stands over me at the stern. He takes my hand in his strong grip to pull me aboard.

'Why are you out of breath?' he asks, his face smug.

'You turned on the engine.'

'Did you think I was going to leave you out there?'

My heart constricts, making it harder to recover my breath. 'What are you playing at?'

'Were you scared I'd leave you? You read too many trashy crime novels.'

And I've spent too much time alone with him in open water.

'I'll never leave you, Jess. You just need to trust me.'

A shudder goes through me. I grab my towel. *Get a grip*, I tell myself. I put my panic down to a fear of deep water and what lurks down there. I want to feel safe and stop thinking bad things about my husband. He unfurls the sails, and I shiver on deck with a sense of disquiet as I realise how reliant I am on him.

He gives me a strange look. 'If you think I'll leave you, you're losing your mind.'

AFTER

I arrived home mid-afternoon after a business trip to Cambridge, and kicked off my shoes. Coming home felt like sweet relief. It always did. My mum and Doug had looked after Darcy. I left my bag unpacked and checked emails on my phone. A client had promised to confirm a focus group budget.

I'm watching you, even if you can't see me. Don't think that dog will keep you safe.

I shut my emails down in a frenzy. Panic needled my chest, and fear for Darcy coursed through my veins. I drove straight over to Mum and Doug's. Not long now until they moved out. A familiar figure came down the path from their bungalow, her lank ponytail flicking in time with her strides.

'Jesus Christ!'

I swerved the car down a side road of similar sleepy bungalows, and jerked to a stop. What was DC Roper doing at Mum's? I last saw her at the police station when she played back

Rachel's recording. Had she seen me just now? I gnawed on a fingernail and checked the rearview mirror.

With Rachel on remand, I'd hoped the investigation had finished with me. But I wasn't the only one with a secret about my ex. Mum had one too. The DC might be asking her to testify. I chewed my nail even harder. Since her stroke, I'd avoided all mention of my marriage and the murder. But now I'd have to talk to her. Mum didn't know I'd discovered what she and Doug had tried to cover up. No one knew. But with the police sniffing round, they were about to catch up with me.

The detective drove away, and I walked quickly to the bungalow, half expecting her to arrive back with handcuffs open by her side. Instead, my mum came to the door, wringing her hands. A cardboard box near her feet was packed with what looked like the framed pictures that had lined the hallway.

Darcy broke the tension by weaving round me in his reassuring way. Mum strained to tell me what a good boy he'd been and about his walks with 'Grandad Doug'.

'Shall I make some tea?' I went through to the kitchen. 'What did the police want?'

'The police?' she said, her voice high and uncertain.

'I saw her leave. The same one who came round to tell me about the murder. Here.' I pulled out a kitchen chair from the table. 'Sit down.' I made a pot of tea and we both sat at the table. She didn't say a word.

'I know what's been going on. I found out when you had your stroke.'

*

In the time after leaving him, I'd been determined to move on, I really had. Confronting life with next to nothing drove me to make up ground. I'd been pulling myself out of the financial hole I'd helped dig, but the emotional well went deeper. And sometimes the past won't leave you alone.

Three days before the murder, my mum had phoned to say they'd decided to move to a flat. When pushed, she said they'd made a bad investment but refused to elaborate. I knew she was covering something up. I told Ben that evening as we cooked together.

'A flat? But she loves her garden. How can they leave it for a flat?' He knew how much she liked watching the birds from the little sunroom at the back.

'Can you imagine Doug without his garage?' I said.

'Are they strapped for cash?' Ben held the knife mid-air as he tried to work it out.

'I don't get it. She says they lost money on their nest egg, but I don't see why they're selling up when they've got their pensions.'

'Let's go round at the weekend, check they're okay. I'll offer to help with the move.'

We didn't get to visit that weekend. Doug called the next day.

'Mia, love, your mum's in hospital. She's had a stroke. They're keeping her in.'

'A stroke?' But she was healthy.

When I saw her in the hospital bed looking so frail, I nearly pulled back in shock.

'How are you feeling?' I kissed her carefully on the cheek.

259

She mumbled replies to questions. I perched beside her, listening and nodding. 'You're in safe hands. You'll be home soon.'

Doug bumbled in with a bunch of grapes and a bag of nightdresses. He looked in nearly as bad a shape as her. After cheerily forced goodbyes, I left them. Back home, I still couldn't work it out.

Early the next morning, I went to see Doug. He still got up at 6 a.m., despite retiring a few years ago.

'She'll be fine, your mum.' He fiddled around in their sun-filled kitchen with the tea caddy and cups, looking like an older version of Ben. He wore his jumper inside out, the label and seams visible. 'Don't worry. She's fit as a flea.'

'What caused it?'

'She's been a bit preoccupied with the move.'

'Why don't you stay put? Keep things stable. If it's money, we'll work it out. I'll pay your bills.'

'No need for that. She won't have to lift a finger with the move.' He didn't look at me the whole time.

'And how are you managing?'

'I'm fine.'

'Why don't you come over after you've visited her? I'll cook us something.'

'No. I'm fine.'

I took a deep breath. 'Doug, why are you moving house?'

'We thought we'd free up some cash.' His voice got firmer and lost its vague tone. 'Your mum doesn't want you worrying and neither do I. Let's leave it at that.'

I couldn't leave it at that, so I went back during visiting times and let myself in. Doug would be at the hospital. He didn't cook, so I made a big pot of casserole for him to heat up, and to conceal my other reason for going there. I shouldn't poke about, but I knew there was something they weren't telling me. I also knew they kept the financial paperwork in the dresser.

'It's all in that big black file,' Mum had told me more than once. 'Just in case you need to lay your hands on it.'

Sorry Mum, but I did need to lay my hands on it. I sifted through their important paperwork, but only found old savings books, passports and ancient current account statements. I couldn't tear myself away, searching the other cupboards and drawers, but nothing. Where was it? I checked under the beds and behind furniture. If I kept on, Doug would catch me rifling through his stuff. I went to leave. On the way out, I looked over my shoulder at the internal door to the garage. Did they keep the bad stuff in there, at a safe distance, the same as my ex had?

I found it in a pile on Doug's homemade shelves. So many documents. My heart contracted at the bankruptcy order. And some kind of guarantor agreement for a loan. Doug had co-signed. I saw the other signature and covered my open mouth.

The fucker, the fucker, the evil bastard. The impact nearly floored me. It felt like my chest caved in. All of me caving in. I bent forward, my vision blurred. Nausea washed through me and I crouched on the floor, but I couldn't be sick, not here.

Everything changed in a heartbeat. He'd conned them into acting as his guarantor and they'd gone bankrupt. He never paid for what he'd done to me because I'd walked away. But I'd come out fighting over this.

I shuffled the documents back into a pile on the shelf and thought of my mum in hospital, who I should be visiting, not snooping round her home. He had to pay. Should I tell Ben? I couldn't, not yet. He might try and stop me. But nothing would stop me.

The next day someone shot my ex-husband dead. And he bloody well deserved it.

BEFORE

July 2015

'Let's stop in Capri,' he says.

I long to lie on a sun lounger. Anything to get away from the boat. For some reason, I envisage white sandy beaches and smart loungers with co-ordinated parasols. It's nothing like the tall, rocky island we arrive at. A noisy backdrop of day trippers surge off ferries at the harbour. The stalls and cafés cater for them with postcards and slices of greasy pizza.

'It's not what I expected.' I mean Capri, but it's true of the entire trip.

'You and your expectations. Nothing ever measures up does it, Jess?'

I burn from the accusation. 'I didn't mean—'

'I thought you'd love it out here. Just be aware of how you're coming across, that's all. I'm trying to help.'

Maybe I do expect too much. He says I need to relax and give everything a chance.

'This is the tourist area,' he says. 'It's better higher up. We'll walk to the highest point when it cools down later.'

He changes into a linen shirt and the smarter shorts that he only wears ashore. 'I need to make a call,' he says, and jumps off the boat.

We have the phone out in the open now, but he says payphone calls are cheaper and the reception more reliable. He strides along the horseshoe shape of the sea wall. Smaller boats like ours congregate at the outer edge, poor relations to the vast motorboats closer to the action. He walks past the biggest boat and flashes a smile at someone on it. I can't see who. Then he disappears from view. He comes back after half an hour, looking agitated. Another phone call about money that never materialises, not that I ask. The gap widens between what I believe compared to his version of the truth.

After the day trippers head back to Naples, Capri cools down and takes on an exclusive feel. We walk to the top of the island and gaze out beyond the rocky seashore, over the Bay of Naples and towards Vesuvius. Even on land, my body sways in time with the boat, keeping me off-balance. We might look like any other couple on holiday but his hand grips mine too tightly, his words barbed and his eyes hidden behind sunglasses.

We drink expensive beer at the *piazzetta*, a square edged with outdoor bars and restaurants for beautiful people to go about their charmed lives. Two men talk at the table beside us. Everything about them looks expensive, from their casual but well-cut clothes to their statement watches. My husband hides his bad grace, watching them with pursed lips. Men with money rattle him. He tensed up earlier when I said Capri wasn't what I expected. It won't take much to set him off again. A vein pulses in his neck, the same one from his angry outburst in Paris.

I stiffen, not wanting him to take issue with anyone. He knows nothing about those men, but they have what he wants: the luxury and respect that come with wealth. That same respect was denied of him when we motored into the marina at Monaco. I tread on eggshells and half expect him to lash out at whoever irritates him. But it's usually only me.

'Tax dodgers, probably,' he says, nodding towards them. 'Over from Monaco.' He leaves money on the table and we walk back in silence.

We draw level with the biggest motorboat; the one he'd taken an interest in earlier. A woman in a tight magenta dress smokes a cigarette on the harbour, one arm resting on the gangplank railings that lead to the motorboat.

'Nice boat,' my husband says, smiling at her. 'We're in a yacht over here.' He motions along the harbour, signalling towards the nearest super-yachts.

I'm surprised he's talking to her; he's usually scornful of motorboats and their owners. Does he only resent men with money, not women? She appraises him, her cigarette poised.

'Thank you. We like it.' She returns his smile, her voice husky and sensual, her accent American. 'It's a very sociable space.'

'You're a long way from home.' He twinkles away at her.

My stomach churns as it does when we sail in rough sea. They talk about how she's come the same route along the

Côte d'Azur. He waxes lyrically about Monaco and the south of France. He ignores me and talks about Monaco marina as if we'd been welcomed there. How would he react if I chipped in? *Darling, the man wouldn't let our tiny little boat in. Remember how he shooed us away?*

It plays out like some kind of routine. Is this what he does when he disappears to make mysterious phone calls and source boat parts? He tries capturing her attention. She doesn't encourage him, but a glimmer in her eyes says she likes him. I see how other women respond to him. Bit of a ladies' man, my husband, and skilled at mesmerising people. Other sailing wives look at me as if to say, 'Aren't you lucky?' Not so long ago, I'd have said yes. Yes, I am.

She takes another drag of her cigarette. An older man in uniform who looks like the skipper comes down the gangplank. She glances at him and blows out smoke.

'Well it's been lovely meeting you. I'm Christina.' She holds out a manicured hand for him to take. He introduces us both by first name, not saying I'm his wife. She turns to the skipper and we walk away.

'I thought you didn't like motorboats,' I say when we're out of earshot.

'Nothing wrong with a friendly chat. She might invite us on board next time.'

'You weren't interested in Rafael's motorboat when he asked us aboard. You seem interested in her, though.'

He leans in to me, his hand on the small of my back. 'I think somebody might be jealous.'

'I'm not jealous.' I pull away. 'But it's weird that you virtually ignored me to win over a stranger.'

'Don't be insecure. It doesn't suit you. You think I'm ignoring you? This whole trip is for you. You wanted to come away. I could see you weren't coping in the corporate world. You're too sensitive. Look how upset you got when your boss pulled you up on one mistake. And you were jealous of your colleague, the one who went to New York.'

'Helen?' I look at him in confusion, wondering where all this is coming from.

'There's times I wonder if it's your childhood that's screwed you up. You have this warped perception. I'm just trying to help. That run-in with your boss was an overreaction and, yes, your . . . *fixation* with Helen. You struggled in the real world, but we've made our own world now. I'll keep you safe, you'll see.'

We reach the boat. He takes my face in both his hands and kisses me softly. Then he rests his forehead on mine.

'Even your mum and Doug said so when they came to see the boat. They didn't say anything around you because they didn't want to hurt your feelings, but they thought a change would be good for you.'

Really? His words throw me.

'I don't think you realise how bad it is. I thought it'd be better out here, in a less pressured environment, but I'm beginning to think your issues will follow you wherever you go. You're creating problems where they don't exist, like thinking I'd motor off and leave you in the water. What kind of husband would that make me?'

'I was only asking about your interest in that woman and you start accusing me—'

'See what you're doing there? You're turning it into an argument. I'm just saying how I've got your best interests at heart, and you twist it and go all emotional.' He puts his hands on my shoulders and looks into my eyes. 'Everything'll be fine when you stop overthinking and relax.'

I go below deck and rinse the glasses we'd left in the sink. He comes up behind me and rubs my shoulders.

'You've had a hard time out here, but I love you for making a go of it.'

His hand roams downwards to my breast. I stiffen.

'Relax. Hey, it's me, relax.'

I turn my head away. 'I'm not in the mood. Not after what you said about me creating problems.'

'Come on, Jess. I love you.' His voice is low and soft, practicing the art of seduction that no longer works. 'C'mon babe, you're gorgeous. Let's go to bed.'

He dries my wet hands with the towel beside the sink, reminding me of back home when he'd wrap me in a fluffy towel when I stepped out of the bath. He takes my hand in his big grip and leads me to the cabin. There's always the chance it'll relax him and bring us closer, the way it used to.

'Your skin's so soft.' He coaxes and kisses me as if he still wants me, but it doesn't feel right, trying to find affection we no longer have.

AFTER

I made tea in my mum's kitchen. When I told her I knew what had happened, her face glazed over and she didn't respond. She looked shaken after her visit from the police. She hadn't fully recovered from her stroke, and the stress of her and Doug covering up what had happened with Rob wouldn't have helped. I knew the damaging effect of keeping secrets.

'I know he conned you.'

She blinked several times and looked at the teapot on the table. 'You know?'

'About the loan.'

'The loan?' She looked older, shrunken. Her face strained.

I paused for her to gather her thoughts and stop repeating what I'd said as a question.

'We decided to keep it from you,' she said. 'You had enough on your plate.'

'You might've known I'd find out.'

'We didn't want you feeling responsible. He messed up your life enough.'

Three months after the murder and he still messed up my life, but they didn't have to shield me.

'Why loan him money in the first place?'

'We didn't loan him money. You'd just got married. He said the two of you were taking out a business loan, and could we act as guarantors. He said it wouldn't cost us anything. It'd tap into our good credit rating to boost the credit rating for the two of you. We wanted to help.'

'But there wasn't a business at that stage. We didn't need a loan. If you'd said, I'd have told you.' I tried keeping the emotion from my voice. I needed to know what happened, but the guilt from them being dragged into his deceit nearly overwhelmed me.

'You never ask for anything. You wouldn't even let us help pay for the wedding. I wanted you to have a good start to married life. Doug and I didn't see the harm. The three of us knew you wouldn't let us.'

'When did you agree to it?'

'That day we went to see the boat.' Her voice shook. She held onto her china mug but didn't drink from it. 'He talked about the business and the safest way to set it up. It was a family enterprise, he said. He asked our advice.'

I thought for a few moments. 'You went to the boat ... I arrived late because he told me to come an hour later.'

'That's it.' She looked into the middle distance and nodded to herself as if recalling it. 'You were late and we arranged it then.'

He'd told me the wrong time, making it my mistake. It left him free to charm them. The bastard. I dug my fingernails into my palms. My anger was as powerful as it had been the day after her stroke, when I first discovered the loan. In a fury, I'd wanted to confront him.

'I hoped your marriage would be better than mine.'

'By arranging the finances with him behind my back?' I shouldn't take it out on her, but I hated him conniving with them.

'It wasn't like that.'

The distress in her voice pulled me back.

'Your dad always had the upper hand with me. I thought you and Rob could have a proper business partnership and be equals. I was trying to help.'

'Didn't Doug see the risk?'

'He said if it had been some get-rich-quick scheme, he'd have seen through it. But it was your new business. It made sense, the way Rob explained it. We didn't know it was unsecured. We didn't even know what that meant. It turned out we were responsible for all his financial obligations. All of them. Not just that one loan.'

I wanted him to die all over again. He deserved worse than a bullet through the heart.

'The police got involved after his murder, trying to unravel his finances,' she said. 'They followed a paper trail of his loans and debts. They said it was fraud, even though we'd signed the forms. But he sort of bamboozled us. It was all a rush and he kept us talking the whole time. You were about to go on your trip, so we had to do it quickly. I know we look like a couple of idiots, but it happened before we could think it through.'

'When did you realise it was a problem?'

She rubbed at her face, looking old and beaten down. Anger overwhelmed me. I fought the urge to upturn the kitchen table and scream in fury.

'When you were in France. He missed the loan payments. Then we found out the extent of it. I was so relieved when you finally phoned us. We needed to speak to him and find out what was going on.'

'The laptop? Oh God.' Her strange phone conversation in France, when he'd refused to talk to her. Then he went off to make a phone call and came back agitated. 'Did he call you back after I'd phoned?'

She nodded and took a sip of lukewarm tea. 'He called back to say it would all be sorted. He said someone let him down. His money hadn't come through, and the boat needed expensive repairs. It was a short-term glitch. We just hoped you'd get sorted soon.'

'If I'd known, I would have come home and started working. I'd have used the money we had left to pay towards the debt, and made him cancel the agreement.' It might have been the jolt of reality I'd needed. Poor Mum. None of this was her fault. She'd suffered so much because I'd brought him into our lives.

'We couldn't tell you. I felt so awful, and Doug still feels responsible for going along with him.'

'We all went along with him. Me more than anyone.'

'It turned into such a mess.' She clutched the sides of her head.

'But the repossession of this place ... why has it dragged on all this time?'

'It can take a while for a home to be repossessed. We're experts now.' She massaged her forehead. 'Our MP and a charity intervened on our behalf to say we were conned. The mortgage company put it on hold for a long time while it rumbled through the system. And the police were pursuing him. That helped us stay on here, especially since the murder investigation, but we were told the best option was to go bankrupt.'

She let out a sob and Darcy stood up in alarm. I pulled him to me and stroked him.

'Now I've messed it up even more.'

I flinched. 'How?'

'We didn't want you to know he'd tricked us about the money. When it came out that he'd defrauded people, the police got involved. You'd split up from him by then. Doug fudged it a bit by saying we'd met him a few times and he'd invited us on his boat. Doug made us sound like a couple of dopey pensioners taken in by a conman.'

'You didn't tell the police we're related?'

'We didn't want you brought into it. If the police had been suspicious, we'd have come clean, but they said he was good at tracking down likely victims. With you and me having different surnames, it wasn't obvious unless they looked into it more closely.'

I braced myself.

'Which they didn't, until now.'

'Okay.' I put my hands flat on the table.

'They came back and questioned us. It got more serious, but we stuck to our original story. We thought that was best, in case, you know, it affected things.'

She stopped short of saying the police might suspect me of killing him. That my ex conning them was a motive for murder. It explained her concern about the police finding the gun and arresting Rachel. She thought I had a stronger motive.

'We saw how they went after that poor girl. They could use it as a reason to accuse you. Someone killed him two days after my stroke. *Two days!* Doug had been visiting me in hospital so we were in the clear.'

I nodded, but that didn't explain her raw emotion. 'How have you messed it up?'

'The policewoman who came just now saw an old school photo of you in a box we'd nearly packed. I meant to put it out of the way. And she recognised Darcy.'

Darcy's alert ear pricked up.

'Darcy, did you grass me up to the police?' I said with a sigh.

He cocked his head. I rubbed his velvet fur. He panted, distressed by all the emotions. I leaned my head on him and composed myself.

'No,' she replied for him. 'But the officer asked about you and I had to tell her the truth. She didn't seem surprised. I think they already knew.'

'It's okay. They would've worked it out.'

As if I hadn't made them suspicious enough. I hadn't told

the police because it gave me a motive and exposed my first lie about not seeing Rob for two years. By keeping quiet, I hoped they would find someone guiltier than me. I had to work out how to handle it. Meanwhile, I didn't want Mum having a relapse. Worrying about the police coming after me wouldn't help her poor health. I left her to rest, and took Darcy home.

I'd thought the real hardship was mine alone, until seeing what he'd done to them. He was to blame for her stroke, brought on by the home repossession. When I'd discovered the loan details in their garage, I visited her in hospital that same afternoon. I'd felt clammy in the overheated ward, as if I might be sick. Blood pounded in my ears, and my mouth dried up. I went along the corridor to an open window and stood with my forehead pressed on the cool glass, one hand on the wall, breathing fresh air to bring myself back.

They said she might have more strokes at any time. I could barely conceal my horror at him reducing her to this. Back at her bedside, we discussed safe topics. She slurred and talked slowly. I talked slowly too. It muted my seething mass of fury, but not for long.

He'd got away with treating me like dirt, but I couldn't rise above this. He thought he could walk all over us, but I wouldn't give him the satisfaction. He was a bad person and he'd turned me bad. But I wasn't as bad as him. I didn't fuck with innocent people. Only him.

BEFORE

That last evening in Capri, we hike back up the hill one last time. I don't know why we stayed here an extra night, given his urgency to get to Greece, but he would take issue with me asking so I leave it.

We walk back under the moonlight and a diamond twinkle of stars, stopping part way down to gaze at the sky. This togetherness is what I'd wanted, but it doesn't feel right. Nothing does, but if I voice it, he'll say I'm inventing problems again. He'll say it's my screwed-up past, my warped way of thinking. I'd complained about him ignoring me, but his attention makes me uneasy. Maybe he's right. Maybe I don't know what I want.

'The sky's so clear.' He stands close behind me, one hand on my shoulder, and points out the constellations. I still don't know what he's up to, with all the phone calls and the way he talked to that woman on the super-yacht yesterday. I take advantage of his relaxed mood, lowering my voice so no one overhears, 'You know when you showed me the gun?'

'Hm.'

He holds me firm with both hands, and we face the black sea.

'You said no secrets.'

'Right.'

'So what's with the secretive phone calls?'

'I'm sorting out the money.' He takes my hand and guides us back down the road to the harbour.

'It's taking a lot of calls.'

He speeds up, his hand grips mine harder. 'It's a mess. My old boss gives me the runaround, so I try the accounts department. Then they say it's been passed on to someone who's not in and to phone back after lunch. Everyone blames the US parent company for holding back the funds. I'm not sure I believe them.'

I'm not sure I believe you. After all this time alone with him and this strange way of living, I no longer trust my instincts. Back at the harbour, a young, tanned crew member stands on the gangplank to Christina's gin palace. He wears a pressed Ralph Lauren polo top and shorts with deck shoes.

'Nice boat,' my husband says, stopping at the gangplank.

Here we go again, I think.

'So how much would this set you back?' he asks.

'About thirty million. Pounds that is.' Turns out he's English. He looks closely at Rob. 'Have we met before?'

'No, but you might have seen us here. We were talking to Christina. I guess she's your boss.'

'She's not the boss,' he says, amused. 'She's his paid companion.'

My husband's jaw tightens.

'Thirty million,' I say. 'Who has that sort of money for a boat?'

'He's in IT, self-made and he's only forty.'

'Wow. Good for him,' I say.

I can see this grates on my broke, forty-seven-year-old husband.

'I remember you,' the man says to him. 'You tried to come aboard in Cannes. When we had that party? You didn't have an invite.'

I look to Rob for a denial. He shrugs and shakes his head in a non-committal way. 'Don't think so, mate. Must've been someone else.'

He clasps my hand and walks us away.

'So, Christina's an escort,' I say as we go back to our little unstaffed boat.

'Yeah. So?'

'Very enterprising of her. I assume she's good at it to snare a multi-millionaire playboy.'

He strides along the harbour, keeping a firm hold on my hand.

'Did you gatecrash their party?'

'He's confusing me with someone else. I wouldn't have gone without you.'

The next morning, we prepare to leave Capri. He stands on deck and sneers at the thirty million super-yacht. Two men try to fly a kite on the boat's spacious deck.

'It's that English bloke we spoke to,' he says, 'doing rich-guy R&R with the boss. What a dick.'

The kite jerks in the air and nose-dives. The staffer holds it aloft again to catch the wind.

'Useless tosser.'

Jealous? I nearly say.

We leave Capri to sail into Italian harbours and old fishing quarters. He restlessly seeks distant horizons, and I look out for Christina's motor boat. I don't know enough to throw accusations, but I suspect his attempt to befriend her was behind our extended stay in Capri. That's why our walks around the island seemed fake and even more tense than usual. Mingling with tourists isn't his style, but he wanted an excuse to pass her boat and strike up a conversation.

At the latest marina, it seems every time I go to jump from the boat, a different twinkly-eyed Italian appears and offers his hand with an enthusiastic *prego*. I don't seek out the attention, but I like it all the same, considering my husband gives me no appreciation. One of those times, the man holds my hand longer than strictly necessary to help me off the boat. Rob comes after me as I walk away.

'Why do you do that?' He walks alongside me and motions back towards the boat.

'I'm not doing anything.'

'You encourage them. Like in Nice when you flirted with the waiter and that guy on the boat next to us.'

'I don't flirt.'

A man walks towards us. Rob grabs my hand.

'Are you guarding me?'

'Well that's very nice. I love you. I'm looking after you. Why do you always have to see the negative?'

I sigh and keep walking to the market.

'You couldn't handle me talking to that woman in Capri, so it works both ways,' he says. 'You're insecure. You don't realise it, but I see how you flirt with men to feel good about yourself. You even did it to Roger in Paris. Marilyn and I spoke about it.'

I stop and stare at him. 'You spoke to Marilyn about me?'

'She brought it up with me, actually. But she was fine. We both knew there was no harm done. I'm flagging it up so you can be aware of it. You don't need other men to feel good about yourself. We're married.'

'I can assure you I didn't flirt with Roger.' I keep walking to the harbour stalls.

'Your clothes don't help. You send the wrong signals.'

My little cotton tops and shorts are non-negotiable in shimmering heat, but I pick my battles and let most of them go, or we'd be at each other's throats.

'That top makes you look fat.'

'I weigh less now than when we met.'

'I'm not saying you're fat. I'm saying the top doesn't do you any favours.'

'Just because someone helps me off the boat doesn't mean you can insult me—'

'Don't be touchy. Your dress sense is a bit odd, that's all. Like those orange shorts you wear. They're not flattering.'

He walks with me to the harbour stalls where I ignore him and choose produce to cook. On one level I know it's not right, but my mind's gone into hiding and I avoid what I can't yet handle. It's easier to pretend none of this is happening, so we blame it on living on the boat, or my expectations, how I flirt, how I make him stressed, if we had more money ... but it's a smokescreen. He's the reason everything is wrong. Him. I should leave, of course I should bloody leave, but I'm scared of what he'd do.

When the boat doesn't move, I cook up risottos and pasta, with focaccia bought with a mixture of pidgin Italian, gestures and smiles. Comfort food to fill the gap of unhappiness. In the lingering heat that evening, we eat on deck, the harbour abuzz with young couples and Italian youths on mopeds.

'This is lovely,' he says about the pasta. 'If you put as much effort into sailing as you do into cooking, you'd be a really good sailor.'

I look at the locals and imagine their lives as an escape from my own, but it makes everything worse. I want to be like them, on dry land with a normal life that's not fucked up. I'd planned to stick with it until Greece, but what's the point?

'I can't do this any more. I don't want to be on a boat.'

If I make it about the boat then he might not take it personally. He'll blame me for not giving sailing a chance, but it's less confrontational if the boat's the problem instead of him. My gaze stays fixed on the people close by.

'I'm going home. I'll take what's left of my money and get a flight.'

'There's no money left,' he says. 'We don't have enough for a flight home.'

'How come? You said it would last until Greece.'

'The boat repairs cost a lot, and it's taken so long to get this far. You don't have to worry. We're living on my money now. I've cashed in part of my pension so I'm taking care of us.'

But are we living on his money? I should have kept a better check on the finances, but he's so slippery about it. He'd said back home that we should take euros so we could pay harbour fees in cash and buy from markets. According to him, I no longer have money of my own, so it's harder for me to leave on my own.

'I haven't been entirely honest with you.' He holds my hand, his thumb circling my wedding and engagement rings. 'The company that owes me money has gone under. That's why they gave me the runaround. They weren't able to pay me.'

'All the more reason to go home.'

'We've enough money for Greece. We'll be there in a few days. We'll sell the boat and get a better price for it in Corfu. Then we'll come home. I'll buy us a new car each and we'll start again.'

I've lost my independence, not that I've had it for a while. I want to go home, but I'm wary of pushing him too far. The safest option is to sell the boat and then I can break free.

AFTER

Once we had it out in the open about the loan, I could at least help my mum and Doug. After leaving my marriage, I'd rebuilt my life, and now I had to rebuild theirs. Back then, I threw myself into work. My first job hadn't been right, but the long hours stopped me dwelling. I hardly ventured out, and didn't spend much money, so my bonuses paid the deposit on a home with the Help to Buy scheme. Nothing came close to my old place, since I'd thrown away my pot of equity. Even so, I pushed myself to find a base and some security.

If I could just afford a little place with a garden for them, that would be enough. The bungalow was lost to the debt, but I looked up options for a second mortgage. If I kept working hard, it might be manageable, so long as I wasn't locked up.

Ben dropped in after finishing a job. We stood and talked in my little garden. Darcy and Stan sniffed around, and birds perched on the branches of a tree, swaying in the breeze. I told him the reason for the repossession.

'That's awful.' He pulled me close and hugged me. 'You poor thing.'

I blinked away tears.

'Why don't you move in with me?' he said. 'And they can stay here.'

'Oh, that's kind of you.' I wanted to say yes, but we couldn't live together, not right now. If the case against Rachel collapsed and the police accused me of murder, Ben would be tainted. Unlike my ex, I wasn't dragging anyone else down with me.

'At least while your mum recovers,' he kept on, taking my answer as encouragement. 'Then she can have a garden to look out on.'

'Thanks, but we don't need to.' I squeezed his hand. 'Sorry. I'm shattered. Cambridge wore me out, and talking to Mum knocked me sideways.'

'No wonder. I should go anyway. I'm watching the match at the pub. They've already got me a pint in.'

I walked him and Stan to the door and waved them off, and then I phoned to check on Mum. Doug answered and said she was having an early night.

'I'd like you both to move in here,' I said. 'I'll go some-where else.'

'No need for that. We're renting a flat with a view of the park. That'll do fine. We weren't sure if we'd get a proper lease, what with the bankruptcy, but a couple from our Scrabble club are going to see their family in Australia for three months, so we're putting everything in storage and house-sitting their place. They're not charging us much rent.'

'Have my house for free. Then you'll have a garden. Shall we ask if I can rent the flat?'

'Your mum can't manage stairs at the moment. The flat has a lift.'

It was even more to feel guilty about. I still reeled from what my ex had done, and I nearly fell apart, seeing how he'd hurt them. They'd say it wasn't my fault, but it was all my bloody fault.

The next morning, I braced myself to phone DS Thornley about Mum's loan. Otherwise, she'd fret about dropping me in it with the police. Darcy sprawled at my feet, dozing after our walk. I called Thornley's direct line and explained what led to them being conned.

'They covered it up with everyone,' I said, 'including you, because they didn't want me to find out and feel guilty.'

'We knew you were related,' he said. 'It's our job to look for connections. We can tell when people are holding back information, Mia.'

I hated the way he used my name when making a point about me. He might as well be saying, 'It's you, isn't it, *Mia*? We know you were there, *Mia*. You're next if the case against Rachel falls apart, *Mia*.' Rachel's dad was wrong about the police not investigating further. They'd certainly been investigating me.

'What they told us didn't add up. We checked it out in case someone was controlling what they said, threatening them. Your name came up. That was after we'd interviewed you. We'd already arrested Rachel Harman on suspicion of murder, and focused our resources on that. Why did they cover up for you?'

'They didn't want me to know about the loan. I suppose they thought it best to deny everything.'

'Clearly being evasive runs in the family, Mia. It's not advisable to lie to the police.'

I sank lower in my chair and wrapped one arm around myself. Good job he couldn't see me down the phone line. 'They felt bad because he scammed them.'

'It's a common reaction. The scammers play on it. People conned out of money often don't want their family finding out. And they think the police will say it was their fault to have been taken in. When did you find out he'd conned them?'

'Only yesterday. I went to collect my dog and saw your colleague leaving their house.' My lies came more smoothly now. 'Then Mum told me, and I realised why they had to move.'

'Didn't she have a stroke? Was that before the murder or after?'

'Um. Before, I think.' Fuck. I didn't want him seeing a motive. He knew. He must know, sizing me up, seeking out evidence.

'When was it?'

'Oh, January.'

He didn't reply. He left it hanging; the fact that her stroke happened just before the murder. In return, I broke my habit of pumping him for information that he wasn't prepared to give, and I finished the call. Thornley knew more about me than he let on. Was he giving me enough rope to hang myself, trying to make me say something incriminating?

I phoned my mum with the update. 'You don't need to worry. He understands why you kept quiet. There won't be any repercussions.'

'Are you sure?'

'We've helped the police build a picture of what he did. That's all they're interested in.'

'Oh. I've been worried sick. I know I'm not supposed to worry, but I do.'

'You needn't now.'

'I was worried about you leaving your job and going away on that boat, but I let him win me over. I should never have fallen for his lies.'

'It's not your fault.'

'I knew there was something about him. I couldn't put my finger on it. Then I realised he reminded me of your father in the early days. Isn't that awful? Trust me to get it wrong when I wanted better for you.'

She hadn't mentioned my dad in years. It threw me. I didn't know what to say, as if we'd broken an unspoken pact. It was the closest she'd come to admitting her own mistakes and how they had rubbed off on me.

'Let's not dwell,' I said. 'I have to go.'

'You and Ben are okay, aren't you?' Her voice turned anxious again.

'Sure. Don't worry. Go and have a rest.'

Ben and I weren't okay, not really. Despite his offer for us to live together, it was strained between us. I couldn't hide my jittery state when we shared a bed three or four nights a week. Lack of sleep addled my mind and I avoided Ben's questions about the investigation. It made him suspicious, but I couldn't risk telling him how close I was to the murder.

BEFORE

August 2015

We sail across the ocean, leaving Italy behind in a two-day voyage to the Greek islands. It's mostly just us in a great big seascape, except when dolphins play round the bow as we cut through waves. If I can just keep nature floating around in my head a little while longer, I'll hold reality at bay.

'Your hair's gone blond in the sun,' he says.

It sounds like a charm offensive coming on.

'You know those phone calls I've been making? They weren't all to chase up money.'

There was probably never any money, but I don't rise to it. Not out here in open water.

'I've been talking to my sister.'

'Your *sister*?' I look at him. 'You never said you had a sister.'

'She's my half-sister. My dad remarried, and they had her. There's a big age gap. We weren't close when she was growing up. I helped her out when my dad died and we became closer.'

'What's her name?' I can't help my curiosity, since I thought he had no family.

'Sky.'

'Why haven't you mentioned her?'

'She disappeared for a while. I didn't see her.'

'Did you invite her to the wedding?'

'She was out of the country. She's been calling the mobile, so we're talking again.'

He looks troubled. There's more to it than he's letting on.

'What's the problem?'

'She's a bit of a drama queen.'

'You don't have to get involved, not out here.'

'My dad treated her badly. She went off the rails when she was younger. I feel sorry for her. I look out for her because I'm her big brother. I've told her all about you. She'd like to meet you.'

I'm not sure what to make of this. He's a hypocrite to be phoning her, after everything he said about us having each other and not phoning people back home.

'I said she could come and stay with us in Corfu.'

'What about selling the boat?'

'She can stay while it's being sold. I've enough money for us to relax for a bit. We deserve it after everything we've come through. We can enjoy ourselves and you'll meet Sky.'

She sounds like hard work, but another person around might lighten the atmosphere. She might shake him from his mood until the boat's sold and we can come home. I'll reserve judgement until we've met.

Not long after, we sail into Corfu in glorious sunshine. Wafts of pine scent float to us on the breeze.

'We're here,' he says, as if holding back emotion. As if life will improve now we've reached the place where the sun always shines, the sea is inviting and life promises better.

I've had enough, but I'll stay until we sell the boat and raise some money. I just need to get home and then I'll work out how to separate my life from his. Once we've moored, we walk along the harbour and he calls Sky from a phone booth. I drink beer in the drowsy shade, staying remote, eyes hidden behind my sunglasses.

'She'll be here on Friday.' He sits down and signals to the waiter for another beer.

'How long's she staying?'

'Forgot to ask. Two weeks probably. The boat might be sold by then.' He scrapes his chair round to face me, working up to one of his big efforts. 'I want to show you my favourite parts of the Ionian before she gets here. I want it to be special for us.'

'What about selling the boat?'

'I'll check out that broker over there.' He nods towards a little shopfront that looks like an estate agent's window, with boats for sale instead of properties. 'We can get them over tomorrow to value it.'

The beer and heat make me lethargic, but I go for a shower that's rigged up round the back of a harbour taverna for tourists on boats. It's dark and pokey but I stay under the jet of warm water for a while. Then I go to try and sleep off the exhaustion of the trip. I doze fitfully in the muggy cabin, jolting awake in a sweat, convinced the boat is sinking. I stumble through to the saloon, where whisky thickens the air. He lies draped on the seating, eyes closed, glass in hand. Not so long ago I'd have asked him to come to bed, but I go back to sleep alone.

We set off the next morning and surf on waves with the wind in the sails. Rob brims with enthusiasm about selling the boat. He said the broker was so interested that he came straight over when I was in the taverna shower yesterday.

'He said the boat's held its value. Someone's lined up to view it at the weekend. That's good news, isn't it? I know you haven't taken to sailing, but let's enjoy our last few days.'

We anchor in a little bay to bask in warm water and the novelty of not pushing on to the next destination. Even my tense husband relaxes. That evening, the sunset reflects a firelight glow on him, reminding me how gorgeous I used to find him. He's turned back into the man I remember from the Canary Islands. It's like a replay of that idyllic first sailing trip, back when I'd joked about coming away for longer.

We probably look like a couple at ease in the world, but my ability to enjoy happier times has been blunted. My life is filtered through murky shades of denial; I blank out the worst of it for fear of acknowledging the truth. A part of me does see, a part of me knows, but the bigger part of me has shut down.

The next day, we set out on a flat calm sea. Part way there, the skies turn dark and we sail into rain. Thunderclouds roll towards us, followed by an ominous low rumble in the skies. It has me in awe of the savage beauty of the sea. Silver bolts of lightning render us vulnerable. In open water, the mast is the most spectacular lightning conductor for miles around, and my wet hands grip the great metal helm beneath a thunderous sky.

The churning sea throws us around and I look up at the pendulum sway of the mast. Water swells round us, the boat battered by waves. I don't know if it's the rain or the sea drenching us, but it's cold, wet and nasty. It brings to mind Becca's tugboat card, my bad weather mantra of the little boat keeping me safe from thunderstorms. I don't trust the sea's moods any more than I trust my husband's.

We come out of the storm and moor. The fragrance of thyme and pine-clad woods drifts down from beyond the pretty harbour where painted wooden fishing boats bob about with nets piled up. In my imagination I climb into the landscape and let pine trees surround me, their scent engulfing me.

That evening, the lights of the harbour bars reflect in the water. He's irritated by loud tourists from a flotilla of charter boats. I'm wary of anyone setting off his temper, not that I want to be cut off in his company. When he's in a dark mood, his presence intensifies with no escape. His half-sister arrives tomorrow. I hope she'll bring some light relief. I don't ask more about her because his jaw is clenched and he nurses a black look. I leave him to it, uneasy about what lies ahead.

AFTER

How do you feel that another woman stands accused of your crime? If the police don't come for you, I will.

Another email. It couldn't be Rachel, not when she was locked up. It might be her dad trying to scare me, or was it Sky? I had to show her I wouldn't be silenced. I did another search on Sky, typing in her address this time. It only turned up the usual few scant references to the murder. Ben walked in and I logged off for the night. I had to stay calm around him, and not get stressed and edgy.

We cooked a stir-fry and then watched TV, the dogs sprawled out on the rug. Ben flicked channels to a documentary about a murder investigation.

'Is this okay?' he asked.

'Sure.'

The documentary drew me in when I'd intended to zone out. I watched the painstaking police work in fascinated horror. My God, they were thorough. All those officers, determined to solve the murder and find the killer. They toiled away, pasty-faced from long hours of piecing together forensics, interviews, and scant CCTV footage. No lucky breaks, just suspects saying 'no comment', and coppers following theories with little to go on.

It made me sweat to think of my ex's murder under a similar microscope. The DCI on the TV promised the victim's family he'd do everything in his power to find the killer. Had Thornley said that to Sky?

'It's actually quite hard to get away with murder,' Ben said during the adverts. 'If you kill someone you leave a trail. These guys are tireless. It's as if they throw everything and the kitchen sink at getting the murderer put away.'

I nodded slowly.

'You're breathing again,' he said.

'I'm always breathing.'

He did an impression of me, serious-faced, his chest rising with a big in-breath that he audibly blew out. 'Like it's a big effort to stay calm around me.'

'Funnily enough, TV murders aren't that relaxing given my current situation.'

'Shall we turn over?'

'No, it's finishing soon.'

'Is that a twitch?' He studied my face.

'It's just my eyelid pulsating.' I placed two fingers on the pulsing vein, and turned back to the TV.

'It's not worth it, is it, murdering someone?'

Why would he say that, as if testing my reaction? I stayed calm, without breathing too heavily.

'It's not a rational act. You don't always do a risk assessment.'

'I bet a lot of murderers regret it. Especially if they know the victim.'

Thornley's words came back to me. *We believe this crime was commited by a woman who knew him.*

The TV police suspected a friend of the victim, who'd fallen out with him over money. The friend took too much interest in the investigation, spouting murder theories to throw the detectives off his trail. I realised the mistake I'd made, asking Thornley all those questions, seeing myself through his eyes, badgering on about Sky. Back on TV, the murderer came to justice, sentenced to over twenty years.

'At least they put him away.' Ben flicked channels to check the weather forecast for tomorrow. 'They got a result.'

'Hmm.'

'Any news on the murder?' he asked.

'No. Just a quote in the paper from that detective we saw at the beach. He called it a difficult case and said they're hoping to secure a conviction.'

'I expect we'll know soon enough.'

Ben went to bed. I said I'd be up in a minute. I wondered what forensics and physical evidence Thornley had, with no CCTV anywhere near the boat mooring. He had footprints, not that he'd followed it up, and he had knowledge of my motive. Was he keeping me as Plan B? I longed to be a fly on the wall in their incident room, and to know whether Rachel would be convicted.

I went to bed and lay awake, my mind churning. Ben slept

beside me, his breathing steady. He'd been pushing a lot about the case and questioning me. My brain created a vivid scenario in which he reported me to the police. The idea grew and grew until it felt bigger than me. Layer upon layer of dread and fear built like waves and pulled me down. I was going under. I could hardly breathe.

My heart raced at breakneck speed. A punch of pain hit me in the chest. Was it a heart attack? I tried to calm my raging heart, scared to move in case it gave out. The palpitations slowed and turned into a terrible ache at the top of my chest. I covered it with my hand to still the hurt.

I sensed the force of it ready to hit again. It happened fast – another bolt of panic right in my heart. Then the fluttering palpitations of an injured bird in my chest, trying to escape from my throat. I shook all over, my face wet with tears when I didn't remember crying.

I told myself it was a panic attack. Even as I tried to rationalise it, the unreality took hold. The murder had sent me over the edge. I began to disintegrate, my body going, a darkness where my heart should be. The bed turned into a black void that swallowed me up. It felt like a freakish dream, but I was awake, hallucinating, with reality gone. My heart pounded and I went mad, the darkness engulfing me. All the bad stuff had got to me, dragging me to the depths. Soon I would be nothing. I'd disappear.

Ben slept on. I touched him with a claw-like hand to check I hadn't disintegrated. My head felt out of sync, all of me out of sync. It terrified me, losing my mind, the divide between sanity and madness breaking down. I'd been here before, after leaving my marriage. Last time I nearly tipped into madness, and then I pulled back, not trusting I'd return.

Darcy and Stan grumbled softly in their sleep on the landing, bringing me back to reality. I found comfort in their noise, but not enough for sleep to come, not with the racing in my chest. I slid my legs off the side of the bed and felt the carpet underfoot. I went down to the kitchen. The overhead light hurt my eyes, but that was better than the dark. I made a mug of tea. Ben and I had only shared a bottle of wine, so I couldn't blame the booze. The murder documentary must have triggered it, along with everything else. Several minutes passed before I breathed more easily.

Too amped up to sleep, I turned on my laptop and looked up panic attacks to remind myself it was only in my head. Mine had a name: a nocturnal panic attack. Ben slept and I walked round convincing myself I hadn't lost my mind, even though it felt that way.

I had to get a grip so I didn't have some kind of breakdown. Ben said I had post-traumatic stress disorder, which brought on panic attacks. He first mentioned it when I started having nightmares. He'd looked it up online and showed me the web pages. Nightmares and flashbacks were symptoms of PTSD, along with guilt, rage and avoiding bad memories. I had the lot, but I never owned up to the murderous rage.

Ben only knew about the nightmares and panic attacks. But calling them panic attacks didn't begin to cover the shit going on in my head. He didn't know that when I closed my eyes I saw my ex's dead body. Ben would want to know why, but I couldn't admit why. I could barely admit it to myself.

I'd read about dissociative states, the term for my alarming tendency to slip into a strange, altered reality. It felt real, like believing the bed would swallow me up, along with my black, black heart. And the nightmares in which I was the killer, not Rachel. I closed my eyes and saw myself at the murder scene as if looking down from above. I looked terrified.

When things turned bad, my ex called me unhinged. Perhaps I was. Unhinged people didn't just hear voices. They saw things. They believed things. They might think they'd done something terrible. It wasn't just in my head. I was there and I'd wanted him dead. No one would believe that I didn't kill him. I was crying again. I only noticed because of the tears streaming down my face.

BEFORE

August 2015

Sky launches into her brother's arms at the airport arrivals, and I stand on the sidelines. She wears oversized sunglasses and a yellow sundress, her hair dyed a shiny shade of burgundy.

'It's so good to be here!' she squeals. 'Gatwick was rammed and the queue at check-in was like, a mile long. I didn't think I'd make it in time, and then they charged me extra for my bag? When I thought it was part of the price? I had to queue up again to pay for it.'

'Sky,' he says. 'This is Jess.'

'Hi!' She hugs me and grins.

We walk out of the terminal with Sky giving us an in-depth account of her flight, and how *amaayzingly* blue the sea was from the plane. She links a possessive arm with Rob as we board the bus back to the marina, so I sit behind them. She barely shows any interest in our travels, but we hear how totally exhausted she is.

'Did I tell you I shared a tent with Tamara at Glastonbury? Oh my God, it was insane. Can you imagine *me* camping? But the bands were totally worth it.'

As an only child, sibling relationships fascinate me, but this is something else. I try to like her, but she starts to grate before we've even got off the bus. She witters on about bands and what do we think of her sandals, which were the bargain of the season. My husband gives her his rapt attention the way he once used to do to me. The realisation stabs at me. I shut down a little and let her monopolise him.

'Where do you live in London?' I ask when we're back on board and settled in the shade of the boat canopy.

'Lewisham, but I want to move.'

'Whereabouts are you from?'

'Hampshire.'

'Me too. What part?'

'Near Godalming.'

'Nice. Do you flat-share in Lewisham?'

She shrugs and doesn't meet my gaze. I wait for her to elaborate, but she picks at her fingernails.

'Shame you couldn't make the wedding.'

'Yeah, well . . .'

He comes up on deck with drinks, and she talks to him about someone I haven't met. The intense heat makes me drowsy. The sea breeze doesn't travel this far into the marina. I leave them talking and go to the shower block.

Standing under a jet of cool water, I look at my arms as if they don't belong to me, surprised by my nut-brown colour, as if I've detached from my body as well as my mind. Maybe the bright white tiles and citrus zing of a new bottle of shower gel sharpens my senses. Sometimes I catch sight of myself in a mirror and don't recognise what I've become: darkened skin, lightened hair, leaner body. The person I'd been before leaving home would be thrilled with my 'beach body', but it came at a price. Beneath the suntan, unforgiving light exposes shadows and fine lines below my eyes. And my vacant eyes say my life has changed.

He holds my hand that evening as we walk along the harbour. Sky grabs his other hand. I pick up strange looks from people wondering about his *ménage à trois*, and let my hand drop. We saunter past crammed-in boutiques, and then circle back to find somewhere to eat. We'd abandoned cooking in the stifling galley, since we can eat nearly as cheaply under an awning at a ramshackle outdoor taverna, so long as we choose carefully.

The two of them face me across the plastic table. Side by side, I see a resemblance in their eye colour. His tousled hair has turned deep gold from the sun, and hers cascades around her shoulders in its vivid burgundy.

He tells Sky that Greece isn't pricey for eating out, so long as you eat like the locals and have moussaka or stuffed vine leaves. I can tell he doesn't like it, since it makes us seem cheap. He'd primed me not to tell her we're selling the boat in case she taps him up for money. She follows our lead and tries the stuffed peppers, telling us about her teacher training course. We share a carafe of house wine and Sky picks out some postcards on sale in the taverna.

'Can these be added to the bill?' she asks the waitress who

clears the table. When we settle up, she twirls her hair and smiles at him.

'Thank you. That was delish.'

'You're welcome, babe.' He sits back with a contented smile.

I look pointedly at him. His smile turns sheepish. Freeloading must run in the family. When Sky goes outside to make a phone call, I stare across the table at him.

'You're very touchy-feely with her.'

He gives me a withering look. 'We're close, that's all.'

'It's weird. Did you see the looks we were getting?'

'Who cares what other people think? She sees me as a father figure.' He checks over his shoulder to see if she's coming back.

'It's strange, the hand holding.'

'Maybe you're insecure.'

'She acts so young. It feels like she's your daughter and I'm the wicked stepmother.'

He sighs. 'I'll tell her you don't like me having physical contact with her.'

She finishes her call and sashays back.

The next morning, Sky reclines on deck and writes her postcards. She wears a bikini top and white denim hot pants that hug her curves.

'Have you got any stamps?' she asks me.

'No. You can get some at the waterfront shops near where we're staying tonight.'

He comes on deck and starts the engine. We motor away from the marina and I show Sky how to bring in the fenders that act as bumpers for when we moor against something solid. She does the minimum required, and then sprawls out on deck and closes her eyes.

'You'd think she'd want to see the coastline,' I say, knowing he planned the trip to show her the views.

'She's tired.'

'From what?'

A frown darkens his face. He looks more haggard these days.

'Teacher training is really tiring.' Her voice comes from behind me, eavesdropping on our conversation.

'Teaching will be too,' I say evenly. *Especially when you're self-absorbed.* We hit the crescent of a wave and a salty cold spray cools my arm, exposed in a strappy cotton top.

'And I look after a little girl.'

'You're a nanny?'

'Not really. I take her to school and go to my course. I pick her up later from her after school club and give her some tea. And I have her all day in the holidays.'

'The money must help, if you're doing all those hours.'

'Yeah, well. I don't get enough money.' She flashes Rob a look that I can't decipher.

He ignores her. She slopes off with one of my books and my sunscreen and slathers it on, eking out the last bit. She lies on her back with bent knees and earbuds in, tapping her feet to music on her phone. The book sits carelessly on the bow, ready to tumble into the sea. She plays a game of acting spoilt and carefree, but I see her hard edges. Her adolescent act masks something deeper that I can't put my finger on.

We drop anchor at a deserted beach and eat the Greek salad and crusty bread I prepare for lunch. Then we swim to the beach and they sit on a big shady rock.

'... and India's really spiritual. Would you like to be a Buddhist?'

Sky tells Rob about some trip she wants to go on. I zone her out. At the water's edge, soft sand clogs round my toes and I wade back in. I dive into the water and take determined strokes until my arms ache and my lungs burn for air. When I surface along the beach, they keep on in quiet conversation. Let them have their secrets. I might have one of my own.

When he'd said we should have a baby, it felt like the most special thing in the world. That was only five months ago, when things had been good between us. So much has changed, but the signs are there: I might be pregnant. I've held off taking a test. I know I'm ready for motherhood, but I'm less ready to be tied to him forever. And what sort of dad would I be inflicting on my child?

AFTER

Ben and I walked the dogs before dark. The wind rustled in the trees lining the path.

'You're not still involved with Rachel's family, are you?' he asked.

'No, I don't want anything to do with them.' I hadn't mentioned that Rachel had recorded me, which would confirm his suspicions about her.

'Those financial scams of his . . . were you involved in any of it?'

I gaped at him. 'What's that supposed to mean?' Surely Ben didn't think I'd con people out of money.

'You were married to him, you might've got sucked in without knowing the truth.'

'I'd no idea what he was up to. He was secretive.'

'And you're not?'

'We've been over this.' I pushed my fists deeper into my jacket pockets.

'It's like you're only giving me half the story, as if you're still playing it down.'

'It's how I cope.'

Ben would think less of me if he knew. And he'd want me to do the right thing when it was too late for that. Not that I meant to deceive him. Not that I told him outright lies, but a voice took over sometimes and gave an acceptable version of the truth. It wasn't a bad voice. It tried to convince me as well as him.

Nearly at the front door, I pulled the key from my jeans pocket and we came inside. I kicked off my boots and went through to the kitchen. The dogs lapped from their water bowl. I took a bottle of wine from the fridge and opened it.

'If you brush me off,' he kept on, 'I only think the worst.'

'Thanks a lot, Ben. That's very supportive.'

'You won't let me support you.'

The cracks grew between us. I poured two glasses and took a swig of wine.

'And you're drinking too much.'

I wrapped my free arm round myself, taking a defiant glug. 'How else am I supposed to get through this?'

He looked as if I'd insulted him.

I put the glass down. 'If I'm so difficult to be around, why are you with me?'

'Why am I with you?' He reached out to me. I backed away. 'I love you, you idiot. When you let your guard down, you're a great person to be with. You're kind and funny and genuine, but you've shut me out since the murder.'

'Maybe you're better off without me.' I could hardly believe I'd said it, giving him permission to leave. All my fault for putting space between us. I didn't want to push him away, but I hated lying to him. Trying to hold it together took constant effort. So tired of it all, I couldn't think straight. God knows why he even wanted to be with me. I'd be doing us a favour, letting him go.

'You'll be better when the trial's over. You can move on.'

Maybe he was hanging on until after the trial, hoping it would improve, the same as I'd hoped my marriage would improve when we reached Greece, unaware it would turn a whole lot darker.

'If you had a holiday and actually switched off instead of pretending to, you'd be able to relax.'

His curly edged travel brochures taunted me from the table.

'Ben, are you not listening to me? I can't keep having the same conversation about relaxing. A holiday won't help.' I pressed the heels of my hands over my eyes.

'Let's go and watch a film. Take it easy. We won't talk about holidays or the trial.' He hugged me, and I blinked away tears. Ben couldn't have been more different to my ex, but he was paying the price for my mistakes. I set boundaries with him that I rarely had in my marriage, as if by staying guarded I'd wipe out the past. God forbid I'd trust him. That's how it seemed when really, I didn't trust myself.

We watched Netflix. Ben dozed off and I checked emails on my phone. Another one arrived, different to the rest. The subject line said *To Ben*, even though it came to my email. Had they sent it to Ben too? I held my breath and opened it.

I'd watch that girlfriend of yours. She killed the last man in her life. Are you next?

307

BEFORE

August 2015

We tie the boat up at a harbour that afternoon. I go to where our stash of money is kept. It's not there, even though he still has a supply of cash.

'Where's the money now?' I ask.

Sky's out of earshot in the tiny forecabin which acts as a guest room.

'I told you. It's gone.'

'Then we need to sell the boat. When's the first viewing?'

'It's been cancelled. The broker's arranging some more.'

I should go to the broker and find out what's really going on. Something else occurs to me. 'Where are the passports?'

'What?'

'We kept the passports with the cash. They aren't there.'

'Oh yeah, I took them in to the yacht broker for them to photo-copy. They needed ID to prove ownership of the boat.'

I eye him with suspicion. 'But I don't own the boat.'

'No, I was just keeping them together. I've moved them to the aft cabin. What's making you suspicious? We don't need them till we go home. You could just trust me like I trust you.'

Sky comes out of her cabin and assesses us.

'We need groceries,' I say to him.

He digs into his shorts pocket and doles out some euros, and then he goes to arrange for the diesel tank to be filled. I make a mental note to find my passport, just in case. Maybe I should sneak off when he's occupied, buy a plane ticket and go without telling him. It feels like too big a step to contemplate right now. I pretend to be normal instead. He doesn't take issue with Sky's nearly-there wardrobe, so I pull out my skimpier clothes. They still look tame compared to the metallic crop top she's wearing with her white hot pants.

I put on a little cerise sundress I'd picked up at a market, and ask if she wants to get some groceries with me. We need more food with her on board, so she might as well help me lug it back. We fill two baskets in the grocery shop, including a few things she wants. At the checkout, she stares into the distance, oblivious to our need to pay. I pocket the change. It's not much, but I still have my bank card for emergencies. Walking back, we pass a kiosk that sells postcards.

'Can we get some stamps?'

'Sure. See you at the boat.' I speed up, my sandals slapping angrily on the hot pavement. When I look back, she trails a few steps behind me.

'Get your stamps?'

'No, I've only got English money, so . . .'

Back at the boat, he sits on the deck. He must have walked past us in the shop but didn't come in. It's hard to tell his mood when sunglasses shade his eyes, but he looks relaxed enough.

'Nice outfits,' he deadpans.

'These shorts are designer,' she says to no one in particular, hands on hips, looking down at them. 'I gave a rich bloke a blow job,' she says testily.

I catch my breath. Her sly eyes narrow at him, challenging him to respond. She radiates a strange, unstable energy. I look from one to the other. He ignores her. She musters all her attitude, tosses her sheen of hair and flounces below deck.

'What's going on?' I pick up a rope.

'She's crazy. I don't respond to that crap. Ignore her.'

I coil the rope into a tight, flat spiral, the way he showed me when I first learnt to sail. 'You invited her. We can't ignore her.'

He laughs, but it's more like a cough than a laugh. 'She invited herself.'

'Did she? But you made the phone calls.'

'Ignore her,' he says, but really, he's telling me to stop questioning him.

Spurred on by Sky's audacity, I don't let it go. 'But why did she say that?'

He shrugs and stands up to rearrange the furled mainsail. 'She's having boyfriend problems. She's getting her own back by coming out here.'

'Why is it your fault?'

He falls silent. I give up and watch him fiddle around with the rigging. After a strained minute, he goes down to her. I stay on deck and try listening in but only catch mutterings through her shut cabin door.

He pays me more attention when we're out that evening, draping an arm round my shoulder. He introduces me to the taverna owner – 'This is my beautiful wife' – before introducing Sky as his sister. She doesn't like it, but keeps her hands to herself. He must have told her to back off. Still, I feel the undercurrent. A secret tension lurks beneath their sibling veneer. It plays out in warning looks from him, which she returns with a defiant stare.

We have a table outside, overlooking the water. Sky blah-blahs on to him about someone I don't know, doing her best to exclude me.

'Yeah, so she's got a Shih Tzu?'

'A what?' he says.

I adopt Sky's inane tone. 'One of those fluffy dogs? They carry them in handbags?'

He gives me a look. I roll my eyes, take my beer and go to look out at the water. When I come back, they mutter to each other and fall silent with my return. I look into the distance, resisting the urge to throw my beer over them. The taverna owner comes to take our order. Sky asks him for a bowl of mussels, followed by king prawns in garlic.

'Sky!' Rob checks the menu. 'That's five times what we normally pay.'

I'm shocked and pleased all at once. She poutily studies the menu. The owner looks away and then allows himself to be distracted by another table.

'Go ahead if you want to pay for it, Sky,' I say. 'Seafood's pricey out here, and we're on a tight budget, but there's nothing to stop you using your holiday money.'

She gives me a tepid smile and carries on browsing the menu.

'Have you still got that gun?' she asks him, not even bothering to lower her voice.

He shoots her a warning look. 'I'd shut up if I were you.'

They barely speak for the rest of the evening.

Shut in our cabin that night, I can only see his face in profile in the dark.

'Hasn't she brought any money with her?' I whisper.

'She expects me to pay,' he mutters. 'I'm that much older, so I always have.'

'But you said there's no money.'

He doesn't reply.

'How long's she staying?'

'A week or two. Just while she makes a point to her boyfriend.'

'Is that what your secret chats are about?'

He turns away. 'She confides in me.'

'It's weird, the way she acts.'

'I'm going to sleep.' His voice is muffled against his pillow.

'If there isn't much money, we'd better book flights home. We can leave the boat keys with the broker.'

'We're not flying home.'

'Why not?'

'There's too much stuff I want to keep. The broker knows

someone selling a cheap car that I can insure to get us home. He'll let me know about it tomorrow.'

I flop back and he falls asleep. The need to leave urges me on. I could try to book a flight, but what if I can't get away from him at the right time? He's always moving us on. He might take us to a more remote island, which would stop me making it to the airport. And it's worse than that. He's hidden my passport. It's not in the aft cabin where he said he'd put it. I'd rather find it than ask him again, because I can't have him suspect me. He can't find out that I want to get away.

Red flags billowed in the wind, but I didn't see them at first. Then I ignored them because that was easier than making Rob angry. I knew I wound him up, but I couldn't seem to help it. He thought I did it on purpose to ruin it for him.

'Don't be one of those girls,' he said. 'The ones who turn their noses up. If you stop moaning and try to enjoy it we could have a good time.'

I didn't say anything that might provoke him; he had such a short fuse those days. I'd no one to tell me that I didn't need to put up with this control freak treating me like shit. All I had was him, but he stayed unreachable, drinking whisky, which didn't improve his mood. By then, I knew our wild romance wouldn't survive the reality of having no money, but I'd nowhere else to go so I was stuck with him on that boat.

He would've married me until he found out I had even less money than him. We had hardly anything to live on, so we only stayed in remote places. If someone came to collect mooring fees, he'd say we'd just arrived and had decided not to stay after all. He was always moving us on, especially if I talked to anyone.

Free yourself from your mother, he'd said back home. But only so he could take over. He promised freedom, and then he became my prison warden. I ended up miles from home with a man who treated me like I was nothing. The less he gave, the harder I tried.

I could just about handle living on the boat when it was sunny, but then it started raining. The Ionian Islands have hot summers and then a lot of rain to keep it lush. He told me this like I was an idiot for expecting the sun to always shine, but I'd never been there off-season so how would I know? Anyway, there's no escape from the weather when you're on a small boat in the water. There's no escape from him either.

AFTER

I returned home from our morning walk to an expensive-looking envelope on the mat. The sloping handwriting looked artistic. No one I knew had writing that nice. I took out the single sheet of paper, scanned through and scrunched it into a ball. *Shit, shit, shit.* It dropped to the floor. Darcy nudged it with his nose a few times. I paced round, gnawing on a thumbnail, and then came back to the crumpled ball and smoothed it out on the kitchen table.

Dear Mia,

I wanted to write to you about the terrible situation with our daughter, Rachel. I'm sure you will understand a little of what we are going through. If there is anything you can think of regarding who might be responsible for the murder, please can you find it in your heart to let us know? I have faith that you will help us.

You will have your reasons for wanting to leave the past behind you. We do understand. At the same time, my husband and I believe Rob's past finally caught up with him. We know very little about that past, which is why we are appealing for your help and insight. Again, I daresay you would prefer to leave the past where it belongs, but we have so very little to go on and you probably knew him better than anyone did.

Alan feels terrible for the way he spoke to you. He's always doted on Rachel, and I'm afraid he was desperate that day and clutching at straws. I'm not trying to excuse his behaviour, but I would like to appeal to you. We don't believe you're involved in any way, but do you know who might be?

I am sure you realise why I need to contact you. Rachel is locked in a living hell. We know she is innocent and we will do anything to clear her name and have her return home. Please help us. You could be our key to unlocking the mystery of what happened that night. I await your reply.

Yours,

Diane Harman

I turned the letter face down and distracted myself by making a cup of tea. The kettle hissed and bubbled, and I clutched a teaspoon, transfixed by steam from the spout. I dropped the spoon in the sink and reached for my writing pad.

Dear Mrs Harman,

My pen hovered over the pad. I'd no idea how to tell her to leave me alone. If I was too tactful she'd keep coming back, but too firm or dismissive would be cruel, or might fuel more anger from her husband. I wasn't the one to save Rachel, but ignoring her mum wouldn't end it.

The anonymous warning 'to Ben' still rattled me. Whoever sent it could have tracked down his contact details, but they hadn't said anything to him. Yet. I hadn't told Ben, driving a bigger wedge between us.

I couldn't handle any more of this. A panic attack welled up. It began with the noise in my ears, the speeding of my heart and the intensifying fear. A hot tingly sensation came before the nausea, along with the familiar grip of constraint on my chest.

I struggled to find air and bent over, lowering myself to the kitchen floor, my back against the cabinets. I had to do my breathing exercises and focus on something real. *Breathe. Look at the vase on the windowsill. What colour is the vase?* Darcy came to my side, his face pushed close to mine. I rested one arm on him.

'It's okay, Darcy.'

He panted in reply.

I thought back to what Rachel said, about the trial failing on the forensic evidence. She couldn't be trusted, but it fuelled my paranoia. Was I next on the suspect list? Thornley had mentioned the need to direct resources in the right way. Maybe they suspected me, but couldn't justify the manpower to follow through on it since Rachel had been charged.

Diane had written her address on her letter. When the panic attack subsided, I hauled myself up and went out. I drove to Haslemere and reached their semi-rural estate, so I could turn the tables on Rachel's dad to stake out his house. Not that I wanted to find him at home. I wanted to talk to his wife. A Ford Focus parked in front of the Harman's garage must have been Diane's, since Alan drove a black estate when he came round. It might be in the garage. I drove off, deciding to go back that evening.

After dark, I returned and pulled up farther along the road, like a fox skulking in the shadows. Alan had parked his pristine Volvo in front of the little Ford. It only took a quick glance to confirm that he didn't keep his car in the garage. I intended to speak to Diane alone, so wanted him and his Volvo elsewhere before I approached her.

I had to be careful, with Alan Harman looking to blame me. Where did Diane stand on all this? Her dignified letter wasn't threatening, but her daughter had fooled me. If I talked to Diane alone, I could find out what she knew about Sky, because my mind kept circling back to her.

My phone rang with a call from Mum. She talked about the park view from the flat they'd be staying in. 'I've decided there's no point worrying about the police going after that poor girl.'

'Good.'

'Did they ever question Ben?' she asked in an uncertain voice.

'Why would they question Ben?'

'Well, you know ... We were worried after Doug told him about the bankruptcy. Doug had never seen Ben so angry.'

'*What?* When did Doug tell him?'

'The day after my stroke. Ben took Doug for a pint and caught him at a low point.'

'Sorry? Ben knew about your bankruptcy before the murder?'

'Yes. Didn't he tell you?'

I stared out at the deserted cul-de-sac, dumbstruck. 'I asked Doug what was going on and he refused to tell me. Why did he tell Ben and not me?'

'He didn't mean to. They had a drink and I expect he relaxed for the first time in ages. He couldn't bear to tell you in case you blamed yourself. He swore Ben to secrecy, but I expected Ben to say something once you found out.'

'I'm meeting someone. I have to go.'

I rang off and lowered the car window for some air. It wasn't enough that Mum and Doug agreed the loan with my husband behind my back. Doug had told Ben about it and not me. I thumped the steering wheel with my palm.

Ben knew all along, and it shocked me to the core. Why keep that from me? When I told him about the bankruptcy, he could have said, 'Actually, I knew but Doug swore me to secrecy'. But he acted surprised. Did he have something to hide? When he'd questioned me about the investigation, I thought he suspected me, but what if he had his own reason to stop me seeking the truth?

BEFORE

August 2015

I brew coffee before Sky gets up, and rub my stiff neck. Rob goes to touch me. I flinch as if he's touched a wound that won't heal.

'Don't.' He stands behind me and places his hands on my neck.

I grip the counter as his fingers apply pressure to my neck. He kneads the knots and my body rocks in time with him. Sky shambles out of the forecabin, hair all over the place, and squints at us.

'I've got a bad neck too.' She presents her back to him in a *ta-daaa* gesture and he takes his hands away. 'Do me, big bruv.'

He starts on her shoulders, saying there isn't enough of him to go round. She claps her hands like a performing seal.

'Is that coffee for me?' She eyes my mug.

I lift it out of her way and go on deck before saying something I might regret. After a minute, they follow me up.

'Yeah, so, they've split up five times or something?'

'Who?' He turns on the engine.

'Patrick's cousin? I already told you. So anyway, he's too good for her.' She looks me up and down. 'He should find someone better.'

Minutes later, we pull away from the scorching heat of Paxos harbour into the relief of a breeze, leaving the sun-baked island behind. I stow fenders and coil lines, and Sky examines her split ends. She sprawls on the deck in a florescent orange bikini that makes her tanned skin glow. Sea air sweeps round us to diffuse the fireball sun. I pull my hair into a ponytail for the breeze to cool my hot neck and angry mind.

'It's lovely to be on holiday,' she calls, rolling onto her front and playing with her phone. She shows no interest in our surroundings.

'I'd like a freeloader's holiday too,' I say, not so she can hear.

'Don't be bitchy,' he says. 'It doesn't suit you.'

Pregnant or not, I'm waking up to reality. I won't tiptoe round either of them any more. I go to take the steps down to the cabin and look over my shoulder at him. 'Can you talk to her about money?'

His face clouds. 'If it stops you banging on. I just wish you'd try and be happy. You said you wanted female company. I don't think you know what you want.'

'I want a shared wavelength,' I say, going below deck. Not some idiot he's foisted on me.

The secret murmur of their voices carries down. I brace myself for her petulance, but she slips back into her girlish act.

Even simple tasks around the boat baffle her, and she kittens round doing everything wrong. It might be deliberate. He explains what to do and what everything's for. Back when he did it to me, I found it endearing. The two of them stand at the helm and he shows her how to steer a course.

'Can't we do something else?' She scowls like a bored teen-ager. With neither of us inclined to love sailing, we at least have that in common. She prefers dry land where she has an audience and can parade around, tossing her hair like a show pony.

'If you're crewing a boat you should know how to helm,' he says.

She purses her lips and swipes away at her phone. 'Can we pull in somewhere for lunch?'

'We have lunch on board, but if you do as you're told we might take you ashore this evening.'

I cringe and look away.

'Fuck's sake, you're such an old bore.' She flounces to the mast and checks her phone. With her back to us, she holds the mast for support on the bumpy sea.

'Take the helm,' he says to me, his eyes shark-like.

He goes and stands behind her, one hand above hers on the mast, bodies touching as he mutters to her. With their backs to me, I can't hear them over the sound of the boat crashing through waves.

'You wanna bet?' she snaps, and goes to the bow.

He follows and stands behind her, big hands gripping her shoulders. I go light-headed at the thought of him overpowering her. My knuckles are tight on the helm. In a blinding moment,

I picture him chucking her overboard. I don't blink, not when he could throw her over in a moment. Is that why I back down from arguing with him? I never push too far. I can hardly see her in front of him. Then her body contorts as she tries escaping his grasp.

'Jess!' She struggles to get free.

He lets her go and throws his hands in the air. She stumbles back, her face like thunder. She must be scared, calling out to me like that, reminding him that I bear witness.

'What's going on?' I say to her.

She storms down the steps. 'Where's the fucking gun?'

He tears after her. I stay at the helm and she pulls the saloon apart in a furious search for the gun. She rips off seat pads and hurls them out of the way. He restrains her from behind, clamping her arms to her sides.

'Fuck off, you bastard! I'll fucking kill you!'

'Calm down.'

'Fuck you!'

She kicks out but he holds firm, talking to her in a low voice.

I negotiate my way around a flotilla of charter boats. By the time the boats pass us, Sky's barricaded herself in her cabin. He comes back up.

'Don't ask.' He rubs his hands over his face.

She stays in her cabin for the rest of the day and refuses his offer of food that evening.

'What now?' I ask, when the two of us are sitting on a sea wall, eating warm Greek pies, fresh from a bakery. 'Will she get an earlier flight home?' In which case, I'd go too.

'She has these moods. It'll pass. She'll be all right by tomorrow.'

'Is it wise to leave her there with the gun?'

'She'll have to beat me to death with it. I've taken the bullets.'

'We need to go home too.' I stare out at the harbour. 'This can't carry on, not with the money situation.'

'The broker texted me. I'm looking at the car tomorrow. If it's roadworthy, I'll take it.'

We return to the boat. Sky lounges on the saloon seating, her phone beside her. She files her nails and looks like she'll kick off at the slightest thing. The hidden gun lies a few feet beneath her.

'Let's go ashore tomorrow,' he says.

She stops doing her nails and looks expectantly at him.

'We'll explore Corfu.' He sits beside her.

I recognise the routine he uses on me, the way he pushes me so far and then pulls me back by trying to appease me. She leans over and clings to him koala-like. Their swirling current of love and hate strikes me as strange. She watches me with a flinty, knowing look.

I wake in the early hours to Sky's raised voice. His side of the bed is empty.

'Shut up about her,' Sky says. 'That bitch is small fry.'

I listen at the door.

'You're the one who won't shut up,' he says in a lower voice.

'You need to know there are consequences.'

'*Quiet*,' he hisses.

'What consequences?' I say, coming out of the cabin. They fall silent, and I fill a glass with water. At least the gun is nowhere to be seen. He turns his head away from us both. Her look tells me to stay out of it. I'm tired of her drama, but there's more to this. I stand my ground, looking from one to the other.

'I'm going to bed,' he says.

I follow him back to the cabin, shutting the door on Sky with a resounding clunk. He turns away from me in bed, tension rising from him. Sky intensifies our problems, bringing out a dark, brooding anger in me. I lie awake for hours, my indignation stoked. My head throbs from the effort of not responding to everything she stirs up. Something's off about her, about the two of them, but I don't know what to accuse him of yet. In the dark hush of night, my suspicions grow like a virus taking hold.

AFTER

I was still parked along the road from the Harman's house, reeling from the news that Ben knew about the bankruptcy before the murder. My phone rang again. I thought it was Mum calling back, but Ben's name came up on the screen.

'Where are you?' he said.

'I'm out. Checking on something.'

'What about the film? I'm at the cinema.'

'Oh God. I forgot.' Diane's letter had distracted me.

'I thought something had happened. I'll wait. Where are you?'

'Haslemere.'

'*Haslemere?* It'll take you half an hour. We'll miss the film. Why are you there?'

I could have made something up, but the lies wore me out. What was the point if we lied to each other? 'Rachel's mum wrote to me. I've come here to talk to her.'

'You have to stay out of it,' he said. 'The police won't like you interfering. It looks bad. It looks like ...'

'Like what? Like I did it?'

'I didn't say that.'

'That's what you mean,' I said. 'Why do you keep digging for information?'

'*Mia.* I'm just saying be careful. You're all over the place emotionally and now you're forgetting about us and going off interfering in the case. You need to take a serious look at yourself.'

'Wow.' I chewed a fingernail. 'I'm all over the place emotionally? Good job you're in control. What are you covering up? It seems you knew about my mum's bankruptcy before the murder.'

He paused and took a long breath.

'She didn't realise you hadn't told me by now. She'd expected you to let on once I'd found out.'

'I was going to tell you,' he said, anguish in his voice. 'But I thought it was triggering for you.'

Triggering. Not quite 'you're crazy', but still. 'You say I'm the one covering up, but what about you?'

'What do you mean?' he said.

'Doug told you just before the murder. You kept it secret from me. Did you act on it?'

'Are you suggesting I was involved? Because if you are, that's screwed up. *You're* screwed up.'

I sighed. 'I'm asking if you went to see my ex.'

'How would I even know where to find him?'

'Doug had his address on the loan documents.'

'Mia, this is insane. Do you seriously think Doug gave me the address to go after him?'

328

'I don't know what to think, other than this isn't working. We're just not good together any more.' I faced a difficult truth: staying with Ben felt harder than toughing it out alone. The self-saboteur in me forced the issue.

'Mia, if you think I'm involved, you're crazy—'

'Is this what it's come to? You calling me crazy to cover your tracks? I don't put up with that shit any more.' If I learnt anything from my marriage, it was to not let anyone call me crazy.

'Take a look at yourself, then, and the way you're acting.'

'Fuck's sake, Ben! Do you hear yourself? My ex would talk like that to deflect blame. What are you covering up?'

'Don't compare me to him.'

I pressed my agitated fingers to my temples. 'I can't do this. I just . . . I can't . . . We have to end it.'

'We don't.'

But we did. How had it come to this? I'd become enmeshed to the point where I barely held myself together and didn't know what to do for the best. Perhaps Ben was right about me being triggered. Stuff like this sent me spiralling down.

'Just leave me alone, Ben, please.' I said it in a small, choked voice and ended the call. Pushing him away felt like severing a part of me, but hiding the truth cut me up. And what else did he hide from me?

The strain had got to me. Even if Ben didn't do it, his interest in the murder stifled me, and his disapproval of how I handled things annoyed me. I never wanted to be friends with Rachel, but that wasn't the point. My ex hated my friendship with Becca and tried to sabotage it. Since then, I'd refused to be controlled. Splitting with Ben cut me up. He resented my ex's hold on me, but surely he hadn't sought retribution. Or had he? Was he in the shadows that night when it all went wrong?

BEFORE

August 2015

I sit in the drunken heat of Corfu, the air heavy with petrol from dusty scooters and cars. Wilting tourists amble past, fanning themselves on the hottest day we've experienced yet. They shoot us envious looks and I envy them back. I have to find a way to return home.

Sky whines that it's too hot. I turn away from her voice. At least her histrionics have put a stop to our sailing. The motor isn't running so our cold drinks are hot, along with everything else. She flops down beside me and reaches over to touch my heart pendant from Becca.

'Can I try it on?'

I undo the clasp and hand it to her.

'Can I borrow it, just for today?'

'A friend gave it to me. I'd rather keep it on. There's probably a jewellery shop near the harbour if you want to treat yourself.'

She flicks her hair, hands the pendant back and goes below

deck. From my vantage point, I watch her through the perspex hatch. She simpers up to him. He goes to a hidey hole behind the seating and pulls out a small wad of notes to give her. It's not our usual hiding place for cash. Is that where my passport's hidden? She throws her arms round his neck and kisses him on the cheek. Then she skips up on deck and off the boat.

In a fury, I go to the cabin and snatch the envelope, holding it to my chest. 'I want that money back.'

He looks at me in shock, and then his face hardens. 'Come off it, Jess. You're better than this.'

'What do you take me for?'

'Don't do this.' He rakes his hands through his hair.

'She's driving me nuts and we're out of petty cash. Where's my passport? I can't take any more of this.'

'You're jealous.'

'Of that conniving freeloader?'

He laughs, his eyes flashing. 'The heat's getting to you, love.' He lunges at me and snatches the money back. 'You're not stable. I should be in charge of this.'

Before I can reply, he's taken off up the steps. The boat rocks as he leaps off. I check on his latest hiding place, but no passport, so I slam into our cabin, infuriated. My head hurts from the effort of it all. It's hard enough contending with him; I can't handle the pair of them. Passport or not, I have to find a way to get home. I go to my tiny cubby hole in the aft cabin for my emergency debit card and mobile. They're gone. The bastard.

I pull on my tired sandals and climb off the boat, bridling at his sheer nerve. My fear of what will happen sends an icy chill through me. The sun presses down as I walk through the cobbled alleys of Corfu town, past dogs that scratch and sleep in the dusty heat. The heat slows me. Washing droops from shuttered first floor windows. A few front doors stand open, revealing ancient decor in dim, fusty rooms.

I could ask a travel agent to call someone back home for a loan so I can book a flight. If I ask Mum, she'll worry. And it feels wrong to beg such a huge favour of Becca, who'll think I've shunned her after all this time. I toy with her pendant and read the inscription again. *Never Give Up*.

When I get to the travel agent, it's shut. They probably won't book a flight without my passport anyway. I keep walking to the beach and work out my next move. I lie on a recliner, hoping no one demands money for it. When I have my passport and a flight, I'll go and wait at the airport so I don't have to put up with their shit. Then I hear her laugh. Sky loiters at a thatched beach bar. She's flirting with a darkly tanned young man with black hair that glistens from a dip in the sea. For someone in a relationship, she acts very available. She spots me, and with a look of sniffy disdain, comes and lays her towel on the sand beside me.

'You wish I hadn't come, don't you?' She sits with bent knees and kicks at the grainy sand with one foot.

'We don't have jobs,' I say, thrown by her sudden openness. 'We don't have money to bankroll you.'

She picks up a tiny stone and rolls it between her manicured fingers. 'Yeah, sorry. I don't have a job either, so.'

'I thought you did child minding? When I was a student I worked in the holidays.'

God, I sound so *old*. She ignores me and rubs sand from her painted toenails. How did I assume the role of pseudo-parent when she's only nine years younger? But she's over twenty years younger than Rob. The man at the bar keeps watching. A friend joins him and they gesture towards her, laughing.

'Why do you think it's okay to act like this?' I keep my voice steady.

She bends over her toes and stifles a laugh.

'What's funny?'

'Oh, you know, nothing?' She looks past me with a sly smile.

How dare you, I want to say, but there's an opening to find out more. 'No, I don't know. Tell me.'

'Well . . . how can I put this? Let's just say some things aren't what they seem.'

I go to speak, but her admirer comes over. Her face signals interest. Before I can find out more, she stands up and leaves.

AFTER

The next morning, I drove back to the Harmans' house. This time I didn't hide in the shadows. I walked Darcy along the road and paused at their pebbled driveway. My ex came here when he'd met Rachel's parents. Had he been excited to start his deception over again? I could almost hear his easy flattery, talking to Alan about cricket or whatever sport he followed.

Darcy sniffed along the edge of the manicured lawn. You could tell a lot about people from where they lived. The Harman house looked a little too perfect from the outside. A woman with neatly styled white-blonde hair drove up and reversed a Ford Focus in front of the garage. She went inside, carrying a rolled-up yoga mat. I walked away to settle Darcy in the car, and then I went back to ring the doorbell. I willed her to let me in before her husband returned. She opened the door.

'Mrs Harman? I'm Mia Fallon.'

She peered at me. 'Alan's not here. He'll be back soon.'

'It's you I want to see. It's about your letter.'

She paused, and then opened the door wider to let me in. She led me through a smart hallway to a surprisingly modern kitchen. It looked like a show home. I thought of her artistic handwriting and eloquent letter, and wondered if she worked. She filled an expensive-looking glass kettle and dropped Earl Grey teabags into a duck-egg blue teapot.

I expected us to sit at the table overlooking the garden, but she laid the tea things on a tray and took us through to a pristine living room at the front of the house. We sat on matching cream sofas positioned around a contemporary gas fire with marble surround. I looked at the studio portrait over the fireplace of a younger, fresher Diane and Alan with Rachel and a boy, who must be her brother. Childhood photos on the mantlepiece showed Rachel as Mary in a school nativity play, cradling a plastic baby Jesus, and another of her dressed as a sweet little nurse.

'She was a lovely child.' Diane saw me looking at the photos. 'She wanted to be a nurse. She doted on her younger brother. I thought she'd be a good mum when her time came. We expected her to settle down and be happy with someone who adored her. All that's been derailed now. She did everything to make it work. She tried so hard.'

I nodded. Close up, Diane's peach-toned make-up concealed ashen skin. Mine was going the same way, with darkening shadows beneath my eyes. We could try and hide our pain with make-up, but there was no escaping it.

'He had no conscience, that man,' she said. 'He didn't care whose lives he ruined.'

'So long as he got what he wanted.'

Her gaze moved to the window and out over the empty cul-de-sac. 'All this has shattered our lives.'

'You asked if I knew anyone from his past. I can only think of Sky,' I said, 'and whether she's involved.'

She looked sharply at me. 'It's because of her that Rachel's locked up, I'm sure of it. She's a pathological liar, helping him defraud that poor widow and taking her savings. The police treat Sky like some kind of victim. Alan's been so angry … They told him to stay away from her.'

'How did it come to that?'

'She's a vindictive young lady.' She poured tea with shaky hands, spilling it on the wooden tray. It spread like blood across the varnished floor of the boat. I stopped the thought before it seeped in.

'Do you know her?'

'No, but I know my daughter and I believe her when she says that woman can't be trusted. Rob and Sky lied to her, and since the murder, Sky's been trying to get Rachel in trouble with the police.' She took a tissue from a box on the sideboard and blotted underneath the cups.

It sounded like they'd only taken Rachel's word for it.

'What happened between Rachel and Sky?' I held my breath for her answer.

'Rachel says Sky was there the night of the murder, but that she's covering her tracks by pointing the finger at Rachel.'

'Is there any proof?'

'You'd have to ask the police.'

'Don't they tell you anything?'

337

'No. Maybe you could speak to them? Make them see sense?'

No thanks. I'd done enough digging with the police and, besides, the Harmans were hardly reliable sources. Of course they believed Rachel when she said Sky murdered Rob. I still couldn't rule Sky out, but it didn't sound like Diane had even met her.

'What evidence do they have against Rachel?'

'Very little. She found his body, so she was traumatised and covered in blood. She knew nothing about his past and all his dealings, except what the police told her. She thought Sky must know, so she went to her. That's when Sky said Rachel threatened her.'

'In what way?'

'Rachel supposedly threatened to tell the police that Sky killed him. She did nothing of the kind. It was the other way around.' She shook her head at the injustice of it. 'Sky sent her threatening emails. She showed me one. It accused her of the murder and said she'd burn in hell.'

Hell hath no fury. Bitch.

'What did the police say?'

She gave a rueful shake of her head. 'They weren't interested. They took her laptop, but I doubt they care about tracing the emails.'

We sat in silence for a few moments. 'What sort of a case do they have, apart from blood stains and no alibi?'

'That's it.'

I didn't ask what Rachel stood to gain from the murder. I knew about his life insurance, but avoided antagonising Diane.

'Your husband spoke about using a private investigator. Did that bring anything up?'

'No, I don't think so,' she said vaguely. She kept looking out of the window, as if watching for him. 'You'll have to ask Alan.'

But I'm asking you. Surely he didn't keep the details from her? Or perhaps she feared saying too much.

'I can't bear that Rachel's locked up for no reason. We have the forensic evidence and experts to disprove their blood spatter theory. She cradled his dead body. The blood came from that, not from firing the gun.' She crumpled back in her chair and turned her face from me, one shaky hand over her mouth.

'I could try and speak to Sky again.'

'Would you?' She looked back at me, her red eyes searching mine, gauging my intent. 'She might talk to you. You might find something out.'

'We parted on bad terms, so don't get your hopes up. She didn't want to talk to me last time. I could try phoning her, but I don't have her number.'

'Alan has it.'

'Why does he have it?'

'Rachel had her details, and Alan's been very proactive in the case.'

I bet he had. I stood up, wanting to leave before Alan turned up.

She stiffened and sat more upright, staring out of the window. 'That's him now.'

BEFORE

August 2015

Sky puts on a coquettish act at the water's edge with her admirer. He seems to want urgent possession of her, but she hip-sways back to me. She casts a glance over her shoulder to check he's watching. Then she sits on her towel and wiggles her toes, a smile playing on her face.

'What's not what it seems?' I pick up where we left off.

She shrugs. I don't let my irritation spill over. Her love interest watches.

'Why does Rob give you money?' I ask.

'He owes me.'

'Owes you what?'

'I promised not to tell you.'

'It's important.' The urgency comes through as I grill her.

There's a long pause while the sun sears into me and she smooths every wrinkle in the towel.

'He's not my brother.'

340

A shockwave runs through me, my suspicions confirmed. They're lovers. Of course they are. The extremes of love and hate, the way they touch and whisper. I didn't confront him because he'd call me mad or jealous. But I'm not. I'm right. Sky fixes her cold eyes on me, wanting a reaction. I sit in grim silence.

'He told you he didn't have kids, yeah?'

'*Sorry?* You're not saying ... you're not his daughter?'

She rolls her eyes. 'Not me, silly.' She smiles, enjoying her performance. 'But he has a daughter.'

'Who?' I swing my legs off the recliner, ready to go and confront him.

She glances over her shoulder at the guy from the bar, and lowers her voice. 'She's called Emily. She's mine. *Ours*. The girl I look after is our daughter.'

The revelation spins in my head. '*What?* Where is she?'

She shrugs. 'Back home.'

I stare in disbelief. 'Jesus. How old is she?'

'Five.'

I press my hands to my face, trying to gain some traction on it. He'd said how special it would be for us to have a child but didn't say he already had one. And now I might be pregnant by a man who doesn't even mention his little girl. 'Why didn't either of you tell me? He could've told me from the start.'

'He doesn't tell people anything he doesn't have to. He's weird like that.'

'Are you still sleeping with him?' I ask.

'No! I've got a boyfriend back home.'

The man from the bar still lingers.

'Why didn't the two of you stay together?'

'I can't be round him all the time. He does my head in. Know what I mean?'

'Does he pay maintenance?'

'Not enough.'

'Why pretend you're his sister?'

'Dunno. Ask him.' She starts to stand up.

'Wait – hang on . . .' I lunge for her arm to stop her. 'Before we went away . . . did he ever see his daughter?'

'When he told you he was working.'

'He wasn't working?'

'Ow!' She twists her arm from my grip and rubs the red marks I've left. 'His contract was three days a week. He saw us the other two days. And he still phones her every week.' She smirks and turns to leave.

I want to push her smug face in the sand. She walks away.

'Some dad, going off for months, and wanting to move out here,' I call after her. A few people turn to stare. He really was just like my dad.

She glares back at me. 'He'll never move out here. He'll spend all your money and come home. I know him better than you do.'

'Nice of you to lie about your child's existence and not bring her on holiday. What kind of mother are you?'

She flicks her hair. I've rattled her. She comes back towards me.

'I needed a break. Why should he have a holiday if I don't?' She nods to my wedding ring. 'If you think that means anything, forget it. He's on the lookout for something better.'

Adrenaline pumps through me. I hold her stare, not letting her get the better of me.

'What with him being so good at it,' she says.

'Meaning what, exactly?'

'It's how we met . . . through a rich older woman.'

All kinds of things run through my mind. 'And?'

She narrows her eyes and looks away. 'Anyway . . . I'm not here for him. I'm only here for the money.'

She turns and walks away, leaving me to fit it together. Sky's capable of making something like this up, but I believe every word. In those first moments of comprehension, it feels like I'm falling.

I slump back on the recliner. A whole stretch of time passes me by and I barely notice. The beach empties and I regain some of my senses. I can't grapple with the impossible business of keeping my marriage afloat. This isn't my life. I don't belong here. I have to find a way to leave him.

We talked about baby names: Jack for a boy, Emily for a girl. My mother went ballistic when she found out I was pregnant. Rob said she'd soften when the baby arrived. I had morning sickness, except I had it all day long from living on the boat. We slept on the boat and ate on the boat and I threw up on the bloody boat.

I wanted to lie on a sun lounger in the shade, with the baby growing inside me. But that meant being around other people, and he didn't like other people. It wasn't even as if he wanted us to spend couple time alone. He just drank whisky and insulted me. What if I went into labour on that filthy boat in the middle of nowhere? I was desperate to come home.

When I was six months pregnant, he took us out in a storm. The boat kept rearing up on these massive waves and plunging down again. I thought we'd drown. I called him a bastard and said he was trying to kill me and the baby. Maybe he wanted me to lose the baby. He grabbed me by the hair and yelled that I was ungrateful after everything he'd done for me. He shouted at me to stop dragging him down.

I tried to sneak away and find the British Embassy. Someone said if you're ever abroad and get robbed and have no one to help, that's where you go. I only wanted a flight home. But he found out.

Rob said my pregnancy hormones had turned me crazy. He said

I was emotional, losing my mind. He said we had to stick together for the sake of the baby. But it was for his sake, not the baby's. He wanted my mum to buy us a house when the baby arrived. Meanwhile, I was alone out there with a man who didn't care about me, and I was scared of what would happen.

AFTER

Diane went to meet her husband at the door. I resisted the urge to slip out the back.

'Mia's here. We're having a cup of tea.' She followed him back in the room. 'Alan's been playing golf.'

He came and stood in front of the fireplace, his pressed polo shirt tucked into chinos. He looked suspiciously at me.

'We were talking about Sky,' I said.

He sat down and motioned for me to sit too. He steepled his hands under his chin. The Harmans had fuelled my suspicions about Sky, though I still didn't know whether she'd been involved. Maybe I did need to talk to her again, really push her this time.

'Mia said she'll speak to her,' Diane said.

'I can try phoning her, but I don't have her number.'

He nodded, less vocal now I'd been the one to show up unannounced. 'Give me a minute.'

He walked out of the room. Diane followed like a nervy pet. A headache nagged behind my eyes and into my forehead, reminding me I hadn't eaten. Craving home and Darcy, I went to the door, aiming for a quick exit.

He came back and held out a folded piece of paper. 'Here you are. She doesn't answer her phone, so I suggest you go to see her.'

'Do the police have anything on her?'

'She has a conviction for handling stolen jewellery. They won't charge her for her part in conning the other women. She's a good liar.' From the beady way he looked at me, those last words felt directed at me as much as Sky.

'Try to find out what he did to anger her,' he said. 'She hassled him about money. Did he say it had run out, which made her see red?'

Diane stood a few steps behind him, hands clasped together. 'Will you let us know?'

'If it's of any use.'

He loomed forward and opened the door for me. I walked to my car without looking back. I took out my keys and noticed how much I was shaking. Darcy woke and I petted him in the back of the car. I should have thought of Darcy, Mum and Doug before tearing off to confront Rob that day on the beach. If the worst happened and I went to prison, it would affect them too.

I sat behind the wheel and looked at the piece of paper. He'd written Sky's address and added a list of the best times to catch her in. He must have been staking her out. No phone number, and I'd no desire to go back and see her. I reached for my seatbelt and jerked back. Alan Harman lurched into my vision. I caught my breath. Darcy growled. Alan tapped on the side window so I lowered it a few inches.

He leaned towards me. 'Talk to Sky for your own good.'

'What's that supposed to mean?'

'I know you were there.'

'What?' My heart pounded so fast I could hardly speak.

'My private investigator has CCTV footage of you in the area. It's in your interest to find out what Sky knows.'

'What are you saying?'

'Just that.' He stared at me.

I forced the key into the ignition and drove off, wanting nothing more to do with him. I'd gone there wanting to find out more about Sky, but Alan was the dangerous one, making veiled threats.

I'd feared all along that CCTV footage would turn up. Even if none existed on the towpath to the boat, there would have been cameras along the route I drove. When the police arrested Rachel, I'd hoped they wouldn't have the manpower to trawl through CCTV for other suspects. But the Harmans had me within their sights.

That night I woke in the darkness, panting. *I've killed him.* I stumbled into the bathroom urgently needing to shower off the blood. So much blood. It took several panicked seconds under the bathroom light to convince myself there was no blood. I couldn't stop the shaking. It was all fucked up. I was fucked up. The nightmare felt real, like a flashback. He'd been shot, and it wasn't Rachel with the gun, it was me. The tears welled up and I couldn't stop them.

Lying in bed the next morning, I wondered if Sky had really played the victim, got Rachel locked up for supposedly making threats. It wasn't that much of a stretch for her to send menacing emails to keep me quiet through fear. That was Sky all over. But keeping quiet wouldn't help me. Whether the emails came from her or not, I had to take the direct approach. If Alan Harman really did have CCTV footage of me, I had to follow through and speak to Sky. Besides, if we had a rational conversation she might realise Rob had treated us all badly and that I wasn't the enemy. I pulled on my bathrobe and went downstairs.

The coffee brewed and Alan's veiled threat hung over me. His PI must have obtained the CCTV from privately owned cameras along the route I'd taken. Had he kept it from the police because it didn't fit the narrative of Sky as the killer? They had to exhaust that avenue first. If the police didn't go after Sky, Alan would change tack to me.

Did the footage show me driving to the beach, and then leaving the murder scene? Did my face look stricken through the car windscreen? If they had CCTV of my car, they could track me to where I disposed of my clothes and trainers after the murder.

My panic turned into anger, reminding me of how I used to feel after my ex's silent phone calls. He'd kept tabs on me when I first left him. Changing my name was a new start. He wouldn't have liked that, so he tracked me down and made silent calls to show he still had power over me. I had nightmares where he would come for me in the dark, I'd be unable to move or defend myself. It scared me half to death. I put a knife under my pillow and told Becca over mugs of hot chocolate on her sofa.

'Use scissors instead,' she said, 'so you can tell the police it's self-defence if you stab him. Otherwise, how do you explain an offensive weapon under your pillow?'

'That's mad. Americans can have a gun by their bed and all I've got is nail scissors.'

'He's still on your mind then?'

'Not if I can help it. Or just to remind myself how stupid I was.'

'The French call it *l'amour fou*, when you're so crazy in love, you almost have no choice. You jump straight in, that's your trouble. You trusted him and he took you for a ride. In my book that makes you the better person, but I knew that all along. At least you got away.'

'He could've pushed me overboard. No one would've known.'

'I'd have known. Anyway, you're alive now, which is a good sign.'

When my marriage broke up, I stopped saying his name. Becca called him 'the bastard', and Adrian called him Walter Mitty. I didn't call him anything, but he still turned up in my dreams. The unnerving stare of those laser-blue eyes would have me shooting bolt upright in bed, gasping for breath as if I'd been underwater too long. In my befuddled state, I'd wake up on the boat, feeling its sway and the swell of dread, until my bedroom came into focus. I hated those freakish dreams that still left me off-balance. It couldn't go on. I had to do something.

Find out what he did to anger her. Alan's theory about Sky rang true. My ex wound her up, and she was volatile enough to pull the trigger. Had she engineered the situation so Rachel was blamed? Rachel was the easy target, but Sky could bring either of us down. And Alan Harman could also bring me down. His piece of paper lay beside the computer with its disturbing rundown of her movements. I would usually take issue with someone spying on a woman, but I couldn't summon the energy for Sky.

I felt a dark pull towards Sky and the truth. I hated my ex for what he'd done, and Sky for colluding in his deception. Whether I could make her talk was another matter, but she might let something slip and I wanted to know. At the very least I could try and get her on side. Tuesdays were best for catching her coming and going. *Today.* My fear of being accused outweighed my reluctance to see her. We had unfinished business. I could be at her flat in time for the afternoon school run.

How had I reached this point? I'd only wanted to keep my life with Ben and Darcy safe, but my ex still stirred up trouble from beyond the grave. I thought back to Ben, how he kept his knowledge of the bankruptcy from me. Is it possible he'd exacted revenge on my ex? Kind-hearted Ben, who took care not to step on insects in the garden. But he'd kept digging into the murder investigation, even knowing how much it upset me. That wasn't like him. Mum's words came back to me. *We were worried after Doug told him about the bankruptcy. Doug had never seen Ben so angry.* No. I didn't want to suspect him, it couldn't be him. I had to find the real culprit.

In a stray moment I considered calling Ben. I missed the way we cosied up in bed, my skin on his skin. I missed his warm earthy smell and the way he murmured to me last thing at night, heavy sentences trailing off to sleep, and I would sink into slumber with him. I missed the way he had me believe everything was fixable, even me.

It all came back to that night, that last time I saw Rob before he died. When I stepped onto the boat, I'd only meant to mess with him. Show him what it felt like. But I went from seeking revenge to letting him push his agenda through, just like before. Or so he thought. Only he didn't get the upper hand because he ended up dead.

BEFORE

August 2015

I return to the boat to get my things. Sky comes towards me along the harbour wall with her travel bag.

'I'm off,' she says. 'You can throw a party to celebrate.'

I could have looked straight through her and kept going, but I stop. This is my last chance to find out, since I'll never discover the truth from my liar of a husband. I knew he harboured secrets, but I didn't know him at all. While the rest of us might keep parts of ourselves hidden, he makes secrecy an art form. One thing she said comes back to me.

'You didn't finish telling me about that older woman.'

'Oh her.' Sky drops her bag with a thud on the concrete harbour walkway. 'She used him ...' She leans forward and emphasises the words. '... *for sex*. They went on holidays. Out for dinner. He makes women feel good, but it's all about him and what he can get. He made money out of her.'

I stare at her in shocked silence.

With a look of triumph, she pulls herself up straighter, enjoying the role of arch provocateur. 'Did he tell you he's been in prison?'

'Huh?'

'He's done time. Ask him.'

What? I believe that they had a child, but I don't know what to make of the rest. His life is a world apart from mine. The woman on the mega-yacht in Capri flashes into my mind, the way he'd charmed her. Did he use the same techniques on me? Of course he bloody did. He'd made me believe we had something special, something worth holding out for. I think of how much I wanted us to have children.

'Oh, and another thing.' She adjusts her bikini under her transparent top. 'If he told you he wanted kids, it's a lie. Emily is the only one he'll ever have. He's had the snip.'

But ...

I step back from the punch to my heart. A vasectomy? I can't believe it, not when he'd held my hand and talked about us becoming parents.

'Liar,' I say under my breath. 'You're a liar.'

She struts past me with her nose in the air. Her admirer from the beach bar walks towards her, arms outstretched. Overcome with tiredness, I climb onto the boat. I feel heavy, all of me weighed down in the stifling heat.

Fucking liars, the pair of them. Don't believe anything they say.

Caught in the tumult, I face the realisation that our sham of a marriage never meant a thing. He's deceived me and I've deceived myself. I stand on the edge of devastation, knowing I have to wake up to the truth.

I root out the pregnancy test that I'd packed, just in case. I'd held off taking it until Sky left, not wanting her anywhere near if I gave him the news of a pregnancy. Then I lock myself in the bathroom and do the test to prove her wrong. A chink of defiance makes me think I can be a single parent. Other women do it. It might be my only chance to be a mum. My heart pounds out a queasy drumbeat as I hold the white stick.

Not pregnant. A false alarm. No wonder my period's late after all the grief. It's a good thing, of course it is. He'd be a useless dad, like my own useless dad. It should be a lucky escape, but relief doesn't come into it. The boat rocks. He calls my name. I don't reply. He tries the bathroom door.

'Jess? She's gone. I wanted to put her on a bus to the airport, but she's taking off on a ferry with some bloke she met.'

I get rid of the little white stick, come out of the bathroom and walk right into him. I take a defensive step backwards.

'She told me everything,' I say. 'All your lies.'

A flicker in his eyes. He turns away and runs his hands through his hair.

'Don't listen to her. She's the liar, not me.' He pushes past me and jumps ashore.

The clammy heat is claustrophobic, so I go on deck for some air. I hold on to Becca's pendant, wanting to hear her voice. I only need to get off the boat and find a phone but I can't, not after all this time.

I go to pack a bag. I take off my wedding and engagement rings, but waver. I might need to sell them to pay for a flight home, so I throw them in the bag with a few essentials. I search all the hidden compartments for my passport, tearing through them in a frenzy. It's not in any of the hiding places, nor is the money or my mobile or my bank card, kept for emergencies, since now is an emergency. Panic flares in my chest.

It turns dark and I crawl over every inch of the boat. I find the gun and see it in a more menacing light than when he first explained it away. Did he show it to me as some kind of warning? I harbour dark thoughts of turning the tables and shooting him with it. The bastard.

It's no use. He must have the passports with him, and he's probably thrown my mobile overboard again. Would the Greek police help me, or would they tell me to go back to my husband?

The boat rocks with his return. The steps groan with his heavy footsteps. He smells of booze, and holds his forwarded mail, a clutch of ripped-open bills. He spreads the red-ink demands and official threats on the table in front of me. The storm builds and I zone out the sense of foreboding.

'We need money.' He sits opposite me at the narrow table.

It's a change from saying the money's on its way. He looks challengingly at me. I turn my head, stupefied by his betrayal. A confrontation brews, but I've no idea where to start: Sky, their child, all the lies.

But I do know where to start, because it all comes back to Sky.

'How could you?' I say. 'How could you lie about who she was, about everything?'

'It's not what you think.'

'Why did you say you wanted a family with me? You've had a vasectomy.'

356

'Did *she* tell you that? Don't believe her. She's a fantasist.'

'Have you had a vasectomy?'

'Christ! This is perverse. Don't lower yourself to her level.'

'Cut the crap. She said you've been in prison.'

His jaw clenches. 'Because of her. Don't listen to her.'

'Because she's a liar, like you? Why the fuck didn't you tell me about her, about the two of you having a child?'

He sighs and rubs at his grey-speckled stubble. 'What's the point? Look how upset it's made you.'

'Because you're a fucking liar,' I shout, tears streaming down my face. 'Our whole marriage is one big lie. This trip is one big lie. Do you not see how bad it is? Do you not care?'

'It's serious, Jess. They're going to take my house.'

'Like you took mine, you bastard. Why did you lie about Sky being your sister? It's sick. And then you bring her here to, what, *humiliate* me?'

'She insisted. She had a boyfriend, so I thought she'd be okay about us. I had no choice. She threatened to tell you everything if I didn't let her come for a holiday.'

'If you hadn't lied, she couldn't have threatened you—'

'Calm down. You're an emotional wreck.'

'What were you in prison for?'

'Ignore her. Whatever she said—'

I cover my face and sob into my hands. 'Enough lies.'

'Forget what you heard. She was blackmailing me about money. She heard I'd got married and came here to play us both. It was only about money.'

'Like persuading me into this trip. Was that only about

taking money from me? Is that what you were up to in Capri, coming on to that woman?' Other women don't matter to me, but his pattern of behaviour begins adding up.

'I love you. This trip was for us.'

'All those lies about money when there was never any money. You lied about going to work when you were with her.' I've worked myself into a fury.

'Stop it—'

'You said Sky was crazy, like you say everyone's crazy, or insecure, or jealous when they come too close to the truth.'

His fist slams on the table and I shrink back. The keys and books and Sky's abandoned hair grip jerk into the air and fall back with an angry clatter.

'You're making trouble for yourself. Push me too far and . . .'

'And what? You'll kill me? Throw me overboard like you nearly did her?'

His eyes flash. I've gone too far. I shouldn't be doing this, pushing his buttons, letting him get to me. I stand up to leave.

'It's over. I want my passport and debit card and euros for a flight home.'

He lurches for me and I take a defensive step backwards. He looms over me and grabs my wrist. I pull away, but his hand clamps onto me.

'I warned you there'd be trouble,' he snarls. 'Why don't you listen to me?'

I twist from his grasp. He pushes me and I spin off balance, fall against the table and hit the floor. A series of small explosions go off in my head as I gulp air, eyes shut tight. I feel his footsteps walk away and the boat shifting under his weight. The bathroom door slams, the noise vibrating through the wooden floor. He punches the wall and turns on the shower.

A desperate wrenching sob catches in my throat and stays there until I gulp it down with a taste of blood. Feeling small, I curl up to absorb the shock. He turns off the shower. I slowly test my body; nothing hurts too much, except the great big fist of pain inside me.

He flicks off the bathroom light and I stiffen. He goes to bed, the cabin door clicking shut behind him. A single tear drops onto the floor. I should be outraged, but I take myself beyond the pain and drift into nothingness. I'm weightless. He's taken it all and reduced me to nothing. At some point, I pull myself onto my feet. I stumble backwards and fall against the wall like a drunk. Then I make it to the seating, where I stay all night.

A stream of sunlight through the open hatch wakes me early, or maybe it's the nagging ache in the small of my back. I sit up and pain throbs into my neck and head. I lurch to the bathroom and the tiny room swims round me. When I emerge, he's making coffee with his back to me. The queasy smell of gas from the cooker hangs around. I sink back where I'd spent the night and close my eyes.

'Here, drink this.'

I open my eyes, startled by his soft voice. He traces a finger over my face and I flinch.

'Hey, easy.' He holds a glass of water to my lips. I take it from him and close my eyes.

'You lost your balance. I didn't mean for you to fall. You never found your sea legs, did you? Even after all this time.' I keep my eyes closed and he places his hand over mine.

'Have a lie down in bed.' The steps creak as he goes on deck.

When he's gone, I drink more water and go to bed. It's true, he didn't hit me. I'm always unsteady on the boat, always off balance. I withdraw, unable to process the bleak reality.

'Hi, sleepyhead.'

I open my eyes to dazzling sunshine and him a hulking silhouette.

'Want some lunch?'

My head's fuzzy. I get up and sit numbed in the shade on deck, and he acts as if nothing's happened. As if squalid violence and intimidation is a natural part of our lives. The glorious weather taunts me. I stay mostly mute, although sometimes when he speaks, I hear myself saying words, I'm not sure what. He says something about leaving the boat and driving home.

'Let's go for one last sail,' he says.

I come to my senses, as if hit by icy water. We can't go out on open sea. Anything can happen. The image of his tussle on the deck with Sky pushes me into action. So easy for him to throw her – me – overboard. And easy for him to charm the authorities into believing it was an accident. *I went below deck and heard a splash. She was nowhere to be seen. Must have hit her head on the way down.*

I stand up. 'I'm leaving. Give me my passport and money.'

'No. We're going home. I know we can't carry on like this.'

360

He reaches for my hand, his eyes imploring. 'I've bought that car to drive us home. That's what you want, isn't it?'

He goes to make the arrangements, and I withdraw to another place. White noise in my head drowns everything out. Hopeless and helpless, if the world stopped turning I wouldn't be surprised. The sun shines, but it's the darkest place I've been.

'Here's what we'll do.' He comes back and crouches beside me, his hands touching mine. 'We'll sell the boat. The broker's coming to finalise it. I've insured the car for the drive back.'

Full of purpose, he loads up the car. I don't bother packing, not caring about anything. All I have is a deep well of unhappiness and no idea how to absorb the pain. Sadness washes around me. For the first time in my life, I can't see a future and I don't try.

We came home when I was eight months' pregnant. I say 'home', but we'd nowhere to stay. He said Mum would accept us when she saw my baby bump. I hoped she would take pity on me and let us stay in the barn conversion, I was her daughter after all. But when we arrived, there was another stable girl there. It gave me a physical ache, seeing that someone had replaced me. I'd been happy there, but he ruined all that.

The housekeeper said Mum was out, so she got her on the phone. She wouldn't even talk to me. I just stood in the kitchen beside the housekeeper, tears streaming down my face, saying that I'd been really stupid to mess it all up, and I wanted to make it good again. The housekeeper felt sorry for me. She held the phone so Mum would've heard me saying those things, but she insisted that we leave.

Rob slipped away while the housekeeper was on the phone. She didn't notice that he'd gone upstairs. She made me a cup of tea and was kind, but I couldn't stop crying. I'd been so stupid to give up everything and get myself in this mess. She couldn't help because it wasn't her house, and it wasn't my home any more. He looked shifty when he came back down and ushered me out.

He'd found us a shabby old houseboat on a grotty stretch of the Thames to look after for a couple who'd bought it to do up. I cried for two days straight and then my waters broke and the baby arrived early. It was the worst pain I'd ever experienced, but Emily and I came through it. He acted the doting dad around everyone at the hospital, but I could see he wanted a way out. Emily and I would never be enough for him.

Then the police turned up and arrested him. They locked him up until his trial for fraud and theft. He'd stolen Mum's jewellery. I was alone with the baby on the poxy houseboat. When I visited him in prison, he said he'd done it because she owed us.

The police said I'd conspired to rob her and had used a distraction technique while he raided her jewellery box. But I hadn't. I said we were desperate, what with the baby and no money. A social worker got a place in a hostel for young mums, and I wasn't so lonely any more.

My own mother refuses to speak to me and hasn't asked about her only grandchild. She thinks he'll reel me in again. He'd have to be dead for her to believe he's not coming back. I wish he was dead. If someone killed him, she might take me back so I could recover what I'd lost. And I wanted that more than anything.

AFTER

I caught the train to London just hours after deciding to speak to Sky again, before my resolve could weaken. I arrived outside her flat and steeled myself. I needed to stay calm, attempt to have a sensible conversation and get some answers. Knocking on her door hadn't worked last time, so I used a different approach. According to Alan Harman's notes, I still had an hour before the school run. Other people came and went. Traffic passed by on the main road close to the estate. I drank a takeaway coffee.

When she didn't appear for the school run, I almost felt relieved. Despite the wasted journey, it spared me a confrontation. Mum and Doug had Darcy overnight, but I could leave now and pick him up before it got late. That wouldn't solve the problem of Alan Harman's threats, though. If I didn't follow through, he might show the CCTV footage to the police. The sky darkened. A sudden rush of movement caught my eye. Sky stormed out, looking harassed. I followed in pursuit, ready to confront her on the go.

She came to a halt at a pedestrian crossing and fished her phone from her jacket pocket. Traffic roared past and people walked up and down the busy street.

'Sky?'

She swung round. Traffic stopped for the red light. She glared at me, turned and strode across the road. I caught up, and she looked sideways at me. Her eyes flashed an emotion I couldn't quite place. Was it fear? The London noise ceased to be, and Sky became my only focus.

'Must be tough for you and Emily, all this.' I didn't want to come across as a threat. 'I'm not here about his death. I'd like to know what went on, back when I was with him.'

She stopped and faced me, her expression hardening. 'Why?'

'I still don't get it. I just want to understand.'

Her shoulders sagged. 'I'm dropping Emily at after-school club. I'll meet you somewhere. Then you have to go. I don't want her knowing anything.'

She pointed me in the direction of a café. At least she was more direct now. The café felt overheated after the cold and damp outside. I shrugged off my coat and ordered a chamomile tea to calm me. Sky might have no intention of turning up, but twenty minutes later, she stomped in with a rush of cold air.

'I haven't got long.' She slung her leather jacket on the back of the chair, poured a glass of water from a jug at the counter and sat down. 'How did you get my address?'

'Rachel.'

'She's a bitch.' She looked at me as if I was one too. *Hell hath no fury. Bitch.*

'I don't know her. We didn't meet until after he died.'

'She's been spreading lies about me. The police locked her up for trying to influence the investigation.'

'If she's locked up, you don't have to worry about her.' I spoke in a placating tone, so she wouldn't lump me in with Rachel. She sneered and looked away. I knew she wouldn't answer direct questions about the murder, but if I could just get her talking she might start spouting off about him.

'I never knew what went on between the two of you,' I said. 'He wouldn't tell me.'

'Why should I tell you?'

'He covered up so much. After everything that's happened, it's good to talk to people who knew him. It helps make sense of it. I'd rather talk to people like you than read some warped version from the media.'

She sighed and leaned back in her chair. 'It goes back to when he was involved with *Deborah*.'

Deborah? I hadn't heard the name before. She must be another woman trapped in his web.

'He liked the whole lord of the manor thing,' she said, 'but she had him under the thumb, which didn't go down well.'

Deborah must be the rich older woman she'd mentioned in Corfu. 'Was he in a relationship with her, or just trying to con her?'

'He didn't con her as such. She had financial advisors. He'd never have pulled the wool over their eyes as well as hers.'

She pursed her lips and looked out of the window, steamy with condensation. 'He made a big play for me. He was a good laugh and we'd slag off Deborah. Pain in the arse, she was.'

'You worked for her?'

She paused and traced a pine knot in the table with her thumbnail.

'She's my mum.' She poked her bottom lip out in a pout, like the petulant Sky from the boat.

'Deborah's *your mum*?' I tried hiding my disgust at the idea of him seducing both mother and daughter. It was twisted even by his standards.

Sky kept tracing the wood grain. 'They met at a polo match at Cowdray. He didn't like horses, but he was always good with the ladies.' She rolled her eyes.

At least she wasn't trying to get one over on me now.

'They hit it off and she ended up paying for everything in return for his *attentions*. I expect he wanted to marry her so he'd have access to the money, but she didn't play along. He was fed up. Pushed his luck. Probably knew his days were numbered.'

'Where do you come into it?'

'She gave me an allowance to look after the horses. We lived in the middle of nowhere and I saw him a lot. He was at a loose end some of the time. I was nineteen and he was, like, *old*, but he had a way about him. Made me feel special.' More eye rolling to indicate how stupid we all were.

'Then what?'

'She found out and tried to stop me seeing him. We took off to Greece without telling her.'

'You don't sound very close to her.'

'We were fine before he came along. Not close. She palmed me off onto nannies and boarding school, but she was still there for me. She loved horses, so we had that in common. She paid me to be the stable girl, which suited us both.'

'And then you went to Greece. How did that go?'

'Obviously money was difficult. Wasn't it always with him?' She pursed her lips and looked away. 'She cut off my allowance. I think she hoped lack of money would split us up. I'd never worked anywhere, other than with the horses, and then I got pregnant and kept throwing up. I couldn't have worked even if we'd stayed anywhere long enough.'

'Did you tell her about the pregnancy?'

'I hoped she'd take pity on me, but she blocked me. She must have hoped he'd leave me and I'd get rid of the baby.'

'Then what?'

'The money ran out and we came home. I gave birth back here and he was arrested soon after.'

'How come?'

'There was an incident with some stolen diamonds and he went to prison.'

'He stole her jewellery?'

'Whatever.' She batted the question away with a flick of her hand. 'She didn't care about the jewellery. She wanted to keep him away from me, so she pushed hard for a conviction. Then I had Emily and we split up.'

'Did your mum take you back in?'

'No. She didn't want to see Emily. She didn't want anything to do with him. It was only last year that she made contact. I swore I'd never get back with him. Now she helps us out. Emily has her own pony that she can go and ride at weekends.'

'You must have patched it up if you visit her at weekends.'

She shrugged. 'There's a barn conversion at the end of the stable block. We stay there. She has her space in the main house and we get to be close to the horses.'

She'd barely looked at me since she started talking, her tone deadpan as if she was reeling off a few mundane facts rather than revealing a squalid love triangle. I could see why he'd go for Deborah, he'd have liked the illusion of wealth at first. But when the power imbalance got too much, he'd turned his attentions to her daughter.

It struck me that if Deborah wanted revenge, she had the means and the motive to hire a hit man. 'Was Deborah involved in the murder investigation?'

'The police would've spoken to her, but that'd be it. She's gone for full confidentiality. Doesn't want to admit he caught her out. She'd rather forget the whole thing.'

'Who do you think killed him?'

'Rachel, obviously.' She folded her arms and glared at me.

'You said he went to prison.'

'Not for long. Then he bought the boat and had this big thing about taking it out of the country in case anyone chasing him for money took it.'

'Like Margaret?' I cocked my head. 'Who he conned out of her savings with talk of Jesus and going on a cruise. You met her, didn't you?'

She didn't answer. I wondered if Deborah had been the first woman he deceived. Then he realised he could manipulate women into giving him a roof over his head. Had he manipulated Sky too or had she always been complicit? When I'd challenged him, he'd said he went to prison because of her. Not that he was a reliable source, but neither was she.

'He only wanted easy money. He was shit at earning a living. He never could stick at anything,' Sky said finally, in the same flat voice.

'Yeah, I guess it's easier to talk widows into handing over their pensions,' I replied. I thought how he had charmed Doug and my mum, who had nest eggs to raid for his short-term gain.

'Do you want to know, or not?' She kept her arms folded and looked me straight in the eye. I caught the same flash of petulance she'd shown on the boat, but it had turned to defiance. Her flintiness in Greece now had a hardened edge of steel.

'Go on.'

'He took off to Greece and you paid for it. Then I came on holiday to make a point. He buggered off when it suited him, so why shouldn't I? If you're thinking of telling the police any of this, they already know.'

'Did they interview you?' I asked.

'I've had the works. They turned up with a search warrant. They took my phone, my clothes. They covered every inch of my car. They didn't find a thing, so they ruled me out early on. I'm going to be a prosecution witness.'

The police had suspected her after all, but Rachel had been the one charged. 'Did you see him before the murder?'

'He said he had some cash for me. I had to collect it from him. When I got there, he denied it. Said he was skint. I called him a bastard and left.'

'Why would he bring you all that way just to make you angry?'

When I'd seen him on the beach, he'd offered me cash too, to give to my mum. Had he been screwing with both of us?

She sighed and ran her fingers through her hair. 'He was a bastard, but I'd no reason to kill him. He's Emily's dad. A useless dad, but it's been tough on her. He gave us money when he had it. He wasn't a total deadbeat. Emily gains nothing from his death. Rachel was the one with life insurance on him. And she lied to the police.'

'About what?'

'About me killing him! Rachel's all butter-wouldn't-melt to the outside world, but don't be fooled. She deserves to be locked up.'

Gone was the monotone; talk of Rachel had riled her up.

'She only cared about the money. He pretended he was loaded to reel her in, like he always did. But unlike you, she made him keep his promises and he got into even deeper shit to keep her happy. Stupid fuckers, the pair of them.'

'But she's in prison. She could be put away for a long time.' *This isn't about petty rivalries*, I wanted to say. I caught her eye but she wouldn't answer. 'You can't give evidence against her just because you're jealous she married him.'

'She's guilty,' Sky snapped. 'The police told her about all his scams before he died. She lost it with him.'

'How do you know?'

'He told me. Said he had enough on his plate with her. He wasn't interested in me. I reckon after he promised me the money, she found out and made him go back on it.'

'Do you really think she shot him?' I said in a low voice.

She leaned forward, palms pressed on the tabletop. 'She's guilty.' She pushed herself up by her hands and yanked her jacket from the back of the chair. 'I don't want you coming back.'

I almost laughed. I'd no intention of coming back.

'If you say anything about me to the police, I'll tell them you were in on it. His scams. I'll say you were guilty too.'

I returned her nasty stare. 'Those anonymous emails I told you about, are they from you by any chance? Because whatever you're trying to do, I won't be intimidated.'

'I don't know what the fuck you're talking about,' she said before turning and walking out.

I strode back to the station in the dark and dissected what Sky had said. I'd never trusted her, so how could I now? She could be lying about everything, and yet her story about Rob and her mum rang horribly true. Somewhere amidst the lies and exaggerations was the real story.

It surprised me that the police had investigated Sky. From what Diane had said, they'd been on her side from the start. If Sky had done it, surely they would have found traces of his blood from the gunshot wound? She would have needed a shower and a change of clothes to make it home without taking any evidence with her.

Two hours later, the train pulled in at the station. I felt exposed walking alone at night without Darcy, who would stay the night with my mum and Doug after all. A prickling on the back of my neck kept me checking over my shoulder. I walked faster. Trees lining the deserted road cast eerie, swaying shadows. I reached the top of my street, out of breath and relieved to be nearly home. A man loomed towards me. I pulled back in horror, gearing up to run, lash out—

'It's okay. It's me.'

Alan Harman. My heart pumped. I clutched my chest.

'What are you playing at?' I backed into the middle of the empty road.

'Sorry!' He held up his hands. 'I just wanted to know if you've seen Sky.'

'Jesus Christ. You're stalking me as well as her.'

I strode down the middle of the road, wanting to get home and away from him.

He came after me. 'Please! Diane and I hoped she'd tell you something. Did she let anything slip?'

I stopped at my front gate, feeling safer under the streetlight in front of my little mid-terrace. Spring buds had formed on the dwarf magnolia that Ben planted in my tiny front garden. I told Alan everything Sky had said, leaving out her threat to tell the police I was involved in his scams, in case he used it against me. I had to keep him on my side. He nodded soberly, his face shadowy in the dark.

'If the police are so hot on forensics,' I said, 'why didn't they find anything when they went over her car and flat?'

'They didn't look hard enough.'

'What did Rachel do to upset her?'

'She married the wrong man and planned a family with him. Sky couldn't handle it when her own life was a shambles.'

It sounded weak. Had Sky told Rachel about the vasectomy? Sky's timing had been impeccable when she told me.

'She said Rachel lost it with him when the police told her about his crimes.'

'Yes, well.' He looked defeated. 'She would say that.'

'Listen, I've done what you wanted. I don't know who killed him, but I know it wasn't me.'

He took a step back, ready to leave.

'I can't do anything more,' I said. 'Can you please leave me alone now?'

He turned and left without acknowledging my words. I watched his dark figure recede into the night.

I went indoors, creeped out by him lying in wait. What else could I do to keep him away from me? Something stirred in the back of my mind. Sky mentioned the barn conversion at her mum's property. She'd told me on the boat she was from Godalming. If her mum still lived there, Sky could have come off the A3 on the way home. She could have showered and cleaned the car at the stables, perhaps without her mum noticing. If she treated it as a weekend retreat, she might have kept clothes there to change into before driving back to London.

If Rob hadn't come along, I'd have been happy in my little home beside the horses, riding Chester along the woodland paths. How did one stupid decision change all that? He had me believe that he loved me, that he could give me a better life. But I realised too late everything I'd lost.

When he went to prison, I was on my own for the first time in my life. I had to toughen up. I toned down my plummy accent, became streetwise and learnt to navigate the system for benefits, which is hard with dyslexia, but Emily and I managed. Later, I stayed alert to his manipulations, I saw what he did to other women, like Margaret. I watched him break out the charm that had worked on me. It helped me wake up to the way he'd sucked me in.

And then he married Jess. I didn't think I'd ever go back on a boat, especially not with him, but things had changed. I had a return ticket and my own home, I wasn't pregnant and I wasn't putting up with his shit again. He had Jess for that. With his new wife in tow, when he fucked with my head, I threatened to tell her everything.

I liked the power balance in my favour for a change, so I could exact revenge. Jess was collateral damage, and I did her a favour by telling her what he was really like. The stupid bitch needed to wake up. That felt good. Like therapy, because I can't afford actual therapy. I played him at his own game and showed him he didn't always have the upper hand. I wasn't under his spell any more.

I didn't know shit back when I first met him, but he taught me that nice, trusting girls get nowhere. Now he's dead and it serves the bastard right. I know I shouldn't think like that, but he made me like this. He made me bad.

BEFORE

I've been lost at sea and it's time to find my way back. We leave the boat in Corfu and travel by car in one glassy-eyed stint, by ferry to Italy, and then through Austria in darkness. After months of heat, the bracing cold revives my senses.

We pull into a layby and sleep in the car. Then at daybreak, he speeds us along French highways. As always, he won't engage with the grief he's caused, not that it matters now. There are no words. I can't articulate the pain so I don't speak at all. We travel in a bleak silence.

I've been hanging on when there's nothing to hang on to. I try to blot it out. I can blot out most things, apart from the sadness that never lets go. Shattering pain adds to grief and I bundle it up and pack it inside me until it's a muffled howl.

'It'll be better when we get home,' he says, driving us to the Channel Tunnel. 'I can access some money in an account. We'll get jobs. It'll be okay.'

I gaze out at the road ahead.

'And you've got money left, haven't you?'

'In my bank account.' I only say it so he'll get me home. Anyway, he has money when he needs it, for the mobile, the car, and the trip home. I'll phone the bank and cancel my debit card that he hasn't returned. I'm not stupid enough to give him anything else. At least I took back my passport when we went through the first customs check. I begin shrugging off my denial, exposing a rawness in me.

Our journey takes us to a gloomy Dover and the strange familiarity of being on home ground while I still feel detached from everything. I must have fallen asleep because when we pull up in front of his house, I jolt awake with a deathly sense of dread.

It's not the relief I expected. We're not on the boat any more, but I still feel trapped by him. His place wasn't like home before, and is less so with our return. His sparse collection of furniture jars with the displaced contents of my house. At least I didn't sell everything in his asset-stripping exercise. He goes off to 'sort out some money'. I curl up on the spare bed and fall asleep.

When he returns, I stir myself but can't get my head into gear. I shamble round, a crumpled version of my former self. I absently touch my work clothes in the wardrobe, as if looking at items on a shop rail. My fingers shake as I touch them.

'We'll make a go of it again,' he says from behind me.

I turn, clenching my fists to stop the shaking.

'Sky messed it up. She put pressure on us. We can pull it together. Don't leave me, Jess.'

Leaving him is the one thing I have to do.

*

The next morning, I wake early. I pick up the landline in the hall, but it's dead. Cut off. Then I see the pile of red bills stacked on the shelf below it. He picked them up when we came in yesterday, but I'd been too tired to notice what they were.

I creep into the bedroom and pick up his mobile beside the bed. It still works. He doesn't wake. I go on the balcony and slide the patio door shut behind me. I shake all over. It might be the cool morning, but I've been jittery since coming home and it's getting worse.

Two chairs sit on the forlorn balcony where we used to have animated chats about going sailing and starting the business. We would look out to sea, sharing hopes and dreams. I call my mum, who answers after a few rings.

'Mum, it's me. We're back.'

'You're back home? What's wrong? You don't sound right.'

How can she tell? I've only said a few words.

'Are you sick?'

'I'm tired. Long journey. I haven't slept much.'

'Is it a bad line? I can't hear you properly.'

'Is this better?' I say a bit louder, checking he's not listening on the other side of the door.

'Why are you back?'

'We decided against starting the business. We'll look for jobs.'

'Are you okay?'

Rob appears and goes through to the kitchen, ruffling his hair. I huddle on one of the chairs, pretending to look at the view the way we used to. Tears prick in my eyes, but I can't tell her anything, not with him almost within earshot. 'I'm fine.'

379

'What about money?'

'We'll get jobs, like I said.'

He'd promised to find work and start paying me back. The money is the only thing I can salvage so I can live somewhere else, not that I believe his promises any more. I end the call. He slides open the patio door and comes out holding two mugs of tea.

'My mum,' I say, laying the phone on the armrest of the wooden chair.

'Right.' He puts the mugs down, leans over and hugs me.

I stiffen.

He keeps one hand on my shoulder. 'I'll make some calls about work. Chase up my contacts. It's a new start, us coming back.'

That might be his new start, but mine means standing up for myself. I don't care what happens when I confront him. I go back inside and pick up a handful of red bills.

'What about these? All the money owed. All the money you took from me.' My voice shakes. 'How's that a new start? You said equal shares for the trip but you've bled me dry. I sold my house and I've nothing to show for it. And all the lies . . .'

'Jess.' He holds his arms out in a conciliatory way.

Does he not see how bad it is?

'And you blame Sky? Seriously?'

He stands in silence. I take his keys and go to unlock the garage. We'd crammed my furniture in there before leaving. The bin liner of brown envelopes still leans against the tatty grey filing cabinet. I pull the middle drawer open. The hanging

380

files are gone, the drawer stuffed with musty unopened post, probably dating back years. His accountant doesn't sort it out, as he'd once said. Nobody does.

I stand in the neglected, damp garage, one hand holding the drawer handle. Buried anxiety bubbles to the surface, causing a breathless, jittery panic. If I stay still and hold on to something solid, it'll subside, but the shaking refuses to go away.

A car pulls up outside. Doug gets out, alone and looking more tense than I've ever seen him. I expect a *welcome home*.

'Are you okay?' He peers at me.

'Fine thanks, Doug. How are you?'

He looks up at the house where my husband stands at the top of the steps, and then he turns back to me.

'You're so thin. Are you ill?'

'It was too hot to eat much.' I wave away his concern, but his horrified eyes say it all. 'Come inside, I'll put the kettle on.'

'Actually, would you mind leaving us alone?' He looks back towards the house, his fists clenched like mine.

'I'd like to stay.' I go ahead of him. Doug coming here won't help. I shoot a warning look at Rob to say *keep it civil*. He pulls himself up straight and keeps one hand on the front door. The two of them stay in the hall with me looking on.

'If you're worried about our finances,' Rob says in a perfectly reasonable tone, 'it's okay. We'll have money coming in soon. Tell Rose it's fine and it'll be sorted. I won't hear anything else on the subject.'

Why would they be worried about our finances? How would they even know?

Doug looks from him to me. 'Jess, your mum says you're very welcome to come and stay with us.'

'She lives here,' my husband snaps. He holds the door wider as a prompt for Doug to leave.

'Bye, love,' Doug says to me, his eyes weary, looking old and hunched up.

I want to cry at his reaction. Rob shuts the door and faces me. At least he didn't ask Doug for money. I don't want them involved, even though I have to get away.

'Why was he worried about our finances?'

'Your mum picked it up from you when you phoned her. This is what happens when other people get involved.'

My mum could tell from my tone that things weren't right. Running out of money is the obvious reason to come home, and Doug must have come over to put her mind at rest. All he'd done was rattle Rob. The house is thick with tension and as claustrophobic as the boat.

I'd made a monumental effort to seem normal on the phone with Mum and just now with Doug, but their reaction pulls me up. It didn't take much on the boat to maintain a veneer of being a couple. Back around people I know, the pretence is obvious and I can't carry on.

'How much money have you got?' he says, his voice cold and challenging.

'None. You've taken it all.'

'You'd better get a place of your own, then.'

I gasp at his nerve. 'Gladly. Pay me back and I'll go.'

He grabs me by the throat and pushes me against the

window. His thumb digs into my jawbone, my neck rigid in his grip. I freeze as his face looms close to mine, his eyes white-hot.

'Watch yourself. If this carries on, I might end up killing you.'

He's chillingly calm, which is somehow worse than his anger.

A crunch of gravel outside. In a blurry moment I see the couple next door, who I've never met. They hesitate. I glimpse their anguish as they wonder whether to intervene. I should be feeling the same, but I don't feel anything.

He lets go and walks out. I sink to the floor and hug my knees. Time passes and I become so cold my blood might have stopped flowing and the chill comes from inside me. From childhood, I've had my life mapped out, but now I've nothing ahead of me and life hurts too much. He's pushed me to the edge, but a tiny, defiant part of me keeps going. I touch the pendant around my neck and grab the mobile he left behind in his rush. I dial a number I know by heart.

Becca.

Becca, who'd never liked him. Becca, the voice of reason.

'Hello?' Years of friendship come through in her voice.

'Becca . . .'

'Yeah, who's that?'

'It's me. Jess.'

'Jess? Jesus Christ, you sound awful. Where are you?'

'I'm back. I don't know what to do . . .' My voice tails off.

'What's happened?' she asks, and I don't know where to start.

That night, I don't make it to bed. I crouch on the floor of Becca and Adrian's spare room and hold on to my ankles. I stay pressed to the wall, needing something solid to stop me falling apart. The next morning feels like death, so I shut myself down some more.

Adrian borrowed a van from a friend, who helped him move my belongings out of the place I'd never considered home. Cocooned in their kind efficiency, I bundle up the shattering pain and pack it inside me until it's a muffled howl. That's where it stayed until the day I saw Rob on the beach.

AFTER

After splitting up with Ben, I put in more hours at work and stopped going out socially. With my mind occupied at work, the waves of panic subsided, if only for a while. I liked dealing with problems that were solvable. It gave me something to hold on to. The managing director of my biggest client phoned to ask me to spearhead another project.

'Our approval ratings have never been higher,' he said. 'You've really changed public opinion.'

He would be less impressed at finding out his expert on avoiding scandal was caught up in one of her own. But the extra work was welcome. Aside from anything else, I needed the money so Mum and Doug would have a place to live.

The sunlight gave way to a gloomy afternoon. I tried to power through with a healthier mind and body, taking a sip from my mug and grimacing at the bitter taste of green tea. Healthy habits didn't ease my paranoia. My brain was stuck on overdrive, my hands shook, and my ragged, bitten-down fingernails hadn't looked this bad since childhood. I went to bed last night expecting the police to break the door down in the early hours. Didn't they do that sometimes, when arresting a suspect? I woke up thinking, *What if they come for me today?*

And they did come for me. The doorbell rang out through the house. Darcy shot up to investigate and I followed. DS Thornley stood on the doorstep with his dour sidekick.

'Can we come in for a chat?' Thornley gave a tight smile.

Fear rained down. They sat in their usual place on the sofa, and I sank onto the other one. My fingers dug into the seat cushion. I fixed my gaze on the floor, willing the dizzy panic to ease off so it didn't become a full-blown attack.

'Are you okay, Mia?'

'Bit lightheaded,' I said. 'I haven't eaten.'

The DC opened her notebook, all businesslike. 'We've come to check on what you previously told us regarding the murder of Rob Creavy.'

They'd worked through the suspects: Rachel, Sky and now me. Had Alan Harman finally shared the footage? What a fucking nightmare, even worse than my actual nightmares. *It's okay. Breathe.*

'Did you see him the day he was killed?'

I couldn't lie any more, but I didn't want to say it out loud. My fingers still gripped the sofa edge. Thornley looked at me as if I were a problem to solve. My mind made giant leaps, expecting the worst. I braced myself for the handcuffs.

'Specifically,' the DC said, 'were you at Stonebeach Head at around 3 p.m., talking to him on the shore?'

I swallowed. 'Is this about the other woman who was seen with him?'

Thornley studied me. 'Are you the other woman, Mia?'

Should I deny it? No one saw me close up. Even Rachel didn't come that close. If she'd changed her story about it being Sky, surely they wouldn't believe her? And she was the one covered in his blood. But I couldn't deny the CCTV if Alan really had tracked it down.

'Did Rachel's dad say it was me?'

Thornley raised an eyebrow at me. 'Why would you think that? Is he bothering you?'

I'd been gripping the cushion so tightly, my hands hurt. I clasped them in my lap instead.

'He'll blame whoever he can so long as Rachel's freed.'

'Strange how your name keeps coming up in the investigation,' DC Roper said.

'Sorry?' My voice thickened with emotion. The room felt oppressively warm.

'Didn't we tell you to stay away from the Harmans?'

'No. You said to stay away from Rachel Harman, which I did. Her dad's been hassling me. He threatened me and followed me the other night. He's trying to point the finger at me.' I blurted it out in an indignant rush. *Pull it back, you idiot. Shut up and act normally.*

Thornley watched me turn into a red-hot mess. I wiped sweat beads from my top lip and wrestled my emotions under control. Sweat trickled down my spine. I had to change the subject from Alan Harman.

'When I spoke to Sky, she said something . . .'

'You spoke to Sky?' Thornley asked. 'When?'

'Tuesday.'

'Why did you speak to her?'

I took a deep breath. 'Because Alan Harman was hassling me. He wants to blame someone else for the murder, so he's got a private investigator onto Sky. I felt intimidated by him. He pushed me to talk to Sky.'

'What did she say that's so interesting, then?' Roper asked, her voice cocky.

'It might not be anything. She said you'd gone over her car and flat but couldn't link her to the murder. Then we talked about her patching things up with her mum. She said she uses a barn conversion beside her mum's stables. It might be in Godalming. I wondered if she'd stopped there on the way home to get rid of evidence.'

'What did she say to make you think that?' Thornley asked.

'Nothing. It was just a thought.'

Roper scribbled in her notebook.

'Mia?'

I looked at Thornley, expecting to be warned off again.

'We know it was you.' He gave me a meaningful look.

'What?' My face burned. All of me burned.

'We know it was you on the beach.'

They didn't understand, or they understood too much.

'I didn't kill him.'

'Is that why Alan Harman's been hassling you?'

I nodded and looked at the floor.

'We need you to come to the police station for an interview under caution. Shall we say 11 a.m. tomorrow?'

I murmured in agreement. I should have been upfront when they first came here, but I'd panicked and dug myself an even deeper hole. They left, and I sat with my hands over my face for a long while. And then I went online to find a solicitor specialising in murder defence.

I scoped out a legal firm and called them to outline what had happened. We set up a meeting for first thing in the morning. Then I made another call, needing a rational perspective.

'Hi, Becca.' I struggled to stop my voice shaking with the rest of me.

'Hi, are you okay?'

'Not really. The police have been round.'

'What happened?'

'You know they did that appeal ... about another woman seen on the beach?'

'Oh God.' Her voice went low and breathless, as if she'd already guessed it was me.

'They think it was me.'

She stayed silent.

'And?'

'They want to interview me under caution.'

She paused for a few beats.

'Bec?'

'Yeah?'

I hesitated. 'You haven't asked if it was me on the beach.'

'No.'

'Why not?'

'If I were you, I'd have killed him.'

'You think I killed him?'

'Honestly? You've been acting pretty weird since the murder. And I wouldn't blame you for killing him.'

That came as a blow. 'I didn't kill him.'

'That's all right then, you're in the clear.'

But I wasn't in the clear. Knowing Becca, she'd suspected all along but hadn't pushed me to tell her. Back when I'd left Rob and stayed with her and Adrian, I'd wished him dead and said as much to them. Adrian had told me I shouldn't say things like that, so I kept quiet ever since. I stopped saying it in the hope I'd stop thinking it. But I did want to kill him. I wanted him dead.

BEFORE

My husband didn't let go easily. A few weeks after I left him, he tracked me down and called Becca's landline, not bothering with a charm offensive. Becca hung up. He sent a letter urging me to remember the good times. He said I'd overreacted, that I couldn't manage without him, and I owed it to us both to give it another chance.

'Another chance? You've got to be fucking joking, mate.' Becca gets her lighter out and makes me burn the letter in the garden.

'Stay strong,' she says. 'We'll help you. That's what mates do.'

I've started a new job at a design and print company. It's a backwards career step, but I'm rebuilding my life. When I put on a suit, I can just about relate to the professional person I used to be, enough to get me through until I shore up my confidence. Underneath the composed layers, I exist in a twilight world where all that matters is getting through the next hour and the one after that, then getting through the day and the one after that. I inch forward, to the outside world at least, while my interior world seethes with hurt and failure.

We burn the letter and leave the blackened scraps to wilt in the drizzle.

'You'll get through this.' Becca locks the back door. 'And when you're ready, you'll find a decent man.'

The thought turns me cold. We sit at the kitchen table.

'Or,' her face lights up, 'a sperm donor.'

'What's a sperm donor?' Ellie trundles through, dragging a tatty doll by its foot, the doll's head bumping on the floor.

We laugh and it feels like a release. Ellie kneels on a dining chair to laugh with us, the glee of being funny outweighing the need to know why. I pull her onto my lap and don't feel alone now I have them back.

Becca gets up to make hot chocolate and Ellie goes along to 'help'. The rain becomes heavier, mingling with the sound of traffic passing by on the wet road. Becca hands me a few pages torn from a glossy magazine.

'Here,' she says.

I start reading the cutting, dated a month before I'd sold up my life and we'd left on the boat. LONELY HEART FRAUDSTERS, the headline says. It highlights the dangers of a certain type of man who targets his prey and sweeps them off their feet with empty promises.

According to the article, he has their joint future mapped out from the start. Reading it in black and white, a normal person might wonder who would fall for that. But I did. Romance, illusions of success and the promise of a new life help the conman wangle his way in. Once he's hooked his victim, he alienates her and keeps her controlled with a dark undercurrent. Caught up in the passion, I'd ignored the signs. I want to scrunch up the pages and shoot the bastard with his own gun.

Becca stirs hot chocolate into mugs and busies herself with Ellie, who hangs off her leg. 'Sound familiar?'

'You can't always see it when you're that close,' I say by way of an acknowledgement.

Becca settles in front of me at the table. 'Will you ever get over him?'

'Yes. But I might not get over what he did.' I sip hot chocolate and smile at her. 'Can we talk about something else?'

'How's the job going, career woman?' She nudges me with her foot.

'I'm getting there. It's not ideal, but I'll work it out.'

'Course you will. You'll make it work.'

I doggedly get back on track, professionally at least. My feelings are a different matter. After suppressing everything for so long, I'm cast adrift on a great big sea of emotion. I cry when cleaning my teeth, waiting in a queue and often after putting on mascara. The tears on tap stretch to crying at other people's misfortunes. I stop watching the news because any kind of tragedy starts me off. I do private emotion best, helpless spasms that go on and on until my head throbs, my eyes hurt and I feel wrung out. Regret crowds in, and it'll take more than crying to get over it.

When I babysit Ellie and Jake the next evening, the phone rings.

'You can't hide from me.' His deep voice sounds danger-ously close.

He catches me off guard. I know he's been drinking from the slackness in his voice. I can almost smell the whisky.

'Come back, or I'll come and get you.'

My heart nearly hammers out of my chest. I scan the pitch-black garden through the kitchen window.

'Don't leave me, Jess.'

I wordlessly hang up, and a fragment of memory returns. Him coming towards me. The smell of whisky. A fall colliding with a surge of pain. The varnished wooden floor of the boat, cool on my cheek as I gasp for air. Rigid with fear. The *boom-boom-boom* percussion in my ears. A wave of nausea subsides by degrees. Metallic taste in my mouth, the taste of blood.

My memories of that time are patchy. Time and sequences dislocate and blur. Some things I remember clearly, but not the worst of it, and those times are my haziest recollections. In my self-preserving mind, they are dreamlike sequences. I flinch from memories – happy, sad and bad – and bury them deep so they'll die of neglect. But his call marks a line in the sand.

Instead of slipping into my pattern of denial, I report it to the police. It turns out the couple next door who saw his aggression through the window had reported it. They worried because they never saw me again. When they asked after me, he acted as if they'd imagined it. The police visited him and he denied intimidating me. My divorce solicitor takes out an injunction, and I vow never to let my ex get the better of me again.

I progress from victim to vengeful, from wanting to die to

wanting him to die. I hate him. The thought of him still living in his house while I lodge with Becca and Adrian makes me clench my fists so hard my fingernails leave purple half-moon imprints in my palms. I've never been a violent person, but I want to kill him with my bare hands. I lie awake trying to summon up the perfect murder. What I really want is to make him suffer and have him know he deserves to die. My secret torrent of revenge runs as thick as blood.

The hating goes on, past anonymous calls when he tracked me down to my new home. It intensifies on the day of our divorce hearing, him all lethal charm in a sharp suit. He flashes a winning smile at his divorce solicitor, then raises his chin raised defiantly, refusing to look me in the eye. I know that whatever is resolved in that room, there will still be a score to settle.

My life is a long way from where I want it, but I begin taking back control. It makes me angry that the person responsible is off the hook. It fills me with a rage so savage that had he been nearby I might tear him apart. But I don't act on the corrosive anger. I had it under control until the day before the murder, when I found out what he'd done to my mum.

AFTER

I arrived at the police station to be interviewed under caution. My newly appointed solicitor had already advised me of the seriousness of the situation, as if I didn't already know. She said I wasn't helping the police, I was being interviewed as a suspect. DS Thornley and DC Roper sat opposite my solicitor and me in the interview room.

'You do not have to say anything,' Roper trotted out the words of the caution, 'but it may harm your defence if you do not mention, when questioned, something which you later rely on in court.'

No more covering up. A strange calm descended on me as I prepared to tell them the truth.

'Mia,' Thornley said. 'We've asked you to come here to answer questions regarding the murder of Rob Creavy.'

I tried to stay composed.

'When was the last time you saw him?'

'I last saw him in January, on the day he died.'

'When we first met you, you said you last saw him two years ago. Is that correct?'

'Yes. Before that day in January I hadn't seen him for two years, not since our divorce hearing.'

'Why did you lie to us?'

'I thought you'd accuse me if you knew I'd seen him that day.'

'Why did you go to see him?'

'I wanted to confront him about my mother and stepdad. He ripped them off.'

I wasn't a violent person, but in the aftermath of discovering the bankruptcy and Mum's stroke, I could have gouged his heart out with a kitchen knife. I'd lain awake wanting to kill him in a murder so perfect that no one could pin the blame on me.

'Did you arrange to meet him there?' Thornley asked.

'Yes. I called him, swore that he'd pay for what he did to my mum.'

'Pay? How?'

'Compensation. Money for them. He agreed on the condition that I meet him face to face, so we met at the beach.'

'What happened?'

I readied myself to tell him what happened. I should have told him from the start, but I'd made some really bad calls. Something about Rob brought out the worst in me and screwed up my decision making. He went round demanding a reaction, culminating with the biggest reaction of all. I'd had enough of paying the choking, all-consuming price of not telling anyone how I'd fucked up. It was time to come clean.

BEFORE

I head to the beach, my heart pounding with rage and fear. He calls my name and I spin round. It's unmistakably him, yet he looks diminished, his faced puffed up with medication or booze. The rugged good looks I couldn't get enough of have faded. His decline startles me, his face ruined. We stare at each other, me in glinty defiance, his eyes bloodshot. Seeing him takes me back to where I don't want to go. But I'm the one who tracked him down.

'Hi,' he says.

I arrived early to get my bearings, not expecting him to creep up. I dig my hands into my coat pockets and feel my phone, which I'd turned off. I didn't want to hear from Ben or anyone else in case I had to sound cheery and normal.

'How are you?' he asks.

I clear my throat to check my voice still works.

'Fancy a brew? We could go to the boat. Old times' sake,' he says.

I back away, even though I'd agreed to meet him here on the shore. He didn't sell the boat in Greece after all.

'Don't go. Let's walk along the beach. Can we?'

He looks as if he needs to talk to me. I tell myself I can just walk away if it gets too much. We crunch over shingle. He walks like a drunk and comments on the sea.

I find my voice. 'I don't need small talk. Not after what you've done.'

'Yeah, right. Turn me into a bastard.'

I stop dead and face him, the wind whipping strands of hair across my face. 'It's bad enough what you did to me. But bringing my mum into it—'

'Heard it all before.' He stares into the distance.

'You said you'd put things right.' My smouldering rage has turned explosive and I don't trust myself. He'd offered to give me the money, but how can I believe that he really will? There's no way of shaming someone who has no conscience. I turn to walk away.

'I'm going to die soon.'

I look back at him, stony-faced at his lame attempt to gain attention. 'Of what?'

'Fatal bullet wound.'

'What?'

'My life's over, I need someone to finish it for me.'

He lowers himself onto a low, rocky ledge, a shadow of the man I first met. He's lost his vibrancy, his good looks ravaged by bad health, or whatever. We're only a few miles along the coast from where we first met, but it seems a world away.

The tide is out, a faint smell of drying seaweed in the air. Two dogs bark in the distance. We look out to sea. He'll do us all a favour if he dies.

'I'm awaiting trial for fraud. I'm going to prison.'

'Defrauding my parents?'

He shakes his head, as if he's done worse than ruin their lives. 'There's enough to send me down for a long time.'

'What goes around comes around.' I kick at the shingle. 'Why kill yourself? Running off to Greece is more your style.'

'I can't run, not now. It's all caught up, the debts and everything. There's no escape, not for long anyway. I can't take any more. Better to end it.'

'Don't exaggerate.'

'My back injury's flared up. The steroids aren't working. I'm in constant pain. I can't sleep, so I medicate with whisky. I've no money, no future. I'm too sick to be locked in a cell on a plastic mattress. Then I'll be too old to start over.'

I stare him straight in the eye. 'Go ahead and blow your brains out.'

'Someone else will do it for me. Lots of people want me dead. Here's their chance.'

I give an ironic laugh. 'Fine, make them do it. You'll be good at that. They might chuck you in a river tied to a lead weight.'

He returns my stare. 'I want it to be instant. Bullet to the head.'

'So do it yourself.' I feel a strange power over him. The man who made a living from trading on his looks and charm has lost them. Most people could handle that, but not him.

'There's a life insurance policy on me. I want someone to benefit. They won't get squat if it's suicide.'

'Gone soft in your old age. Who's it for, Sky?' I say with a sour note.

'No. I don't see her these days. She hardly keeps in touch.'

No wonder. He's no use to her as a sick convict. I sit on a large rock and the cold from the stone seeps into my jeans.

'How will Emily feel when she finds out her dad is dead?'

He hunches forward and puts his head in his hands. 'Be better for everyone in the long run.' He starts to cry, crumpling in on himself. I didn't think him capable of tears, even in self-pity.

'You're going to prison. Deal with it.'

He wipes his face with the palms of his hands. 'The pain's getting worse. And I've got no money.'

'Neither have my mum and Doug.'

He turns his head away.

'You conned them like you conned me, except they really are too old to start again.'

'It wasn't personal.'

'Of course it's fucking personal!' I get up to walk away, and then swing back to face him. 'They worked hard for everything and you stole it. You put my mum in hospital, and you moan about losing sleep? Why isn't the insurance money for Emily?'

'It's for my wife. Got married last year.'

A dull ache thuds through me. He used his charms to snare another wife. Poor woman.

'So you have got something to come out for.'

'She'll leave me if I go inside. The house is being repossessed. At least this way she'll have enough for a flat. She took out the insurance herself. She might as well benefit.'

'Your wife gets a home while my parents lose theirs?' I clench my fists harder.

'I've changed. And she's not like you. She's weak. You're strong. I've got some cash on the boat. Five grand. It's not much, but give it to your folks.' He looks past me, further along the shore. 'Look. That's her now.'

I turn. A young woman with her back to us clips up the steps built into the sea wall, her body stiff, as if she's seen us and marched off. She disappears behind a sprawling patch of brambles and I lose sight of her.

'That's your wife?'

He nods. 'She's been trying to track me down. She'll have seen my car parked at the house and come looking.'

She seemed to be stomping away on some kind of mission. She didn't look weak, not that he can be believed. And she's taken out a life insurance policy on him. Hardly romantic optimism.

'What'll she think, seeing you crying to me?'

'She'll be upset. She's insecure.'

'Aren't we all.'

He gazes off.

'Why not just take off with the cash? Have another season in the sun on a fake passport?'

He shakes his head. 'Like I said, it's too late for me. I can't sail with my bad back. And you don't get whisky in prison.' He looks at his hands. 'You still hate me, don't you?'

'I used to lie awake at night thinking of ways to kill you.'

He almost smiles. 'What was your favourite?'

'Multiple stab wounds, slowly inflicted.'

'Do you still want to kill me?'

I give a hollow sound, like a laugh but more of a cough.

'You haven't answered.'

'It's not a rhetorical question?' I say.

'It's a straightforward question: do you want to kill me in return for the cash, yes or no?'

I sway a little from the wind buffeting me, or maybe I'm just light-headed.

'Your wife can kill you if she wants the insurance money.'

'She's not strong like you. You can shoot me with the gun. I've worked it all out. Let's go to the boat. It's hidden away where no one goes. Do it there.'

AFTER

In all my nights of grimly fantasising about the perfect murder, I never anticipated the scenario of assisted suicide that he presented to me. The man I'd married had big plans for the future. The man on the beach had no future.

Once I'd started telling the police what happened, it all came out. Thornley and Roper stayed silent as I accounted for my actions. My every word was recorded, possibly to be used against me.

'So that's what happened on the beach.' I told the officers. Now they knew that I'd agreed to shoot him. I wanted to keep going but the upset of it overwhelmed me and I crumpled up in the chair, sobbing quietly into my hands. My solicitor offered me a tissue. I wiped tears from my face, expecting them to arrest me.

'You do realise,' Roper said, a look of disgust on her face, 'that an enormous amount of police resources have been spent on this investigation and you've been covering this up the whole time?'

'We need a break,' my solicitor said. 'I'd like to talk to my client alone.'

Roper took us wordlessly to another room and brought me a plastic cup of water.

'I want to tell them the rest,' I said to my solicitor when we were alone.

'When you've had a breather, they'll finish questioning you.'

'Then what?'

'It's possible you'll be charged so they can keep you here and question you for longer. Then they're likely to submit new evidence to the CPS.'

Part of me believed that what I'd told them strengthened the case against Rachel. She discovered his betrayal the same time as I found out what he'd done to my mum. She had the life insurance and he wanted to die. She must have seen me on the beach before his murder, but she couldn't admit it in case another woman turning up and giving him grief suggested he provoked her into murder. Her dad knew it too, so he held back the CCTV footage of me. They went after Sky instead.

Hard to believe Rachel still loved him, as she claimed on the day we met. The police arrived just days before and told her the extent of her husband's deceit, including his sideline in 'romance fraud'. And he'd conned my mum, which brought me to his door around the same time that Rachel started adding it all up.

He only brought Sky and me there knowing his life was

imploding. It all caught up with him – the police investigation closing in, my mum's stroke, Rachel discovering the truth, Sky demanding money – the three of us angry and bearing down on him.

'I want to finish telling them what happened.'

BEFORE

Straight after making the arrangements on the beach, Rob goes to the boat, and I head along the path to my car. No one sees me waiting for darkness to come. Rain starts to fall. I give it thirty-five slow minutes, and then drive along the sleepy road to the track that leads to the mooring. He kept the boat by a quiet riverbank, away from prying eyes and debt collectors.

After dark, there aren't any streetlights or passing traffic, just the occasional dog walker to be mindful of along the deserted towpath. It's dark now, properly dark, but a dim light on the boat guides me to him. I kick off my shoes, leave them on the muddy grass and climb aboard. The boat dips to announce my arrival. It feels oddly familiar being back on board. I've returned to the place where everything went wrong. My determination masks the shakiness.

A light burns below deck. The smell of whisky fills the cabin. A glass and a nearly empty bottle stand within arm's reach of him. Has he got blind drunk in the time I've been gone? He slumps, ungainly on the banquette seating, his head at an awkward angle. I swear for putting myself through this when he's probably too pissed to take it in.

'It's me.'

I balance on the steps, clutching the handrail through my gloved hands to stop the shaking. In the faded light, I see pools of thick, dark liquid. Reality hits. *Blood, it's blood.* At the same moment, I see it trickle from his nose and mouth. Then everything happens too fast: I see the gun on the floor, the flesh wound in his chest. I turn and run, stumbling from the boat.

My heart pumps out of my chest and into my throat. I pull on my trainers, flee to the car and fumble with my keys. Urgent breathing makes my mouth too dry to swallow. Rain falls, washing away evidence. My whole body shakes and I hear a noise that sounds like a desperate faraway animal. It comes from me. My chest hurts, as if my lungs are denied air. I drive off, hunched forward, clutching the steering wheel to steady myself, just how I'd sailed through the storms we'd faced five years ago.

Back home, I pull off my clothes inside the front door and pile them on the mat. Everything goes in a bin liner, including the mat. I shower off every trace of what I touched. But I can't wash away the sight of him and all that blood. The freefall of discovering his body slows and turns into a film my mind can't erase.

I pace the house, agitated. *Stop it*, I tell myself. Focus. I drive out again to ditch the evidence. I dump the bin liner in a wheelie bin behind a crappy parade of shops, miles from home and put the car through a car wash, all the while pretending everything is normal.

The next day I scrub the inside of the car for invisible specks of blood, unsure if it's penance or purification. I scrub and scrub to try and subdue the uncontrollable shaking and the sick feeling in my stomach.

He's dead, and I was there. I'd gone there wanting retribution, only someone else got there first. I don't know what happened on the boat, all I know is that he goaded me and tried to make me kill him, and now he's dead and I'm implicated. No one except the killer knows I didn't do it.

AFTER

DS Thornley picked up the police interview where they'd left off. 'Why didn't you go straight to the boat?'

'Rob wanted us to go straight there. I said no. Not till after dark. Less chance of anyone seeing me.'

That thirty-five minutes saved me from murder. As I drove to the boat, adrenaline pumped all thoughts from my head. If I'd been rational I'd have said no, but I stopped being rational when I saw those documents at my mum's. I only wanted payback for her and Doug.

I'd pulled in at the riverbank and turned off the engine. Panic overwhelmed me, a tightness across my chest, and I struggled to breathe. My heart beat ahead of me towards the boat. A rushing noise filled my ears. What was I thinking? What if I was caught? My breathing slowed and the dark impulse receded, along with the heavy dose of adrenaline. The chill evening air enveloped me and brought my sanity back.

Revenge was a dish best served cold, but when the heat

subsided, the madness went with it. It wasn't revenge. He'd manipulated me into carrying out his demands, same as always. I wanted to blow his brains out, but why do his dirty work?

My resolve built and I wouldn't go through with it. I'd been looking for some kind of compensation, when my best revenge was telling him the only life he'd destroyed was his. Not mine, not my mum's. I didn't have to *earn* a payment. He owed them. I'd get on that boat and mess with him a bit. Make him hear me out because I held the power, not him. Then the fucker could shoot himself.

Turns out I wasn't cut out for murder. And why would I trust him? I hadn't considered the danger at first, and once in my right mind, I knew I couldn't do it. But put in front of a jury, they might not believe I'd changed my mind and found him dead. I hardly believed it myself. The police might not believe it either. I only knew that up to the time he died, I'd still wanted to kill him.

Thornley sat back and gave me that narrow-eyed look of his, the one where he tried to work me out.

'I know how bad it sounds,' I said, 'but I didn't kill him. I'd never have gone through with it. My revenge was walking away. That's what I went on the boat to tell him. He was dead when I got there.'

'Mia, you've been lying to us for months, ever since the first time we interviewed you,' Thornley said. 'Even when I advised you to tell the truth, you still concealed your involvement.'

'But I wasn't involved. I don't know who killed him.'

DC Roper sneered and looked away. No wonder I'd concealed it, given their scepticism. I'd done a bad job of managing the damage Rob caused and now I'd given them enough to charge me.

'I was scared to tell you earlier because I didn't want to be wrongly convicted. Everything I've told you in here is the truth. It's everything I know.' I laid my palms flat on the table. 'What's going to happen?'

'A decision will be made on whether you're charged,' Thornley said.

Two nights before the murder, Rachel kicked off about Emily's maintenance payments. She played me a recording of Rob on her phone, the gloating bitch. She only played his words, but I know they were both slagging me off.

'Sky's volatile as fuck,' he'd said in the recording. 'She's crazy. Is she crazy enough to kill me? I doubt it. She loves me too much. She'll never give me up. She pretends it's about the money, and yeah, she's a grabby bitch, but it's me she wants.'

His devious bitch of a wife played a dangerous game, rubbing their marriage in my face. I bet she sent those emails too. Jess, who now called herself Mia, thought I was sending them, but my dyslexia would've given me away. Rob used to make out I was stupid, so I told Jess I was in teacher training, to feel clever for once. But I'm not stupid. I can lie as well as the rest of them.

Rachel got what she wanted in the end. The night he died, Rob told me to be at the beach. He said he'd hand over my money, Emily's money. But he just brought me there to humiliate me. It was all his fault. He'd fucked me over one time too many. I could only take so much. He might be Emily's dad, but he pushed me too far. I know I should have walked away, but I pulled the trigger.

I did it. I killed him.

AFTER

Thornley and I locked eyes across the table in the interview room. His words about charging me hung in the air.

'Charged with what, exactly?' my solicitor said.

'Perverting the course of justice.'

I breathed out. I didn't want any kind of conviction, but that was nowhere near as bad as a murder charge.

'It's a serious offence,' DC Roper said, reading my expression. 'It carries a maximum sentence of life imprisonment.'

Oh fuck.

'Do you accept that my client did not commit murder?' the solicitor asked.

'We've charged someone else with the murder.' Thornley said. 'Sky Rasson.'

I gasped and sat back in my chair.

'Your tip-off led officers to a property in Godalming where evidence was found.'

'What evidence?' I asked.

'We found the remains of a small bonfire, along with a beanie hat nearby. She probably dropped it in the dark, thinking it had gone on the fire with the other evidence that she burned. CCTV shows her wearing the hat when she drove away from the area. It held her DNA and blood spatters consistent with firing the fatal shot.'

Thornley's open response didn't fit his usual 'we can't discuss the investigation with you' stance.

'Sky Rasson has admitted the charge,' DC Roper said.

'Really?' It floored me, that she had confessed after staring me down in that London café, accusing Rachel.

'It spares her and everyone else a trial,' Thornley said.

'Do you have any further questions for my client, or can she leave now?' my solicitor asked.

'You're free to leave,' Thornley said to me with the trace of a smile and a nod of his head. Perhaps he was glad I wasn't the guilty one after all.

Rachel got what she wanted. The police dropped the charges against her and charged Sky with manslaughter. I pictured the scenario between Sky and Rob. It played out in my mind, like watching a film. He'd have provoked Sky one last time, hunched forward, eyes fixed on her, or not, depending on how drunk he was. Hardly grounds for murder, but did it trigger something in her?

She might have tried to stop the shaking, the same as I had, not long after. She'd have held the gun with both hands and braced herself against the shot. His breathing might have been frayed as she took a step closer and aimed for his heart. One shot punctured the dead quiet. His body jolted and his arms splayed out. She dropped the gun and ran off in a panic. After I'd left, Sky must have returned to throw the gun in the water.

Once Sky was convicted, the whole story came out in the media. I opened the double page newspaper spread to a photo of the gun used to blast his heart away. *Yes*, I thought, *that's it.* A forensic psychologist in the paper said a woman is more likely to shoot someone in the heart. *A man is more likely to shoot to kill through the head, as there is a higher chance of it resulting in sudden death.*

The piece was accompanied by the photo of Sky and Rob that I'd given to Thornley. She met him as a 'naïve nineteen-year-old, in thrall to the man who preyed upon attractive younger women'. It said she'd been diagnosed with PTSD from his violence towards her, and he'd manipulated her for years. She was given nine months in prison, when the typical range was between two and ten years.

When I went to see her, I'd had an inkling that he'd lured her there to make her angry enough to kill him. Only because he'd done the same to me. By that stage I wouldn't have put anything past him, including pushing the mother of his child to commit murder. He knew if he provoked us all, someone might actually do it. *I'm a bastard, here's a gun, now shoot me.* He preferred to die in a crime of passion than a lonely suicide.

A photo of Rachel was used in the feature, on the boat with him, smiling gamely as I once had. Perhaps they had honeymooned in Greece and sailed around the islands. Perhaps he became angry with her for not knowing how to do the sails. He might have knocked her to the floor in a drunken rage over money. She might have wanted children as much as I had.

Part of me had died from loving him. You can't go back to your old life after a relationship like that. You change, move on, and learn to live with it. I'd been in pieces for a while, and now the pieces fitted back in a different way. I wanted the grief to burn out. The glint of hope was there, and I needed it to haul myself forward.

At least we'd had good news about Mum and Doug's housing situation. The council had allocated them a retirement bungalow, taking that particular weight off our minds. Mum's voice shook with emotion when she told me the news. And then came the confirmation that I wouldn't be charged with perverting the course of justice.

Ben had left two messages, checking I was okay, saying he wanted me back. He talked as if we'd never split up. I wanted him back too. He'd only ever been looking out for me. Rob was finally in the past, he had no hold over me now. I had got away.

EPILOGUE

Rachel

When the police barged in with a search warrant, they told me what Rob had done. I confronted him, ready for his worn-out denials, expecting him to call me crazy. You'd have to be crazy to put up with his shit. But no. He slumped with his head in his hands and said he wanted to end it all. It threw me.

He deserved to go to prison, but I wanted revenge. He'd dangled Sky in front of me, and would push it until I became upset, and then he'd call me jealous. He knew I planned to leave him, and he used the threat of suicide as a bid for sympathy. It was mostly the whisky talking, but I hatched a plan to get them both back. With the right approach, I knew I could make Sky shoot him.

'Why not have another woman do it in a crime of passion,' I said, 'and die the way you lived.'

I knew he'd gain perverse pleasure from playing us off against each other. I could put up with it, helped by the life insurance as compensation for what he'd put me through. And defrauding the insurance company from beyond the grave would appeal to a man like him.

'Ask Sky. She'll do it,' I said. With her short fuse, if he gave her the gun, she might fly into a rage and shoot him.

I loathed Sky with a passion. She'd tried to turn him against me from the start. Jealous bitch. She'd barge in wanting money, looking me up and down as if I were the trashy one. Fuck knows why he had anything to do with her. Okay, they had the kid, but he was hardly a responsible dad.

'Sky can't be convicted because of Emily,' he said.

Bastard. 'You need someone volatile enough to do it. Sky's volatile.'

'Sky's volatile as fuck. She's crazy. Is she crazy enough to kill me? I doubt it. She loves me too much. She'll never give me up. She pretends it's about the money, and yeah, she's a grabby bitch, but it's me she wants.'

I doubted that. Of course, he'd no idea that I recorded the conversation.

'Find someone else then,' I said. 'Bring them to the boat and goad them. You're good at that. Go out with a bang, to suit your style.'

Unbeknown to me, he did just that, bringing Mia to the beach. Meanwhile, I set Sky up behind his back, playing them both at their twisted game. I swiped his mobile, which wasn't difficult when he left it lying around and rarely checked messages. He never took it to the boat, wanting to escape from all the people hassling him for money.

I knew I could convince him to let Sky do it. A few comments here and there about Sky being a bad mother, Emily being better off at her grandmother's. It wouldn't take much. He always put himself first, even before his only child. If Sky presented herself, he'd go with it.

Sky was even easier to wind up. I took his phone and fed her lies, supposedly sent by him. I deleted the evidence so he couldn't find it, but the police would. When she heard him call her 'crazy', she lost her shit. No wonder. It used to make me lose my shit too. One furious voicemail later, Sky was in the frame.

I followed up with one more text, the most important one. A contrite message from my dear husband with a peace offering of £5,000 from his secret stash.

Come to the boat and get it now before Rachel finds out. Don't bring Emily because it's all kicking off here. The police might arrest me at any time. x

It brought her running. I'd whipped up a toxic mix: Sky demanding money that didn't exist from a semi-drunk and abusive Rob, who had a gun to hand.

Everything went to plan, until I 'discovered' the corpse. Being a caring wife, I went looking for him. I touched his body to check he was dead. The police throught the blood stains incriminated me. They thought I'd set Sky up, or Mia, or both. They were half right, I suppose.

Poor, naïve Mia. The look on her face when I first showed up! She thought I'd come to accuse her. But I played the long game. *I loved him. I just wanted him to get better.* Yeah, right. But she swallowed it. I'd gone there wanting to see if it really had been her on the beach that evening. She knew. I knew. But we never said anything. Hilarious really, not that I could laugh as a grief-stricken widow.

Mia soon became my Plan B. I let her believe Sky had it in for her, but Sky had it in for everyone. When it looked as if they'd lock me up, I programmed the anonymous emails to delay-send so Mia kept on receiving them. I wanted to make her paranoid and it worked.

Sky told me ages ago that she'd hold hands with Rob just to wind Mia up. How she'd exposed all Rob's lies. She enjoyed telling me the specifics. She said it as a power trip over me, so I knew she could do the same to me. I used it against her, making the emails appear to come from Sky. Bitch. For a heartless killer, she got off lightly.

Mia bought into my fragile widow act. She lapped up the sensitive, tearful shit. I reeled her in, two battered wives together. Fuck that. I was only in it for myself. Mia proved useful in the end. She found the vital clue to nail the bitch. We both knew Rob deserved to die. I did us all a favour.

ACKNOWLEDGEMENTS

Thank you to my agent, Camilla Bolton, for her unswerving belief and for using her superpowers to land me a book deal. I couldn't believe my luck when Sphere adopted me! Special thanks to Lucy Dauman for her clear editorial gaze, and to Lucy Malagoni, Thalia Proctor, Sophie Wilson, Abby Parsons and Rosanna Forte at Sphere. Thank you to Charlotte Stroomer for designing the front cover.

Thanks also to the team at Darley Anderson, including Roya Sarrafi-Gohar, Sheila David, Mary Darby, Kristina Egan, Georgia Fuller and Rosanna Bellingham.

I would like to thank my family and friends, and my astute and thoughtful readers including Dawn Warrington, David Blunden, Dorothy Wright, Chris Moore, Rita Rooke, Robb Grindstaff and Simon Forward. My wise and wonderful writer friends at Grey Havens have been a long-time inspiration. I'm grateful to Tim Hodges from Sussex Police for walking me through the police procedural aspects. Any inaccuracies are my own. Thank you to everyone else who has been supportive. It means a lot.

Lastly, a special mention to James for celebrating every success, always with a glass of something. Despite your love of sailing, I'm glad you're nothing like Rob.